Jane Blanchard is Fea_____ Born in Hampshire, s_____ London as a music publicist, working with bands such as Status Quo and Thin Lizzy, before training as a journalist with Mirror Group Newspapers. She worked as a reporter and columnist for regional and national newspapers and magazines, before joining the news desk at Television South West. Since then she's worked extensively as a writer/producer/director on news, current affairs, outside broadcasts and documentaries on subjects as diverse as ballet, football and barbershop singing. Her *Consumer File* series was the highest rating programme in TSW's history. At Westcountry TV, she was a finalist at the New York Film and Television Festival for her programme about the plight of Romanian orphans. Recent successes have included a documentary series on the history of ITV in the south-west.

Jane lives in Devon with her partner Iain Blair (alias best-selling romantic novelist Emma Blair). For more information on her books, please visit her website at: www.janeblanchard.com

Getting It!

JANE BLANCHARD

A *Time Warner* Paperback

First published in Great Britain as a paperback original in 2003
by Time Warner Paperbacks

A CIP catalogue record for this book
is available from the British Library.

ISBN 0 7515 3364 5

Typeset in Berkeley by M Rules
Printed and bound in Great Britain by Clays Ltd, St Ives plc

Time Warner Paperbacks
An Imprint of
Time Warner Books UK
Brettenham House
Lancaster Place
London WC2E 7EN

www.TimeWarnerBooks.co.uk
www.janeblanchard.com

For Mark
Grown up now but still my baby!

Acknowledgements

There may be only one name on the cover of this book, but believe me, there is a whole support system out there without which *Getting It!* would not have been possible. This is my chance to thank them all once again.

I've dedicated this book to Mark who, as well as being simply the best son in the world, patiently sorts out all my computer tantrums and has created the most wonderfully groovy website for me:

www.janeblanchard.com

Sincere thanks to my partner Iain (alias best-selling author Emma Blair) who provides unlimited supplies of love and support; to my agent Pat White for her tremendous warmth and wisdom; and to all the team at Time Warner for their constant encouragement and faith in me.

I'd also like to send huge thanks to all my friends for putting up with my lack of cooking and appalling communication while I wrote this book. In particular: Rene, Jane, Elayne, Wendy, Kathy, Ian, John, Sally, Christine, Janet, Jennie, Jill, Susie and Trina. Not forgetting the Curry Night Girls: Liz, Gill, Jenny, Cherry, Deirdre, Judy, Jean and Angie.

And finally a big thank you to my friends in television dotted around the globe, especially those who spilled the beans about some of the goings-on at shopping channels. Probably best not to name them . . .

Chapter 1

**WANTED – FUN PEOPLE FOR THE
TV CHALLENGE OF THE DECADE!**

Do you love shopping? Do you want non-stop excitement?
Then join Getting It, TV's newest and most exciting shopping
channel. Getting It is going to kick all its rivals straight off the
screen with cheaper, brighter, bigger and better products you
never knew you needed – until now! We're looking for
presenters, producers, writers, camera operators, sound
recordists, buyers, accountants and admin staff.

Fran slammed down the phone for the tenth time that
night. The dippy female voice in a pseudo-transatlantic
drawl got halfway through a recorded announcement
giving an address for application forms and then abruptly
cut out. Fran lit a cigarette, took a deep drag and cursed
aloud. Only two more days before she was giving them up,
along with chocolate, red wine and an incurable addiction
to celebrity magazines. It had become a New Year ritual.
She knew that by mid-January latest she'd have
encountered some horrendous office crisis and would be
back on them all again. Her roots would need doing by
then as well, so she could cheat on the magazine bit by

catching up with two weeks' worth of *Hello!* and *OK!* at the hairdresser's.

She picked up the phone and dialled once more.

'Hi and welcome to Getting It. Are you? If so, we'd like to hear from you. Leave your number after the tone or drop us a line at this address: Getting It—' At exactly the same spot, it cut out again. The answering machine was either full or faulty. Apparently nobody would be getting it that night.

Fran surveyed the huge pile of shirts in a basket in the corner of her kitchen. Should she just pack it in and join the Mile-High Ironing Club tonight? Or indulge in her favourite fantasy? The fantasy won hands down and soon she was completely transported, flipping through an article on celebrity brides of the year, relishing all the syrupy detail, the designers, the guests and so on. Knowing that the marriages were more likely to be limping into injury time long before the wedding dresses went out of fashion. Fran just loved celebrities. She was almost ashamed of how much detail she knew about Posh and Becks, Catherine and Michael, Sir Paul and Heather or Madge and Guy. She could name all Earl Spencer's wives and ex-girlfriends, yet her mind went momentarily blank when she tried to think of the name of the Foreign Secretary these days. Not impressive, she constantly told herself, considering she was a journalist with twenty years' experience. Admittedly not a top-flight reporter on a national paper or magazine. *The Hartford Evening Echo* didn't have quite the same cachet. And any celebrity visiting Hartford had probably just taken a wrong turning. But she knew she should have been able to whip through the names of the cabinet without drawing breath.

'Can't seem to retain anything these days,' she

murmured aloud to herself. 'Except water.' Oh well, at least her current job writing and editing the weekly women's pages and property supplement meant she could indulge a few secret celeb fantasies, like snooping around the occasional dream home that came on the market or encouraging a postbag of views on Victoria Beckham's latest hair extensions.

She was also the newspaper's clairvoyant, Madame Chita, a secret so closely guarded that even her fellow reporters didn't know her identity. Unbelievably, nobody had twigged the joke in the name either. Then again, if you were a budding investigative reporter the *Hartford Echo* probably wasn't the place to stay for too long. The majority of the reporters had been there longer than Fran, and were grappling with the will to live as opposed to sniffing out a good story. The Madame Chita deal involved an extra few grand a year, disguised as a long service increment, with the copy written secretly at home and posted in a plain white envelope. Madame Chita regularly provoked a huge postbag on account of her rather risqué predictions, and the *Echo* news editor had no intention of blowing her identity and wrecking what had become a talking point around Hartford.

Fran lit another cigarette from the butt of the previous one. Where had the last twenty years gone? she pondered. Am I starting to regret staying on the same paper all these years? Fran already knew the answer to that; she was stuck in a rut. Bob, her husband, had a steady job with a local bank and they lived in a suburban three-bedroomed semi with its own small drive. Unfortunately, Bob possessed no drive whatsoever, except where his tool kit was concerned. Bob had been 'doing up' their house for the past ten years. With hindsight, Fran should have insisted they got a quick loan and then called in a builder. But it was far too late for that now. With the half-finished kitchen, the untiled bathroom, a yet-to-be-installed shower room, the hall missing several floorboards, a sitting room that hadn't been decorated since pop art had taken a dive, doorbell and burglar alarms still in their packets, yes, Bob wasn't exactly honed by the wind.

She thought back to how they'd met. She'd applied to the bank for a mortgage on a small flat and he'd been the sub-manager arranging it. She'd liked him then and she still liked him now. Bob had never been in the drop-dead gorgeous category – he was tall, thin and a bit gangly, with a shock of thick, still-brown hair. Oh, and a bit boring, but he was as steady as a rock. When they'd married, she'd imagined life would be in a fairly ordered household on a smart estate on the edge of Hartford with a couple of children coming along at some stage. She was happy to tick over on the *Echo* until the babies arrived. But, sadly, the stork never visited and both of them were too shy to pursue the fertility problem. Now, at 42, Fran had quietly accepted her fate and just got on with her little bit of showbiz at the *Echo*. And Bob took off to his tool shed.

At first, Fran could understand why he did that. After a predictable day at the bank, having meaningful discussions with customers about their overdrafts, Bob found his hammering and banging a kind of physical outlet. Fran grew to enjoy having the house more or less to herself. The constant state of unfinished projects had got on her nerves initially, but as the years went by she ceased to notice. Bob wouldn't hear of a penny being spent on anything he could make himself – eventually. So, bit by bit, Fran gave up. A reporter's salary on the *Echo* didn't run to major renovation so instead she quietly blew her spare

4

cash and Madame Chita's fee on some fairly decent clothes. Friends who visited for the one and only time – they always suggested eating out after that – couldn't understand how this well-dressed woman (Marella, Planet and the odd bit of Mondi) could emerge from such a mess of a home. Then they couldn't wait to get out of the door and exclaim: 'Did you see the state of the bathroom? The window's practically falling out. And all those books heaped up gathering dust because he hasn't got around to putting up the shelves. I don't know how she lives with him, let alone the chaos.'

Fran's reverie was interrupted by a sharp blast of December frost and Bob appearing at the kitchen door. 'All right, darling?' He kissed her fondly, as he always did. 'Thought you'd be watching all those reviews of the year on the box.'

Fran stubbed out her cigarette and got up to put on the kettle. 'Just savouring one of my very last cigarettes ever,' she grinned.

Bob smiled back knowingly. Fran giving up smoking had almost become part of their Christmas tradition, as seasonal as mince pies, putting up the tree and cursing when the fairy lights didn't work.

'Oh, and I'm applying for another job,' she announced dramatically. 'Or rather, trying to.'

She pointed to the ad in the *Echo* which she'd circled with a red pen.

Bob looked completely shell-shocked. He wasn't good on change. Speechless, he blew the wood dust off his hands and picked up the paper. There was almost a full minute's silence. Fran grinned to herself as she spooned his favourite Kenyan high roast into the cafetière. She'd known he would be taken aback. It might just kick-start

5

him into doing something about the state of the house. Then again, probably not.

'Strewth, Fran,' he spluttered once he'd read and re-read the ad several times. 'This sounds a bit racy. Do you think it's you?' He peered anxiously at her.

'Time for a change,' she announced firmly, hoping it might include the house. 'I'm getting to the stage where I'm just waiting for the moment they ask me to write my own obituary. I can already picture the headline: "Echo Mourns Veteran Reporter". I'd be buried at the bottom of page thirteen.'

'I didn't realise you were so unhappy there,' said Bob, aghast at what he was hearing.

'Darling, I'm not unhappy. I'm in a rut. Quite a happy rut, actually. But I just saw this ad and thought: new year, new job.'

She paused to light another cigarette and drew gratefully from it. 'I probably don't stand a hope in hell,' she continued. 'Far too old, been in the same job too long, but what do I have to lose? Nothing. Except that I've tried that number all evening and the bloody answering machine cuts out every time.'

Bob re-read the ad while she put the coffee down in front of them. He ran his long thin fingers through his hair several times. It was always a sign that he was uneasy or under pressure. 'It sounds a bit tacky,' he confessed, 'especially the name. Getting It, I ask you. Isn't that a bit naff? I hope it's not anything sleazy.'

'Well, there's only one way to find out,' Fran retorted. 'It's typical that it appears in our jobs section rather than on the front page, but that's the *Echo* for you. First with the ads, last with the news. I can make some legitimate enquiries tomorrow, like ringing up *Broadcast* magazine to see if they've heard of it and what they think about its chances.'

'Hmm, OK, I take your point,' said Bob, 'but it's a terrible title. Sounds like a swingers' magazine or a strip club. I can just imagine taking you to the bank's annual dinner and saying, "This is my wife, Fran, who's working at Getting It." People might ask for a list of your rates.'

Fran threw back her head and laughed. 'What? At my age? Don't be ridiculous.'

Bob gazed admiringly at her still-trim figure and blonde highlighted bob. 'Darling, to me you're a gorgeous, good-looking woman. You don't look your age at all. You could easily knock ten years off without any trouble.'

'And you're hopelessly biased, Bob Hallgarth. But you're very sweet and I love you. And I'm listening. Don't worry, I'll check it out very carefully. But I'm determined to have a go.'

He finished his coffee and kissed her tenderly on the forehead. 'Back to the shed, just to finish a couple of things. Won't take long.'

She watched him amble back up the garden path. Finish a couple of things, she thought to herself, yeah right. She stubbed out her cigarette somewhat guiltily. Well, only two days left and there were three packets in the drawer. She might as well finish them before Big Ben started its countdown. As she heard the faint whine of Bob's jig-saw starting up again, she turned back to her celebrity magazine and was soon engrossed in a feature on yet another soap actress 'welcoming us into her sumptuous home'. Fran allowed herself to fantasise about suddenly being catapulted to celebrity status and having a society photographer literally begging to take her photo. She could just imagine the magazine copy:

Fran Hallgarth welcomes you into her uncomfortable but intriguing home, tucked away in a boring suburb of the market town of Hartford. Fran, who's forty-two (no, make that thirty-nine), is the *Hartford Echo*'s star showbiz writer and it's here in this shabby little study with peeling apricot paint, sitting at an antique Imperial typewriter (a snip at a car boot sale), that her best ideas magically come to life.

'I love collecting old things,' Fran says proudly, showing off her set of non-stick saucepans that she stacks artistically on the floor. Fran keeps her enviable figure trim by smoking incessantly and occasionally giving up red wine and chocolate. The secret of her long and happy marriage to her banker husband Bob? He virtually lives for his tool shed, where the handmade Shaker-style kitchen cupboards and shelves will eventually emerge.

The couple met and fell in love through their shared joy of interior design. They are both avid readers, as you can tell from their fine collection of yellowing paperbacks, seen here heaped up in the dusty corner of the sitting room. Note the authentic pop art wallpaper, so evocative of the seventies with its brown and orange swirls. And their creative imagination will eventually run riot when Bob gets around to ripping out the avocado bathroom suite and doing the tiling.

'We've been debating for the last seven or eight years about actually retaining the bathroom suite because it's so wonderfully retro,' says Fran, whose keen sense of style is everywhere to behold.

As in most homes, the kitchen is the hub of the

household and it's here that Fran and Bob spend romantic candlelit evenings eating supper on this delightful plastic foldaway picnic table. No twenty-first-century gadgets for Fran. She firmly eschews the modern cook's microwave, split-level oven or Aga. You'll find no breadmakers, juicers or turbo woks in the Hallgarth household. Her magic tip for producing food to die for is this simple and traditional Baby Belling. Just two rings balanced on an old work bench are all you need, says Fran, whose Patak curries and Sara Lee desserts are the talk of four counties.

Meanwhile, the couple have exciting plans for their garden. Old sinks are just waiting to be planted up and a fascinating sculpture of rusting bicycles evokes a bygone age. Glass panes of different sizes are attractively arranged around the outside of the tool shed, reflecting the light on even the dullest of days. Inside, Bob is engrossed in his work. He's been making some exquisite elm door handles with his lathe. Two finished so far and only another sixteen to go. He is, of course, a perfectionist and so only the best will do. The floor is littered with attempts that went wrong or pieces of wood that simply didn't come up to scratch.

'The secret of our success?' say this delightful couple. 'Take your time. Homes should evolve gradually. Let a year or two lapse between each decision and remember that a job done properly will be a job that lasts a lifetime.

Perhaps he should make a start on our coffins, thought Fran. She glanced out of the kitchen window. There were times when she'd personally love to jig-saw that shed – or even nuke it.

She reached for the phone and dialled the Getting It number again. Once more, Miss Deeply Dippy drawled through her message and cut out at the usual spot. Fran suddenly realised she wanted to be part of this new shopping channel more than anything else in the world.

Chapter 2

Fran couldn't quite believe she'd done it. She'd got up at the crack of dawn, dashed off her weekly Madame Chita copy, predicted 'doom, gloom and a funeral' for a Taurean reporter in the newsroom who'd been particularly bolshy to her lately. And foreign travel involving non-stop sex for the two blonde bimbo Virgoans in telesales who were off at the weekend to terrorise Goa. Couldn't have picked a better place for a couple of goers had been among the more printable remarks from the newsroom.

She put her copy in a plain white envelope marked for the editor and popped it in the postbox at the bottom of her road. Then she turned her silver Peugeot 205 (leather seats, her little luxury to make up for the state of the house) in the opposite direction to the newspaper office and headed out of town. Her pathetic little girl voice 'phoning-from-her-sick-bed' to say she wouldn't be in the office that day hadn't gone down too well. She'd been put through to the news editor, Guy, who'd been in a very expansive mood, recounting all the jokes he'd read on his email that morning. Fran had completely forgotten her plot and laughed raucously. She'd realised to her horror that she couldn't then revert to her little girl voice.

Miraculously, Guy had been interrupted by news coming in of a body found in a squat on Hartford's most notorious housing estate and had just slammed the phone down. She, too, was now off the hook.

The journey to an anonymous hotel twenty miles from Hartford went by in a flash. Fran tried to rehearse what she would say at her interview aloud in the car until she was caught giving it her all, including arm movements for emphasis, by two spotty youths in a boy-racer as they sat at traffic lights. But she knew exactly what her major stumbling block would be. One look at her CV would be enough. Age, followed by 'too long in the same job'.

Then there was the inevitable dress code dilemma. What did a potential employee of a wacky new TV channel wear? No rule book on that one. Black skirt, black polo neck, purple jacket and long black boots, she decided, plus a slight jewellery overload. She was still stunned to have been called for an interview but, of course, she hadn't yet told them her age. When she'd finally got some sort of sense out of Getting It's recorded message, all she'd had to do was to send in a CV. So she'd decided to say bye-bye to the forties, hello thirty-nine. Big hooped silver earrings, then, and a couple of chunky bracelets.

Fran had set off ridiculously early, certain that in her nervous state she would overshoot the turnings and end up late or stuck behind a learner driver. In the event, she was there in under an hour and ensconced in a parking space right outside the hotel, until she decided she'd be too conspicuous and appear desperate. So she drove straight out again, around the town a couple of times and then arrived back to find she'd lost the space. Panic ensued while she did three laps Le Mans-style of the hotel's small car park and then combed the back streets. By the time she arrived back at the hotel at the appointed hour she was windswept, sweaty and panicking.

An anaemic-looking blonde in killer heels, a short black leather skirt, black lace blouse and a Wonderbra so visible through the blouse that you could practically read the washing instructions, was busily brandishing a clipboard and ticking off names as people arrived. Obviously not used to working around her jacked-up tits, her chest kept getting in the way.

Fran took a seat in a small room crammed with around thirty people perched uncomfortably on orange plastic chairs. She glanced around surreptitiously at the other candidates and realised they'd had the same dress code problem. Some of the women were in top to toe black, while a couple of girls in their early twenties had come in what could only be described as clubbing gear. Two neat young men looked very serious and earnest, in contrast to their media ties, one featuring the Teletubbies and the other Pokémon. Another chap of around thirty looked as though he'd just popped in from the gym. Slicked-back hair, perma-tanned face, one earring, bulging muscles, faint smell of liniment and a snake tattoo just peeping over his much-too-tight shirt collar. One stunning-looking girl with a mane of straight pale blonde hair, dressed in a floaty green chiffon number, looked as though she might whip out a chocolate Flake or a bottle of Timotei shampoo at any moment.

To begin with, everyone adopted British Standard Lift Behaviour: total silence and absolutely no eye contact. All that was missing was some muzak and a disembodied voice saying 'Third floor, Ladies' Underwear and on to Bedding'.

After ten minutes, Teletubby and Pokémon broke the ice by sighing, looking at their fake Gucci watches and speculating as to where the nearest pub might be. Fran took this as a signal to open her bag and fish out her make-up and comb. 'Oh shit,' she muttered as she surveyed herself in her powder compact mirror. The wind and rain had completely ruined her two-hour face and hair battle that morning. Travelling mascara, deathly pale skin, blurred lipstick and limp and lifeless hair. In this state she'd probably have more success applying for a pensioner's extra heating allowance than for a job as a producer on a new hip-hop and happening shopping channel.

As Miss Wonderbra ushered two more people into the room, Teletubby and Pokémon demanded to know what was happening. 'Look, I'm going to have to go out for a fag break in a minute,' said one. Suddenly everyone was muttering complaints to each other. Fear and ambition had suddenly evaporated. Looking helpless and sensing a riot brewing, Miss Wonderbra wrestled with her clipboard once more. When she'd finally manoeuvred it around her chest, she announced breathily that she didn't know and teetered out of the room, muttering vague promises to find out.

'Should have known better after that shambolic answering machine,' said Teletubby. 'I bet that was her on the recorded message.'

'We've been waiting for over an hour,' one of the disco girls chipped in. 'I'm on a meter and it's already run out.'

'I'll get my agent to ring up and find out what's occurring,' said the Timotei blonde, whipping out a tiny mobile phone from her Fendi Oyster bag (which clearly wasn't a fake). The word 'agent' sent shivers of in-adequacy around the room. Fran's eyes met those of the only other woman in the room around her age. She had short dark hair, olive skin and was wearing a black trouser suit with a huge burgundy dévoré scarf wrapped around her. They exchanged silent looks of desperation.

Suddenly the door swung open. A slim man in his early thirties with cropped blond hair, deep sapphire blue eyes and wearing a dark and clearly very expensive suit swept confidently into the room. As he beamed at everyone, his eyes bored into them like lasers.

'Hi, I'm Paul Dyer, head of production,' he announced amiably, clearly not expecting a word of protest. And he was right. There wasn't as much as a whisper. What moans and protests there might have been simply died on everyone's lips. Fear and ambition were firmly back on the menu again.

'Hello and welcome to Getting It,' he continued, blue eyes glittering. 'Today we're looking for presenters, producers, writers, buyers and floor managers. But we don't want just any old people. We want team players with fizz and buzz, people who have a sense of fun. And let me tell you, guys and gals, you'll need a sense of humour when we tell you about the salaries. Ha ha! So we're going to set you a little test. I want each of you to pick something unusual from your handbag – or guys, if you don't have handbags, stick your hands in your pockets. But no pocket billiards, guys. If you haven't anything in your pockets, borrow something off the girls. Everyone will get a chance to sell their chosen object to the panel in the next room for a couple of minutes. Just describe it, why you bought it and why you think the panel ought to buy it. And then you'll have a chance to talk about yourself and why you want to work here. OK? Kelly-Marie will call you in one at a time. Random basis.'

15

And with that Laser Eyes was gone. A moment's silence was followed by pandemonium as the women started scrabbling in their handbags and the guys began frantically rattling the change and car keys in their pockets.

Miss Wonderbra, now Kelly-Marie, reappeared and summoned one of the disco girls. Moments later she called in the girl in green chiffon. As the numbers whittled down, small conversations broke out around the room. Fran looked helplessly at the woman in the burgundy scarf.

'I don't know about you but I haven't got anything worth flogging in my handbag,' said Fran.

The woman smiled back sympathetically. 'Me neither. Two old taxi receipts, some out-of-date Tesco vouchers, bag of make-up and a rather toothless comb. I think I'm going to have to resort to extolling the virtues of my key fob.'

'Same problem,' said Fran. 'The most unusual thing in my bag is an old bulb from a lamp I've been trying to match up for ages. I'm Fran Hallgarth, by the way.'

'Stella Robinson.' They shook hands. 'What are you applying for?'

'Script writer/producer,' said Fran helplessly. 'But I've absolutely no experience in telly. I work on the *Hartford Echo*.'

'Sounds pretty impressive to me,' replied Stella, rewinding her scarf for the umpteenth time out of sheer nerves. 'I'm going for a buyer's job. Can't be any worse than what I do now.'

'What's that?'

'I'm the manager of Bias on Fashion in Hartford and I'd do anything – well, almost anything – to leave. I'm fed up with spending my waking hours squeezing overweight

16

women into large floral prints with industrial-strength seams. Do you know it?'

Fran nodded. It was known locally as Bypass on Fashion, or the Shop That Fashion Forgot. 'Well, I hope you get the job,' she sympathised. 'I'm sure you've got the right experience.'

'Tell you what,' said Stella, nervously eyeing the door in case Miss Wonderbra tottered back in, 'why don't we get in touch after all this and compare notes? At least we could look back and laugh about it.'

'Good idea,' said Fran, fishing in her bag for a card. 'Please don't take offence but it was terrific to see someone, er, more mature in the room. Everyone else seemed young enough to be at school.'

'Absolutely,' replied Stella. 'My heart sank when I saw those girls in *Saturday Night Fever* gear. Mind you, they didn't ask my age when I phoned them about the job. Just as well as I'm thirty-seven.'

'I'm thirty-nine,' said Fran, trying to mean it. Well, at least one of us is lying, she thought.

The door swung open. Fran and Stella hardly needed to look around. Miss Wonderbra stood in the doorway grappling with her clipboard.

'Fran Hallgarth,' she breathed. 'Follow me.'

Fran stood up like an alien being summoned back to the mothership, muttered a goodbye to Stella and marched down the corridor after Kelly-Marie, her heart thumping, her mouth suddenly dry. What on earth had made her get into this? Thank God I have told no one about this, she congratulated herself. No one will ever need know. She had even begun to think about treating herself to a new suit from the Planet sale when she was thrust through a door and ushered to a seat.

The room came abruptly back into focus. There was Paul Dyer, together with an older man and a woman whom he didn't bother to introduce. They were all sitting in armchairs around a low coffee table strewn with files and sheets of paper.

'Bit chaotic, lost your CV, but let's press on,' Dyer beamed, indicating by his tone that speed was of the essence. 'Your two minutes on something out of your handbag starts now.' He mimed an imaginary stopwatch.

Fran delved into her handbag, hands visibly shaking. The silence – all of three seconds – seemed like hours.

'This light bulb,' she spluttered, 'could change your life. And your light. Well, I mean both really. It's so important to me that I carry it everywhere. Now you might think that I'm carrying it around just to match it up with another one next time I'm in an electrical shop. But you couldn't be more wrong.'

Fran flashed a fixed smile at the three of them while pathetically scanning the room for a secret escape route. She spied a large open window with billowing net curtains, Hitchcock-style. Pity they weren't on the ground floor.

'This light bulb is so utterly brilliant,' she ploughed on, 'that I want to spread the word. By carrying it around in my handbag, anyone I meet can see it, examine it and then go and buy one of their own. When people discover just how great, how cheap, how safe and how long-lasting this bulb is, do you know what they do? They do the same as me. They carry one around with them to spread the word.'

I wonder if they've got any jobs going for trainee missionaries at this channel, she thought miserably.

'Do you know how much this bulb cost? No, neither do I. It's so cheap, it's not even worth mentioning the price.

Go on, take a look, pass it round.' She handed it to Paul Dyer. 'Feel its shape, its wonderful design. It could change your light. And your life. So many celebrities have seen the light too. Claudia Schiffer in her Majorcan home, Catherine and Michael in theirs, Hugh Grant in Notting Hill, Richard and Judy at home in Cornwall.' At least all those celeb gossip columns she loved to pore over were coming into their own. 'So why don't you light up, just like the stars, and use this light bulb,' she finished.

Silence. Three seconds felt like three hours. Fran could feel her cheeks burning with embarrassment.

'That was great,' said Paul Dyer, smiling, yet his laser eyes betrayed nothing. 'Thanks. We'll let you know.'

Fran picked up her bag, mumbled her thanks and shuffled out of the room. Back in her car, she took a couple of sharp intakes of breath. What a complete fiasco that had been. She looked at her watch. Nearly lunchtime. She'd park in the town centre. It was sufficiently far away from Hartford that she wouldn't run the risk of bumping into anyone from work. And she would definitely treat herself to something from the Planet sale to make up for it all. But first she needed a cigarette – and a drink – after that ordeal.

She plonked herself down in a corner of Café Rouge and lit up. New Year resolutions blown again but this was probably the best excuse she'd had for years. Oh the sheer relief as the smoke hit her lungs! She ordered some penne with artichoke hearts and aubergines and, oh to hell with it, a large glass of red wine. She then sat back and surveyed the scene. Shoppers flushed with success in the January sales were starting to pour in. After lunch she'd head for Planet, one or two of her other favourite shops, pick up another of those difficult-to-match blasted light bulbs, head home, have a miraculous recovery from her illness and return to work tomorrow as if nothing had happened.

Except that she'd left the damned bulb with the interview panel. Hell, that would mean carting the whole bloody lamp out next time. Oh well, served her right.

Chapter 3

'Just going out on a fag break,' Fran announced to Guy.

'Bit early for a ciggie, isn't it?' he enquired, eyes glued to his computer screen.

'I've been in here since seven this morning,' Fran retorted. Mostly out of guilt from the previous day's skive but she wasn't going to admit that. I've just finished my page on New Year fitness.'

'No, I mean the smoking,' he replied, still engrossed in his screen. 'Bit early for that. You normally keep off the fags till around mid-January. We always look forward to you throwing your toys out of the pram for at least the first fortnight.'

'Yeah, well, I've resolved to resolve not to give up smoking this year.' Fran didn't want to get herself into a corner over yesterday. Nor did she want to discuss her big resolution this year: to do anything but this.

Fran trotted out to the smoking area, grateful for the daylight and fresh air that a fag break ironically afforded. The smokers' hut was a pathetic lean-to affair which involved a trek around two sides of the building. One or two of the old die-hard reporters who couldn't last out until lunch or evening pub opening times used the hut for a swift tinnie and dumped their cans in there. Alcohol was strictly forbidden in the building but no one wanted to test the rules to see whether they applied to the smokers' hut. Now and again, someone took it upon themselves to clear out the empties in a black plastic bin bag and spirit them away. The system was once severely tested when one of the sports writers was caught *in flagrante delicto* with bin bag by the *Echo*'s doddery old chairman, Harold Smithson. Fortunately Mr Smithson was as hard of seeing as he was of hearing, and failed to notice a couple of stray Stella cans casually rolling across the car park. Instead the reporter got a lecture from Mr Smithson on not using company time to go to the launderette.

The biting January wind made an impact even on the short walk to the hut. Fran blew on her hands to warm them up before reaching in a pocket for her cigarettes.

'Bit early for that, isn't it?' remarked Des Ryder, the *Echo*'s permanently scowl-faced chief crime reporter, hunched in a corner over his Capstan full-strength.

'Don't you start,' Fran replied. 'Already had that script from Guy. I'm not giving up this year, OK? Anyway, what are you giving up for New Year?'

'Driving, it seems,' replied Des bitterly. 'Got stopped way over the limit yesterday. Up in court tomorrow.'

'Oh shit, I think I'm down for Hartford Magistrates tomorrow,' said Fran, horrified. 'Guy's really short so I said I'd do him a favour.' Guilt trip again about yesterday's bogus sickie.

'Actually,' said Des, brain suddenly cranking into gear, 'if you are there tomorrow you could do ME the biggest, most gi-normous favour.'

'What's that?' Fran was immediately suspicious. She

and Des weren't that close. In fact, not close at all, thanks to his horrendous halitosis.

'Well, if you somehow miss my case, you know, be out phoning copy for the late edition, then Guy and all the suits won't find out. I've already worked out I could manage with lifts from the photographers and the odd taxi here and there. That way the management won't find out and I won't lose my job.'

He flashed Fran a wicked grin featuring nicotined teeth of various sizes. 'Do that and I'll buy you dinner.'

Fran shuddered. It had never occurred to her that Des did food at all. She suddenly felt a great burden weighing down on her. Des wasn't someone you argued with. An ex-*Daily Mirror* heavyweight, it had been downhill all the way to the *Hartford Echo* where the pace was so leisurely in comparison that he could spend a large proportion of his waking hours in licensed premises. It was a sheer miracle that he hadn't been caught over the limit before. About as miraculous as fifteen-games-without-a-win Hartford Hotspur lifting the premiership.

'No, that's not necessary,' she replied. 'Look, Des, I'll do my best but supposing—'

'No supposing,' hissed Des, 'just do it.'

Fran scurried back to the newsroom, heart thumping. This New Year wasn't getting off to a very good start. Failed miserably in her attempt to give up fags, placed in impossible situation regarding a work colleague. And, yesterday, couldn't even make the case for a blown light bulb.

'A woman called Robinson rang while you were in the fag hut,' Guy shouted across at her, his eyes still transfixed by his screen. 'I've emailed you the number.'

Fran dialled, scanning her gym membership copy one

last time while the number rang several times. 'Thank you for calling Bias on Fashion,' announced a female voice. 'How can I help you?'

It suddenly dawned on Fran that the Mrs Robinson in question was Stella from the job interview.

'I hope you didn't mind me calling,' said Stella, 'but I just wondered how you got on yesterday.'

'Complete shite, actually,' Fran replied, lowering her voice so as not to be overheard. 'I made a total idiot of myself trying to sell a used light bulb so I don't expect to hear anything.'

'Ditto,' said Stella. 'I did a minute or two on the history of my key fob and that was it. I was out on the street. Pity, I got quite excited at the thought of working in telly.'

'Me too. But it was such a shambles. They'd lost all my details, so they cheerfully informed me. So even if I was the light bulb salesperson of the year, I doubt they'd be able to get in touch with me anyway.'

Fran glanced up and spotted Guy unashamedly trying to catch the gist of the conversation. 'Listen, sorry to be rude,' she continued, 'but I'm a bit under the gun here. Let me know if you do hear anything.'

Guy was now glaring at her across the newsroom. He'd obviously twigged that it was a personal call. 'No time for girlie talk. Your property pages this week – get a bloody move on,' he shouted. 'You can see we're short-staffed. I need them done by close of play today. And let's have something a bit swanky for the first page. It's New Year, it's a long time till pay day – let's be aspirational. And don't forget, I've put you on court duty tomorrow.'

How could I forget? Fran thought bitterly to herself. What a wonderful Catch-22 situation that was going to be. She'd have to do as Des said, otherwise he'd make her life unbearable. Knowing Des, he'd survive. He operated by his own rules – nobody knew what he did day to day, other than help subsidise Hartford's licensed trade. Just when everyone began grumbling about his very different agenda to theirs, Des would come up with a really good exclusive story about some heinous crime. And then promptly head straight back to the pub again.

Fran started dialling estate agents' numbers and sifting through endless details. Nothing aspirational about this lot. 'In need of extensive renovation', 'some structural work required', 'appeal for TLC'. A bit too close to home. She rang Bob at the bank to tell him she'd be late home tonight on account of the workload. He was with a client, one of the secretaries informed her. Probably granting someone a loan to do that 'extensive re-novation', she thought enviously. Pity he couldn't grant himself one.

By the time Fran wearily steered her Peugeot into her driveway it was nearly eight o'clock. The light in the shed indicated Bob was home, shedding the cares of the day with a spot of therapeutic hammering and banging. She'd cook some pasta and a cheat sauce for quickness. Soon the pans were bubbling precariously on the Baby Belling as she laid up the picnic table.

'Did you pick up that message on the answering machine?' announced Bob as he came into the kitchen. 'Something to do with that interview you went to yesterday.'

'What?' gasped Fran in shock. 'What did they say?'

'Play it back yourself,' said Bob with a grin. 'Seems you made quite an impression.'

Fran rushed out into the hallway, avoiding a large gap in the floorboards. She bent down to where the machine lived, balanced precariously on a pile of CDs awaiting shelves.

Up came Kelly-Marie's pseudo-drawl, saying unconvincingly that she had been 'faaabulous' and would she go back to the hotel at ten tomorrow morning for another interview. Sorry about the unavoidable short notice, blah blah blah.

Fran's throat went dry. She could hear the blood rushing in her head. It was a mixture of total excitement and panic. Excitement that she had actually succeeded at something and that the dream was still alive. Panic that if she went along she'd have to phone in sick again tomorrow. Tomorrow of all days, when she was due in court covering – or avoiding covering – Des's driving case. At least it got her neatly out of that particular dilemma. Fate, without the help of Madame Chita, had intervened.

Of course she'd go. She knew she didn't have a choice. As she cleared away the plates after dinner, she enjoyed a brief fantasy of never having to write another of Madame Chita's regular double-page spreads on 'Your Summer Fate' (once changed to Fête by a mutinous sub editor who was leaving). Or, with her property editor hat on, 'Dream Homes at Nightmare Prices' (same sub). No more trotting out for ciggies in the fag hut, or putting up with Des's snake breath. Instead she pictured herself at glamorous showbiz parties, product launches and photocalls. She'd miss Guy though. He worked everyone hard but at least he was fair and made sure that everyone did their share. Except Des, of course.

Next morning she was off once again in the opposite direction to the *Echo* offices. She'd persuaded Bob to ring in sick for her – they agreed that an emergency trip to the dentist was a bit more plausible and it meant that she could go in to work later on and reduce the guilt factor.

Same hotel, better parking spot this time. Hair passable, make-up not bad. Suit light grey with dark blue polo neck. Handbag now full of more interesting things, just in case.

Kelly-Marie greeted her with as much enthusiasm as a lamb in a queue for the abattoir. Today's killer heels were red to match a pelmet-length skirt and a cross-over black cardigan straining at the seams over another triumph of underwiring. Bleached blonde *Footballers' Wives* hair untidily piled up and topped off with a large red feather. It would certainly have clinched her pole position at a Spearmint Rhino Club.

She ushered Fran into the same room, but this time there were only four people occupying the orange plastic chairs. One, to her delight, was Stella, whose face broke into a huge smile as she entered the room. Another was Mr Six-Pack with the bulging biceps and the snake tattoo on his neck. Miss Timotei was also there, this time in shocking pink, together with one of the women in black. Apparently Teletubby, Pokémon and the disco girls hadn't made the cut.

No pep talk from Paul Dyer this time. They all sat in stony silence, wondering what was going on in the interview room. This time Fran was the first to be called. At least it would soon all be over. She offered up a silent prayer as she followed Kelly-Marie's clippy-cloppy footsteps down the corridor.

Please help me to get this job, she begged the Almighty. And I promise I'll never moan about Des Ryder or the plastic picnic table ever again. She heard the door close behind her. The same three pairs of eyes bored into her.

Chapter 4

When Fran got back to the *Echo* offices, she knew immediately that something was amiss. Two of the telesales girls were whispering animatedly in the corner of the reception area. Then Shirley, the *Echo*'s ultra-smart chief receptionist, tipped her off that some kind of war had broken out upstairs in the newsroom.

'Weapons of mass deception,' she whispered as Fran sashayed past the reception desk. Shirley knew everything that went on inside and outside the building – not only who was doing what to whom, but how, why, when and where. However, she was the soul of discretion. She only dealt out information when she deemed it absolutely necessary.

Fran climbed the stairs, trying to practise deep breathing at every step. She had her suspicions about the 'war'. Pushing open the glass door into the newsroom and reading all the body language, she knew she was right. Guy, red-faced and clearly incandescent with anger, was standing over an equally smouldering Des, apparently dictating him a news story. It was the account of his drink-driving case and Guy was making Des type it up himself.

'Ryder, who's fifty-one and the *Echo*'s chief crime

reporter, admitted driving while three times over the limit . . . no, make that *more than* three times . . .' Fran caught enough to get the picture. Des had somehow been found out and she knew he'd blame it all on her. He'd bide his time and catch her in the fag hut at some point.

Wrong. Des erupted immediately on seeing Fran, sprang up from his desk, brushed Guy aside and began chasing after her around the desks.

'Hold the bottom of page nineteen,' muttered one of the subs.

'Anyone got a camera?' murmured another, trying not to laugh.

'And where were you, you bitch?' ranted Des, who was now positively steaming. 'You skived off on purpose.' The whole newsroom had downed tools, unashamedly listening.

'I don't know what you're talking about,' Fran stammered as she dodged around the block of desks where the sports writers sat. Des was gaining ground, still shouting and shaking his fists at her. But suddenly his lunchtime consolation session of three pints and a few whisky chasers got the better of him. Red-faced and gasping for breath, he pulled up short, just as several pairs of arms had reached out to stop him in his tracks. Instead of the expected punch-up, Des simply crumpled into an undignified heap on the floor. To add insult to injury, when he peered up from the floor the entire sports department was standing there laughing at him.

'Serves you right, you bloody drunken sod,' muttered Jeff, one of the football writers. 'Leave her alone. What's she got to do with any of this?'

'Exactly,' intoned a voice from behind them. It was Derek Callaghan, the managing editor. He'd obviously heard the commotion and come out of his office further up the corridor. Everyone suddenly went silent.

Mr Callaghan, who was secretly relishing the drama, drew himself up to his full height – all five feet six inches in his socks. 'Security are on their way to escort you out of the building,' he boomed imperiously at Des. 'You are suspended until further notice. And, Guy, I suggest you get to the bottom of this disgraceful episode.'

He then looked around for Fran, who was now cowering on the other side of the newsroom, white-faced from shock and dying for a cigarette.

'Fran, I hope you're all right and not too shaken.' Then he turned back to the newsroom: 'May I remind you all that physical violence is a sackable offence?'

With that, he swept back to his office, secretly congratulating himself on his bravura performance. The next bit of drama was the sight of Des being escorted from the room as if he'd just been sent down at the Old Bailey. Finally, Guy beckoned Fran into his little glass booth at the end of the newsroom.

He opened a filing cabinet drawer, pulled out a half empty bottle of vodka and two rather manky glasses, and proceeded to pour them a couple of fingers each, topped up with tonic. Momentarily stunned at the blatant breaking of the alcohol rule, Fran hoped people leering at them would think they were drinking fizzy water. She hated vodka but she needed the instant effect it had on her. Soon she began to relax from the shock and related to Guy what had happened in the fag hut the previous day. In return, Guy explained that in her absence that morning he'd sent a trainee reporter, Rob, up to cover Hartford

Magistrates. Blissfully unaware of Des's impending driving ban, Rob hadn't even recognised Des's surname on the charge sheet. So when Des took centre stage for his case, instead of the press bench being empty as he had confidently expected, he saw Rob sitting there, keen as mustard and brandishing a shiny new pen and huge notebook.

By the time Des had paid both his fine and a visit to the pub next door, Rob was halfway back to the office with his story.

'We'd already had one fracas before you arrived,' grinned Guy. 'Des thought he could nobble Rob when he got back to the office. But I walked in and caught him red-handed. When I discovered that Des had been up in court and had gone to various lengths to keep it out of the paper, I decided he should type up his own story. That is, of course, when you chose to make your entrance. Hence fracas number two.'

Fran listened intently. She was still waiting for the inevitable question. And finally it came.

'Just what had you intended to do if you'd been in court this morning?' Guy gave her a piercing look.

'I, er, hadn't quite decided,' said Fran truthfully, biting her lip. She gazed down at her glass, searching the bottom of it for the right answer. 'In the end, the decision was made for me when I had to go to the dentist,' she added untruthfully. Please don't let my teeth drop out in punishment, she silently prayed. At least she could pass off her face flaming with embarrassment as a rough morning at the dentist followed by the effect of the vodka.

'Anyway,' continued Guy smoothly, 'I'm running the story at the top of page three in tomorrow's early editions.'

'What about Des?' she asked, trying not to giggle at the thought of Des being a page three boy. 'What'll happen to him?'

'Personally I think we should sack him, but that's a matter for Mr Callaghan. In any event, I think Des may have to revise his working arrangements quite radically if he wants to stay on. He's been banned from driving for two and a half years. He'd have to start turning up here every day for a start.'

Fran shivered. The thought of old Snake Breath being in the office every day was the stuff of nightmares. He'd have optics installed in the fag hut before they knew it.

Guy drained his glass, signalling to Fran to do the same so they could remove the evidence. Then he suggested she wrote off the rest of the day.

'Have a good long soak in the bath with a glass of wine and then relax beside the fire,' Guy said kindly. 'Get that husband of yours to cook you a lovely candlelit meal. Then come back tomorrow refreshed.'

Fat chance of that, thought Fran, in a freezing bathroom with the plumbing hanging out of the yet-to-be-tiled wall and the radiator not connected up. The plastic picnic table might not look too bad by candlelight though.

She was just heaving in the last of the big blue bags of washing from the local laundrette (washing machine still merely a fantasy) when Bob made his big announcement.

'You've had another message from that mob.'

'What mob?' replied Fran, sensing her life depended on it.

'That shopping thingy,' he replied with a small grin.

'What did they say?' She stopped herself from grabbing him in anticipation. 'Any hint of what it was about?'

'Nope, just to call them,' said Bob mysteriously. 'Anyway, must get on with those door handles. Give us a shout when supper's ready.'

She watched Bob's angular form lope up the garden path. She'd like to have loathed him and left him, but she couldn't. Bob was actually the nicest person she'd ever met. He'd do anything for anybody – it might take him several years, but the thought was there.

She went into the hall, side-stepping the missing floorboard. There she confronted the answering machine, took a deep breath and played back the message. Sure enough, it was Kelly-Marie. Getting It wanted to make her an offer and could she ring back any time up until midnight? She took another deep breath and dialled. Eventually Kelly-Marie answered, in between audible drags on a cigarette.

'Paul Dyer wants to speak to you,' she drawled. Pause, agonising pause.

'Hi, Fran Hallgarth?' a familiar voice enquired. 'Congratulations. Welcome to the wonderful world of television shopping. We'd like you to join the Getting It team.'

Fran felt her throat go dry, her knees buckle. She wanted to sink to the floor but without a carpet it might have been painful. She stayed upright, clutching a pile of books for support, muttered her thanks and tried to sound coherent.

'Not brilliant money, I'm afraid,' Paul continued. 'But, to be fair, you're not a telly oppo – yet.' Fran could almost feel his laser eyes boring into her down the phone line.

He then proceeded to offer her, as he put it, a Martini contract. Any time, any place, anywhere. And a salary of a third less than she was getting on the *Echo*. She choked, momentarily disappointed. Suddenly Des lurched into her consciousness. No, she'd willingly take a cut – anything to avoid his little bullying sessions in the fag hut or his forthcoming stale-sweat-and-alcohol presence in the newsroom. She'd just have to cut back on Mondi and Planet for a while and shop at Next or Principles. Not the end of the world. Once she'd recovered sufficiently, she put candles all around the kitchen and on the picnic table, picked up the telephone and ordered an Indian takeaway. And when Bob finally appeared in the kitchen doorway, his thumb bleeding profusely from a collision with a stanley knife, she could not hide her delight. Even Bob, who wasn't prone to vast displays of emotion, expressed genuine excitement at her success. Much later that night, as Bob snored for Britain, she couldn't sleep for excitement. A new job in television! And at her age! This was the stuff of dreams.

Next morning, Fran awoke with the sentimental sadness that accompanies any big life change. Bob showing such enthusiasm last night for her job offer had been a great help. But here she was, saying goodbye to the *Echo* where she'd served twenty years, where she'd met most of her friends, shared the most laughs. She'd been there even longer than she'd been at school. And, of course, it had provided her with an income and the sanity to cope with the Un-Real Rooms scenario going on at home.

She almost crept through reception, trying to avoid Shirley's gaze in case she gave the game away.

'Don't worry, hon,' said Shirley, impeccable as ever in a grey suit and white blouse, and doing her usual mind reading act, 'Des isn't in. He's suspended for a week and then booked for a meeting. You know, THAT sort of

34

meeting.' She winked conspiratorially. How did Shirley do it? She practically knew what everyone ate for breakfast. Mind you, that was quite easy where Des was concerned. The egg on his tie wasn't hard to spot.

Fran had insisted that Paul Dyer put the job offer in writing before she gave in her notice. He'd offered to fax it to her at the *Echo* office at 10 a.m. on the dot so that she could then announce her bombshell as soon as possible. It meant hovering over the fax machine, but as her desk was nearest she felt she could take the risk.

As she logged on to her computer, she began to ponder some of the advantages of leaving. No more boring old property pages, or women's pages dispensing annual advice to summer brides, winter widows, spring cleaners or autumn de-clutterers.

She was still musing about all this in the morning meeting when she realised she hadn't been paying the slightest bit of attention to the day's list of stories.

'You all know what happened here yesterday,' Guy was telling the fifteen or so reporters in the room. 'If you don't, then you're rotten journalists. But here, I'm afraid, is where the story stays. I don't want to hear or read anything about this in *Hartford Life* or any other of our rivals. Geddit? And if any of you are planning to top the bill at Hartford Magistrates in the near or even distant future, kindly let me know. Journalists are not entitled to any sort of papal dispensation or diplomatic immunity over their crimes. They make the papers, same as everyone else. Des's case will appear on page three, top story. End of story. Now let's get on. We've deadlines to meet. Let's write that fish and chip paper.'

Fran went back to work, trying to concentrate while keeping an eye on the fax machine. After Getting It's previous form, she was not convinced the fax from Paul Dyer would arrive at all. (10.05 – it was already a bit late.) She was also aware of newsroom eyes still on her after yesterday's fracas. She decided to flip through a couple of celebrity magazines for a bit of fashion inspiration. Here was just the thing – stars in leather trousers. Perhaps she could run a readers' poll on when are you too old to wear them. (10.18 – definitely late.) She could ring a couple of boutiques that she knew stocked leather trousers and find out the average ages of their clients. (10.27 – bloody late.) She started dialling Stella's number.

'Going out for a fag break?' enquired forty-a-day Felicity who, somewhat ironically, was the *Echo*'s environment correspondent.

'Nope, not yet,' replied Fran.

She was so preoccupied with dialling Bypass on Fashion that she failed to notice the fax machine spluttering to life. Stella answered after the first ring.

'Hi Stella, it's Fran at the *Echo*. I'm thinking of doing a feature about leather trousers and I wondered if your shop—'

'Do me a favour! Bypass ladies are only just worshipping at the shrine of control top tights.' Stella shrieked with laughter. Obviously there wasn't anyone in the shop. 'We've a long way to go before we can cope with leather trousers.'

'OK, well, it was worth a try,' said Fran, quickly scanning the immediate desks to make sure she wasn't being overheard. She lowered her voice. 'They made me an offer last night.'

'Wow, me too!' said Stella. 'I've just heard this morning. I'm over the moon about it, but the money's crap – worse than here. Are you going to accept?'

'Yes, except the bloody fax confirming all the details that they promised on the dot of ten hasn't bloody well arrived. And they haven't got their email up and running yet.'

'Oh, I've just quit anyway,' Stella announced. 'Phoned the boss about ten minutes ago. He's furious, I'm pleased to say. I can't wait to see the back of this place. And all my enormous clientèle. Don't worry about the fax, it'll come. Let's face it, they've been fairly shambolic up to now. I can't imagine Kelly-Marie having the va-va-voom to operate a fax machine even if it were designed by Fisher Price. Let me know when it arrives.'

Fran promised she would. Bitterly regretting not telling Paul Dyer just to post the details to her home, she picked up her bag and headed out to the fag hut. Felicity was still there, lighting a new cigarette from the butt of the old one. She got straight to the point. 'So if you hadn't been at the dentist, would you have shopped Des or turned a blind eye?'

Fran knew they'd all ask sooner rather than later. She decided to stick to what she'd told Guy yesterday, which was the truth – up to a point. 'Des did make threats. It was a terrible dilemma and I didn't know what to do. It was the only time I've ever been glad of toothache,' she finished rather unconvincingly.

'Well,' Felicity continued, 'you've done us all a huge favour by outing Des.'

Fran muttered her gratitude. I must get Madame Chita to predict me a holiday, she thought, to get away from all this fibbing. Being the centre of attention in the newsroom had not been in her plan. Joining the new and exciting world of television certainly had, except they couldn't even operate a fax. She could hardly jack in a job with twenty years' service and pension behind her on the strength of one late-night phone call.

As she climbed the stairs with Felicity huffing and puffing behind her, Fran began to mentally list the advantages of staying at the *Echo*. The money, for a start, was better, and the hours more regular. She could even Return to the Forbidden Planet – she allowed herself a laugh at her own joke.

'Fax for you,' said Rob, the cub reporter who'd covered Des's case. He pointed to a curling roll of paper on Fran's desk.

Fran rushed over to it, hands shaking. It was exactly what she'd been hoping for, including a barely legible note from Kelly-Marie saying she'd put the paper in the wrong way round the first couple of times and had jammed up her machine. Fran looked up at her colleagues, half expecting them to know the fax's contents and be busily turning it into the front page lead. But no, they were all pounding away on their keyboards or had phones tucked between ear and shoulder.

'Can I see you in your office?'

Eyes still riveted to his screen, Guy gave his standard 'wrong-time-of-day-for-this-type-of-nonsense' grunt. Then he glanced up, realised it was Fran and dramatically changed his mind. 'I suppose it's about Des. We'd better talk.'

'Sorry, Guy, it's not about Des,' said Fran, her voice squeaking with sudden nerves, just as it had at the Getting It audition. 'I wanted to tell you that I'm leaving. As soon as possible because I've been offered another job.'

Guy was momentarily ashen. 'You can't do that,' he spluttered. 'You've been here since clocks were invented. You're part of the furniture.'

'Oh thanks! Is that why I've often felt sat upon?' replied Fran. 'Anyway, this old bit of G-Plan has had enough.'

'Look, Fran, we're sorting the Des problem,' said Guy, trying to regain control of the situation by leaning forward on his desk in an attempt to look more caring. 'Confidentially, he's coming in next week for a full and frank chat about his future – and believe you me, it won't take long. But I need you to do the property and the women's pages. You're one of my stalwarts – you churn out more than most of them put together. You can't be serious.'

Fran owned up to her dentist fib the day before and explained all about the job. Once he'd got over the shock, Guy seemed genuinely pleased for her and almost envious, but he was clearly very concerned about finding a replacement quickly. Especially as Fran then calmly announced that she had two weeks' leave owing so could effectively finish in just a fortnight.

'Tell you what,' continued Guy, somewhat desperately, 'how about staying on as Madame Chita? That would fool all that lot out there.' He indicated the newsroom who had not, to date, rumbled Fran's alter ego. 'How about me upping the Chita money?'

'Hmm, I'll think about it,' she said, wishing she could dismiss his offer out of hand. A pay rise for Madame Chita – that would make up some of the deficit of the new job. A future without the odd bit of cashmere, Wolford tights and Lulu Guinness handbags would be hard to contemplate.

'I'd like to leave as soon as possible. No point in hanging around.'

The more she explained about the new shopping channel, the more Fran got excited. At last, an escape after twenty years. Never having to type the words 'des-res' or 'low-cal' ever again. Never having to tour around neat little semis and wonder why she couldn't live in one just like it. She couldn't wait.

Chapter 5

Fran had never known a month go by so quickly. Despite the *Echo*'s insistence that she work her full notice and be paid for the holiday she was due, she was anxious to leave things tidy when she left – just in case Getting It didn't work out and she might want to knock on the *Echo*'s door again. She spent long days preparing all her usual columns, plus mapping out ideas and lists of contacts for her successor, in between popping into a neighbour's who had a satellite dish to watch all the shopping channels. At home, as Bob hammered and banged his way through a few more abortive door handles, she hammered away at her old typewriter, writing as many Madame Chita columns as she could get through to give herself a head start in the new job. She'd given into Guy's pressure and agreed to write the horoscopes for the time being. She deliberately wrote herself a terrible horoscope – 'Stay in, it's terrible out there' – just in case someone finally twigged.

Des had turned up for his meeting a week after his court appearance and been promptly fired. That had sent a frisson of panic around the newsroom. Despite being the most unpopular man in the building, and possibly the whole of Hartford, his sacking had shaken up some of the biggest bastions of complacency. Even forty-a-day Felicity had suddenly found the wherewithal to produce almost double her normal rate of copy. It was all thanks to fear, plus a new environmental magazine that had just been launched from which she was cribbing all her ideas.

Suddenly Fran's last day loomed and it was time to say goodbye to twenty years' life at the *Echo*. She spent most of the day in tears. Mid-afternoon, Guy rose to his feet and clapped his hands to get everyone's attention.

'Do you want the bad news or the even worse news?' he asked the assembled throng. Muttering and quiet jeering broke out from every direction. 'Well, the bad news is that Fran Hallgarth is leaving, as most of you already know. She's going to join the wonderful, glamorous world of television where she will be a huge success and never speak to the likes of us again.'

He then proceeded to give a short account of Fran's two decades at the *Echo*, mentioning some of the scoops she'd found and how popular her columns were.

'Fran,' he beamed, 'we never thought you'd leave us. I don't think even Madame Chita and her crystal ball could have predicted that one.'

There was a ripple of laughter. Fran found her fixed smile had curiously got stuck to her teeth. Surely he wasn't going to reveal her alter ego. She'd be so embarrassed. Her horoscopes were wild, imaginative and daring – really not like her at all – and they'd occasionally grabbed the front page lead when she'd successfully predicted a lottery rollover for a Capricorn (not all Capricorns, just one of them, living in Hartford). On another occasion, a woman had written in obviously pleased that her husband had

42

actually been struck by lightning, after a warning that sparks might fly for Arians.

Fortunately Guy ploughed on with the tribute. Fran was presented with two parcels, two envelopes, a card signed by all the staff and a huge iced cake with a replica of a television screen on the top. She hastily opened the presents so everyone could see them. A beautiful Yves St Laurent silk scarf – they'd obviously clocked her expensive tastes – and a huge leather organiser for all her contacts in her new and more exciting life. The envelopes contained subscriptions to *OK!* magazine and *House Beautiful* to remind her of the *Echo*. *House Beautiful* also reminded her rather painfully that her own home was anything but. The staff weren't to know – she'd never dared invite them round. Everyone cheered and clapped as Fran made a short speech of thanks and then cut the cake.

'If that was the bad news, what's the even worse news then?' chorused two subs. Everyone turned to Guy, who started to look a bit shifty.

'Hhhhmm,' said Guy reluctantly, staring at the floor. He didn't want to rot up Fran's last moments in the job. 'You won't like this. Not my idea at all. But apparently they couldn't get anyone else to take Fran's place. I'm afraid I have to tell you that Des is back, starting on Monday.'

A huge wave of disbelief and unrestrained swearing swept around the room.

'Sorry folks,' Guy continued, looking horribly embarrassed. 'I advertised for two senior reporters to replace Fran and Des – and not a single applicant. We had no choice but to take him back. Don't worry, folks, Des will have a different brief. There won't be any more of Des Ryder Investigates . . . occasionally!'

'That's what you get when you don't pay enough,' was the audible mutter around the room.

'Will Des be writing Fran's columns then?' chipped in one of the subs. 'Hey, I can see the headlines now – "Des Ryder's Des-Res" or "Drink Yourself Healthy with Des's Ten-Pint Plan".' Everyone screamed with laughter.

Later that evening, when most of the newsroom had piled into the local pub, Fran asked Guy for his take on Des's reinstatement.

'I've no idea,' Guy confessed, 'but I suddenly got a directive from the management. All I can conclude is that Des has something over them – inside knowledge on some extra-curricular rumpy pumpy or arrears on their golf club bar bills. Des loves revenge, he makes no secret of it. It's his *raison d'être*.'

'That's exactly what I'm afraid of,' Fran conceded.

Getting It's induction week was – to put it bluntly – a farce. The sixty chosen people gathered for five days of training at the same hotel where they'd endured their auditions. The atmosphere was a highly charged mix of raw ambition and nerves. Fran and Stella were fascinated by the fact that Six-Pack had survived the cut, together with Timotei girl. At first it was difficult to work out everyone's job because they all attended the same briefing sessions, whether they were on principles of camera operation, libel, script writing, or health and safety. It was a huge amount to absorb.

'Why on earth do WE need health and safety training?' Stella demanded during one of the very short coffee breaks.

'Just suppose we were flogging frying pans,' replied Fran. 'Would you want old Six-Pack over there installing a cooker for your use during a live programme?'

'Hmmmm, see what you mean,' said Stella.

Coffee break over, it was time for yet another interminable seminar – this time on studio techniques. To their surprise, Paul Dyer walked in to take the session. He'd been conspicuous by his absence, but appeared to take great delight in the shock reaction he'd caused. Soon everyone was split into groups and role-playing like there was no tomorrow.

Suddenly Paul Dyer consulted an expensive watch. 'Enough,' he pronounced. 'I have a special announcement to make.'

A projector screen appeared from nowhere and the fearful sixty found themselves confronted by a very rough mock-up of the Getting It logo – a drawing of a very curvy blonde girl with a wanton look wearing a leopard skin bikini and sitting inside a shopping trolley.

'Exactly what I wear when I go shopping,' remarked Stella under her breath to Fran. 'Very Bet Lynch.'

Everyone clapped and cheered furiously. They were already showing signs of being completely brainwashed. At this rate, Hartford's Jehovah's Witnesses would be signing up for Ann Summers' parties.

'Let's hear it for cheap and tacky,' Fran replied. 'That's why they picked Hartford for the location, conveniently up the motorway and far enough away from expensive London. Right now, I don't care how truly awful it is, it is just so exciting being in on the birth of a television station. I would never have dreamed this could happen.' Which goes to show what a rotten clairvoyant I am, she smiled to herself.

The next two weeks were nothing short of a nightmare. The action moved from the hotel to a shabby warehouse on the edge of Hartford where miles of electrical cabling were hurriedly being installed. Two studios were being created, one small one which featured a permanent kitchen set and a larger, multi-purpose studio that could accommodate a range of multi-gym equipment and other bigger items. As for the office areas, they appeared to have been relegated several leagues down the priority list. A selection of desks and chairs, hot from a liquidation sale, plus a range of reconditioned computers. Amid all the building chaos, the courses, the mission statements, the lectures and the seminars continued. And as the rehearsals proper began, it became apparent what everyone's roles were to be.

Six-Pack, whose name was Piers, had been hired as scene shifter and floor manager. He was obviously going to be terribly good at heaving bits of scenery around but as a floor manager he was having problems. Responsible for interpreting all the director's instructions through his headset to those on the studio floor, he had to be able to give mimed commands to the presenters and count backwards. Already Piers had been heard practising to himself: 'Ten, nine, eight, seven, five, fuck, six, seven, fuck, three, one, two, oh whatever.' It also transpired that Timotei girl was called Tracey and she was to be one of the main presenters.

Despite the training, the pep talks, group bonding and all the rehearsals, the prospect of broadcasting live became more and more scary. Fran couldn't imagine how the shambles she was now witnessing on a daily basis could possibly work. She was installed in a production office writing copy about all the various products, but even as a division three shopaholic she could see very little that warranted a flutter with the credit card.

Stella, meanwhile, was already knee-deep in dealing with clients, or vendors as they had to call them, who were anxious to sell their products on air. Everything was wildly talked up, even if it was obviously rubbish. She found the lack of guidance quite baffling. Should she go with the multi-purpose saucepan/steamer combination, the organic doggie beds or the seaweed body exfoliant? It was all a mystery.

Fran turned her attention to some bullet points about a self-cleaning deep-fat fryer. This time next week, some of the rubbish she was writing would actually be uttered on live television. It might be a boring old deep-fat fryer but, hey, this was showbiz.

Fran fell into a blissful reverie which involved Getting It winning lots of television awards. The fantasy had just moved on to a swanky dinner at the Hilton, sitting alongside her favourite celebrities, when she was suddenly aware of a tall, lanky man of indeterminate age standing by her desk.

'I'm Steve McGuire,' he smiled, somewhat nervously, offering a rather wet handshake. 'Er, we're going to be working together.'

Fran looked blankly at him. This was all news to her.

'Er, copy, product back up and so on. And you are?'

'Fran. Fran Hallgarth. I, er didn't know you were arriving,' she added, trying to wipe her hands subtly on her trousers without him noticing. 'No one told me about you.'

'Oh, s . . . s . . . sorry,' he stammered. 'Didn't they tell you?'

No, you numpty, otherwise I wouldn't be asking, thought Fran. How on earth had he convinced an interview board of his ability? He must be some amazing whizz kid.

'Where have you come from?' she asked, bracing herself for a Bill Gates-type CV.

'Potters Bar,' he announced. Not the answer she was expecting. 'Just trying to get a h . . . h . . . handle on all this,' he finished eventually. 'What makes you t . . . t . . . tick?'

'Batteries,' she replied with a forced smile, trying to put him at his ease. He failed to see the joke. It suddenly occurred to her that he looked just like Clark Kent in his thick dark-framed glasses, but – just possibly – without the Superman connection.

'I'm a journalist,' she announced with forced cheerfulness. 'Came here from the *Hartford Echo*. Oh, and I'm thirty-nine.' She must keep remembering that bit. It sounded so much healthier than forty-two. She'd had to reduce the time she had spent working on the *Echo* accordingly.

'I've, er, come from telesales,' said Steve nervously. Just as well, thought Fran. Those glasses would have frightened off any potential face to face customer. 'I c . . . c . . . couldn't start before because they m . . . m . . . made me work my full notice,' he continued. 'And then my m . . . mum had to go into hospital. So I've missed most of the training. I'm a bit w . . . w . . . worried about it.'

'Oh, I'm sure you'll soon catch up.' Fran tried to sound soothing. Clark Kent was going to be an uphill struggle. But, she warned herself, for all she knew he could be a management spy. Or perhaps he was just one of those librarian types who quietly got on with things without the benefit of personality. He certainly didn't fit into Paul Dyer's original pitch for Getting It when he'd advertised for people seeking non-stop excitement. Perhaps Paul had fulfilled his quota of constantly pre-orgasmic people and was now looking for a few boring ones to create a balance. Steve looked as though his idea of a top night was a discussion about Latin poetry over a large mug of Horlicks.

The *Hartford Echo* had just started running the knocking stories. To begin with they'd been very supportive of a new television station springing up virtually on their doorstep. Night after night they'd run stories about the new channel, how many jobs it would create, how much it would pump into the local economy, how much the company was saving by not setting up in London. Then the stories progressed to speculation about which famous faces might be signed up to appear on the station. The answer was, of course, none, but the speculation made for some good headlines.

But then suddenly the tide turned. 'Chaos at New Shopping Channel'; 'Staff Fear They're Not Getting (the hang of) It'; 'Panic-Buying Channel' were just some of the headlines. A couple of the stories, Fran noticed, had Des Ryder's by-line on them. Perhaps he was getting his revenge. At least the old soak must have got off his backside and made a bit of an effort.

The only trouble was, as an ex-employee of the *Echo* Fran sensed everyone at Getting It thought she'd been feeding him the lines. Some of Des's copy had, in fact, been hitting the spot. The station had been plagued with technical problems. The graphics suite that would generate all the on-screen information about product codes, prices and the all-important phone number for orders was nowhere near up and running. One of the newly delivered studio cameras had developed a fault so they couldn't do a proper camera line-up. This meant that the shots from the rogue camera made everyone's skin tone look bright orange, as though they'd just flown in from presenting travel programmes. To add to everyone's dismay, Kelly-Marie was suddenly announced as office manager, in charge of reception, telephones, stationery, rotas and expenses. For someone who'd not yet mastered a fax machine properly this was an Olympic-sized leap of faith.

But Fran didn't really care. She was secretly entranced by the whole concept of television. She was in love with the idea that, come the end of next week, people would press buttons, activate cameras, check sound levels, powder last-minute noses – and suddenly they'd be on air. After years in the same old *Echo* newsroom, this was so exciting she could hardly speak.

Chapter 6

With six days to go, Paul Dyer called everyone into the studio for a pep talk.

'As soon as we're on air,' Stella muttered to Fran as they filed in, 'we must go out one evening, get slaughtered and compare notes. Life in the buying department is a complete nightmare. The products are utter rubbish. Who on earth would want to buy an organic doggie bed with its own plug-in fragrance to match your pooch's birth sign? We must be importing half of Taiwan.'

'That bad?' Fran enquired.

Paul Dyer pulled himself up to his full height to address them. 'Well, folks,' he announced, eyes flashing with unconcealed anger. 'You're really not Getting It – at all. We're on air from next Friday, twenty-four hours a day, seven days a week. I would like to say we're on schedule. But we're not. We're total shit. And most of it's just plain bloody carelessness. Just remember that every programme we record will be shown again and again and again. Then again and again and again. So even if it's a pile of rubbish, it'll keep on rolling for up to six months. Mistakes and all. So we've got to get it right first time.

'Everyone has got to pull their weight. Graphics

people – time you learned to spell. During rehearsals this week I have already seen on screen a deep-fat fryer spelled f – r – i – a – r.' He paused for effect. Several people tried not to laugh. 'We're talking about something that makes chips, not an overweight monk. And presenters and scriptwriters, for goodness' sake think a bit more carefully about what you're going to say. Yesterday alone we had a "high fibre" optic lamp. This is a lamp, not a health food. Presenters must be briefed more fully. And to top it all, some dickhead thinks we're selling fat-pack furniture. The product might be the cheapest, the biggest or the best thing since sliced bread. It might also be the worst thing BEFORE sliced bread but we've still got to shift it.

'Camera angles – I saw a lot of backs of heads. Unless we're flogging hair restorer, wigs or toupee tape, I don't want to see them. And let's take an axe to that hammock before it claims another victim. I'm already one presenter down before we've even started.'

Fatigue and nerves had finally spilled over during the previous night's demonstration of a rather cheap garden hammock. Try as she might, Tracey couldn't get the hang of it – literally – for love nor money. The idea was that she should lie in the hammock and sway gently while extolling its virtues to three cameras. But after several attempts to get on board she'd spectacularly fallen to the floor. There was no mistaking the sound of the crack as she broke her elbow. They'd all gathered at the edge of the scene dock to watch her being bundled off to Casualty. Fran prayed that the story wouldn't reach the ears of the *Hartford Echo* and prompt another round of silent finger-pointing.

Everyone shuffled away, very despondent and vowing

under their breath to get wrecked that night. Stella sidled up to Fran.

'You know we said just now about meeting up once we were on air,' she whispered. 'I think I could do with comparing notes tonight.'

'Yes,' Fran agreed, suddenly grateful not to be going home immediately. After a day like today she just wasn't in the mood for Bob's Black and Decker moments or yet another pasta and sauce meal knocked up on the Baby Belling.

Having both phoned home to tell their husbands to fend for themselves, they were soon sat in the corner of a little French bistro a couple of blocks from the Getting It studios – if you could call them that. They still looked like a run-down warehouse from the outside.

'Apparently someone's complained anonymously to the management about Paul Dyer shouting "diarrhoea" all the time in his office,' Fran announced as she buttered a crisp brown roll.

'Really? I mean, does he have a problem?'

'Nah. He was merely answering his phone. Dyer here. Diarrhoea.'

They both burst out laughing.

'Personally, I haven't had so much fun in years,' said Stella, wiping her eyes. 'When I think back to all that time in the bloody shop saying, "Yes modom, no modom", at least I'm allowed – even paid – to have an opinion.'

'The whole set up is rather weird though, isn't it?' said Fran, the wine loosening her tongue. 'I thought it was going to be ever so glamorous working in television, celebrities practically popping up out of the drains. A real step up from the *Echo*. But it's not. Here we are, all cooped up in a dreary biscuit tin on the edge of nowhere in particular. And I've taken quite a big salary cut. Thank God they gave me a year's subscription to *OK!* when I left the *Echo*. It's the nearest brush I'm going to get to with celeb-dom.'

Stella, her mouth full of pâté, nodded in agreement. 'But I just wanted to be out of that bloody shop and into something more exciting,' she finally explained, putting down her knife and fork. 'So in that respect at least I've achieved it. But I agree, it wasn't what I was expecting. I know it sounds a bit daft but I always imagined being famous when I was a little girl. Probably just wanted to find out what it felt like.'

'Yeah, me too,' said Fran. 'When I was on the *Echo* I used to dream about writing a column for the *Mirror* and being invited to previews, film premières or even the opening of an envelope. Just be famous for being famous. I've always wondered what it's like to have people rush up to you in the street for autographs or raid your dustbins.'

'Nearest I've got to that kind of treatment is being hustled by market researchers and timeshare touts in Hartford High Street on a Saturday morning,' replied Stella wryly. 'I'd love to ride around in a stretch limo, appear on chat shows and get the best table at the Ivy.'

'And another thing,' said Fran. 'When you get to that celebrity status, everyone gives you things. Just when you're wedged up and could actually afford lots of lovely expensive kit, people fall over themselves to get you to wear their clothes, borrow their jewellery, ride in their cars and go to their parties. I could cope with that.'

'Do you think we're too late?' asked Stella wistfully.

'Definitely, and even later in my case,' said Fran, lighting a cigarette, eyes downcast with sudden embarrassment. 'Please don't tell a soul but I lied about my age to get the job. I'm actually forty-two but I did a bit of subtraction. Somehow thirty-nine sounds a whole generation younger.'

They paused while their starter plates were cleared away.

'Actually,' Stella half-whispered as she leaned across the table, 'I have a confession to make too. I did the same thing. I'm forty-one and counting but couldn't bear the idea of the forties. Just sounded like the war. I knew we had a lot in common!'

'So how "old" are you?' Fran grinned.

'Er, better at takeaways than you. I'm coming up thirty-eight. I look at it like this – if the Queen can have an official birthday, I'm bloody well going to have an official age.'

Over the main course, they shared their disappointment in the shopping opportunities at Getting It. Both had been hoping for a healthy discount on some really top-notch stuff. But a world of cheapie rotary mowers, home multi-gyms and seaweed supplements for all the family wasn't quite what they'd been expecting.

'I am enjoying this confessional so much, I think we should order another bottle of wine,' said Fran, lighting up again. 'But first I'll ring Bob and see if he can pick us up. We don't want to be banned from driving the first week Getting It's on air.'

She produced her mobile from her bag and made a quick call to Bob.

'No problem,' she announced, 'he'll drop you off and take us both in to work tomorrow so we can leave our cars.'

Stella thanked her enviously. 'Ray wouldn't do that,' she said. It was the first time she'd really mentioned her husband. 'He's such a pig, thinks only about himself. All he's done is whinge since I landed this job. Especially as I've been working until ten most nights the last few weeks. I think he liked me stuck in the shop, regular money, set hours, dinner on the table on the dot. It was all routine, routine, routine. Now it's just chaos. And of course he can't cook, won't cook.'

Fran drew heavily on her cigarette and flicked a long line of ash into the ashtray . 'No kids, I take it.'

'Omigod, no.' Stella looked at her in horror. 'Ray's far too set in his ways. He whips through the weekly telly guide in the *Daily Mail* with a highlighter pen to decide what we'll be viewing: football or gardening. Do you know, I'm probably the only living person in Britain who's seen every episode of *Gardeners' World* and can describe the current home and away strip of every team in the premiership. I mean, how sad is that? Now you can understand why I was so keen to get this job. We're not talking bit of a rut here; we're talking one hell of a trench.'

'I suppose Bob's in a bit of a rut too,' Fran confessed. 'I love him to bits but he's not exactly fast-lane fodder. He's doing all right at the bank but he's not a go-getter. Instead of footie and gardening, where Bob's concerned read DIY. Our place is more of a job creation scheme than a house. I've even thought of secretly writing to *Real Rooms*.'

'How about *DIY Disasters From Hell*?'

'No, couldn't do that to him,' said Fran. 'Too cruel. Bob's heart is in the right place – right next to his tool kit.'

'At least he's prepared to down tools – literally – to come and pick us up,' Stella laughed, taking another huge glug of wine. 'Ray wouldn't dream of doing anything like that, not unless the entire Spurs squad were on the next table and Charlie Dimmock was out front watering the window boxes.'

'What's his job?' Fran asked as she topped up their glasses yet again.

'Estate agent,' replied Stella. 'But the way he whinges on, you'd think he spent all day measuring up sink estates. By the way, have you got kids?'

'No, never happened,' said Fran sadly. 'Wanted them but they never arrived.'

'A blessing where I was concerned. Ray wouldn't have taken kindly to a baby having the temerity to cry during a penalty shoot-out.'

The last of the wine drunk, Fran phoned Bob to tell him to set off while Stella indicated to a passing waiter that they'd like to settle the bill. Twenty minutes later they were in the warmth of Bob's car, boot laden with wood off-cuts and rattling tools, and heading for Stella's house on the edge of Hartford.

'Omigod, I'll be in the dog house,' Stella shuddered as they pulled up outside the smart Victorian red-brick semi, shrouded in darkness. 'He must have gone to bed.'

They air-kissed goodbye. It had been a good evening. A new and enduring friendship had been forged.

'She seems nice,' remarked Bob as he steered the car homewards. 'I was quite worried about you leaving the *Echo* after so long but you already seem kind of settled. She strikes me as a good friend.'

'Yes, I believe she is,' said Fran. 'It's funny – in all the years I was on the *Echo*, I never had a really good pal. But it's great to have an ally so early on in a new job. Someone you can confide in a bit, especially when the going gets rough.'

They pulled up outside their house. 'If I could get a

move on with the kitchen,' Bob turned sideways in the driver's seat to look at her in the lamplight, 'maybe we could invite Stella and her husband over for dinner. Would you like that?'

Fran kissed him tenderly on the cheek. 'Lovely idea, but don't put yourself under unnecessary pressure,' she said, suddenly feeling guilty about the sarcasm in her voice that implied the pigs were being cleared for take-off.

As they crossed the doorway, carefully avoiding the gaps in the floorboards, Fran realised with an enormous pang of guilt that she couldn't just fall into bed immediately. Her Madame Chita copy had to be posted in the morning.

'I'll make the coffee, you get out the tarot cards,' said Bob smoothly when she'd explained that she had work to do. Now bitterly regretting ordering the second bottle of burgundy, a slightly befuddled Fran sat down at her typewriter. 'Pisces,' she wrote. 'Bad week. Someone breaks into your house and steals all your clothes. So you have to go out in a cardboard box. Make sure it isn't raining.'

Oh dear, the wine was playing havoc. She'd barely got as far as typing the word Aries when the phone went. Bit late for a phone call, she thought, half immersed in thoughts on Aries' prospects for the coming week. Bob would answer it upstairs. Suddenly she heard his voice telling her to pick up the phone urgently. A rush of potentially life-threatening situations flashed past her eyes, ranging from her elderly mother dying to being outed as Madame Chita.

It was Stella, sobbing her heart out. She could only catch odd words or phrases between the sobs. 'Caught the bastard ... should have realised ... thank God ... cameras.'

'What on earth's happened?' Fran asked unnecessarily, trying to decipher what Stella was on about. 'Shall I come over?' she eventually offered.

'Yes, no . . . yes, oh hell, I don't know what to do. Never suspected . . . photographs, I've got the photographs.'

Fran took charge of the situation. 'Look, Stella, I don't understand what's going on but Bob will drive me back to your place immediately.'

She replaced the receiver, grabbed a coat and briefly explained the situation to Bob. Within fifteen minutes they were back outside Stella's house with Fran on the doorstep ringing the bell and wondering what the hell she was going to be faced with.

Stella finally opened the door, looking wild-eyed and very dishevelled. She immediately broke down into racking sobs and looked on the verge of collapse. Fran took one look at her and indicated to Bob to go home and she'd call him later on. The two women went inside.

Even to Fran, who'd never set foot in the house before, it was obvious there'd been some kind of incident. Cushions had been thrown around, and a jardinière had been knocked over, spilling a potted palm and wet soil all over the pale green carpet. A side table, on which a collection of silver-framed photographs must have sat, was now empty, the smashed pictures all over the floor.

'I'm sorry, I'm so sorry,' Stella kept mumbling, her face now awash with travelling mascara. Fran handed her a wadge of tissues and announced she would make them a cup of tea. So typically English in a crisis, she reflected as she scoured the tiny kitchen for teabags and a couple of mugs. Bit like the imperious call for hot water and towels in film scenes where someone's about to give birth. Surely a shot of morphine for the mother and a stiff brandy for the father would have been more useful.

Soon they were sitting down, one on each sofa, nursing steaming mugs of strong tea. Bit by bit, Stella poured out what had happened after she'd come home. As she'd guessed from his car parked outside and all the lights out, Ray had gone to bed. Except that he'd gone to bed with someone else.

Chapter 7

'I walked into our bedroom and there they were, cavorting in OUR bed,' Stella sobbed angrily. 'Both completely naked, silly grins on their faces, champagne bubbling away in MY glasses, sat on MY bedside table in MY bedroom. And do you know, she was even on MY side of the bed.'

For a second, Fran had to suppress a smile. 'Did you recognise this woman?' she asked, recovering her composure.

'Nope, never seen her before in my life. Bright red hair, masses of it. Just proves what a thoroughly rotten bloody liar Ray is. He's always said he loathes redheads, says their skin smells funny.'

Surely that particular lie was now the least of Stella's worries. 'So what did you do?' Fran asked.

At that point Stella broke down again. Fran quickly scanned for sight of a drinks cabinet. Then she remembered seeing a wine rack in the kitchen. Handing Stella another pile of tissues, she got up and went to find it. A rummage through some drawers produced a corkscrew. She decided that red wine might bizarrely remind Stella of her unwelcome visitor so she picked up a bottle of Frascati, a couple of glasses from the nearest cupboard and went back into the sitting room. There she poured out two big glasses and then lit herself a cigarette.

'Could be just the night to take up smoking again,' said Stella ruefully.

'Hey, don't start. Not worth it,' Fran begged her. 'I begin every New Year's day with a resolution to pack it in and I fail miserably by about January tenth. I didn't even bother at all this year.'

'OK, you're right, I suppose. I've got enough problems to deal with now,' said Stella, gratefully taking a huge slug of wine.

'Now,' said Fran gently, 'what happened after you discovered them?'

Stella hung her head and gestured for a cigarette. Fran reluctantly passed over her packet. Stella lit up and took a deep puff. Seconds later, she was doubled up coughing. 'Nah, maybe not,' she said, stubbing the cigarette out in the ashtray Fran had found.

'Good girl. Now tell me what happened and then we can decide what to do.'

Stella took a deep breath, opened her mouth to begin her account and was left in mid-air. The shrill sound of the doorbell might well have been the crack of rifle fire. They both sat still for a few seconds. The bell rang again.

'I'll go,' said Fran firmly, coming to her senses. 'You stay put.'

She marched purposefully to the front door. The light of the moon gave an outline of a tall, well-built man. She prayed it wouldn't be Ray but couldn't think who else it might be. What on earth would she say to him? 'Hello, do come in to your own home. I know what you've been up to with that redhead . . .'

She grappled with the door catch and then suddenly the door was open.

'Evening, madam. Wondered if I could have a word with Mrs Robinson?' A police officer in uniform stood on the doorstep, brandishing his identity card.

'She's in here,' Fran found herself stammering. She led the officer into the sitting room. Stella's face was a picture. From the white of her shock and distress, she suddenly turned a deep shade of red – the red of acute embarrassment.

'I gather there's been a bit of an incident here tonight, Mrs Robinson,' said the officer, surreptitiously getting out a small notebook. 'Just wonder if you could help me with a few details.' He glanced towards Fran, implying that she ought to leave the room.

'Fran stays,' said Stella firmly, pulling herself together by blowing her nose noisily. 'She's come over to help me.' Curious, thought Fran. Stella doesn't seem as shocked about the police involvement as I am.

'Do you, er, know the other lady in question?' the police officer asked tentatively.

'No, never seen her before in my life. Don't even know her name,' Stella's eyes flashed with anger. 'Didn't know my husband was knocking off somebody else, come to think of it.'

'Well, the woman in question, a Miss Marilyn Rougemont, was found in, er, a bit of a state,' he continued delicately.

'Yes, I'm sure she was,' said Stella defiantly. Fran was on the edge of her seat now. What on earth was this about? She suddenly felt she'd stumbled in halfway through an Agatha Christie mystery.

'Could you tell me what happened here tonight?' the officer continued.

'Spent an evening out with my friend, Fran here. We work together. Told my husband I'd be home late as we were eating out. Came home to find him in bed with a redheaded slapper. There were words. Arguments. Shouting. Then I grabbed the bitch by the hair and dragged her downstairs.'

'And what did your husband do?' enquired the policeman, making swift notes. Fran lit another cigarette, riveted by the events unfolding before her.

'Oh, he did his usual impression of a complete waste of DNA. I kicked her out the door. Then Ray and I had a big argument here in the sitting room. As you can see, tempers frayed, things got broken and then he stormed off. I assume he took his car and went after her.'

'Well, er, possibly, but he didn't catch up with her. We found Miss Rougemont wandering around a couple of streets away. Someone spotted her and reported the matter to us.'

'Serves her right,' said Stella. 'All I did was throw her out. Am I in some sort of trouble?'

'Don't expect so,' said the policeman soothingly. 'Unless people get hurt, we don't generally intervene in domestic incidents. Did anyone get hurt in this, er, argument?' He glanced around at the mess in the room.

Stella shook her head and held up her right hand. 'I don't think a cut finger amounts to much. Broken heart's a different matter.' She started sobbing once again.

The policeman put his notebook away and turned to Fran. 'Are you going to be around for a while?' he asked. 'I think she'll need some support.'

'Of course,' said Fran. 'Are you going to take this any further, Officer?'

'Doubt it,' he replied. Then he paused and looked at her closely. 'Don't I know you from somewhere?'

'Used to work on the *Echo*. Probably seen me in court,' said Fran.

'Oh, that's it,' said the copper, vastly relieved. 'Don't think this one will make it to Hartford Magistrates,' he continued, half whispering to her, 'but it would have made a great yarn for your lot.'

'Why?' said Fran, completely confused.

'Oh, you haven't heard the full story then. Your friend's husband's redheaded pal was reported running down the street stark naked. We thought we were on to a rape case but once we'd talked to the lady in question it became obvious that this was a rather, er, unusual domestic incident.' He glanced at Stella's sobbing form on the sofa. 'I'll just take my leave quietly,' he added.

Fran showed him out. Naked women running down the street – this was more happening than Getting It. With her *Echo* hat on she'd have been straight on the phone to the newsdesk, but not any more. Besides, this was too close to home. Tonight she and Stella had forged a friendship.

Fran walked back into the sitting room and refilled their glasses. Stella looked much calmer. Perhaps the policeman's visit had jolted her out of the initial shock.

'I must say I admire you, Stella,' Fran said gently. 'I didn't realise you'd thrown her out *sans* clothes. That took a bit of panache.'

Stella, who'd been nursing her glass, looked up at Fran and managed a small smile. 'I didn't really set out to do that. It just happened so quickly. All I could think of was that I wanted that bitch out of my house.'

'Ray didn't go after her then?' Fran prompted.

'No, he didn't. Not immediately. The irony was that he obviously felt embarrassed to be naked in front of me so he just stayed under the duvet while I hauled her out. By the time I'd got her through the front door, he'd got himself sort-of dressed. Then we had our little scene in here.' She pointed to the damaged pots and ornaments. 'I'm not even sure he realised she'd left the house minus her kit, otherwise he might have rushed after her.'

'Pardon me for suggesting this,' said Fran, 'but wasn't it a bit crass of him to be discovered tonight? After all, we only arranged our meal on the spur of the moment. He must have realised we wouldn't be out all that late.'

Stella took another sip of wine and then wiped her eyes again. 'I think,' her voice wobbled, 'he actually WANTED to be found out. Things haven't been right between us for so long I can't remember when they were. I suppose I suspected he was having an affair but I tried to blot out the evidence. I didn't want to do all that credit card statement-checking, or ringing the office to see if he really was measuring up houses at eleven p.m. I think I just didn't want to confront it. And looking back now, me joining Getting It, with its irregular hours, was going to make his secret life a bit more difficult. He was seething when I got the job and I couldn't understand why. When I was at Bypass he knew exactly where I was all the time.'

'Are you sure he wants out?' said Fran. 'Don't jump to conclusions too soon.'

'He went after her, didn't he?' said Stella emphatically. 'As soon as we'd had our row, he was off. No, he's made his choice. He wasn't anything like as shocked to see me as she was. No, I think it was Ray's typically lazy way of telling me it's all over.'

Stella broke down into shuddering sobs. Fran sat down next to her and put a comforting arm around her. 'I'm going to ring Bob now and get him to pick us both up. Let's get you some clothes together, lock this place up and you can come and stay with us while you have a think about things. Sitting here won't help much. Leave all the mess, just get enough stuff for a few days.'

To her slight surprise, Stella made no protest at all. She silently went upstairs and came down a few minutes later with a plastic carrier bag and a small suitcase. Meanwhile Fran found some coffee and a cafetière, plus cups and saucers, and brought them in on a tray. They flopped back on the sofas, sipping their coffee while they waited for Bob. A small ring on the doorbell indicated he'd got there in record time.

Fran picked up the suitcase and Stella the plastic bag. 'The bitch's clothes,' Stella explained. 'I'd like to drop them in a litter bin on the way, if you don't mind.'

They made their way out to the car, and Stella was just about to climb into the back seat when she stopped. 'I've forgotten something,' she said, turned tail and went back into the house.

'Nearly forgot the camera,' she announced on her return.

'Camera?' Fran turned round from the front passenger's seat, sensing another revelation.

Stella did not disappoint. 'How I had the presence of mind to do this I'll never know, but this little beauty was on the hall table. It's a point and click job, belongs to Ray.'

Fran looked puzzled.

'I took photographs,' said Stella, waving the camera.

'After I'd kicked her out of the front door, I grabbed the camera and ran out into the road after the bitch. It's funny how much faster you can run with your clothes on than someone who's completely naked and trying to find somewhere to hide.'

Chapter 8

Three days to the launch of Getting It and the tension was palpable. You could almost smell the fear stalking every corridor. More and more smokers joined the huddle outside.

That day's dry run had been the most disastrous to date. With the station's main presenter, Tracey Timotei, still out of action thanks to her broken elbow, the other presenters were being put through their paces with a vengeance.

A blond lookalike couple called Jason and Charleena had rehearsed the same products over and over again until they sounded like nursery rhymes. A speak-your-weight cycling machine, a novelty peanut butter-maker and a range of organic carpet deodorants with incongruous fragrance names like bark, petal and pith.

Despite having names like Aussie soap stars, Jason and Charleena generated so little sunshine and warmth they might as well have just met at a bus stop in Siberia. They were completely devoid of any chemistry, not to mention brains. But they'd just managed to fill ten minutes on a rather dull range of face creams. Paul Dyer was prowling around the gallery, listening to all the instructions and looking very tense. They weren't getting much help from Piers, who was still grappling with the art of counting backwards in his role as floor manager. He'd also just had his tongue pierced and it had swollen as a result, giving him a terrible lisp.

'Cue graphics,' the director shouted as the onscreen display miraculously appeared showing the product numbers and prices, plus a close up shot of the In Your Face moisturiser and Atomic Spot Bomb. 'Keep selling,' he commanded. 'It's going well. Another two minutes.'

But Jason and Charleena had peaked. They looked desperately at each other.

'Just a few more tips on how to use this wonderful range of skin preparations,' Jason said slowly. 'We've looked at how you can use them on your face, but you can use them on other parts of your body too.'

'Yes,' chipped in Charleena with forced jollity. 'Forehead, nose, under-eye area, cheeks and neck. Plus on your hands, arms, elbows, legs, ankles, big toes, smaller toes and all your favourite fingers, both hands. Isn't that amazing! And don't worry if you have any skin allergies, they've been fully tested on animals.'

'Absolutely,' replied Jason gratefully. 'So that means they're completely safe for us humans to use.'

They smiled inanely at each other. In the gallery, all hell broke loose.

'Who wrote up their product notes?' demanded Paul Dyer. 'Fully tested on animals, my arse. We'll have half the animal liberation mob descend on us like a pack of wolves.'

Mercifully, the rep from the face cream company wasn't in the gallery. Paul snatched up the product notes and went even more apoplectic when he saw the next item coming up in rehearsal: A 'do-it-yourself electrocution kit' for pain-free facial hair removal.

'For God's sake,' he roared, 'I'm a bloke and even I know it's electrolysis, not bloody electrocution. And whoever wrote this deserves to be plugged into the National Grid.'

A shiver ran around the gallery.

'And another thing,' he ranted, pushing down the talkback button so that Jason and Charleena could hear him in their earpieces. 'You're BOTH wearing black jackets. For chrissake, doesn't someone around here notice these things? You look like two pissholes in the snow. I want glossy, glam presenters on this show, especially flogging beauty products, not two numpties who look like part-time funeral directors.'

Fran and Stella went home exhausted from all the tension, vowing to flop down in front of the television and chill. But a tell-tale envelope addressed to Stella lying on the doormat swiftly changed that agenda. They both knew immediately what it contained. The photographs of the redheaded streaker.

Stella hadn't wanted the embarrassment of handing in the roll of film to a local photo shop or chemist and then having to go back and collect the pictures. She'd opted for the anonymity of a postal service, hoping they wouldn't reject the photos because of their content.

She opened the envelope, glanced through the pictures and handed them to Fran without a word.

'It's a bit like the Readers' Wives section at the end of men's magazines,' Fran concluded, trying to make light of the situation. 'You know, where grotesque fat women get their husbands to take photographs of them in the buff, legs akimbo, tits touching their waists. And then, for some strange reason, they block out their eyes instead of the really gross bits. I must say, she looks distressed.'

'Too bloody right,' said Stella. 'Don't forget, I'd just hauled her downstairs by her hair.'

'Not using any of our Tressed Out hair products, I note,' said Fran sarcastically. 'If she did, she'd get much more shine on those split ends.'

'But what do I do now?' asked Stella as she screwed the envelope up into an ever tighter roll.

'If you want my advice,' Fran said firmly, 'you'll have a good long think about it. Let's get Getting It on air first. Then see if Ray plans to carry on getting it from our streaker here, or decides it was all a colossal mistake and comes crawling back. Then, if you still feel you want out, it's time to go to a solicitor.'

'What about the pictures?'

'File them away for a rainy day and forget about them.'

Next day there was a very different kind of pandemonium. Paul Dyer suddenly summoned the entire staff to the main studio. After his angry outburst the previous day, everyone braced themselves for a serious dressing down. But a very different Paul Dyer stood before them. The gaunt, haunted look and the anger had gone. The laser blue Terence Stamp eyes were firmly back in business.

'Well, we're nearly there, folks,' he announced. 'Yesterday had its moments but we're getting there. We have at last achieved our first technically clean show. And in two days' time the nation – or at least those enlightened people with satellite dishes – will be Getting It – well and truly. Now that I can sleep easier in my bed, I can tell you that there will be a fantastic champagne launch. Please come dressed to the nines – as over the top as you like – as the station will be formally opened by Vanilla Montgomery.'

A loud buzz went around the room, neatly divided into those clearly impressed and the rest who mouthed 'Who's she?' at each other. One of the ignorant few was Piers, whose tongue still hadn't subsided after the new piercing. He sidled up to Fran.

'Whoth sthe?' he whispered.

'Huh,' scoffed Fran, her subscription to *OK!* magazine paying off yet again. 'If *Footballers' Wives* had an It girl amongst them, it would be Vanilla Montgomery. She's a cross between Victoria Beckham and Lady Victoria Hervey. Oh, and you could throw in a bit of Normandie Keith as well.'

Piers looked even more confused.

'Sorts out the *OK!* crowd from the *Biceps Monthly* mob, doesn't it,' Fran whispered to Stella. 'This is a bit more like it. Proper showbiz at last. Maybe there is a God after all.'

The whispers died away as Paul Dyer indicated that he was resuming his speech. He certainly had a great gift for rallying the troops.

'Obviously we've invited the media to the launch. So be prepared for a few photographers. Plus, we're inviting a couple of journalists to do high-profile behind-the-scenes pieces about the new station. So over the next few days they may want to talk to you about your job and the weeks leading up to us going on air. Think before you speak is probably the most obvious thing to say. I don't want to gag people. We want the pieces to be fun, interesting and realistic but we don't want to look stupid. Any queries on that, come and see me.'

He paused while this bombshell was assimilated.

'Now, before you all clear off for the day, I am going to unveil to you the graphics department's worst-kept secret – our finished logo. This will now be used on all screen idents. You'll have new stationery, letterheads and so on arriving by the end of the week. And here it is. Cue imaginary roll of drums.'

The plasma screen behind him suddenly sprang to life. Up came the logo. It was basically the same design they'd all seen before, only now it was animated. The wanton blonde in the fur bikini, crammed into a shopping trolley, was now Tracey Timotei. When the trolley reached centre screen, it stopped and she blew a kiss to the camera. Then the slogan – 'You should be Getting It too' – appeared on screen.

'Hope she doesn't fall out,' shouted one wag from the back. A ripple of laughter went around the studio. No wonder Paul Dyer had gone ballistic after the hammock incident. His leading lady had almost swung herself out of action.

'Yes, Tracey will be here for the launch,' he continued. 'She's had her elbow pinned so our viewers will never know. Obviously she won't be able to use her arm for a while so we'll have to choreograph things a bit carefully. So this, folks, is our image.'

'Hard to reconcile fur bikinis with non-stick frying pans,' Stella whispered to Fran.

'Remember this is Hartford, not Hollywood,' she replied with a grin.

They all trooped out of the studio, heading back to their offices.

'I don't think I've ever been so excited,' said Stella as they reached the buyers' office. 'It's really taken my mind off the whole Ray thing.'

'I'm pleased to hear it,' said Fran as they plonked themselves down on the nearest chairs. 'I must say I never thought we'd have this swanky launch. Trust Paul Dyer to announce it today. Typical bloke, doesn't realise that it takes weeks of effort for women of our age to look good.'

'You can't do a proper detox in two days,' Stella said, gathering up her handbag ready to leave. 'Barely time to have a bath and do your nails.'

'Especially in my home,' said Fran, instantly embarrassed at the thought of her terrible bathroom. 'I'm so sorry about the state of the house. You looked so shocked when you first saw it.'

Stella paused for a second and looked her straight in the eye. 'Stop apologising. It was just a surprise, that's all. Especially as – how can I put this tactfully – you're always so smartly turned out. But you're surrounded by, er, things that don't work.'

'Oh don't worry, I'm not the least bit offended,' Fran replied. 'Funny thing is, although I loathe the place being like it is, you do somehow get used to it after a while. Keeping things in cardboard boxes, dodging the holes in the floorboards, wrapping the shower curtain around yourself because of the lack of tiling. In the end it becomes a way of life. Along with, I suppose, the acceptance that Bob just will not entertain the idea of anyone else doing the work. Do you think I'm being weak-willed about this?'

Stella smiled at her. 'Not in the slightest,' she replied. 'I had exactly the opposite – a lovely home with a rotten husband. You and Bob are rock solid. You can replace a floorboard but you can't replace a person.'

'Pity that particular person won't replace the

floorboards,' said Fran ruefully. 'But you're right about him, I wouldn't swap him for the world. Just wish he'd get a move on with the work, or admit defeat. Do you know what they gave me when I left the *Echo*?'

'No idea. What?'

'Subscription to *House Beautiful*.' They both roared with laughter.

'The irony is,' Fran continued when they'd recovered, 'I used to write property pages and traipse around fantastic houses. Nobody had any idea I live in this dilapidated state. It's a measure of our friendship that I invited you to stay. And I guess it's a measure of YOUR friendship that you're still putting up with it.'

Stella glanced around the office. Most people had already cleared off home. 'I've had an idea,' she said. 'You go and get your stuff while I make a phone call.'

She fished out her Filofax and started dialling. By the time Fran had returned she was just winding up her chat.

'. . . yes, half the world's media is going to be there . . . Would you? Fantastic. You don't mind re-opening? Wonderful. We'll pop by in about half an hour. Ciao.'

She replaced the phone and turned to Fran triumphantly. 'We are going to look like stars on Friday. That was Ginette; you know her shop?'

'Do I!' Fran exclaimed. Ginette's was the most expensive boutique in town. 'I only ever dare look in the window during sale time – and preferably when it's closed.'

'She's a friend of mine and she's going to sort us out. Lend us a couple of really drop-dead gorgeous outfits. We'll give the young ones a run for their money.'

They set off, giggling like teenagers, for Ginette's. Even the relentless drizzle couldn't dampen their spirits as they wove through the Hartford rush hour. When they finally arrived at the boutique, only a short dash from the nearest car park, they looked like a couple of drowned rats. Ginette, the epitome of Parisian elegance, unlocked the door and welcomed them without seeming to notice their bedraggled state. She greeted them with air kisses in a cloud of Diorissimo.

'Dahlinks, I 'ave some wonderful leetle numbers, just ze job for your beeg day,' she announced, beckoning them with long, much-ringed fingers over to a rail near the till. 'You 'ave a look while I make ze coffee.'

As the delicious aroma of strong percolated coffee began to fill the boutique, Fran and Stella tried on some of Ginette's suggestions. She'd put out a range of suits and dresses, some casual, some formal and others definitely aimed at cocktail hour. In the end they all decided that as it was an office day a suit was most appropriate. They each shortlisted three suits and agreed to take a majority vote.

Ginette sat elegantly sipping coffee and nodding approval at every twirl. Now and again she'd point them to a blouse, a scarf or a piece of jewellery that would add the finishing touch. In the end the choice was easy.

Stella did a final catwalk swagger in her chosen outfit. A deep burgundy velvet trouser suit with a cream silk shirt and turned back cuffs which looked wonderfully dramatic with her short dark hair. Ginette suggested string of pearls and earrings to match.

Fran, too, couldn't believe her luck. She was wearing a mid-calf straight navy pin-stripe skirt and matching jacket with a price tag that could have warranted a mortgage. Ginette steered her to a lilac silk camisole top that matched the jacket lining.

Next thing Ginette was deftly packing the clothes in tissue paper and cardboard boxes before despatching Fran and Stella back out into the drizzle.

'Maybe this was all meant to be,' Fran mused as she drove them home. 'Wouldn't it have been awful if we hadn't seen the ad, met at the interviews and got the job? We'd never have got to wear these fantastic outfits. I'd still be at the *Echo* and you'd be stuck at Bypass.'

Stella managed to wipe away an unseen tear in the darkness. 'I wonder if I'd still be with Ray. I suppose the whole situation might have drifted on much longer.'

The drizzle had now turned into heavy rain. Stella was grateful for the noise of the wipers drowning out the wobble in her voice.

Fran continued: 'At least you found out sooner rather than later. Another ten years down the line would have been much worse. Maybe your job change prompted something in Ray. He saw you having the courage to make changes and took his cue from you, although he got a bit more drama than he bargained for. This is fate taking a hand.'

Stella nodded miserably. She eyed Fran's cigarettes on top of the dashboard. Fran caught her glance.

'No,' she said. 'You've done very well up to now.' After a short silence she added, 'Talking of that four-letter word fate, here comes another of my big secrets. You've already seen the state of the house so that's one out of the bag. But there's another that you're bound to discover sooner or later. I don't think I can keep it from you as you're staying here. It's actually so hush-hush that only two people in the world are in on it. Ever heard of Madame Chita?'

Stella looked blank for a moment. 'Clairvoyant in the *Echo*? The horoscopes with attitude?'

'Yes.'

'No, it can't be.'

'Yes, it is. It's me, and in a minute I've got to sit down at my rackety old typewriter and bash out the next instalment.'

Stella sat back in her seat, momentarily lost for words. 'That's amazing. I mean, everyone always talks about them because they're so, er, outrageous. I hope I'm not offending you.'

'No, not at all. They're meant to be over the top. I've been doing them for years, but no one at the *Echo* knows except Guy, the editor. And Bob, of course. And now you make it three.'

They pulled up at Fran's house. Stella was still incredulous. 'I remember ages ago the paper ran a massive campaign to try to find out who she was.'

'Yeah,' smiled Fran. 'I wrote some of that story myself! It was rather bizarre, trying to discover my own identity. It all started when the previous clairvoyant popped her clogs, due to unforeseen circumstances of course! They didn't have anyone to step in. So for a bit of a laugh, I secretly wrote an outrageous column of horoscopes and posted it anonymously to the *Echo*. It was stuff like: "Capricorn – do you want a divorce? No? Then cancel that holiday immediately. You'll only row all the time." They printed it and then I confessed to Guy. We struck our little secret deal and it's being going on for years.'

They got out of the car and went round to get the

precious boxes from the boot. 'What's Ray's star sign?' Fran asked as she put the key in the front door.

'Taurus. And the Chinese New Year of the Rat.'

'Had to be, didn't it,' said Fran with a grin as she pushed open the door. 'I'll make sure he gets the message then.'

Chapter 9

Getting It's launch day did not get off to an auspicious start. Fran and Stella decided to get up early to allow more time for hair, make-up and nails. In the event it was just as well. The shower that had been hanging on by a thread finally gave up the will to live and came away from the wall, along with several large chunks of masonry. As a precaution Bob insisted on turning off the water supply, so they both had to make the best of a flannel wash and shampooing their hair with bottles of mineral water over the kitchen sink.

'I bet Vanilla Montgomery doesn't start her day like this,' said Fran, shivering as the ice-cold Evian hit her scalp. 'It's all very well Bob slaving over elm door handles but it won't help us to look like celebrities for a day.' She was overcome with anger and embarrassment about the state of the bathroom and tried to contain herself. This was not the day for a row. This was supposed to be showbiz.

Eventually they reached the moment they'd been looking forward to – donning their fantastic outfits. They emerged in Fran's sitting room where she pulled out a full-length mirror from its permanent resting place behind the door.

'Pretty ace, I'd say,' said Fran. 'I think you look amazing.'

Stella did a twirl in her burgundy trouser suit while Fran strutted up and down in her pin-striped suit.

'She's a star, Ginette,' said Stella. 'These outfits are perfect. Not too over the top, just right for the most important working day we've ever spent. And if we get pictured in *Hello!* or *Heat* or something then Ginette will display the pictures in the shop.'

'I now understand,' said Fran, lovingly touching the fabric of her jacket, 'why you really can justify spending nine hundred pounds on a suit. It makes me feel so much more confident.'

'Me too,' replied Stella. 'But we must remember they're on loan. So no red wine or rogue flakes of greasy pastry from vol-au-vents at the launch party.'

'Don't worry,' said Fran with a grin, 'I shan't be eating anything. This waistband's a bit tight.'

'So what does Madame Chita predict for today then?'

'Oh, fame, fortune and absolutely no lunch.'

The tension was so high that out of sheer nerves two cars collided in the car park amid angry scenes. Fran and Stella took deep breaths, calmed themselves and strode purposefully through the main entrance. And stopped dead in their tracks in total shock. Not just because the reception had been transformed overnight with deep pink carpets, burgundy leather furniture and floor-to-ceiling banners of Tracey in her fur finery. No, it was the sight of Kelly-Marie manning the shiny cream leather reception desk, or rather, sprawling across it. Clearly the message about the media and the 'go for it' dress code had registered and Kelly-Marie had decided to do it large.

Dressed in a token sheer black top over the inevitable black Wonderbra and pelmet leather skirt, she'd added thigh-length black patent boots with four-inch silver spike heels and a pink feather boa. A pink feather concoction on her head, complete with black net fascinator, topped off the ensemble.

'Nobody told me it was a gangsters and molls party,' Fran muttered under her breath as they swept past, avoiding eye contact with each other in case they laughed.

'She looks like a cross between Julia Roberts in *Pretty Woman* and Faye Dunaway in *Bonnie and Clyde*,' Stella observed. Once they reached the production office they finally broke down into fits of giggles. But there was more to come.

Steve had also risen to the challenge by coming dressed as 'Clark Kent trying very hard to be Indiana Jones'. He was wearing a sand-coloured safari-type linen suit and a tan leather hat. The only thing missing was a rope coiled in his waistband and a gang of Nazi art hunters in hot pursuit. Unfortunately he didn't have anything like the bearing or personality to carry it off. The trousers were a natz too short, the plastic pen tops showing over the breast pocket of his jacket didn't help and the thick black glasses ensured it was more a case of Buddy Holly meets John Wayne.

But it was Piers who took the award for Best Attention-Seeking Outfit. Tanned to the point of dayglo orange, he'd had blond streaks put into his black hair, which was now sticking up in tufts. He'd managed to add a few overnight piercings to his tally. There were another couple of earrings and a new nose stud. His outfit owed its inspiration to Elvis Presley. A white stretch bodysuit with a huge collar and covered in tiny studs confirmed his continuing love affair with lycra. Rumour was that Piers had got somewhat confused by Paul's 'dress up to the nines' speech and had interpreted it as fancy dress.

'Is he trying to tell us he's a stud?' asked Stella out of the corner of her mouth. 'Leaves very little to the imagination.'

'Absolutely. Leaves very little altogether to the imagination,' Fran replied. 'I'm not an expert on lunch-boxes, but in this case I think the matchbox has landed.'

'And that tan. He could guide in stricken tankers with that colour.'

'He'd certainly get work as a doorman at Graceland.'

Transmission was due to start at noon. Tracey Timotei, looking amazing in a butter suede dress, was in place to launch the station and present the first live programme, selling a range of gold jewellery.

The minutes ticked away until Kelly-Marie's drawl announced tentatively over the tannoy that it was eleven o'clock, one hour to go. A frisson of panic went round the offices and studio. Fran sat at her computer putting the finishing touches to some good copy lines about a new seaweed body wrap, trying not to be overwhelmed by the wonder of her expensive suit-for-a-day and the occasion itself. It was a heady mix of fear and excitement that she'd never experienced before. Stella was feeling the same, completely caught up in the tension oozing from every corner of the building. She was shocked and then delighted to realise that she'd forgotten about Ray and the redhead for two whole hours. This telly lark was certainly diverting.

As noon nudged nearer, everyone started to congregate in groups as they watched television screens showing a still-empty studio. At ten to twelve, Paul Dyer ushered everyone not involved in the studio production into a viewing gallery high above the studio floor where there were crates of champagne and trays of glasses laid out on tables covered in white tablecloths.

'Just to tide us over until the press arrive,' he announced with a grin.

Tracey Timotei could now be seen on all the monitors, ready to promote the jewellery using only her good arm. Camera angles and shots were being practised for the last time. Five to twelve.

On the studio floor, Piers was having difficulty fitting his headphones over his very swollen ears, thanks to the new studs. In the studio control, Adrienne, the production assistant, was now shaking so much she looked as though she'd been on tequila all week. Suddenly the viewing gallery was filled with the bustle of journalists and photographers. All in a day's work for them, thought Fran, and that used to be me. But now I've crossed to the other side. The studio director started to intone the words they'd all been hearing every day for the past few weeks, except that this time it was for real. 'Fifteen seconds to air. Coming to camera three in ten, nine, eight, roll VT, seven, six, five, four, three . . . cue music . . . cue Tracey.'

'Hello and welcome to a brand new television station. You're watching Getting It, and if you hadn't been before, you certainly are now. Well and truly. My name's Tracey Starburst and I'm delighted to be part of this momentous piece of televisual history.'

'Who wrote that shit?' Fran whispered to Stella. 'Momentous piece of televisual history, my arse.'

'No idea, but it sounds impressive,' Stella whispered back. She was feeling terribly overawed by the occasion. 'By the way, what's her real name?'

'Crump,' replied Fran. 'Tracey Crump. Makes Starburst seem quite normal, doesn't it?' Their conversation was then drowned out by the sound of flash guns and champagne corks popping, not just in the viewing gallery but on screen too. Tracey was deftly pouring out champagne one-handedly for a couple of vendors on screen and toasting the success of the station. As she then neatly plunged into a sales pitch for the glasses themselves, Paul Dyer toasted the assembled group in the office, a grin stretching from ear to ear.

'To the success of Getting It,' he proclaimed expansively. 'May we all be Getting It regularly from now on.'

'To Getting It,' they all mumbled, gratefully swigging down the bubbly as fast as they could. Another barrage of flashes, then suddenly there was a stampede. The media had already had enough and were descending on the buffet like a swarm of locusts. Tracey and the studio crew were left to plough on through their historic televisual moment while the rest of the pack went off for a serious drinking session and the chance to mingle with Vanilla Montgomery and a clutch of B-list celebrities.

Every woman over thirty in the building noted with relief that Vanilla Montgomery, wearing a tight black leather dress, was showing the first signs of cellulite. Every man under the age of thirty didn't know or care what cellulite was. And if she could drink a pint, lay a patio and discuss Man U's rest-of-season prospects then better still.

'Well, I think the first day was a success,' said Fran, sprawling out on her charity shop sofa. ('No point in replacing the sofas until I get that ceiling rose done,' Bob had said ten years ago.) 'And I confess that my day was made by that utterly divine suit.'

'Ditto,' said Stella, raising a glass. 'Handing it back will be the hardest bit. I just adore this whole outfit. Would look great in a divorce court, yah?'

'Now come on, don't spoil a fabulous day,' said Fran firmly, lighting a cigarette. 'Worry about all that tomorrow. I don't know about you, but I felt part of something really important today. It's one of those days we'll probably never forget. Especially if we make it to *Hello!*. Can't wait to see the photographs.' She instantly regretted those last words, seeing Stella's instantly stricken face.

'The photographs,' repeated Stella. 'I wish I hadn't taken them now. They're so – so tangible. It's like the proof right in your face. I can't give Ray the benefit of the doubt, or kid myself it didn't happen. It's all there staring at me.'

'You could chuck them out,' said Fran quietly, but I don't think that would be a good idea because they're proof of what happened. Whatever the future throws up, it'll never be as bad as that time. If the going gets a bit rough, you've at least got pictures of the bit of rough.'

Even Stella managed to laugh. It had been a long day and she was now too tired to cry.

Chapter 10

A new kind of panic was setting in. Opening day on *Getting It* had been rehearsed into the ground. That just left day two to take care of, plus all the others that followed, twenty-four hours a day, all year round.

An atmosphere of controlled hysteria pervaded every area of the building. Steve seemed permanently confused in his secret world behind those terrible specs. He was struggling with some copy for a range of travel goods 'you never knew you needed' – even after purchase. Cockroach repellent, elastic washing line for your hotel balcony and a calorie counter for twenty different cuisines and languages. He was trying desperately to look nonchalant while frantically hoping Fran would help him out. When she finally arrived, pretending absolutely not to have a hangover from a late-night drinking session and confessional with Stella, he pounced on her.

'At last, Fran,' he beamed desperately. 'I really don't know what to say about baby's own leather passport cover in p . . . p . . . pale pink or blue. You'll do this one soooooo much better than I would.'

Oh really, thought Fran, noticing a nervous tic in his neck and a copy of *Bluff Your Way In Television* half-hidden at the back of his desk. She recognised it because she'd bought a copy herself several weeks ago. Steve appeared to be constantly terrified of getting things wrong but blissfully unaware that his insecurities just created more work for everyone else. It was time he found a few things out for himself.

Steve handed Fran the file, trying to disguise his desperation. She glanced at it briefly and handed it straight back.

'Sorry, Steve,' she said with a half-smile, 'I'm just too busy with the Crinoline Lady Collectables Show. This one's definitely got your name on it.'

Before Steve could come up with another excuse, she turned away from him, picked up her phone, dialled her home number and had an animated conversation with her answering machine. Frantic to find something to do other than accept defeat, Steve managed to knock the offending file on the floor, scattering all the brochures and pieces of paper over a wide radius. Universal tutting broke out around the office. It was tense enough without having someone like Steve on board. As he knelt down to gather up the paper, a mobile phone began sounding the James Bond theme. To everyone's barely concealed amusement, Steve reached in his pocket and retrieved his phone.

'Yes, Mum, it's going fine,' he said, straightening his glasses. 'Ah, now you might just be able to help. Have you ever used one of those travel elastic clothes lines? What about cockroach repellent?' Everyone rolled their eyes to the heavens. Clearly Steve couldn't do anything without someone's endorsement. Fran found herself wondering who'd given him the go-ahead for the 007 theme for his mobile.

Today was more than just day two. It was Getting It's first fashion programme and Stella, as the fashion buyer, was desperate for it all to go well. The two-hour stint featured a couple of models showing a range of cruise wear called In The Bag. Twenty different outfits could be created from seven basic pieces all produced from one co-ordinated flight bag. Allegedly.

It reminded Fran of all those summer holiday packing articles she'd written for the *Echo* over the years, involving sticking false glittery flowers on to your flip-flops to turn them into evening wear and using your swimsuit as an evening top with a sarong. Not all that delightful for your nearest and dearest if you've been swimming, sweating and slapping on sun oil in it all day long. Fran had once tried out her own advice by travelling to Menorca with Bob for a fortnight with only one small bag. To her eternal shame, she'd had to go out immediately and stock up on clothes – and a large suitcase. She'd only admitted that to Stella last night.

Stella had carefully rehearsed with Karen, the presenter, and the models to get all the looks. Her previous life at Bypass on Fashion was standing her in good stead. And it was a treat to work with professional models who would have looked amazing even if they'd worn plastic rubbish sacks. A far cry from the fat old bag ladies from Bypass, for whom a bin liner would, at the very least, have hidden a multitude of sins.

So far so good. The blonde model in the black range and the brunette in the fuchsia pink were showing off the different facets of the garments on a mini catwalk. On deck, by the pool, a casual walk, smart for lunch, relaxing in the afternoon sun and dancing the night away – the outfits certainly worked hard. For each 'scene', the models added the appropriate jewellery, hats, scarves, bags and shoes. As they built up to the grand finale, Karen visibly relaxed. This was her first live stint and she'd managed to keep going despite being incredibly nervous. She hadn't missed out a single combination either, helped by Stella's off-camera sketches as a prompt. The final twirl was to be an evening ensemble. Both models emerged looking stunning in the long flowing jackets and loose trousers. They'd added dramatic jewellery and sparkly high-heeled sandals to finish off the look. Stella, gazing at the bank of television screens in the gallery and sitting next to a representative from In The Bag, heaved a silent sigh of relief. The rep, too, was delighted. Calls to buy the whole kit had been a little slow to start but had really picked up in the last half hour.

Karen was just telling viewers to hurry as stocks were disappearing fast when her words took on a more literal meaning. One of the models caught a slender heel in a gap in the makeshift catwalk and crashed down, bringing the other girl with her. Instead of two glamorous women supposedly dressed for a ball on a cruise ship, they'd become a black and pink heap, legs akimbo, accompanied by a great deal of muted swearing. Karen immediately froze, the colour draining from her face.

'Wind up, wind up,' shouted Jon, the director, in her earpiece. 'Then we'll to go to a recap.'

'Well, er, er,' struggled Karen, completely thrown by the mayhem and the moans of pain going on beside her.

'Sod the bloody models. Recap the prices and wind up,' shrieked Jon.

'I, er, er . . .'

'Oh for fuck's sake, you stupid tart. Roll a preview then.'

Up came a couple of minutes' promotion for the next swathe of bargains. Gold rings and pendants, followed by a range of Super Suck vacuum cleaners and I Can't Believe It's Gone stain removers.

'What happens now?' asked Stella, ashen with shock. 'That programme's supposed to be repeated later tonight and several times this month.'

'Goes out as it is,' snapped Jon. 'No time or budget for editing. Look, love, the bloody thing's selling, that's what we're here for. I can't help it if the fucking models can't stay upright. Right, clear the set, thirty seconds to air. Monica, hold that first ring up to camera two so we can take a look at it. Yes, that's fine. Just buff it up a bit, Piers, there's a love. OK folks, here we go.'

The production assistant started a countdown. Ten, nine, eight . . .

Down on the studio floor, Piers had had his work cut out clearing the studio of a snivelling Karen and two angry models nursing bruises, already on their mobiles to their agents, moving the dodgy catwalk out of shot and re-setting the studio for a jewellery display. And then helping Monica to give the jewellery a final polish ready for transmission. All in two minutes flat.

'Who needs to go to the gym with a job like this?' he muttered, sweat visible on his vest.

'Cue music, cue Monica,' shrieked Jon. And she was off. Monica, poached from a rival channel, had several years of television shopping under her belt and it showed. Romance the rings, Paul Dyer had emphasised to all the presenters. Jewellery is romance. It's not the everyday stuff of saucepans, detergents or rowing machines. It's the happily ever after bit of life – but only if you ring the number at the bottom of the screen with your credit card details.

For the next two hours the cameramen and gallery crew relaxed as Monica glided effortlessly through ring after ring. When she got to the part about how the signs of the zodiac related to the stones Fran, watching on a monitor, couldn't resist a small grin. Monica seemed to know far more about the zodiac than Madame Chita. Talking of which, she'd sit down and write her next column tonight after dinner. She was in the mood to make it really controversial.

Tapping away on her ancient typewriter balanced on the picnic table, Fran was absorbed in a 'stay in bed and out of trouble week' for Taurus. She was just giving some 'take the phone off the hook' advice when her own phone rang, giving her a jolt. Who could that be at 10 p.m.? she thought, glancing at her watch. To her surprise, Kelly-Marie's drawl came down the phone.

'Starp, starp what you're doin' and watch our channel,' she breathed and then hung up.

Fran flicked on her TV and her new perk of the job – her brand new satellite receiver. What on earth could be that important to prompt Kelly-Marie to use any form of technology? She scrolled down to Getting It with a deep sense of foreboding.

Tracey was in full swing, presenting a home cleaning show which included the much-hyped vacuum cleaners and stain removers. Because of her broken elbow, she'd obviously had to co-opt Piers into helping out on screen. Spread out in front of her were several pieces of cream carpet with various things spilled on them, including ketchup, ink, coffee and red wine. Muscles rippling and sweat pouring, Piers was scrubbing away with the 'revolutionary' stain remover I Can't Believe It's Gone.

Tracey was desperately trying to extol the virtues of the product as Piers scrubbed and scrubbed. But the stains were in for the long run. They showed no sign of lifting.

Tracey hastily moved on to the 'outstanding' Super Suck vacuum cleaner, so powerful that its suction could lift up an average-sized dining chair.

Fran dragged herself away from the screen for a few seconds to call out to Stella, who'd gone to bed early after the stress of the day.

'Quick, quick. You've got to see this,' Fran shouted up the stairs. 'This is history in the making. I feel a stampede for the film rights coming on.'

Stella made it downstairs in time to see Tracey, aided by Piers, rig up the vacuum cleaner and a chair for the big experiment. It was more like watching a circus act with a couple of magician's assistants. Even a drum roll would not have been out of place as the tension built. Tracey then recited the manufacturer's Olympic-sized claims about the suction power of the machine.

'I didn't see this in rehearsal, did you?' enquired Fran.

'No,' Stella replied. 'I don't think they had time to practise this one. Looks a bit risky.'

They were ready for the Big Lift. The machine was switched on, up went the chair – and down it came again with a thud on to Tracey's foot. Through grimaces of pain, she tried to plough on. Even Piers, not known for his scintillating wit, was trying to keep a straight face and wondering whether to seize the moment and give himself a speaking role. The final shot was of Tracey, clutching her foot and yelping, and Piers in a tangle with the chair, the vacuum and its various leads.

Fran went into the kitchen to put on the kettle, still quaking hysterically. 'I'm sorry I dragged you out of bed but the potential for disaster was too glorious,' she said to Stella, re-emerging with the tea things.

'I wouldn't have missed that for the world,' said Stella, wiping her eyes. 'That was uncharacteristically clever on the part of Kelly-Marie, wasn't it? Mastering the art of the phone again. She usually only manages walking and talking at the same time, with occasional breathing.'

'True, but I will thank her,' said Fran. 'Anyway, I can tell you that the Super Suck vacuum cleaner show was one of Steve's claims to fame. And I can definitely say that it sucks. But it's not necessarily super.'

'Why would anyone want to buy a vacuum that lifts up chairs?' said Stella. 'I mean, what's the point of that? Personally I've never felt the urge.'

'Steve again, I'm afraid. A right old anorak in the making there. I'm sure chair-sucking is probably the national sport in some obscure country he visits on caravan holidays. What do you make of him?'

'Total mystery. But one that I have no interest in solving. All we know is that he came from Potters Bar, did some sort of telesales and has a mother. Most of us can stump up at least one of those three.'

Chapter 11

It was the talk of the office the next morning. Thanks to telephonista Kelly-Marie just about everyone had caught the chair-sucking incident and was gossiping about it openly. All except Tracey Starburst, of course, who was signed off sick again, having added a selection of broken toes to her tally.

'Didn't realise it would be quite so dangerous working here,' Fran chided Steve, who'd arrived in his Indiana Jones meets Crocodile Dundee leather hat. It still didn't swing with the goofy glasses and the white sports socks. 'I suppose it's all quite tame for someone who's used to a bit of adventure.'

She indicated his hat with a nod of her head. The feeling around the studio was that Steve was a bit of a sad fantasist. Or maybe he really was Superman disguised as Clark Kent. The heavy black-framed glasses never came off. There had been a flurry of office speculation about underpants – under or over the trousers.

'Well, as a matter of f . . . f . . . fact,' Steve started, but they were both cut short by the fire bell going off. For a few seconds everyone stood stock still, waiting to see if it was a false alarm. But it carried on ringing.

'Out, out, everyone get out,' bellowed a security guard through the open office door. 'Quickly please, folks. Assemble outside for a head count.'

Fran snatched up her coat, handbag and car keys, well schooled after the endless fire alarms that occurred at the *Echo*. Mostly started by Des having a surreptitious fag too near a smoke alarm.

They all assembled outside, Kelly-Marie already turning blue in today's outfit of tan suede micro skirt, off-the-shoulder white gypsy-style top and deep orange scarf wound into her hair. She looked as though she'd collided with a can of tomato soup. Fran and Stella huddled together, grateful that they'd found gloves in the pockets of their coats.

'We must be off-air,' said Stella, glancing around at the crowd. 'All the tekkies are out here. They must have abandoned the programme.'

She was drowned out by the arrival of a fire engine. All the women leaned forwards involuntarily, anxious for a gawp at a hunky hero in uniform. Black smoke was now pouring from several windows of the building. Speculation was rife as to the cause of the fire – Piers putting into practice what he'd learned on a crash course in gas fitting, a revenge arson attack by Tracey or too much static produced from Steve's Superman outfit.

Eventually the truth was out.

'A peanut butter-maker caught fire,' Colin, one of the cameramen, told them. 'Monica was trying to demonstrate how it worked. Instead of perfect peanut butter there was a terrible smell, all this black muck and smoke pouring from the machine, followed by a bang. The viewers must have thought they'd switched over to *London's Burning* by mistake.'

'I hope it doesn't catch all of our Useless Plastic Objects,' remarked one of the household buyers, gratefully lighting up a cigarette. 'We've got forty thousand UPOs out the back.'

'Jolly good job if they did,' remarked another. 'Let's face it, we were never going to shift those horrible plastic whizziwhisks. Not to mention that truly awful hubble-bubble soap holder. Still, it's good to be off the phone for five minutes. It's been going berserk since Tracey's chair-sucking stunt last night.'

'Really?' said Fran. 'What sort of calls?'

'Disastrous, mostly. Companies ringing up to cancel their slots. It makes us look incompetent if we can't demonstrate the goods properly. And this fire palaver won't help either. We've already had "presenter drops chair on foot". Now we've got "presenter sets fire to peanut butter machine". It's really, really not good news.'

Fran glanced back at the studio, very depressed, just as a familiar silver Beetle pulled up several feet away. Out stepped Larry the Lens, one of the *Echo's* most sleazy photographers. The rumours about his 'private' work had never gone away. Fran found herself shrinking back among the crowd. She was still very anxious to play down her *Echo* origins, especially after all the speculative stuff Des had written before Getting It went on air.

'What's up?' said Stella, immediately reading Fran's worried expression.

'My previous life catching up with me again. And to think we were both hoping for fame and fortune. Here we are, in the freezing March cold, standing in a car park watching our workplace burn down and about to be captured for posterity by Larry.'

'A couple of weeks ago I'd have been thrilled to have

my photograph in the *Echo*, but now the very mention of the word photograph sends shivers down my spine.' Stella suddenly betrayed the emotions she was still feeling. Fran nodded sympathetically.

'But I've had an idea,' Stella continued. 'I want to bounce it past you tonight when we've got over this little lot.' She indicated the fire, which suddenly gave off a roar. 'That'll be the UPOs.'

'It's amazing the whole place didn't go up,' Fran reflected that evening. 'I really thought we'd be out of a job by tonight. But it's amazing how a blaze as dramatic as that didn't do more damage. There's a lot to be said for the cheap and nasty building syndrome. If it had been stuffed with comfy chairs, sumptuous curtains and knee-high carpet it would have gone up much more quickly.'

'Maybe that's a good selling point for UPOs,' said Stella. 'Even if your house burns down your whizziwhisk will remain intact. Cue Gloria Gaynor singing "I Will Survive".'

They both burst into fits of laughter as they tried to remember the words of the song.

'Which brings me,' said Stella finally, wiping her eyes, 'to my idea. I want to know what you honestly think before I do anything about it.'

With that, she disappeared out of the kitchen and came back waving a magazine.

'This was lying around the buyers' office,' she said. 'Shows what a sad lot we all are. It's a new magazine called *Handbagged*. It's dead tacky. It's for women who either want to hook the object of their desire or boot him out. A sort of hump or dump scenario – all in a mag.'

'I could see myself plundering it for ideas on how to get

rid of Steve,' Fran said somewhat suspiciously. What was this leading to?

'Well, it's the first issue and they've got this amazing competition to launch it,' Stella continued excitedly. 'They're asking for real-life revenge stories with photographs. And the prize is amazing. Some serious dosh plus a swanky night out in celebrity London.'

Fran put her head in her hands. 'Bloody hell, Stell, I can see which garden path you're heading for. Is this wise? It's fraught with problems, not the least of which is libel.'

'Look, read it,' Stella said emphatically, shoving the magazine into Fran's hands. 'It's all been thought out. They doctor the photographs and the text so people can't be identified.'

Fran conceded defeat and lit a cigarette. She read the article in between deep, thoughtful puffs. 'And you want to submit your story of Randy Ray and the Redhead? Listen, hon, they can do what they like about airbrushing the pictures but how often are naked redheads seen running down the streets of Hartford? It's not like: Oh, there goes another one.'

'OK, but how many people know what happened? You, me, Ray, carrot-top and PC Plod.'

'And all the people who phoned the police thinking it was a rape.'

'There can't have been that many. It was around midnight. How many people drag themselves away from the telly to stare out of the window just in case a naked woman runs past?'

'You're opening a big can of worms here,' Fran warned, taking another puff. 'If there's the slightest hint of who she is or where the picture was taken, take my word for it, the net closes very quickly. Could you cope with Des and

Larry on your doorstep, or, worse, the boys from the nationals?'

'That's why I'm asking what you think,' said Stella. Then, with a nervous little grin, she added, 'Actually, it would be on *your* doorstep. I've already made up my mind. I think. Sort of.'

Fran re-read the article in bed that night. What would she do if she were in Stella's position? As she gazed at Bob's sleeping form and inhaled the faint smell of wood that accompanied him whenever he'd spent the evening in the shed, she realised once more how lucky she was. That she couldn't imagine life without him, despite the state of the house. One day she'd somehow persuade him to give up the DIY so they could move to a brand new house *without* a shed on some modern estate, where, deep joy, they could get the builders round to fix anything that went wrong.

Next day, the building looked remarkably unscathed considering yesterday's inferno. Most of the fire had been contained in the studio area. The offices, the warehouse and most of the UPOs had survived. The studio was crawling with technicians and engineers working flat out to get the station back on air as fast as possible.

Paul Dyer called a meeting of the entire staff in the biggest room available, the buyers' office. It was standing room only as everyone listened expectantly.

'There's good news and bad news,' he announced, fixing the room with the familiar but still scary laser eyes. 'The good news is that we should be back on air in under a week. We have lost only minimal stock. But we are wise after the event. We're going to move some stock to an alternative warehouse on the other side of town and use the space left to build another back-up studio here. That should ease some of the problems we've had in turning around programmes. It also means we can introduce some bigger items, like fitness machines, without the problem of clearing the set in a couple of minutes. Unbelievably, the peanut butter machine not only caught fire but also caught the public's imagination and sold out. So that's the good news.

'The bad news is that we are about to get a roasting in the press. The fly-on-the-wall journalists I told you about at the launch have, of course, witnessed first-hand the various disasters of the past few days. This story is a gift for them. We made the late ITN news last night and I suspect some channels will take the story a bit further today. Can't blame them and I think we should try and view that in a positive way. At least our name is reaching a much wider audience than we ever envisaged. Just sit tight for this week's newspapers.

'Oh, and one last thing. You'll probably read about this so you ought to hear it from me first. Tracey, Karen and Monica have resigned. So I shall be auditioning replacements. That's it. Back to work.'

Everyone trooped out, rather subdued. 'Wonder what they'll do about the logo,' said Fran to no one in particular. 'This must be the end of Tracey's trolley days.'

'Pity,' remarked one of the cameramen, 'I thought it was so bad it was almost good.'

Fran went back to her desk. A shiver of disgust went through her as she read a message saying Des from the *Hartford Echo* had phoned and would she call him back. Yeah, right.

Chapter 12

The stand-in jewellery presenter, Caroline, was having a tough time. The gallery team that day were half way through a ten-hour shift and were bored and cracking jokes, all of which she could hear in her earpiece. Her programme guest, Isabella Velasquez, who 'designed' her own pieces from an address which sounded very much like an industrial park on the edge of Madrid, didn't quite have the command of English necessary to keep any sort of conversation going.

As Caroline fingered a silver pendant featuring an amethyst, she tried once again. 'This is such a beautiful piece. What inspired you, Isabella, to create this fantastic setting for the stone?'

'Eez beeyootiful,' smiled Isabella.

'Absolutely. So unusual. So what gave you the idea for this design?'

'Si, si, because eet eez so beeyootiful.'

'And the amethyst is the birthstone of Pisces, isn't it?'

'Que?'

'Sign of the zodiac. Fish.'

'Si. Like feesh very much.'

'Er, yes. And the matching ring. Now tell us about that.'

'Si. Ees matching. But no weeth feesh. Si.'

'Can you tell us about it?'

'Beeyootiful.'

Not helped by hoots of laughter from the gallery coming loud and clear through her earpiece, Caroline ploughed on. Thankfully, the watching public must have felt sorry for her because they phoned in in their droves and snapped up the pendant and ring sets so quickly that Caroline was put out of her misery. Time to move on to a 'fabulous Hollywood cocktail set'. She walked across the studio to the kitchen area where a tray of drinks, glasses and an ice bucket had been set up.

'Ever wanted to mix your own cocktails at home? Well, now you can relax with a Singapore Sling, or knock up your very own Margarita or Manhattan. Just like the stars,' she announced.

In her earpiece came the gallery team's version of events. Clearly they all preferred a Slippery Nipple, Sex On the Beach or Between The Sheets. It sounded as though they were actually throwing their own cocktail party up there. Caroline wished they'd shut up; she could hardly hear herself think, let alone drink.

'Now, you've got everything you need in this fantastic set to make any cocktail party go with a swing. The cocktail shaker, swizzle sticks, even little umbrellas and sparklers to make your drinks look really stylish and showbizzy. But the best bit of all is this guaranteed, one hundred per cent non-drip jug in which to mix your drinks. Yes, one hundred per cent non-drip.'

'Coming to camera two,' said the director. This was a full frame of Caroline's face.

'Now, I expect like me you've got really drippy jugs,' she

announced. There was a pause and a fleeting look of panic on her face. In her ear, the gallery team was completely convulsed. Talk-back was hastily switched off. Caroline, grateful for the abrupt silence in her ear, regained her composure. 'So this jug is a God-send. No more wiping up or endlessly washing tablecloths with this one. And now I'm going to make a jug of sangria and show you just how brilliant it is.'

She ran through the ingredients, realising as she did so that there were no cinnamon sticks nor any sliced fruit on the table. Thank you so much, Piers.

'Going awfully well, isn't it,' she joked as she mixed the drink, minus the fancy bits. 'We'll have to use our imagination on the fruit. And now I'm going to add a few ice cubes, pour myself a delicious glass and pretend I'm in Barcelona. Remember, this amazing set is only twenty-nine pounds ninety-nine, delivered straight to your door. The jug is one hundred per cent guaranteed non-drip. And now, the moment you've all been waiting for. Here goes.'

The director ordered a close-up shot on camera three, amid mock drum rolls from the gallery team. Caroline was still oblivious to their antics.

She held up the jug and poured. 'Well,' she smiled, 'it only dripped a tiny bit. That certainly knocks my jugs into touch. I'm definitely going to order one of these myself.'

The second they threw to a promotion, Caroline stalked out of the studio and straight out of the building, never to be seen again.

The weekend headlines were worse than expected. The *Sunday Mirror* devoted a double-page spread to *Getting It – In The Neck. TV's New Disaster Channel.*

The first line was: *Is television's latest shopping channel, Getting It, already heading for the final check-out?*

'Doesn't get much more depressing than that, does it?' said Fran wearily as she put the paper down. 'Good of Tracey's agent to seize the moment and threaten to sue. Mind you, I suppose I don't blame her.'

'Me neither,' replied Stella. 'I'd have done the same. It's quite a hatchet job with all the hints about the share price tumbling and jobs being axed. And to think that we both believed Getting It would propel us into the public eye.'

'Well, we did make a brief appearance at the back of the crowd in *Hello!* when they covered the launch,' said Fran. 'I knew it spelled trouble when Paul Dyer announced he had a couple of journos in on the ground before we went on air. I never actually met them. They were rather subliminal, weren't they? I read one of their articles and realised why I never made it to Fleet Street. Just couldn't do the hype. This woman actually wrote "failure is the new success". Yeah, right.'

'Here's to failure then,' replied Stella, holding up a cup of coffee. 'Cheers hon. Let's see what tomorrow brings.'

Monday morning heaped even more column inches of misery on the station. The *Sun* carried a report on Caroline's swift departure. 'Why I'm no longer Getting It' shrieked another headline. The article went on to detail the lack of gallery discipline, not to mention the rubbish array of products she'd had to promote, including the infamous non-drip jug. It was all uncomfortably close to home.

In the production office everyone was huddled into corners, talking in soft voices and spelling out doom and gloom. In the buyers' office the phones were going solidly.

Firm after firm rang to cancel any involvement with Getting It. Soon there'd be nothing left to sell. Stella, booked to attend a trade fair later in the week, wondered whether to get it over with and cancel now. Just to add insult to injury, the programme going out at the time included the infamous stain remover. Everyone sat around looking more and more depressed. What was the point of doing anything?

Fran was just beginning work on that evening's late-night bargain hour. This involved a recap of a whole mish-mash of products, often at a cheaper price. Tonight, she thought, we have the stain remover that thinks it's a carpet remover, a guaranteed non-drip drippy jug in a cocktail set, the iron that makes light work of your clothes by burning them and, of course, the now legendary Super Suck vacuum cleaner. The bargain hour was billed as 'Suddenly Essential: things you never knew you needed – until now.' What bitter irony.

Just as she was wondering whether the station would totter on to the evening, an email came round from Paul Dyer summoning the entire staff to the studio at 5 p.m., during a repeat hour. Well, this was really it. Getting It – your P45, that is. For the first time she began to speculate as to whether she'd get her old job back on the Echo. All those make over your house/garden/face/fingernails features began to take on a very tempting aura. She almost salivated at the thought of knocking out another couple of columns on the bijou cottage, loft living and barn conversions – although she very much doubted there were any barns in the Hartford area left to convert. She'd do more Madame Chita copy tonight. That would get her in the mood for a chastened return to the Hartford Echo.

As the afternoon progressed, the production office grew

more and more like the Rue Morgue with people unashamedly calling up their CVs on their screens and tinkering with them. Blatant conversations broke out on how to explain to future employers why the job at Getting It had ended. One joker even suggested having a reunion at the local Job Centre.

'At least you've got your little sideline,' Fran remarked to Steve.

He looked blankly at her.

'Well, you can just nip into a phone box and turn into Superman,' she chided him. The Clark Kent jokes were out in the open now because Steve didn't seem to mind. He seemed almost pathetically grateful for any kind of attention.

'Oh you may say that but I couldn't p . . . p . . . possibly c . . . c . . . comment,' said Steve, attempting the immortal line from *The House of Cards*. It just didn't work with a stutter.

Fran didn't even laugh. She still couldn't work him out at all. She made a mental note to suggest a profile on him if she managed to get back at the *Echo*. At least the headline was easy: 'Steve McGuire – Man of Mystery'. Working out who or what he was was another story.

Five o'clock finally came and everyone reluctantly left their desks and shuffled into the studio. It was a bit like going to the dentist with rampant toothache, hoping to get away with a check-up.

Chapter 13

Paul Dyer swept in on the dot of five, sapphire blue eyes sweeping the room like radar. Conversation immediately ceased with everyone desperately straining to interpret the blank expression on his face. The Armani suit teamed with Doc Martens was a master stroke of style thought Stella as she stood next to Fran. How unlike Steve, whose bizarre selection of clothes made everyone wonder if they were picked out at random like lottery numbers.

'Well, it's been a strange day,' Paul began. 'This morning it looked as though our warehouse would be virtually emptied out by the time I stood here. Sadly it was because the buying department was receiving more calls cancelling new contracts than our call centre was getting from customers ordering the odd tea towel.'

A groan went around the room. People started shaking their heads in disbelief. Get it over with quickly, thought Fran. Just announce closure and let's get to the pub.

'But suddenly,' continued Paul Dyer, 'a miracle happened.'

'Strewth, not feeding the five thousand out of that awful fish kettle we were flogging last night,' sniggered Colin the cameraman. Everyone giggled nervously.

Paul Dyer beamed, much to everyone's relief. 'The ratings came through. And they're amazing. For a small new shopping channel we notched up a record share of the available audience. Nothing short of a miracle, as I said. This means, ladies and gentlemen, that we have been granted a stay of execution.'

Everyone broke into low whispers of delight, followed quickly by disbelief again.

'Obviously we'll have to analyse this, but it seems our huge publicity in one of the Sunday tabloids, plus a follow-up article today, has forced us well and truly into the market place. This is the kind of profile we just couldn't buy. OK, at the moment it's because the public want to watch our mistakes. It's a kind of Eddie the Eagle situation, that very British thing where we almost celebrate and cherish failure. But if it means people are tuning in, if it saves the channel and our jobs, let's not knock failure. It's a bit early to say for sure but our accountants are telling us to hold tight. You can only sell if you have the products in place and the customers to see the goods. At least our chequered short history is pulling in the viewers. Whether the viewers will convert into loyal customers remains to be seen. But if they do, it'll be a testament to the presenters and the production team. So, folks, our eleventh hour appeal has been granted. We are not yet out of the woods, but we're certainly chopping down trees.'

That night during supper, Fran and Stella celebrated with a bottle of champagne left over from Christmas. Even Bob managed to drag himself away from his shed to join them briefly. They drank a toast to 'survival and success'.

'In fact,' said Fran, now mellowing by the minute from the champagne and lack of lunch, 'if Getting It keeps getting it for another couple of months, I am personally going to ditch this picnic table and buy something decent. Well, half decent on my reduced salary. I've waited ten years for it so there's no rush. How about you? Any aspirations?'

'To win that competition,' said Stella, immediately regretting she'd confessed. You old blabbermouth, she mentally scolded herself. Her plan had been not to mention it again, just announce it out of the blue if by chance she won.

'Not *Handbagged* magazine?'

'Yep, I posted my entry this morning. Couldn't resist it in the end. I was so fed up with the situation at work, and that redheaded bitch's face was beginning to haunt me.'

'I should imagine that's the last thing the readers of *Handbagged* will be gawping at,' replied Fran, who was still uneasy about the whole thing, convinced that it was deeply flawed and that it would rebound on Stella. But ultimately it was Stella's shout, and maybe, just maybe, it would be therapeutic. It was certainly one way of dealing with her new and very raw anger.

Next day was a non-stop flurry of activity at Getting It. Thanks to another newspaper story about the amazing ratings, everyone was running around like serial killers who'd just cheated the gallows. The phones wouldn't stop ringing, especially in the buyers' office where for every contract cancelled yesterday three more arrived today. Stella was drowning under a sea of paperwork.

As if anyone needed a signal that it was 'business as usual', Paul Dyer was now auditioning replacement presenters. Model after actor after presenter, male and female, seemed to be practically camping out in the corridor outside his office. A couple of the guys looked as though they were camping it up very nicely as well.

Clearly the interview panel was giving each candidate a rough ride. Every so often the odd scream or indignant outburst would be followed by the loud slam of a door and the sound of flouncing footsteps in the corridor.

By late afternoon, rumour had it that one girl, a well-known network presenter, had been told the funky clothes she was wearing were not suitable for a Getting It audience. 'Too wacky for here. Think Kenny G rather than Ali G,' she'd apparently been advised.

Another was allegedly told she was too fat and would have to begin a strict diet if she wanted to get to the next round of interviews. 'I didn't get to the top of the food chain to nibble on some rotten old lettuce leaf,' she'd proclaimed loudly as the door was opened to signal her departure.

The comings and goings went on for several days, with the nosier members of staff reduced to corridor-crawling to find out what was going on.

'Bit like replacing the Pope,' Fran remarked to Piers during a fag break. 'We're all waiting for the smoke to come out of the chimney.'

Piers looked blank. Obviously picking a Pope wasn't the talk of the gym.

'Whenever they've chosen a new Pope, it's signalled by smoke,' Fran explained. 'Everyone just sits back and waits for the signal.'

'How bad does the old one have to be to get fired?' queried Piers.

'Not bad at all. Just dead.'

'And then they set fire to him to make the smoke signal? That's a bit primitive.'

'Oh for goodness sake, Piers. What did you expect – selection by Pope Idol?'

Piers shrugged and went back inside. It was time for him to buff up the new Glitterati range of jewellery that was being demonstrated next.

Back in the studio, however, there was another panic going on. Faced with the non-arrival of the model who was to wear the jewellery, an emergency replacement was being sought. Kelly-Marie made an appeal over the tannoy for anyone with multi-pierced ears to get to the studio as quickly as possible.

Having had no response, she was despatched around the building on an model-hunt.

'Anyone here with pierced ears?' she announced timidly. A couple of girls nodded. 'But how many holes do you have?' she then enquired. 'You'll need more than one hole if you want to do this.'

'None of your bloody business,' came the swift reply. Kelly-Marie looked faintly puzzled.

The minutes ticked away. Bitterly regretting the fact that she didn't have multi-pierced ears, Fran turned away to get on with her new collectables slot. It might have been fun to appear briefly on screen. She'd been wondering lately what it would be like and whether she'd get stopped in the street after one appearance. Probably not, she concluded. She was so engrossed in her thoughts that she didn't clock the programme starting up on screen. It was only the sudden hoots of laughter around her that made her glance up. There on a candlelit set was Francine, one of the new jewellery presenters, busily putting earrings into a slightly red-faced Piers. The director took a close-up of two diamanté earrings side by side in Piers's right ear, set off by his bulging, overworked neck.

'Now this matching set would look great with evening wear,' said Francine. 'Or even going to the gym, as Piers is demonstrating. And look how the light sparkles on it and sets off that magnificent snake tattoo that Piers is sporting. You really will be the talk of the treadmill if you wear these . . .'

Francine could barely keep a straight face. She was studiously avoiding all eye contact with Piers in case she burst out laughing. Piers, however, was growing in confidence by the second. Used to staring at himself in the mirrors at the gym, this was merely an extension of admiration of the body beautiful. He was also secretly congratulating himself on the fact that he'd cleaned his ears that morning.

The gallery crew were now in an advanced state of hysteria so talkback had been switched off. Hearing five people squawking with laughter would not help Francine one bit.

Fran briefly wondered whether it was too late to nip out at lunchtime and get her ears pierced. Stop it, you silly girl, she berated herself. You've not been hired as a presenter, so remember your place in the pecking order.

Chapter 14

That night a rare event took place in the Hallgarth household. Fran and Bob had a row. As always, it was a one-way screaming match. Fran had held off until she knew Stella would be out visiting a girlfriend. Suddenly it started – her mouth opened and her brain couldn't control the flow of pent-up anger. Every once in a while she had to let rip about the state of the house.

'I can't go on in this mess,' she shouted, feeling her face going purple with rage. 'Look at this kitchen – wobbly worktops, shuddering plumbing and stuff still in boxes. It's like cardboard city. We might as well start selling *The Big Issue*. It's brought it all home to me again since Stella's been staying. We're not living here, Bob, we're camping. After ten years.'

Bob, who wasn't capable of uttering a cross word even if he tried, just hung his head. 'I know I'm a bit slow on everything, sweetheart, but it will be wonderful when I've finished.'

'There won't be any wonderful, Bob. Just unfinished.'

'But think of the money we're saving . . .' Bob's cautious banking background was never far away.

'Think of the pittance we'll get for this house when we

move,' retorted Fran, a pulse now going in her neck. 'A potential buyer viewing this dump would probably knock twenty grand off any asking price we came up with. Let's face it, you're hardly Bob the Builder. Trouble is, now that I've taken a pay cut we couldn't afford to get someone in even if I could begin to persuade you.'

'Yeah, yeah, I know you're right,' Bob said meekly.

'I'm just fed up with living out of packing cases and juggling meals on that bloody Baby Belling. We can't invite anyone around . . .'

'You invited Stella to stay.'

'Only because she was desperate. And the fact that she *has* stayed shows just how desperate she must be. Sorry, hon,' Fran started to relent, to her own annoyance, 'I know your heart's in the right place, and I know how much you love pottering in that shed – which I'd personally like to nuke. But it isn't happening, is it?'

'Well, not as fast as I'd have liked,' Bob conceded as he fumbled in a drawer. Fran paused while he rummaged some more. And some more.

'Er, is the bottle opener in here somewhere?' he asked eventually.

'Yes, that's exactly where it is,' she replied. 'Somewhere.'

They said nothing while Bob continued to rummage in the drawer. Eventually the bottom fell out, sending a cascade of knives, wooden spoons and other kitchen paraphernalia into the abyss of the cupboard below. Now he was on his hands and knees, red-faced, grappling not just with the utensils but with baking tins, steamers and saucepans as he searched for the bottle opener. At last he found it, opened a bottle of beer and took a grateful swig.

Fran finally broke her silence. 'Time is money,' she said coldly. 'I rest my case.'

They suddenly stopped glaring at each other across the table and burst out laughing. Fran and Bob's rows always went like this.

'Now I've had an idea,' said Fran, lighting a cigarette and looking Bob firmly in the eye. 'There are some cheap kitchen cabinets being offered in a promotion at work next week and I was thinking we could buy some with my staff discount. And before you protest at the word cheap, cheap is at least a happening word. In fact, it is music to my ears. And I might even ask one of the guys at work to come round and help put them up.'

A flash of piqued pride whipped across Bob's face. 'We could store them in the shed until—'

'Nope. They're going straight in and up,' said Fran firmly, not quite believing her own voice. 'If those cupboards make it to your shed, you'll start taking them apart – in less time than it takes to find the bloody bottle opener.'

'OK, you win,' Bob grinned affectionately. 'I do love you, Fran. You know that, don't you?'

'Yes, I do, and I love you too,' said Fran mischievously. 'But now you have a rival for my affections. Just at the moment I'd love some kitchen cupboards even more than I love you. Remember tonight and how long it takes to get a drink in this house.'

Fran then started to cook supper. Normally Bob would have retreated to his shed while this was going on but tonight he knew he'd better stay put. And Fran put him through his paces, rummaging through the cupboards and cardboard boxes yet again for all the things she needed to make a simple pasta and carbonara sauce. He was even more ashamed when he realised that the infamous Baby Belling – only ever a stop-gap – was now on its last legs, having done ten years of unsteady service. Fran instructed him in the art of shoving bits of newspaper under the wobbly legs to make it more stable.

As they consolidated their peace over a bottle of wine, they fell into conversation about life at the bank and also the U-turn in fortunes at Getting It.

'Your channel's the talk of the bank,' Bob informed her. 'Much more exciting than the world of direct debit. One of the girls in my office even bought that terrible cocktail set, you know, the one with the drippy jug, on the basis that it would be a good laugh at dinner parties.'

'Well, there's no accounting for taste, and just wait till you see the new collectables series I'm working on at the moment.'

'Bad, eh?'

'The word naff doesn't even come near. I couldn't begin to recommend it too lowly.'

'Do you regret leaving the *Echo*?' asked Bob, suddenly more serious. 'It was a huge step after so long.'

'Yes and no,' said Fran, immediately pensive and lighting a cigarette. 'I took a huge pay cut, don't forget, but it was a rut and I'm glad of the change. I did think by now I'd be leading a more glamorous life with a little bit of stardust. Stella and I had this pathetic hope that we'd make fleeting appearances on some of the programmes. But other than the presenters of course, the only person who's made the big time is dear old Piers Tongue. And that was scrubbing carpets and wearing earrings. And, thankfully for all of us, it was a non-speaking part.'

Bob sat back and laughed. 'Perhaps it's just as well, love. It seems to be quite a dangerous profession, this presenter lark. You've had one falling out of a hammock and dropping a table on her foot and another complaining about her drippy jugs.'

'That's true,' Fran conceded. 'It's like working for Shopping For Dummies. Even the trade papers have started referring to us as the Idiots' Lantern.'

'Pity, you were so excited about it at the start,' Bob continued. 'I really thought you were going to end up mixing with the stars from the pages of all your favourite magazines.'

'Yeah, well, I suppose I did have a brief flirtation with that idea,' she said, tipping her ash into an old saucer. 'However, I have an awful feeling Stella might still pull that one off.'

She gave him a brief account of Stella's entry into the *Handbagged* competition. Bob was suitably horrified.

'Strewth, hell hath no fury and all that,' he said, pouring out the last of the wine between them.

'Absolutely,' replied Fran. 'I think she must have a good chance of winning simply because of the pictures. Fortunately, or unfortunately, the prize is perfect: we get to fulfil our silly mid-life ambition to be famous – for one night only.'

'But the fall-out could be disastrous. It could jeopardise her divorce case, couldn't it?'

'I don't even want to think about the implications. Talking of fall-out, I'm going to have great difficulty falling out of bed tomorrow morning after all that wine.'

Within five minutes they were upstairs, cuddled up in bed and both snoring for Britain.

Fran was working flat-out on the new Collectables strand. It was hard work waxing lyrical about a neo-Georgian silver-plated unicorn rearing up around a clock of nylon blue suede with pearl buttons to mark the hours and a paper butterfly perched precariously on the end of the second hand. Or a pink and white crinoline lady crocheted toilet roll cover. Or a collection of red glass clowns that wouldn't have looked out of place as the booby prize on a coconut shy.

What really spooked Fran was a set of dolls with china faces, all dressed in frou-frou dresses and poke bonnets. The first time she confronted them they were all sat in a row on one of the sofas, apparently glaring at her. It reminded her too much of *Child's Play*.

'Now I AM going bonkers,' she said, half-aloud. She took a deep breath and promised herself a fag break soon. Suddenly she was aware of someone else in the studio. She whipped around to find Paul Dyer behind her with two visitors, one male and one female. Both mid-twenties, both very beautiful, impossibly slim, impeccably dressed, overacting like mad and gushing like Buckingham Palace flunkeys. Fran guessed them to be new presenters.

'Aha! Just the woman,' said Paul Dyer.

Alarm bells instantly began ringing in Fran's head. She knew she wasn't going to relate to either of them very much. For a brief moment she regretted not having put on a natz more make-up that morning.

'Brilliant timing,' said Paul Dyer to the glamorous pair.

Brilliant fluke, thought Fran, but she was too sensible to say anything.

'May I introduce Fran Hallgarth, one of our star producers,' said Paul expansively. 'Fran, this is Tiffany and this is Kiefer.'

Fran shook hands with them, grateful for the unexpected compliment and wishing he'd stopped at the word star. Tiffany and Kiefer sounded as though they had trod the same road as Tracey, the woman who'd put Stardust into Crump.

There was no denying they were a good-looking pair. She was tall and tanned with white blonde hair in a trendy style, wearing obviously expensive clothes. He was half a head taller with light brown hair allegedly bleached by the sun. Impossibly beautiful in an almost stereotypical beefcake sort of a way. Both oozed a practised confidence, yet they knew exactly what side their bread was buttered. They were hanging on to every word Paul Dyer uttered, especially when it was about them.

'Tiffany and Kiefer begin on Monday and they'll be co-presenting the main evening showcase,' continued Paul. 'Then they'll alternate on Suddenly Essential: products you never knew you needed – until now. And of course they're just a phone call away.'

Paul Dyer had a rather endearing habit of lapsing into the style of his own adverts and press releases. He probably wrote them, Fran mused.

'Where are you from?' she enquired, trying not to sound too fascinated.

'I'm an actress,' said Tiffany in that pseudo-self-effacing 'look at me' way that only actresses can. Suddenly she was Ophelia, Anna Karenina and Hedda Gabler rolled into one and playing to the back of the gallery. 'Theatre, commercials and several films.'

'Me too,' Kiefer chipped in, not to be outdone. 'Plus ex-National Theatre, ex-West End, ex-American soap and ex-Royal Shakespeare.'

But not *The X Files*, thought Fran. How long would it be before he was ex-Getting It? Come to think of it, what the hell were they doing here anyway if they were that grand? She took an uncharacteristically instant dislike to both of them, but conceded that they'd probably look knockout on screen.

Fran smiled back, steeling herself not to laugh. The thought of Tiffany wrestling with the unicorn clock or Kiefer extolling the virtues of the crinoline lady loo roll holder was just too side-splitting to contemplate.

This could be fun.

Chapter 15

The eyes of the media were now firmly on Getting It. Day after day, journalists in all the national papers from the broadsheets to the red tops commented on the goings on, reviewing the programmes as if they had been full-scale dramas or major storylines in soap operas. Every gaffe, mistake or double entendre was faithfully reported in all the TV columns, which had the effect of making Getting It's dozen or so presenters extra nervous. Most thought they could learn their trade – live telly and ad-libbing – in the twilight zone of a shopping channel. After all, there were more than twenty similar channels to choose from and plenty of places to hide. But, it seemed, there was only one Getting It. Day after day, the headlines screamed: GETTING IT WRONG, STILL GETTING IT WRONG or NOT GETTING IT AT ALL. The products and the presenters were criticised mercilessly but still the viewers stayed with them. The more ridicule they got, the higher the ratings – and now this was having an effect on product sales.

The board of Getting It now found itself in the invidious position of having to take a gamble on the new-found fame. They had to decide whether the boom would last long enough to warrant extra staff at the warehouse and call centre to cope with the vastly increased demand. Then there was a policy decision to be made. Should they go through hoops to stop the on-screen gaffes, or keep things as they were? Would viewers switch off if they finally got all the camera angles right, the products actually worked on air and the presenters sounded coherent?

Even Piers had started getting fan mail, much to everyone's secret fury. As well as his unscheduled appearance modelling diamanté earrings, he'd accidentally appeared in shot so many times – usually in a nasty nylon vest – that he'd become cult viewing. It all started when a camera caught him crawling along the floor to rescue a standard lamp that had fallen over during yet another violent demonstration of the Super Suck vacuum cleaner. The director had been so mesmerised by what Piers was doing that he'd forgotten to cut to a different camera. Result, letters from hordes of middle-aged women who thought Piers looked rather scrummy on his hands and knees. One even went as far as to feature him on a website dedicated to tight buttocks. Paul Dyer, never one to miss a trick, was straight on to the public relations company to announce that Piers would be demonstrating a new range of home gyms they were planning to promote.

Fran and Stella quietly admitted to a rare attack of jealousy. There he was, no brains, no personality. Just a sweaty singlet and a set of bulging biceps – and yet he seemed to be landing on his size twelve feet without even trying. He'd developed a screen profile without even opening his mouth.

The U-turn in the station's fortunes threw most of the

staff into a state of confusion. Having shouted at them on a regular basis for all the mistakes, it now seemed that the management wanted them to carry on making them.

Eventually Paul Dyer called a staff meeting to clarify the situation once and for all.

'OK, we've all had a laugh,' he acknowledged. 'We've dined out on it and the papers have rubbished us into success mode. But it cannot last. Eventually even the worst of us are going to get the hang of our jobs and then there won't be any mistakes. At that point, we'll lose our huge audience. So while we've got them, let's keep them. Ultimately it's down to good products, good research and good presentation.'

To a murmur of anticipation, he introduced Tiffany and Kiefer and talked up their impressive CVs. The pair responded by flashing brittle smiles at the assembled throng.

Back in the buyers' office, one of the secretaries was straight on the phone to her mum to check out Tiffany and Kiefer's acting credentials in her copy of *Halliwells*. A few minutes later the call came back. No trace. A ripple of laughter went around the office.

Stella immediately phoned Fran to tell her that little snippet. Fran wasn't the slightest bit surprised. One or two producers in her office had tapped their names into search engines without a result either. Fran's alarm bells were still ringing out loud and clear. There was something about them she really didn't like. Steve glanced up from reading what they all referred to as *Geek Weekly* (usually some computer or internet-type magazine) and came up with a rare bit of logic, which almost redeemed the fluorescent tie he was wearing.

'If they're that m . . . m . . . marvellous, what the hell are they doing here in some deadbeat part of the country in a glorified b . . . b . . . biscuit tin?' he managed.

'I constantly torture myself with that question,' said Fran with more than a touch of irony. 'Along with the meaning of life.'

They might have been imaginative about their previous careers but there was no disguising first-night nerves for Tiffany and Kiefer. Fran was certain the pair of them would go into orbit when they saw the Collectables products because they were so tacky and out of keeping with the endless walk-in wardrobes of clothes they both appeared to own. She wondered how Tiffany would look in one of her fabulous Annabel Wakeley suits flogging a pack of two T-shirts, one peach and one turquoise, at a 'you can't afford not to have it' price of a fiver. Or Kiefer, the immaculately tailored Man From Dormeuil, waxing lyrical about a pair of purple check beach shorts.

Certainly first-night nerves overcame any potential protest from either of them. Fran ran through the products with them, patiently explaining all the details and handing them their cue cards. Then she went to the production gallery to watch. Up came the new music for the slot and they were off.

'Welcome to Getting It. I'm Tiffany Shire.'

'And I'm Kiefer Reeve and we're here to welcome you to our exciting evening slot called Suddenly Essential . . .'

'Every evening at this time we'll be bringing you some fantastic bargains for your home, your car, your wardrobe or your garden.'

'Everything you see tonight is of course covered by Getting It's money-back guarantee. But we can guarantee you won't want your money back. Guaranteed!'

They paused to mock laugh at their 'joke'. It involved lots of tossing of shiny John Frieda haircuts.

'So welcome to Suddenly Essential – all personally selected by us.'

They both paused to beam at the camera.

Like hell, thought Fran. It was cheesy but they both looked so good on the monitors that, at that moment, she'd have forgiven them anything. She watched as the pair of them wafted effortlessly through the first section of the show, linking seamlessly from saucepans to silver jewellery, from luggage to garden lights. Word from the warehouse was that all the items were selling out fast. Paul Dyer, who was also sitting at the back of the gallery, allowed himself a small grin as he saw the figures rocketing. This was more like it, this was what he'd intended the station to look like. At last it looked as though Getting It could shed its dubious reputation as most-watched comedy channel.

Fran allowed herself a little daydream that perhaps, at last, the channel would win some respectability. Maybe even an award. Perhaps she and Stella would, after all, attend some star-studded media events, clad head to foot in Ben de Lisi, proudly representing Getting It as they mingled with the likes of Terry Wogan, Michael Aspel, or even, phwoar of phwoars, Des Lynam. Fran felt mildly faint at the prospect of such celebrity red carpet rolling out ahead of her.

Her reverie was loudly interrupted by universal swearing around the gallery. She glanced up abruptly at the bank of screens. Tiffany appeared to be flustered and pink with embarrassment. No mean feat through that deep St Tropez tan.

'Oh shit, there goes another one,' grumbled the director.

Fran struggled to see what was going on. Tiffany was grappling with the neo-Georgian silver-plated clock, trying to extol its virtues. Then it dawned on her what was happening. Tiffany's long, beautifully French manicured – and now obviously fake – nails were pinging off loudly, one by one. In an effort to distract viewers from her plight, she started talking about the paper butterfly on the second hand.

Camera three moved in for a close up of the poor old butterfly staggering around the clock. Just as the shot settled, the butterfly gave up the will to live and fell to the bottom of the perspex clock case. Meanwhile, off came another perfect nail, this time ricocheting from the camera lens with consummate ease.

Instead of coming to her aid, Kiefer said nothing. When they finally got to a promotional break, the fur started flying. For two minutes the pair spat venom at each other, much to the horror of the gallery.

'You should have helped me out there.'

'Not my fault you had false nails, sweetie. How was I to know?'

'Never you mind. If it had happened to you, I'd have bailed YOU out.'

'No need, darling girl. I don't wear false nails.'

'Pax, pax,' the director shrieked in their earpieces. 'Back to you in fifteen.'

Suddenly the perma-tanned smiles were switched back on for the final part of the programme. This included a range of gas-fired barbecues complete with vacuum packs of speciality beefburgers and sausages. Kiefer lit the first barbecue with great aplomb while Tiffany placed some of the burgers and sausages on the metal grill. They spent a couple of minutes talking up the barbecue, how easy it was to light, cook and clean. Meanwhile, Kiefer did the blokey thing, put on a striped apron and did a lot of business with the burgers, turning and basting them with olive oil. Tiffany prepared a salad, thanks to a revolutionary salad shaker so enormous you'd have to have had an extension built on to the average kitchen. Suddenly they were ready for a tasting.

Fran, up in the gallery, prayed the smoke alarms wouldn't go off as the sausages looked decidedly burned. For once, the gods smiled. Until, that is, it came to the moment of truth.

Kiefer, with consummate ease, put the sausages and burgers out on a plate. Grinning in his suave way, he invited Tiffany to sample his cooking.

'Sorry Kiefer.' She smiled a brittle smile. 'Can't help you there. I'm a vegetarian.'

'Deuce,' muttered just about everyone in the gallery.

Chapter 16

The rumour didn't take long to circulate. The few seconds it took to type the email were enough. Everyone's computer went ping simultaneously as the message appeared on the screen. Tipping them off about Getting It's own unofficial website.

In the production office, all conversation ceased as everyone tapped in the web address. Silence followed as they navigated their way around the site. Then, finally, sniggers led to giggles, which in turn led to loud guffaws. Fran laughed so much she had to mop her eyes with a tissue.

Some computer boffin had obviously been having a field day with the station. There were pseudo profiles on all the presenters, and their past careers, plus speculation as to whether they were 'Getting It' on a regular basis. Then, throwing all copyright rules and regulations to the wind – and cyber space – clips of all 'your favourite disasters' were available at the click of a button.

'Brilliant,' said Tim, a producer who had only started last week. 'I'd heard about the drippy jugs but I'd never seen them in action. Amazing. Pity she's left. She's a corker!'

There was even a chatroom and a noticeboard where 'fans' of the station could post their comments. Most of the remarks so far were of a speculative nature about Tiffany and how she'd perform off camera. Even Piers had attracted quite a following, with viewers asking for the contact numbers of his body piercer, tattoo studio, gym and personal trainer.

Coming soon, proclaimed the home page, was Getting It Babes, which promised the sexiest bits from the home fitness shows. And also The Body: 'Your chance to add virtual tattoos to Piers'.

Omigod, groaned Fran inwardly. This would send Piers into virtual telly orbit. His starring role in a series of home fitness shows, as promised by Paul Dyer, was looming. The general feeling was that he'd be more successful on the Abdo Fabbo stomach trimmer than buffing up diamanté necklaces, or being caught on camera rescuing Tiffany's false fingernails. Piers had still not mastered the art of counting backwards, nor had he succeeded in getting Kelly-Marie, the apparent object of his desire, into the pub, let alone the sack.

The only person in the production office to be sniffy about the website was Steve. Sense of humour failure probably, Fran decided. She wondered for a few minutes whether he was a virgin. He was certainly the least touchy feely member of the office. That might explain why he didn't somehow fit in.

Fran rationed herself to one last look at the website. There was a page of speculation about whether Tiffany and Kiefer were having a sizzling affair. Well, they had got that bit wrong, she laughed to herself. They positively loathed each other and were not showing signs of building any bridges. In fact, Fran was attending a production meeting later that afternoon where she was certain that particular problem was likely to be top of the agenda.

Fran, Steve and three other producers sat around the table looking expectantly at Paul Dyer. He shut the file he'd been reading and came straight to the point. As he always did.

'What is discussed at this meeting is to be totally confidential,' he announced, laser eyes on full beam. 'So no need to spare any hurt feelings. It's quite simple. Tiffany and Kiefer loathe each other's guts and it's showing on screen. We're getting sackfuls of letters from viewers asking why they hate each other. It's only a question of time before we get the press on our backs. The trouble is, we've courted publicity from the word go. Our gaffes won us the kind of coverage that we could only dream about. But now we have a new type of problem on our hands. Do we exploit this hostility or nip it in the bud? Round the table views, please.'

'You mean, we make a virtue of it? This lack of chemistry?' asked Irene, a normally unruffled, bleached blonde thirty-something who produced the kitchen-based shows. 'Doesn't get my vote, not with cooking programmes. All that gas, hot pans and sharp knives. It's asking for trouble. I'm always on the edge of my seat in the gallery watching those two glaring at each other over the gas hob.'

'I agree with Irene,' said Fran. 'This cooking with attitude isn't an easy watch. It's a bit like Fanny Cradock being horrible to Johnny all over again. Having two people who loathe each other isn't ultimately funny and I doubt it's helping business. If either of them had any sense of humour we could play up the funny side of it. But they just behave like one long hostile takeover bid.'

Everyone around the table nodded.

Irene continued: 'I honestly thought we were about to have a fight on our hands the other day. They were demonstrating a low-calorie frying pan and Kiefer actually suggested Tiffany should snap one up immediately. Implying with all the subtlety of a block of lard that she was fat. I thought Tiffany was going to explode but she came back with, 'That's YOUR Christmas present solved.' Later on she demonstrated a fondue set and at the proverbial tasting session Kiefer retaliated by announcing how much he missed his mother's cooking.'

'How did Tiffany react to that?' asked Fran.

'Well, apart from leaving us in no doubt that she wanted to ram the whole thing down his throat, she came up with something along the lines of, "Yes, it must be so terribly hard for you to manage being miles from a decent chippie."'

Paul Dyer had been listening attentively to all the comments, taking an occasional note with a very expensive fountain pen. 'They could, of course, become cult viewing,' he said. 'We could allow them to really let rip. Would that intrigue viewers? It's certainly different – the station you tune into to watch the presenters slugging it out, sparring over the saucepans. Steve, you haven't contributed. What's your view? Should we sack them, split them up or make them bond?'

Steve looked as though he hadn't been listening. A faint pink tinge of embarrassment crept up his cheeks. He opened his mouth but nothing came out. Fran suddenly felt rather sorry for him. He seemed completely terrified of saying the wrong thing.

'I'm sorry to see we're depriving some village of an idiot,' said Paul Dyer tartly, without waiting for a reply.

'Next time you come to a meeting, try to master the art of breathing, listening AND talking. OK, I think we're all in agreement. Let's not throw out the baby with the bath water. We'll try a bit of bonding first. I'll have a gentle chat with them and then we'll arrange a series of lunches and pep talks. Then we'll review it in a fortnight.'

Driving home alone that night as Stella was working late, Fran savoured the opportunity to reflect on the meeting. She'd been convinced they'd split Tiffany and Kiefer up. Not effectively give them a second chance. The thought of having lunch with two people for whom the ends of the earth could never be far enough apart didn't appeal. And worse, trying to make them bond. That was more a job for Superglue. And why didn't Steve have any opinion on the subject?

Pulling into her road and parking her car carefully on the drive behind Bob's, Fran didn't notice a man in a long dark raincoat standing in the shadows of her garden hedge. She picked up her briefcase, locked the car and began to walk towards the front door. As she did so, Des Ryder took a step forward out of the darkness.

'Hello Fran,' he smiled through his familiar nicotined teeth. 'I'm working on a story and you owe me, remember?'

Chapter 17

Stella and Tim, the new producer, were having a laugh about Kiefer and Tiffany's latest row. The gallery crew had been entertained the previous evening by an argument that continued through all the short promotional breaks. In between flogging verdigris herons, solar-panelled water features and a job lot of pink fluorescent patio heaters, their fixed grins had turned to almost spitting hatred every time the camera was off them. Paul Dyer's bonding plan was clearly coming unstuck.

'That pair are like computer viruses,' said Tim, who was responsible for home fitness. 'The Kiefer virus – only boots up if he's in the mood.'

'What about a Tiffany virus?' responded Stella. 'No memory at all despite lots of expensive upgrades.'

'I'm sure there's a Kelly-Marie virus too – trendy new computer, looks amazing, all the lights flash but nothing inside actually works.'

'What about Piers?' queried Stella.

'That's easy – pages permanently under construction,' Tim replied triumphantly.

'Talking of construction, how do you think Piers is going to cope on his first fitness programme?'

'Well,' pondered Tim, who'd obviously done his homework on the subject of Piers, 'provided he hasn't had something important ringed, tattooed or pierced, he'll probably be more than adequate. I had been hoping he'd have another stud inserted into his tongue so he'd be rendered thpeechleth again.'

'Let's face it,' Stella agreed, 'when Piers opens his mouth, it's only to swop feet.'

'Can't understand what any woman would see in him,' said Tim. 'Who on earth would want to be seen out with a man in a singlet with "I Love Blackpool" tattooed on one arm and who must be worth his weight in . . . er . . . piercings?'

'Exactly,' Stella replied. 'Most men don't realise that all that muscle-rippling stuff doesn't generally appeal to women. They always leave out the most important exercise of all.'

'What's that?' asked Tim, suddenly nervous. His daily exercise regime consisted of an hour's rigorous pint glass-lifting in the pub after work.

'Well,' said Stella lowering her voice and glancing round, 'those body builders are always so busy with their biceps, they ignore more important places. Not much going on in the underpants department.'

'Huh, so size DOES matter,' scoffed Tim.

'Well, we can only hope,' replied Stella, laughing. She liked Tim. She judged him to be mid-forties with deep brown eyes and a craggy charm. Another plus point was that he was a good listener. They'd hit it off from the day he'd joined, and he was the only person other than Fran whom she'd confided in about the Ray situation. He'd immediately sympathised, having gone through a divorce a couple of years previously. He'd also confessed that he'd been made redundant from his job selling radio airtime and had had to tell a few white lies to secure the job at Getting It.

Stella reluctantly turned back to her latest project, determined to keep her mind off her divorce proceedings. Beachwear and travel accessories, including a foldaway deckchair you could carry in your hand luggage that she knew would spell a near-death experience in the wrong hands. Let's hope I don't get landed with Tiffany and Kiefer on this particular project, she thought as she dialled up one of the companies involved to begin arranging shipments. While she waded through the various push-button options she treated herself to another quick look at the unofficial Getting It website. Steeling herself not to enjoy the vacuum-sucking episode for the umpteenth time, she looked on the noticeboard. Some crank had posted loads of messages about Tiffany, saying what a cracking piece of crumpet she was and how, shock horror, Kiefer didn't deserve her. Didn't deserve her, Stella chuckled to herself. More a case of walking over broken glass to avoid her. Must be the work of a nutter.

Fran had spent all morning running through the ins and outs of yet another Suddenly Essential night, trying to work out how she could possibly link from a set of porcelain dolls dressed in Victorian costume to a blow up paddling pool. Well, she could think of one way, but it wasn't fit for broadcast. But her mind wasn't totally on the job today. Des's spooky appearance had really shaken her. She'd made heavy weather of her Madame Chita column last night as a result. Des'd put his arm around her but it hadn't been a hug. More a sinister warning. His closeness had been vile and he'd almost knocked her out with his death breath. Now that would have made a good *Hartford Echo* front page lead: Former *Echo* Reporter Found in Gutter: Police Hunt the Halitosis Killer.

'I've been having a long, long think about you,' Des had snarled at her, eyes flashing and his hair in particularly greasy ringlets. 'And you still owe me big time. Time to call in the debt. I want the lowdown on this Kiefer character and his very pretty girlfriend.'

'I don't know anything,' Fran had stammered, shocked and ashamed that he frightened her so much.

'Of course you do, and if you don't give me some hard facts for a really good story I'm going to make one up and quote an "insider". Everyone will know it's you because you used to work at the *Echo*. So give in gracefully, sweetie. Now what's going on? Are they shagging? They do a lot of pretending that they hate each other. I don't believe it for one minute.'

'They'll all believe it's me giving you the story anyway,' Fran had managed to mutter. 'Whatever I do or don't tell you, they'll all think it's me spilling the beans.'

'Exactly. You'll have nothing left to lose once my story goes into print. They'll kick you out so fast you won't have time to check your watch. Then you'll find out just how I felt.'

Fran had brushed him aside and marched up to her front door. Mercifully he hadn't followed. She'd slammed the door so hard the glass panels had quivered precariously.

Revenge, that was what Des had been after. She'd gone into the kitchen to put on the kettle, angry with herself for being so upset. A faint whiff of woodchip indicated Bob was in his shed. She'd made a pot of tea, poured out two mugs and then made her way up the garden path. Bob had looked round, startled for a moment. Fran rarely visited the shed. It was non-negotiable space – like a teenager's bedroom.

'Look,' he'd said triumphantly, his face breaking into an ear-to-ear grin. 'I've got it right at last.' He'd held up a perfectly formed elm door knob. Fran had tried to avoid looking at all the failed knobs on the floor.

'Brilliant,' had been her unconvincing reply.

Bob, her rock, had suddenly taken in her white face and slightly shaking hand as she handed him a mug of tea. He'd downed tools, given her a big hug and made her perch on the workbench while she told him in detail of the events of the previous five minutes.

Do nothing had been Bob's advice. Ignore him, he was just trying to stir things up unnecessarily. But she'd known that Des wouldn't leave it at that. It was only a question of time . . .

Back to Suddenly Essential, which was really only a posh title for a warehouse clearout. Fran gazed hopelessly at the incongruous range of products she was expected to include. As well as the dolls and the paddling pool, there were some packets of sausages, a compilation of completely unknown 'chart toppers' from the swingin' sixties and some horrible bean bags in swirly patterns. The paddling pools didn't have pumps, the sausage packets were printed only in German and most of the hot hits from the sixties came from a band called Matt Vinyl and the Undercoats.

The phone rang. There was no mistaking Des's voice. He was straight back on the case. She could almost smell his foul breath down the phone and imagine his greasy hair flopping over the handset.

'Just jogging your memory,' he snarled. 'Tiffany and Kiefer. Are they Getting It? I want the lowdown and I don't like waiting.'

'Sorry,' said Fran defiantly. 'The answer's the same. Not a chance. And anyway, there's no story to tell.'

'Have another think. In fact, have a good long think over the next couple of days because I hear rumours that your precious station isn't doing too well financially. I want to know about that, Fran. Your job must be in jeopardy. I'll put in a good word here when you get the boot. You know what I need so get it quickly. If I don't hear from you, you'll regret it.'

Fran gripped her phone so tightly her fingers went white. She was determined not to give into temptation and slam down the phone. That would alienate Des even more – if that were possible.

'Des, I have nothing to tell you. Even if I did, I wouldn't be allowed to.' Or be that bloody stupid, she thought.

'One more thing,' came Des's menacing voice. He was beginning to sound like Vincent Price in a Hammer Horror movie. 'I'm having another crack at the mysterious Madame Chita. You're one of the longest servers at the *Echo*. Any thoughts? Any clues as to who she is? You must have a theory.'

'No, none at all,' Fran replied rather too quickly. Her heart almost skipped a beat. No, not that lark again. She was beginning to feel like a cornered rat. Except that in this case, Des was the rat, not her.

'You know the number to call. Au revoir, sweetie.'

Fran put down her phone and gazed at it for a full minute. This was getting out of hand. Bob's advice to do nothing had been kindly but unrealistic. She gazed around the office. OK, so joining the station hadn't quite been the glamorous step into celebrity-dom that she'd hoped for. But she'd grown to love it over the past few months. There was a huge shot of adrenaline every time the cameras focused on something she'd produced. Now they were becoming more ambitious with themed shows, she'd been thrilled when several of her ideas had been taken up. She was enjoying discussing how to dress the set and introduce the products in a logical and yet fun way.

All that was missing was a little bit of personal fame. There'd been no stampede of autograph hunters in the high street. No Stella McCartney or Nicole Farhi on the phone, clamouring for her to wear their clothes. Not even a sniff of a Jimmy Choo sandal or a Mulberry bag.

But she was determined she wasn't going to have a slimeball like Des rot it up for her. After all, she hadn't done anything wrong. It wasn't her fault that Des had been pissed, caught driving and then featured in the *Echo*.

Her gaze still on her phone, she dialled Paul Dyer's number and made an appointment to see him soonest – which his secretary Fiona announced was the next day.

The cheap kitchen cupboards that Fran had ordered were due to be delivered in the next few days. At last, the prospect of one habitable and respectable room beckoned. After all those years of fantasising as to how it might look, Fran was almost scared that she wouldn't like the reality. Tonight she and Stella had decided to begin painting the kitchen in readiness for the arrival of the cupboards.

It was likely to be a triumph of eagerness over experience. Fran, who of course hadn't wielded a paint-brush for a decade, was determined to enjoy it. Stella, on the other hand, wanted desperately to make it up to Fran and Bob for gatecrashing their home. The first thing they did was to order Bob out of the kitchen, banishing him to his shed.

'He's not exactly kicking and screaming,' Fran observed as Bob scampered happily up the path. 'Right, the first rule of decorating, I think, should be to have a drink. So let's find a bottle and then we'll do something about all that sizing and sanding.'

The kitchen units were to be in the style of American ash, or real veneer as Fran put it. She'd already ruled out any bright colours in case they didn't work. Having got this far, she couldn't bear the thought of having to do it all again. Instead, she convinced herself that magnolia was a non-offensive colour and would be easy on the eye when they came to sell the house. Sell the house? That, too, seemed like a fantasy. Fran levered open the paint pots with an old kitchen knife while Stella whipped the cork out of a bottle of Muscadet. They clinked glasses and drank to the kitchen.

Half an hour later, they were staggered at the results.

'Omigod,' said Fran, amazed. 'Already it looks so different.'

'Well, that's two, going on three, glasses of wine talking,' replied Stella, 'but I do think you're right. And you've cheered up, which is even better. You've been very preoccupied today, Mrs Hallgarth.'

Tongue now loosened, Fran outlined Des's sinister visit last night and subsequent phone call. Stella was horrified, immediately blaming herself for working late.

'You don't think . . .' Stella paused agonisingly as she lit a cigarette. She was now firmly back on the weed, using her divorce proceedings as the excuse. '. . . that perhaps it's just a case of Des having the hots for Tiffany, do you?'

'No way. Des couldn't make overtures to a symphony orchestra – let alone a woman.'

'But we don't know that,' said Stella wisely. 'From what you say, you know no more about this idiot than I do. Maybe he has a secret pash. Most men do, even if they appear to be total benders. Up to now, he's never been seen with a woman. But that doesn't mean he's as camp as a row of pink tents. It might mean he's not all that bothered – that is, until he meets the right woman and then, *coup de foudre*, ker-pow, wham bam, he's hooked.'

'Can't see it,' said Fran. 'His only passion as far as I know comes in the form of licensed refreshment.'

Stella shook her head knowingly. 'Just because no woman of sound mind would put up with Des and his dental nasties,' she continued, 'doesn't mean that he's not a man of emotion. Tiffany might be his secret obsession, and the only way he can fuel it is to talk to you as you work with this screen goddess.'

'You mean he's quivering away, secretly salivating?'

'Exactly.'

'But surely he realises she's out of his league?'

'Ha! Unlike women, men don't feel the need to look in mirrors very often. I bet Des thinks he looks pretty drop-dead gorgeous.'

'Maybe he ought to take a look then,' said Fran ruefully.

'Of course,' said Stella suddenly, clapping her hands, paint and brush discarded for the moment. 'Why didn't I think of it before?'

'Think what? You are going to tell me, aren't you?'

'Des could be the guy who puts that screen worship stuff on the unofficial Getting It website.'

'Not possible,' said Fran, picking up her paint brush again. 'Des grappling with technology is about as likely as

Christine Hamilton turning down a stint on *Parkinson*.' She carried on, oblivious to what Stella was doing. Minutes later they both burst into uncontrollable laughter. On one of the unpainted walls, Stella had used her brush to write in big letters of fresh paint: MARK MY WORDS.

Chapter 18

Fran marched down the corridor to see Paul Dyer at the appointed hour. Her pounding heart reminded her of those nerve-racking interview sessions that had got her the job.

Paul, immaculate as ever, sat with his feet up on his vast red-leather-topped desk, surrounded by heaps of papers, files and VHS tapes.

'Diarrhoea,' he announced down his intercom. 'Get me those figures on the camping show. Quick as you can. Hi, come in, Fran, sit down.' He beckoned her in and turned back to his intercom in one easy movement. 'And Fiona, get us some coffee in here, right now.'

He swung his legs off the desk and gesticulated to all the tapes.

'Show reels,' he said. 'Lots of losers who think they can get on telly. They all want to be a star. Some of them are quite terrible. If you want a laugh sometime, help yourself. Just remember to chuck them in that bin afterwards.'

'That bad?' Fran gulped, envying them for at least *having* a show reel.

'Oh, worse,' he replied. 'There's one guy who looks and

sounds like an alien, not to mention a girl who's doing a piece to camera while she's changing some bloke's colostomy bag. Brave effort and meant to shock, I suppose, but we're hardly likely to feature them on *Suddenly Essential*, are we? It's all about knowing your audience.'

Fran couldn't suppress a grin. But before she could reply, Fiona, Paul's secretary, scuttled in and banged down a tray with a cafetière, cups and saucers. She was a peculiarly sexless girl, probably mid-twenties, with a permanent scowl. Everyone in the canteen had long given up on her, sitting in the corner glaring over her gluten-free sandwich and *Daily Telegraph*.

Paul watched her stomp out again with a strained smile.

'She does my head in,' he said when the office door had closed. 'I think she came here thinking the job was just a fast track to stardom. She's my biggest mistake. Of all the people I hired at the start of this, she's certainly one I got wrong. She manages very successfully to combine being bitter with complete stupidity. She's so bloody dense I'm surprised light doesn't have to bend around her.'

Fran burst out laughing, nerves forgotten. She'd never realised Paul Dyer could be quite so amusing – or indiscreet. He poured out their coffee and handed her a cup.

'Hope you don't take sugar, as Fiona's forgotten again.' He rolled his eyes to the ceiling. 'Now, what can I do for you?'

For a moment she'd almost forgotten. Then, at the thought of Des, her face fell immediately. She took a deep breath and recounted as briefly as possible the story of Des's drink-drive conviction, how he was sacked and then reinstated, the confrontation at her house, the threats and the impossible situation he'd put her in. Paul listened intently without betraying a flicker of emotion.

'So you see,' Fran concluded, staring at her rather chipped nail varnish, 'whatever I do, the finger of suspicion is always going to be pointed at me. That's why I felt I had to talk to you.'

'You've done all the right things,' he said, breaking into a smile. 'I'm glad you've told me, Fran, but there would never have been any finger of suspicion. I trust you implicitly. You're one of the real stalwarts here and I don't want this Des character giving you a hard time. Now tell me,' he paused, 'do you think this guy is capable of being a stalker?'

Fran found herself almost blinking at the directness of his gaze.

'A stalker? Sleazy old soak, yes, but stalker? I've never really thought about it,' she managed. 'Why should he be a stalker?'

They each took a sip of their coffee. Paul leaned forward across his desk. Fran noted long, lean fingers and cufflinks shaped like tiny television sets.

'What I am about to tell you is confidential. It goes no further than this office. Tiffany is being stalked. It's not just those silly smutty messages being posted on that bloody website. She's getting phone calls here, on her mobile and at home. Nothing kinky or heavy breathing. Just silence.'

'Can they be traced?' Fran was staggered.

'They appear to come from different payphones but all from the Hartford area. Then there are letters, some posted locally, others just put through our letterbox here. Again nothing kinky, probably just some old saddo who fancies the idea of a bit of a bunk-up with a pretty girl. But it's freaking her out. She's a bag of nerves. I'm thinking of getting the police on to it.'

'Oh, THAT serious.'

'Yes, the last two weeks or so have been relentless. She's so screwed up about it she now has an escort from the building to her car and I'm getting an expert in to talk to her – and the other presenters – about personal security here and at home and dealing with difficult fans. This guy has obviously been watching her movements. One of the reasons I'm telling you this is that it has just occurred to me that this Des character might be the stalker.'

Fran thought back to the conversation she'd had with Stella the other night. Stella thought Des might be the obsessive nutter on the website. But was he capable of making silent phone calls and writing weirdo letters as well?

'I honestly don't know,' she confessed. 'I must say I've never thought of Des as a ladies' man. I can't remember him ever showing interest in any female. His *raison d'être* is to be obnoxious and to get to the pub as fast as possible. But I'll tell you what I do think he's capable of.'

'What's that?' Paul was intrigued.

'Des is perfectly capable of creating a story. He'd have no conscience about upsetting someone, especially if it gave him a good front page lead. If Tiffany's off screen for a few days over all this, and Des gets wind of it, he'll come up with some sort of story. It's his currency, don't forget. And of course, if he IS the stalker, he'll secretly know the real reason why she's off. Because he's caused it.'

Paul nodded and poured them some more coffee.

'Funnily enough,' he continued, 'to begin with I thought it was Kiefer doing all the kinky website stuff. There's some kind of silly competition going on on this site and I happen to know, because I've seen our phone bills, that both of them have been mass voting for themselves as the sexiest star on the station. They're certainly not being subtle about it, but then we didn't hire them for their grasp of nuclear physics. I began to wonder whether Kiefer might be taking it a step further in the hope it would freak her out. But in a funny way, I'd rather the culprit was your newspaper chap. From my point of view it would be one helluva lot easier to deal with if it were him.'

Fran nodded and then drained her coffee cup. 'I can see that. But there's one flaw in all this, now I come to think of it. I don't see Des as a website whizzo. He's an old-style reporter who'd still rather use a typewriter and paper than a computer. He absolutely hates technology.'

'Well, I am definitely going to call in the police,' said Paul. 'Whether it's an internal or an external job, we need to know who's doing this. I'm really glad we've had this conversation, Fran. You've done all the right things. But don't forget, what we've discussed is totally confidential.'

'Absolutely,' said Fran emphatically.

'Good,' said Paul. 'And there's one other thing. You're getting a pay rise. Not much, but it might make life a bit easier. And that's confidential too. Don't breathe a word or they'll all want one. And I've got enough screen divas to cope with as it is.' He indicated the pile of show reel tapes again.

Fran was aware of Fiona glaring at her as she sailed

back to her office. Having gone in a picture of doom, convinced that she was in a completely untenable situation which would result in the sack, here she was with a pay rise and the backing of the man who all but ran the company.

The big day was nearly upon them and Fran was so excited she thought she'd implode. She issued strict instructions to Bob not to touch the kitchen cabinets when they arrived. She didn't want them disappearing up to the shed for a ten-year makeover.

'In the unlikely event of my death,' she announced imperiously to Bob over breakfast, 'I don't want to find these cupboards popping up in your shed. They are going to live on that wall and nowhere else.'

'Yes, Milady,' said Bob in a Parker-from-The-Thunderbirds accent.

Fran opened the *Daily Mail* and skimmed it as she sipped her tea.

'Good grief,' she exclaimed, flinging down the paper. 'A new survey says men spend more time in their sheds than in the shower. I could have told the market research company that and saved them all a fortune.'

Bob pretended to look wounded. 'Alan Titchmarsh writes books in his shed,' he replied valiantly, 'but I believe it's quite a posh one.'

Our shed's pretty posh compared to our house, Fran wanted to snap back, but she thought better of it. Now that the kitchen cupboards were in her sights she was determined not to let up. She hoped this would be the first of several DIY projects to make the house respectable that didn't involve Bob. She kissed him goodbye fondly as he set off to work.

Stella appeared in the kitchen doorway. (It was just that – a doorway. Bob had removed the door to sand it down about five years ago.) She sat down as Fran buttered toast. She was just pouring out coffee for the pair of them when the phone rang, and Fran answered it.

'Hello sweetie,' came the familiar voice. 'How's things at Getting It? I'm hearing all sorts of interesting rumours and I think I must be hearing them from you.'

'Des, you're wasting your time,' Fran said firmly. 'I've told my boss about your calls. So you can print what you like but he'll know it didn't come from me.'

There were rasps of mock laughter from Des. 'Oh, he'll change his mind when he sees the story,' he snarled. 'I know you're going to enjoy reading it too – Big Cash Crisis at Hartford's Troubled TV Station. And where was the lovely Tiffany last night? Off with stress? Well, frankly, I'm not surprised.'

Fran gulped. It really WAS him. Des the Stalker. She steeled herself to stand firm.

'Des, you disgust me. Get off my back. You do your job and I'll do mine. And I am now going to put down the phone. Goodbye.'

She stared at the phone for a few seconds, then grabbed her coffee mug. At least he'd dropped the Madame Chita line. Or maybe he just hadn't got as far as that.

Stella looked at her. 'It's that horrible bloke from the paper again, isn't it?' she said quietly. 'What's he after?'

'Doing another story about the station. He wants to rubbish us. I'm just relieved I went to see Paul about it. He said that whatever story gets printed, he knows it will not have come from me. But whether anyone else at Getting It will believe me is another matter.'

'Oh, they will,' said Stella. 'I'll make sure of that.'

It's going to be a challenging week, thought Fran, almost slipping into Madame Chita mode. What rubbish will Des dredge up this time and how will my kitchen cupboards look?

Chapter 19

Various jokes were doing the rounds about the Ark being built by amateurs but for the *Titanic* and Getting It they'd brought in the professionals. The gags were undoubtedly prompted by the news that Getting It's first full-blown home fitness programme was about to be recorded. A clue for visitors might have been the ever hopeful Kelly-Marie languorously stretched out over the reception desk in purple lycra on the morning of transmission.

Throwing caution to the wind, Paul Dyer had invested in the services of a marketing company to give the new show a boost. As a result, there'd been major advertising in magazines and newspapers, plus invitations to journalists to come along and cover the first day, warts and all.

'Our reputation for cock-ups still goes before us,' he'd told a production meeting the day before. 'Every time we open our doors to journalists there's a bloody stampede. So we might as well capitalise on it. I don't think we'll ever shake off our reputation so I'm beginning to think we might as well nurture it.'

'Let's face it, Paul,' a voice came from the back of the room. It was Jon, the director who'd borne the brunt of the

Tiffany/Kiefer war. 'In terms of warm and friendly presentation, we are at rock bottom and starting to dig.'

'I appreciate your professional reputations are at stake,' Paul Dyer fired back, not amused. 'Whether we like it or not, we're still wiping the floor ratings-wise with virtually all the other shopping channels put together because of our mistakes.'

The latest embarrassment to the station had been a home steam-cleaning machine that had practically gobbled up a set of curtains during a demonstration. Due to contractual obligations the programme had to be repeated in all its awfulness several times a week. A witty mention in the *Daily Mail* Wicked Whispers column had ensured its place in television history. The Unofficial Getting It website had had a field day and there was almost a surge on the National Grid every time it was shown. Despite the steam cleaner being wildly over-enthusiastic, it had now completely sold out and the vendor was apparently thinking of demanding more awful repeats as soon as he could ship in more supplies.

Today, of course, belonged to Piers. This was his defining moment. With Kiefer presenting the show, Piers would be demonstrating just what he was made of – literally – in lycra. All those hours and hours spent in the gym and at the tattoo studio and piercing parlour were about to be enjoyed by the nation's shopaholics. He was being backed up by a chorus line of leggy models in thong leotards. The hour-long programme was to take the form of a mock work-out with music and exercises going on in the background while Kiefer talked about the range of machines demonstrated by Piers.

A wildly expensive 'personal trainer to the stars' had

been recruited to choreograph all the exercises, choose the music and rehearse the models.

'What could possibly go wrong?' Tim was asking himself as he paced up and down in anticipation. This was his biggest project to date.

'Stupid question,' replied the rest of the office in unison.

'Piers opening his mouth?' offered Stella, who was nursing a colossal hangover. She'd succumbed to a big sobbing session over her marriage the previous evening and had ended up drinking far too much brandy. It was all she could do to concentrate on not throwing up. She desperately wanted to support Tim but knew she wasn't going to be much use.

'He's been told to keep his comments minimal,' replied Tim. 'Arnie-style grunts are acceptable, discussions about Maastricht are not.'

'Then you're bombproof,' said Stella, wishing her stomach was too. 'Kiefer's a good-looking bloke, he's solo presenter on this so you've ruled out any sparring opportunities with Tiffany. Dear old Piers Tongue and his kit will appeal to our tackier audience and all the blokes will drool over the thong leotards in the background. So – something for all the family.'

Tim wasn't convinced but appreciated her encouragement. She kissed him lightly on the cheek and wished him luck with the programme as he made his way to the main studio.

Meanwhile, in the production office Fran too was nursing a hangover from hell, having joined Stella on the brandy. Steve was being particularly irritating. Today's sweater in canary yellow just wasn't doing it. Trinny and Susannah would have cut a very large swathe through his Billy No-Mates wardrobe.

'Steve,' Fran said, clutching her forehead. 'For goodness sake, give me a break, will you? I've got a blinding, self-induced hangover.'

Steve turned tail and disappeared out of the office. A couple of minutes later he reappeared with two mugs of coffee, both black.

'I thought you could use this,' he said, handing her a mug. Fran was totally taken aback. Steve NEVER made coffee. Or got anything right first time. Somehow it made him seem even more irritating, she thought to herself. A bit like finding out that Dracula was actually a registered blood donor.

She was just muttering her thanks when the opening music of the home fitness show boomed out of the monitors. Everyone cranked up the volume to show support for Tim by watching the show.

'Hi, my name's Kiefer Reeve and welcome to Getting It, TV's liveliest shopping channel. We hope you're not only Getting It, but getting fit too. Tums and bums going south? Are your thighs going east and west? Then this is the show for you. Getting It says Getting Fit – and you can trim away those unsightly bits of body fat in the privacy of your own home. This programme will show you how easy and how painless it can be to lose weight. And change your life.'

Thank goodness he's not on with Tiffany, thought Fran. They'd not waste a second in locking horns on this one. The scope for insult would have been infinite.

The models in the background were all busily working away on the rowing and ski-ing machines, the treadmill and weights. All smiling with perfectly capped teeth and trying to outdo each other just in case there was a casting agent watching . . .

Kiefer had now launched into a one-way conversation with Piers, carefully asking him closed questions that required only the answer 'yes' while Piers pumped away on one of the machines. It was deemed reasonably safe territory for Piers now that his tongue had just about recovered from yet another infection – this time from having the stud removed.

'So, Piers, you look pretty fit.'

'Yeth.'

'I expect it's taken many hours of working out to look this good.'

'Yeth, it—'

'And of course it's all thanks to this Abdo Fabbo stomach trimmer, isn't it, Piers!'

'Yeth, defin—'

'Would you recommend our viewers buying one?'

'Yeth, I think—'

'Absolutely.' Kiefer turned to another camera. 'Now,' he continued smoothly, 'Piers is going to demonstrate just how versatile this piece of kit is. Not only does it trim your stomach as we've seen – and very successfully too, Piers, if I may say so. You'd never mistake that six-pack for a Party Seven, would you?'

'Yeth. No.' Piers corrected himself hastily. He then grinned to the camera, showing off his new gold tooth amid groans from the office.

'But it also doubles up as a mini rowing machine. Watch Piers now convert the Abdo Fabbo trimmer in one deft movement. Blink and you'll miss it, it's honestly that easy.'

The camera zoomed in to capture the 'one deft movement'. There was a pause, followed by a strangled cry of pain. Piers, trying not to let on that he was in agony, had somehow twisted his back. Kiefer, being the hardened professional that he was, homed straight in on the models at the back of the set, abandoning Piers and virtually stepping over him. Ignoring the odd stifled cry from Piers as he was carried out of shot, Kiefer chatted away to the girls as though nothing had happened. Meanwhile, out in the scene dock, Piers was lying on the floor in the recovery position, screaming his head off while one of the studio hands dialled 999 for an ambulance.

The phones in the building were buzzing. On screen, Kiefer lingered with the girls in lycra, talking about fitness and the equipment they were using. Because they'd been hired as set dressing, it was an uphill treadmill struggle. None of them had a clue what the equipment they were using was for. The ability to talk as well as work out had escaped most of them.

Suddenly Kiefer walked back to the front of the set where miraculously there was another lycra-clad figure busily working out on the Abdo Fabbo trimmer vacated by Piers. The bleached blonde stack of curls looked strangely familiar.

'So Kelly-Marie, how is it for you?'

'It's faaaaaaabulous,' replied Kelly-Marie, her drawl exaggerated for the benefit of the viewers. The inevitable Wonderbra, today in red satin, was just beginning to creep into view over her purple cropped top as she moved up and down.

'Strewth, she must have sprinted in from reception, the crafty cow,' said Fran. 'She was wearing that kit this morning. I thought she'd come in fancy dress.'

In the production gallery, everyone was similarly transfixed. Tim had sat with his head in his hands in total despair and disbelief as Piers was carted off. As had the directors of the company supplying the machines. This was their first television venture – and it now looked as if it might be their last. To add a touch of irony, the siren from the ambulance coming to fetch Piers could just be heard faintly on set.

But suddenly the atmosphere was wall-to-wall smiles. It was all down – or rather up – to Kelly-Marie's ubiquitous Wonderbra, which was now making its presence felt in a big way.

'I love that Erin Brockovich look,' said the boss of the Abdo Fabbo. 'Shows she's a real woman. Shows you can work out AND have tits. That's exactly the right sort of message we want to put across. Better tits than that Gym Junkie guy.' He rubbed his hands with even greater glee when the warehouse reported sales of the Abdo Fabbo suddenly going through the roof.

When the programme finally came to an end, Tim felt he too had spent a solid hour on the treadmill. Spontaneous applause broke out in all the offices. Everyone seemed to have forgotten poor old Piers, now in agony at Hartford Hospital's casualty department with a suspected slipped disc. Meanwhile, a screaming match was now in full swing between the models who'd been upstaged not once but twice.

Fran went immediately to find Stella. She found her clutching a cappuccino in the canteen.

'Shame about poor Piers,' Fran said, sitting down opposite her. 'I wonder how he'll feel when he hears that Kelly-Marie took over so successfully.'

'I should imagine it'll put his nose – not to mention his back – out of joint,' she replied. 'Although he's rumoured to be very keen on her. This might change things.'

Chapter 20

A very tender Piers had now been discharged from hospital but was signed off work for at least three weeks with strict instructions to rest his back. No punishing sessions at the gym for a while so his much vaunted six-pack was going to need the plastic stringy bit to hold it all together. He'd literally had his fifteen minutes of fame, thanks to the Abdo Fabbo trimmer. But not one to miss an opportunity where the object of his desire was concerned, he'd sent Kelly-Marie a huge bunch of red roses to congratulate her on stepping in so successfully. Kelly-Marie's immediate response to her new-found fame, both on screen and in all the national newspapers thanks to the invited journalists, was to strut around Hartford during her lunch hour hoping to be recognised. Not difficult anyway, given Kelly-Marie's dress code.

Stella had other things on her mind, however. She was embroiled in what was turning into a very bitter divorce. She'd found going to a solicitor to discuss all the legalities quite a distressing ordeal. But on the plus side, she'd found a pretty little garden flat that she'd instantly fallen in love with. She now hoped Ray would be amenable to selling the house quickly so they could both move on. She hadn't seen or spoken to him since that fateful night. Everything was being handled through their respective solicitors, and although she went through highs and lows about the situation, she was already beginning to think that she was better off without him.

'And don't even start on the subject of fish in the sea and cod quotas,' she warned Fran as they strolled around the town during their lunch break. 'I don't like fish anyway. I wouldn't mind a pound for every time someone has trotted that one out. No, I don't want to meet anyone. The idea of going out on a date after all these years is far too scary. I like my life as it is, thank you very much. Talking of which, where's Tiff?'

Fran couldn't help but look shiftily at her boots. Stella was straight on the case, immediately asking questions.

'Oh all right then, strictest, strictest confidence, our Tiffany's being stalked. Paul Dyer told me.'

'Any idea who?'

'I suppose, in view of all the mischief-making in the *Echo*, there's a slight chance it might be Des,' said Fran.

'See! What did I tell you! I said he was the website nutter, didn't I?' Stella announced triumphantly.

'We might find out for sure soon. Paul was thinking of calling in the police.'

'Omigod, THAT serious.'

Back at the studio, Kelly-Marie, in very restrained tight maroon leather trousers, sheer black top with maroon satin Wonderbra, and just back from doing another recognition tour of the town, glanced up briefly from her copy of *Heat* magazine. From her body language, being back on reception clearly didn't suit any more.

'Oh, Fran,' she drawled, 'call for you from Shirley at the

Echo. She said you'd know the number.' She went straight back to her magazine.

'This smells of trouble,' Fran whispered to Stella as they walked down the corridor and then went their separate ways. Hating herself for feeling so full of foreboding, Fran picked up her phone and without giving herself a nano-second to chicken out dialled the *Echo*, her happy lunchtime mood instantly evaporated.

'Just thought I'd tip you off,' said Shirley in stage whisper. 'We're running some knocking story about your shopping channel tomorrow.'

'Thanks Shirley, you're a star,' Fran replied, wondering how Shirley always stayed so brilliantly ahead of the game. She should have been a journalist.

'Any idea who's the reporter?' she asked, trying to sound as though she didn't really care about the answer.

'Des,' came the prompt reply.

Fran replaced the receiver and immediately dialled Paul Dyer's number. She was summoned to his office.

'Come in, come in,' beckoned Paul, Doc Martens up on the desk as usual.

Fran went in and shut the door firmly behind her. 'Bad news,' she announced. 'I've just had a call from the *Echo* receptionist to say they're publishing some kind of knocking story on us tomorrow.'

'Hey, don't worry,' said Paul, instantly reassuring. 'We've been in the headlines all week one way or another.'

Fran managed a half laugh. 'But it's apparently Des who's writing the story,' she continued, 'so that can only mean one subject, can't it? The relationship between Kiefer and Tiffany. Also, where is Tiffany at the moment? People have started asking.'

'Off with stress from this stalker business,' Paul replied,

taking his feet off the desk. 'I've got the police on to it now and they're giving her some personal safety training as well. You know the sort of thing, going home by different routes, changing phone numbers, having two mobiles on different networks in case of emergency, and so on. She's now recording all her calls and the cops are also trawling through her phone records.'

'Any leads yet?'

'No, none, but I'm sure there soon will be. It'll be interesting to see what this Des character writes about tomorrow. If he writes about Tiffany and Kiefer loathing each other's guts, that's one thing. But if he writes about her being stalked, doesn't that probably rule him out as being the stalker?'

Fran thought for a second. 'Not necessarily,' she reasoned. 'I think he's devious and sick enough to write about himself. After all, if he *is* the stalker, he'd be the world's expert on the subject.'

Paul looked a bit perplexed. Fran continued: 'We had a typesetter years ago whose part-time hobby was stealing women's underwear off washing lines. The *Echo* ran a massive campaign for weeks hunting the "Hartford knicker-knocker" and of course what we didn't realise at the time was that he had been calmly setting the stories about the hunt for himself! So, believe me, it's possible.'

And I had to write stories entitled Who Is Madame Chita?, she thought to herself. It was definitely possible.

'Well, we've already lived through some tough times,' said Paul. 'I am not the least bit worried about what Des might or might not write. My only concern is the effect it might have on Tiffany. I know she's a pain in the arse but she's one of our stars. And, by the way, don't you start worrying as well.'

'OK,' Fran breathed a sigh of relief. 'Thanks, Paul. That's good to hear.'

'Now remember, whatever Des or anyone prints, I know it hasn't come from you.'

Fran nodded as she left the office. But she didn't sleep a wink that night.

Chapter 21

Just as the rumour machine was moving into the realms of Interpol, Tiffany turned up for work the next day looking as gorgeous as ever. With her choppy cut blonde hair and dressed in a pale pink trouser suit, she bore no resemblance to the victim of a maniac.

She swept into the studio and presented two hours of what everyone referred to as 'stuff you never knew you needed' – a nose-hair trimmer in the shape of Pinocchio, a My Little Pony sonic tooth flosser, his and hers yoga mats and a guaranteed no-mess paint roller. Everyone held their breath as Tiffany demonstrated the paint roller loaded with dayglo orange paint. Some of the production gallery staff actually got down on their knees to offer prayers that it wouldn't spill all over the obviously expensive pink suit. Their prayers were answered.

Fran was watching on screen in her office. Tiffany had certainly been impressive and did not look as if she were under any kind of stress. It had probably helped that she was presenting on her own, Fran guessed. Teamed up with Kiefer, there would undoubtedly have been the usual fireworks.

Fran checked her watch for the umpteenth time.

Coming up to midday. Any minute now the *Hartford Echo* would be hitting the streets. She just hoped that somehow Shirley had got it wrong. That Des had been making empty threats. That it was all just a hideous nightmare. Like being given the Pinocchio nose-hair trimmer for Christmas by the man of your dreams.

She glanced up at the screen again. A couple of Getting It's presenters were struggling to fill. They'd been ad-libbing about a pot of face cream for the past five minutes and were beginning to run out of steam. Clearly the cream was selling its face off and they were being instructed via their ear pieces to carry on talking.

Fran tried to distract herself by thinking about the kitchen cupboards going up this weekend. It was a dream come true and she knew she should be really excited about it. But all she could think about was Des's loathsome breath and the awful stigma of being associated with the *Echo*. She decided to take an early lunch and pick up a paper in town.

Outside the studio, the air was deliciously fresh from a recent shower. The pavements were still glistening and covered with millions of pink petals from the late spring blossoms. Fran walked slowly over to her car, taking deep measured breaths to try to keep calm. She was still angry with herself about this whole Des thing. She no longer worked at the paper. Paul had assured her he believed she had no involvement in the story. And anyway, what WAS the story? She didn't have a clue. Why do women always feel guilty, even when it's not their fault? she asked herself repeatedly.

As she drove into the centre of town, she dreaded seeing the billboards with headlines such as 'Mole at TV Station' or 'My Stalker Nightmare'. She finally found a parking space, headed for the nearest WHSmith, bought a copy of the *Echo* and steeled herself not to look at it until she was back in the safety of her car.

Relief swept over her in waves. 'Top TV Girl Off With Stress' was the headline. It went on to detail Tiffany being overworked and under pressure at a 'shopping channel in crisis'. The main source appeared to be Tiffany's agent, who had seized the moment to remind the world of her client's 'illustrious film and television career to date'. But there was no mention of a stalker. Des had then cribbed some of the city analysts' comments to paint a gloomy picture of a TV station facing eventual falling ratings and a slump in sales. He then gleefully went through a selection of viewers' favourite cock-ups and gave the unofficial Getting It website a hefty plug. The nearest he got to anything controversial was mentioning the 'friendly rivalry between top presenters Kiefer Reeve and Tiffany Shire'.

Fran heaved a sigh of relief. Tame stuff and now totally discredited because, as the papers were literally being printed, Tiffany had, of course, made her comeback on screen this morning. Probably deliberate after Des's call to her agent. So Des hadn't exactly covered himself in glory.

She took a grateful puff of her cigarette and began idly flipping through the rest of the paper, reminiscing. It now seemed so predictable. Photographs of men dressed up as babies on charity fun runs, thief sought for missing lawnmowers, Hartford Players doing yet another Alan Ayckbourn ... when suddenly it caught her eye. She could feel her throat go dry and the colour drain from her face.

Centre page spread, big bold headline: Who Is Madame Chita? The article chronicled the *Echo*'s secret clairvoyant's career. How her 'horoscopes with attitude' had so often captured *Echo* headlines, plus a selection of letters from readers for whom her outrageous predictions had come true, and others heavily criticising her after they'd followed her advice and it had all come to nought.

Then came the worst bit. Staff at the *Echo*, the article claimed, had no idea of her identity. It was apparently the management's most closely guarded secret, right up there with the size of their pay packets. But, proclaimed the article, the *Echo*'s chief crime reporter, Des Ryder, was on to the case. 'In what could be his most far-reaching investigation to date, he's pledged to find out just who is the elusive Madame Chita.'

Fran reached for her mobile and dialled with shaking hand. Shirley answered on the second ring.

'Seen the piece?'

'Oh yes,' said Fran, panicking for a second over which piece she was referring to. 'Not too bad, actually, but thanks for tipping me off, Shirley.'

'Pleasure, dear.'

'Is Guy there, by any chance?'

'Sorry, sweetie, he's on leave for a couple of weeks. Rhodes, I believe. Villa just outside Lindos with old friends from his Portsmouth schooldays. Only three hundred quid a week so I'm thinking of booking it myself for later in the year.'

'Shirley, you should have been a reporter,' Fran half grinned as she ended the call. That would explain it. If Guy had been around this week he'd never have commissioned that story. This was Des going for a bit of glory, plus getting back at her over the court case yet again.

She then allowed herself a brief horror that Des actually

knew her identity, or that someone in accounts had put two and two together and decided that the monthly cheque Fran now received for her Madame Chita column was not just a retainer for story tips as she and Guy had agreed.

She drove back to work as the heavens opened once more, downloading more pink and white cherry blossom in its wake. Going back into the studio, she bumped straight into Paul Dyer.

'We're off the hook, I think,' he said quietly to her with a half-smile.

'Yes, thank goodness,' she replied. You might be, she thought, but Madame Chita's nightmare is only just beginning. As she got back to her office, her phone was ringing. She grabbed it with one hand as she struggled out of her raincoat with the other.

Des's voice smirked down the phone. 'See my piece?' he demanded.

Which one? she thought desperately. 'Yes,' she replied, trying to keep her voice firm. 'But unfortunately it's been a bit overtaken by events.'

'What?' he snapped.

'Well, clearly you didn't realise that Tiffany presented two hours of live telly this morning. She looked in pretty good shape to me. Ciao.'

She put the phone down and took a deep breath. She could hardly go out for a fag break as she'd only just come in. But right now she felt like whipping through a pack of Des's Capstan Full Strength in one go. Oh, and a large gin and tonic.

Clearly Des, fully reinstated as the *Echo*'s chief crime reporter, was also back to his old habits. Fran knew full well he wouldn't have watched the programme this morning – as soon as the front page deadline had been reached he'd have been straight to the pub. Besides, the only television was in Guy's bollocking room and Des had seen quite enough of that recently. At least she hadn't given him the chance to quiz her about Madame Chita. But he'd be back, of that she had no doubt.

The weekend passed in a wave of mixed emotions. Exhaustion from the events of the week, stress about what would appear in the *Echo*, shock about the Madame Chita investigation and exhilaration about the kitchen cupboards. Bob had been a real star. He'd let the carpenter get on with installing the cupboards and just helped where he could. It was a novelty for him to see a job actually completed. Witnessing Fran's complete ecstasy at a finished kitchen made him appreciate the frustration she'd suffered over the years. He now vowed to crack on with the door handle project with renewed vigour.

Stella, meanwhile, had completed on her garden flat. In between oohing and aahing as the kitchen took shape, she and Fran ferried car loads of Stella's vast collection of clothes over to her new place. Her relief at finally having a home of her own was right off the Richter scale, together with the knowledge that Ray didn't know she'd even bought a flat, let alone the address. Ray had been very bolshy, considering the circumstances in which the marriage had so abruptly ended. Letters had been flying back and forth between their solicitors without much progress, apart from rocketing legal bills. At one point, Stella had thought she'd have a fight on her hands about everything down to the ashtrays. They'd finally lapsed into an uneasy truce through their solicitors. Ray had reluctantly agreed to allow Stella to return to the house to collect the rest of her personal things. But this was only after Stella had announced formally through her solicitor that he could 'stuff the furniture'. Her only demand was that he wouldn't be there. She was anxious to move on as fast as possible – she'd even taken out a bridging loan to speed up the purchase of the flat.

Five car trips later, Fran and Stella flopped down on the springless sofas in Fran's sitting room and opened a bottle of champagne to celebrate.

'You're getting to be a habit with me,' sang Stella as she popped the cork and poured them each a glass.

'Well, at least champagne doesn't involve spending five hours trying to find a corkscrew,' said Fran, raising her glass.

'Not any more,' Stella replied. 'By tonight, your corkscrew will have its own drawer. And not a bottomless one. That's not a prediction, Madame Chita, that's a fact.'

Fran bounced back to work on Monday. She was still so excited at having a kitchen at last that she'd almost had withdrawal symptoms at leaving it behind. She'd even managed to cook the very first roast they'd ever had in the house, now that she had an oven. Admittedly Fran, Stella and Bob had all crammed around the plastic picnic table to eat it as a new pine table and four chairs, heavily discounted by a visiting rep, weren't being delivered until next week.

Her happy mood continued when she opened her pay packet and saw that the rise Paul Dyer had promised had in fact materialised. And not only that, it was heaps better than she'd been expecting. She'd celebrate with a new outfit. Since she'd been on Getting It's lower salary she'd not even ventured through the doors of her favourite shops just in case she was tempted. Perhaps this signalled the Return to the Forbidden Planet?

Or maybe, now that there were improvements going on at home, she could persuade Bob not to shore up the dangling electrics himself and get a qualified electrician in to do the job. Then she could get a plasterer to fix the bathroom, followed by a tiler; a power shower would be nice . . . oh, the list was endless.

The studio was just gearing up for the first live broadcast of the day. Amid the sound checks and camera line-ups, all eyes were on Tiffany and Kiefer, co-presenting for the first time in days. The programme was selling a range of quite upmarket (by Getting It standards) beach and cruise wear, all to be modelled on a low and heavily inspected catwalk. The director decided to place Tiffany and Kiefer on either side of the catwalk in an attempt to cut down the mutual aggravation factor. Tiffany would reel off the prices and details while Kiefer would give comments from a male perspective.

Stella, who'd been the chief buyer on this show, knew all too well that the set up gave the pair plenty of scope for sarcasm or arguments. Everyone was crossing their fingers that somehow Tiffany and Kiefer would get through the programme without being nasty to each other.

'Five . . . four . . . three . . . cue Tiffany.'

'Hi there. My name's Tiffany Shire and welcome to Getting It, the shopping channel that really does change your life.'

'And I'm Kiefer Reeve and we're here to bring you the latest, the best and the most glamorous beach and cruise wear you'll ever find. In fact, Tiffany, I think you'd look great in some of the fashions we're going to show in a minute.'

'How very sweet of you, Kiefer,' she gushed. 'But I'm not taking my clothes off today.' Kiefer did quite a good impression of feigning disappointment.

She continued: 'We have a team of models backstage who are going to bring you the best beach wardrobe money can buy. Forget the high street. Get it at Getting It.'

They both fixed cheesy smiles to camera two. Everyone in the gallery breathed a sigh of relief. They appeared to have declared some kind of truce.

Stella sat at the back of the gallery thanking her lucky stars. The companies supplying the clothing were top notch and they'd insisted on Tiffany and Kiefer as the presenters because they looked so impossibly beautiful. The fact that they were impossibly loathing of each other didn't come into it. The first hour was simply whizzing by and so far things were going well. The range of bikinis, swimsuits, matching sarongs, flip-flops, beach bags and hats were doing a roaring trade. Even the company reps were sitting there in disbelief as sales figures started coming through. As some of the sizes completely sold out, their grins got wider and wider.

They were just coming up to the one-hour mark and everyone in the gallery was congratulating themselves on a fantastic presentation. Stella was allowing herself a brief reverie about becoming a stylist for a glossy magazine and wafting around the world's hotspots in search of perfect locations. It could all be within her grasp. Tiffany was introducing a new section of the programme – a very expensive beach bag that contained a whole collection of equally expensive goodies.

'Now this is just what I'd go for, being a lazy shopper,' she crooned. 'In this totally gorgeous bag, look what you get. Beautiful bikini, matching pareo and sandals.'

The camera zoomed in for a close-up. 'On top of that you get a handy pack of sun protection creams, this fabulous pair of sunglasses, this beautiful beach towel, a co-ordinating pillow and, look, they've even thought of a magazine to help you while away the – aaarrrrrgggghhhh.'

Tiffany dropped the magazine hastily and burst into tears. But there was no mistaking what it was – everyone had seen it on camera.

'Cut to a promotion,' yelled the director. As a pre-recorded run of the day's schedule was broadcast, pandemonium broke out in the gallery and on the studio floor. Tiffany was out of the studio as fast as her Gina heels would let her.

'Who the hell knows the products?' shouted the director, purple-faced with rage. Suddenly all the technicians who'd been facing the bank of screens turned around to look at Stella, who was perched on a stool behind them.

'Get down on that studio floor,' he commanded an open-mouthed Stella. 'You're the only one who knows this stuff.'

'Two minutes to the end of this item,' announced the production assistant, glancing up from her stopwatches.

'Move it,' shouted the director.

Stella never remembered the short walk down the corridor to the studio floor. She never recalled a make-up girl appearing with brushes to make something of her face, nor the floor manager rigging her up with an earpiece and microphone. Nor someone handing her Tiffany's clipboard with the running order of all the items that Stella herself had prepared.

Kiefer smiled at her in a tense fashion. She could see

the fear in his eyes. Heaven knows what hers said. 'You stick with the fashion crap and I'll do the prices, codes and all that stuff. OK?' he announced imperiously. She nodded, unable to speak. The studio began to sway.

'Coming to you in fifteen seconds,' she suddenly heard in her ear. The countdown competed with the pounding of her heart like some kind of drumming competition. She felt sick. Her lips suddenly froze as though she'd forgotten how to talk. How on earth was she going to get through this?

And then a miracle happened. It was as if she'd travelled through a time warp. Forty-five minutes of live television whizzed by as if on fast-forward. Suddenly Kiefer was winding up and they were both saying goodbye. She almost panicked that it was all over so soon. Gone, disappeared into the ether.

Everything went quiet for a few seconds, then twenty people stormed through the studio door, shouting, screaming and cheering.

'Brilliant Stell!'

'You were fantastic!'

'Amazing!'

Stella, on the other hand, stood completely stunned, unable to move. She felt she'd run a marathon and was too tired to acknowledge the cheers from the stadium. Now it was all over, she started to shake.

Sales of the range had gone through the roof, despite the quick change of presenter. And Stella, of course, had saved the day. Kiefer couldn't resist being magnanimous in his praise, grabbing the opportunity to have a swipe at Tiffany.

'Thank God you knew all the clothes,' he said. 'The only thing I know about sarongs is that David Beckham sometimes wears them. And as for sandals, all I know is that my sister had a honeymoon there.'

Everyone started muttering about going out for drinks and an impromptu Chinese to celebrate Stella's feat, but all she wanted to do was crawl home.

In the end she relented, and next thing she knew about twenty people including Fran were all sat at two huge tables in the Hartford Jade Garden discussing the events of the afternoon. After glasses had been raised to Stella, there were cries of, 'Speech, speech.'

Stella rose wearily to her feet. It was the first time she'd really been able to get her mind around the whole experience.

'Listen, thanks to all of you. I can't really say much as I feel absolutely zonked after all that. Thank you for just getting me through it. I'm not sure I actually want to see it played back though.'

Everyone roared with laughter. 'You'll have to,' said one of the cameramen. 'It's being repeated at least four times this week alone.'

'But they'll have to cut out THAT bit though,' another chipped in.

'Sorry to be a bit thick on this one,' said Stella, 'but I wasn't actually looking at the screen when Tiffany broke down. What was it that upset her?'

There was an amused silence. Fran finally broke it and supplied the answer.

'Probably just as well you didn't know. It was the most hideous porn magazine. The works, you know, horses, sheep, blow jobs, the lot. Someone must have planted it.'

Chapter 22

Stella insisted she was going home to her new flat. She just wanted to sleep and sleep and then wake up the next morning to see if she'd dreamed it all. Was this the start of some new and high-profile career or just a figment of her imagination? Sleep the dream, she decided.

Fran, meanwhile, drove home wide awake with a mixture of emotions. She was delighted for her friend, it had been an incredibly brave performance. After all the previous catastrophes on the channel, she doubted viewers would more than blink a couple of times at the sudden change in presenter. But she had to own up to a small twinge of jealousy at Stella's stint in front of the cameras, as well as concern as to who had planted the magazine. Was it the work of the stalker, and if so, how on earth had he got that kind of access? She could well understand Tiffany's reaction, given the recent history.

She sat down at the picnic table for probably the last time (the new pine table was arriving tomorrow) and admired her new kitchen. She made herself a cup of tea, lit a cigarette and pondered some more. Bob was still in the shed, cracking on with the door handles and uttering hitherto unmentioned words like 'urgent'. She'd take him out a cup of tea.

Just as she reached for the teapot, the phone rang. Bit late for a call, she thought, looking at the clock. Probably Stella with some final thoughts on the day.

'Hi sweetie,' drawled Des's voice. 'So what's occurring?'

'What do you mean?' asked Fran, realising instantly this was the most naive remark she could have made in the circumstances.

'Come on, sweetie, we're all on to it. That magazine. Who planted it and who's got it in for the lovely Tiffany?'

Fran decided to take the short cut. 'Sod off, Des. It's nearly eleven o'clock and I've had a busy day.'

'Who's trying to upset her? Is it that smarmy co-star of hers, Kiefer?'

'Why don't you just shut up? And why are you so fascinated by her anyway?' Fran couldn't resist.

'Good story, darlin'. You ought to know me well enough by now.'

Fran certainly did. The horrible greasy hair, stinking breath and shirts that went on all week. How could she forget?

'I've heard she's being stalked,' he continued, 'from a very, very good source.' Fran caught her breath at this revelation.

'Oh really?' she tried to reply calmly. 'How did you know that?'

'Contacts, sweetie. And judging by that magazine, it sounds like an inside job. What's the security like in your place?'

Fran tried not to laugh, thinking of Kelly-Marie in her disco outfits fending off terrorists in reception.

'Come on, Des, even if I knew you're just about the last

person on the planet I'd be telling. Anyway, it's late, I'm tired, I've had a long day and I'm just summoning up my last bit of energy – to put this phone down.'

She banged down the receiver, took a sip of tea and shivered. At least he hadn't asked her about Madame Chita.

The next day, the story about the porn mag made all the nationals. How much more controversy? asked one prominent columnist. Are they doing it on purpose? asked another. How much longer will the viewers find it entertaining?

How long indeed? thought Fran as she scanned the morning papers. Some had carried a quick mention of Stella stepping into the breach, but because there was no publicity shot available of Stella their interest had been minor.

Meanwhile Stella had been hauled in for a chat by Paul Dyer. He felt she had potential as a presenter, but she'd taken a deep breath and refused. Over a coffee in the canteen she discussed it with Fran.

'I almost can't believe I turned it down,' said Stella, 'but the trouble is that I'm still in shock from yesterday. When you think how we joined this station hoping we might make a fleeting appearance in the background, now I've been offered this opportunity and what have I done? I've turned my back on it. Am I mad? Do you think I did the right thing?'

Fran paused for a second. 'No, frankly,' she said firmly. 'You're nuts not to give it a go. Most people would donate interesting bits of their bodies to get that opportunity. And let's face it, Stell, you're the wrong side of forty. You're going through a miserable divorce. This is a chance of a lifetime and you've already had quite a chunk of lifetime. So think about it. I'd take it like a shot if it were offered to me.'

'Yeah, but you don't know just how scary it was. How people do that every day I don't know.' Stella hung her head, exhausted and confused by events of the past twenty-four hours.

'By the way,' Fran changed the subject. 'I had a late-night call from Des last night.'

'Omigod,' said Stella, perking up. 'What was he after this time?'

'Oh, Tiffany again. He seems to know about her stalker. He was asking what I knew. Said it was an inside job because of the magazine.'

'It HAS to be Kiefer then, doesn't it?' Stella said, secretly grateful to be off the subject of her new career direction. 'Perhaps he's just jealous. She does get an awful lot of attention, especially on that stupid website.'

'Maybe, although I can't see his motive for sabotaging a programme that he's appearing in,' Fran replied. 'I'm just relieved that Dirty Des didn't start asking questions about a certain clairvoyant.'

'Sounds like it's only a question of time though. Be careful, Fran. He sounds dangerous.'

The unofficial Getting It website trumpeted a new campaign that day – Bring Back Tiffany. Whoever was responsible for the website was convinced that Tiffany had been set up and that Stella had somehow ousted her. Visitors to the site were invited to vote online and also to write letters of support to the station. It blithely gave out Paul Dyer's name and the full address of the station.

And, of course, the moment when Tiffany made her

fateful discovery had already been cheekily uploaded and was available at the click of a button. You could even zoom in on a still of the porn mag.

It was the only topic of conversation all morning in the buying department. And it continued in the local pub over sandwiches and pints.

'Stand by for a postal invasion,' said Tim. 'Let's just hope Piers's back gets better so he can lug that enormous postbag up to Paul's office.'

'I quite miss Piers,' said Stella wistfully. 'I mean, I don't miss the sweaty singlets, the muscles on permanent parade and that constant whiff of coconut oil. But he's a nice chap, very willing. His heart's in the right place.'

'Yeah, hidden somewhere behind those pierced nipples.'

Stella screwed up her face in disgust. 'Bleugh, just the thought of them makes me feel squiffy.'

Tim looked at her and laughed. 'Hang on, I've got to make a phone call. Must cancel my appointment.'

'What's that for?' asked Stella.

'I'm booked into the Hole In One to have my nipples done. Thought you'd find me more attractive.'

The Hole In One was Hartford's new trendy body-piercing shop. Jokes were always flying that Piers visited so often he must have a reward card. And that points meant piercings.

'Oh puhleeze,' said Stella in mock disgust. 'You cannot be serious.'

'Well, I'm not John McEnroe but how about having dinner with me instead?'

Stella was completely taken aback. She hadn't seen that one coming at all. She was suddenly aware that she'd gone red in the face. She glanced around to see if the rest of the gang were listening. They all seemed intent on laughing and slurping beer down their throats.

She took a desperate sip of her mineral water as her brain whizzed. She'd been so caught up in the discovery of Ray and the redhead, the photographs, getting divorced and buying her flat that she hadn't given a thought to going out on a date. It seemed incredibly scary.

Tim immediately saw the fear in her eyes.

'Hey, it's only a meal, nothing more,' he said gently. 'Also, now that you're a big star I want to be seen out with someone famous.'

'I think not,' Stella laughed, relaxing a little. 'You won't be seeing me on the box again. This morning Paul Dyer offered to train me up as a presenter but I found the whole experience a hazy nightmare. To do that every day for a living is not for me. I'd spend so long in a trauma ward I'd practically be paying council tax on it. So I've turned him down.'

'You're a mug,' Tim remarked immediately.

'That's what Fran said. Are you two in cahoots or something?'

'Well, don't make it a double and turn ME down too,' Tim pleaded.

Stella paused, lit a cigarette and looked at his craggy features. She was suddenly overwhelmed by the most ridiculous pang of guilt. It was just too soon after Ray. She prayed that she'd misheard him, but he repeated his offer of dinner.

'I . . . I . . . look . . . I'm not divorced yet,' she stumbled, 'and—'

'—it's too soon,' Tim finished for her. 'Look, Stell, I think you're terrific. And not just because of yesterday. OK, one day I'll ask you again. Meantime, I hope we're still friends.'

She nodded silently, running her fingers nervously through her hair, too confused to say any more. They all trooped back to work.

Going into the buyers' office, Stella noticed a large white envelope sitting on her desk. The contents made her heart skip a beat and her hands started to shake.

'Eugh,' she gasped in a tone so distressed that everyone else in the buyers' office turned around to look as she dropped the note and the envelope.

Everyone rushed over to see what was wrong. Stella burst into tears as the note was retrieved. They all gasped in horror as they read: 'Tiffany's the star. You're scum. Get off the screen, you ugly cow.'

Tim immediately put his arm around her and commanded someone to ring Paul Dyer. Five minutes later, she was sitting ashen-faced with Fran in Paul's office.

Paul was very calming and told her not to worry. He outlined in detail the account of Tiffany's stalker. Stella already knew most of it from Fran but she managed to feign ignorance. Paul suspected that the author of Stella's little bombshell was the same person. It was a similar style – newspaper headline cut-outs, hand-delivered in a white envelope.

'It's some fanatic who thinks Tiffany is some kind of screen goddess and that anyone who might get in her way must be frightened off,' he said. 'Tiffany's had some personal safety training and I'm going to get some organised for you, Stella. In the meantime, don't go home alone tonight.'

'At least I made the right decision about the presenting bit,' Stella stammered.

'On the contrary,' said Paul. 'I've had another look at your tape. You're going to have to re-think that. But perhaps not today.'

Stella had turned white again. Fran leaped to the rescue.

'Stella won't mind me saying this, Paul, because I think it's relevant. She's going through a terrible divorce at the moment. Just not a good time for her, especially with all this.'

Paul leaned forward on his desk, the picture of concern. 'Sorry to hear that Stella, I'd never have guessed. Shows just what a trooper you are. But please think about it some more. I can't remember ever having to beg someone to try a bit of presenting. They're normally queued down the corridor and around the street.'

'Come and stay with me again,' Fran offered immediately. They left Paul's office with his assurances still ringing in their ears. By the time they left the studio that evening, a big burly security guard was sitting at Kelly-Marie's reception desk, ready to escort Stella to her car.

'Didn't believe I'd be back here so soon,' Stella managed to smile as they sat down at Fran's new pine table, cups of strong coffee between them. 'Oo-er, this is posh,' she continued, trying to cheer up. 'We'll get you into *House Beautiful* yet, Fran.'

The kitchen did look terrific. But it had the adverse effect of making the rest of the house look completely absurd. Even Bob was now muttering about getting an electrician and a plasterer in.

'Stay as long as you like,' offered Fran, who'd really missed Stella since she'd moved into her flat.

'Thanks, hon,' Stella replied. 'Oh, by the way, I had another shock today.'

Fran looked mystified. Stella explained about Tim asking her out to dinner.

Fran's face immediately broke into a smile. 'Fantastic. That's lovely. He's such a nice guy.'

'Sorry to disappoint yet again, but I said no. Just felt far too frightened and guilty,' Stella confessed. 'I know it's stupid but I ask you, middle-aged woman going out on her first date in nearly twenty years? I should be at evening classes making baskets, or doing jam and Jerusalem at the WI. And if he knew my real age he'd probably not have asked me anyway. So I've saved myself heaps of embarrassment. Anyway, what do people talk about on dates these days?'

'Don't ask me. I've been married for two decades. I guess you could pretend it's another ordinary everyday work-type chat.'

'Yeah, ordinary like my forty-five minutes of fame, stalkers, hate mail, newspaper headlines and personal safety training.' At least Stella was beginning to see the funny side.

'I just think you're saying "no" to too many things right now,' said Fran firmly.

'That's what Tim said.'

Tiffany's stalker was the front page headline on the next day's *Hartford Echo*. Des was clearly warming to his theme. The level of accuracy in the report, Fran decided, indicated that Des had somehow got himself a mole. Staff were 'huddling in frightened groups', all presenters were receiving 'top-level security training' and, possibly with a bit of Des's legendary top-spin, 'the building was being swept for bugs and phones were being tapped.' Everyone at Getting It had to admit it made quite a gripping read.

Inside the paper was another speculative piece about the Mystery of Madame Chita, Fran noted with a heavy heart. It featured several interviews with longstanding members of staff, all claiming they had no idea of her identity – and probably cared even less. The investigation revealed that the horoscopes arrived in a plain white envelope once a week, posted locally. The 'Letters to the Editor' page was devoted to the same subject, with one or two deranged claims that readers had seen Madame Chita in their dreams, on the check-out in Safeway, or that she was actually a man, possibly a vicar trying to drum up trade for his Sunday services.

Fran couldn't help but smile at some of the speculation. She nipped out at lunchtime, armed with her mobile, to phone the *Echo*, hoping Guy would be back from his Greek holidays.

'Guy? Thank God. It's Fran. Can we meet tonight? No need to ask why.' They arranged to meet after work in a quiet pub.

'I'm going to resign,' Fran said immediately, before she'd even taken a sip of her glass of rioja. Guy paled, even under his newly acquired suntan.

'Hang on a minute, Fran,' he urged, realising he had a fight on his hands. 'I'm sorry the story came out while I was on holiday, but it did. So neither of us can turn back the clock.'

'Yeah, but I can still pack it in.' Fran was very firm.

Guy offered Fran a cigarette and then lit them both. Through the smoke, he continued: 'Look, love. We've ridden out this storm before. Remember a few years ago when the *Echo* went big on Madame Chita's identity? No one rumbled you then. Why should they do so now?'

'Because that was then and this is now,' said Fran. 'Things are different, technology has advanced beyond our wildest dreams. I bet the paper on which I typed this week's Madame Chita column is off for DNA testing even as we speak. I could be just hours away from infamy.'

'"Infamy, infamy, they've all got it in for me",' said Guy in his best Kenneth Williams voice. 'Sorry, love, couldn't resist. Look, bottom line is this – the Madame Chita story is selling its socks off. We've put on twenty thousand copies since we started running the Mystery of Madame Chita. It's business.'

'Don't you think the public will be furious when they discover that she's exactly what her name suggests? A cheater?'

'Don't be ridiculous. If Des hasn't fathomed that one, why should any of our readers? Don't forget, everyone has a right to be stupid. And that includes Des.'

Fran took another puff, sipped her wine and thought for a few seconds.

'But surely the circulation's only gone up because of all the Tiffany stalker stuff,' pleaded Fran. 'You know, TV drama on your doorstep.'

'Sorry, Fran, but our postbag alone suggests that you have one helluva following. Clearly you're the talk of the twitching net curtain set around here. You bring a little excitement into the hum-drum lives of Hartford wives.'

'Oh, spare me the responsibility,' Fran replied. 'I'm sure someone else could write the column. It's not that difficult.'

Guy looked at her pleadingly. 'God, you women are all the same. Never rate yourselves. I'm sorry, Fran, but you bring a bit of magic to that column. You're outrageous, tongue in cheek, witty, sarcastic. People like that. Madame Chita's column sets the *Echo* apart from all others.' He sipped his pint and went in for the kill.

'No one will guess it's you. Look at you, blonde hair,

sassy suit, killer heels. You're hardly flogging heather wearing a gypsy skirt and hooped earrings. And another factor,' he dropped his voice to a half-whisper, 'is that we've kept this arrangement completely secret for years. If I commission another person to write the column, will he or she have the same sense of secrecy? I'm not sure I'd want to take the risk.'

Fran gazed into the bottom of her wine glass, straining to read the beer mat through the red dregs. Giving up the column would wipe out her recent pay rise. There'd be no Return to the Forbidden Planet after all.

'Besides,' Guy continued, 'the whole town is now searching for Madame Chita. If I started trying to block the stories I'd have Des on my back asking pertinent questions. Fingers would point. At me.'

Fran nodded in reluctant acceptance. She had to agree that the campaign was not only clever but it was also making money. And even Des was clawing his way back into favour.

'Tell you what,' said Guy kindly. 'Live with this for another couple of months and then we'll review the situation. Meanwhile, let's have the real lowdown on your friend Tiffany. Is there anyone she's pissed off?'

Fran pretended to take a swipe at him. 'Guy, don't YOU start. You're getting as bad as Des.'

'Long way to go,' Guy grinned back, gathering up their glasses to buy another round. 'It would take me years to build up that level of hair grease.'

Chapter 23

A week in politics is a long time, but an uneventful week at Getting It seemed like a lifetime. There hadn't been any horrendous on- or off-screen arguments, all the products had actually worked, no one had ended up in hospital and there hadn't been a glimpse of a porn mag nor a single headline from Des. The only ripple came from a couple of newspaper columnists who ventured to suggest that Getting It was 'the station that was finally Getting It right'. Even office gossip and speculation about Tiffany's stalker had gone off the boil.

Producers and buyers were getting together for their weekly catch-up. There was some cheeky speculation that a lack of drama might prove demotivating for the staff, now used to a daily diet of crisis.

'Hope us Getting It right doesn't make the viewing figures drop off,' said Stella, putting down the *Daily Mirror* and taking a sip from a mug of coffee. 'Mind you,' she continued, 'how could anyone resist these?'

She held up a set of dumb-bells disguised as fake designer vanity cases.

'Look,' she announced, 'all your favourite designers, Louis Vuitton, Burberry, Versace. Fashion and fitness all in the bag. You look as though you're carting all your stuff around in a designer bag when actually you're working out and getting rid of your taxi arms.'

'Taxi arms?' asked Tim. 'What the hell are they?'

Stella smiled nervously. She was hoping Tim wouldn't bring up the subject of dinner again. 'It's that mid-life moment when you hail a taxi and you notice for the first time that the top of your arm wobbles.'

'Yeah, right,' said Tim, instantly sceptical.

'Or there's the down-market version.'

'What's that?' Tim was now very suspicious.

Stella was beginning to enjoy this. 'They're also known as bingo wings!'

'God, you women are so cruel about each other,' he said as he exploded into laughter. 'But YOU don't have bingo wings.'

'Don't you believe it. This sweater hides a multitude of sins,' she announced, regretting the way the conversation was going. She quickly changed the subject. 'Anyway, Steve's back this morning.'

Several of the team broke into the theme from *Thunderbirds* because he reminded them of Brains on account of the glasses. Steve had been on leave for a week, which had prompted renewed discussion about what would make him tick. Apart from a timebomb, the general feeling was nothing.

'He's just the sort of bloke we'll read about in years to come when he's outed as a Russian agent,' said Irene, busily setting up a revolutionary new juicer she was going to demonstrate at the meeting. 'He could be a closet astronaut for all we know.' Everyone nodded in agreement and then looked horribly embarrassed. Steve was standing at the door.

Fran hoped he hadn't overheard that last bit. It was rather cruel. She noticed he was sporting quite a tan yet he hadn't said he was going anywhere hot or exotic. The Indiana Jones brown leather hat was having another outing. It just didn't quite go with the Tesco carrier bag containing his lunch.

'Hi, er, everyone,' he said nervously. 'M . . . m . . . miss me?'

'Yeah, but my aim's getting better,' replied one of the buyers. Everyone started to laugh. It took Steve a couple of seconds longer to get the joke which prompted a second roll of laughter.

After the meeting, everyone went back to their normal tasks. While waiting to be put through on a call, Fran idly clicked on to the unofficial Getting It website. To her horror, the Bring Back Tiffany campaign had been updated. She prayed Stella wasn't reading the bit about 'the middle-aged frump' who had stepped in after Tiffany had found the fateful magazine.

'She's after your job, Tiffany,' warned the website. 'Watch that beautiful back of yours. We don't want some old bag appearing on screen, we want Tiffany.' There followed page after page of testimonials as to how brilliant, how beautiful, how amazingly intelligent Tiffany was. As if she was Pamela Anderson crossed with Carol Vorderman, with a bit of Mother Teresa and Princess Diana thrown in.

Fran was suddenly aware of Steve hovering to speak to her. It was one of his more annoying habits. Rather than speak or wave, he'd stand there pathetically for ages, waiting for her to glance his way. She felt a mixture of irritation and pity for him, and put the phone down.

'So where did you go on holiday?' she asked politely. 'Anywhere special?'

'N . . . n . . . no, not really.'

'Well, you must have,' Fran persisted. 'You've got quite a tan there.'

Steve blushed furiously through the tan. He was saved from further questioning by his mobile phone ringing its 007 theme. Too inept to disguise the nature of the call, Steve was clearly having a bit of a problem with a credit card company. Then Fran noticed the nut brown colour ended in an abrupt streak by his left ear. Clearly a triumph of St Tropez – but only in a bottle. Fran reflected on the irony that whenever Piers slapped on fake tan it was just accepted as part of his body-conscious image, streaks and all. But on Steve it was just incredibly naff and a bit sad.

Steve regained some of his composure when he realised Fran was listening. 'Look, I'm a very busy man. I'll have to get back to you.'

He ended the call and stuck the phone back in his pocket. 'These bloody Visa people just don't leave you alone, do they?' He looked to Fran for some sympathy. She gave him none.

'Since you're straight back from the beach,' she said, 'you can give me a hand on this morning's latest project, the Getting It On The Beach show. No, it's not bikinis and swimsuits, I'm afraid. In a nutshell it's a whole pile of useless crap that people buy because they think they should have it on the beach.'

Steve's face was a picture. He looked as though he'd just been voted out of the *Big Brother* house. Before he could summon up an excuse, Fran handed him a fat file of notes and flounced out on a fag break.

She scooped up Stella on her way out and they were soon having a puff outside in the early summer sunshine. After they'd shared a chuckle about Steve's latest adventures in fake tan, conversation inevitably turned to the stalker. Mercifully, Stella hadn't received any more hatemail. Over the past week she'd gradually come to the conclusion that perhaps it was just a one-off. She'd made a decision not to look at the website comments. Tiffany and her supporters could be safe in the knowledge that her star was still firmly in its ascendancy. There was no going back on screen for Stella.

'So when are you going to say yes to Tim?' Fran shot her a piercing look.

'Hmmmm,' said Stella, inspecting her newly polished ruby nails. She'd suddenly found she was inflicting a time-consuming beauty routine on herself. Bath bombs, lengthy manicures, hot oil and wax treatments. Then hours fiddling around with outfits deciding what to wear to work. Was this a symptom of interest in Tim?

'I can't go out on a date with him because I work with him,' Stella continued. 'Besides, it's now too late. He knows too much about me. I can't do the Woman of Mystery bit. I've bored him senseless with the fat, frumpy world of Bypass on Fashion which he found hysterical. He knew all about that. Turns out he'd married one!'

'Omigod,' Fran gasped.

'That's more or less why they divorced. She turned into a beached whale and refused to do anything about it. Apparently it was all he could do to get her to take a bath, let alone get her back down the beach and into the water.'

'Poor Tim,' Fran replied. 'No wonder he's keen on you. You always look a million dollars. Are you sure you just want to be good friends?'

'Funny you should mention that,' Stella confessed, looking at Fran from under her long dark lashes. 'I'm thinking of investing in some new underwear . . .'

*

Fran and Stella sat dumbfounded in Paul Dyer's office. In their silence, they desperately tried to grasp what he'd just outlined.

'Look, you two,' he said firmly, 'you can both talk a donkey's hind leg off, you both love shopping, you both know more about the bloody products than just about anyone around here. For God's sake, give us all a break and give it a go.'

Paul had just offered them some presenter training with a view to a regular fashion slot aimed at, as he tactfully put it, the more discerning female shopper.

Once they'd regained some composure, Fran managed to get out the inevitable question: 'Aren't we a bit old for this lark?'

Paul was ready with his answer. He gave them a half smile as he shook his head vigorously.

'Sorry, girls,' he grinned, 'not at all. You two are quite a double act. You could talk your way out of a nuclear war. You both look right, too. You're both sharp dressers and I think you'd really appeal to viewers of your age. I should have spotted it much earlier.'

He was met with continued blank expressions. 'I've watched you two casually yapping about the Super Suck vacuum cleaner as though your lives depended on it. It's good, it's what we need.'

'Yeah, but it's one thing chatting in the pub and quite another blathering on in a studio with a camera trained down your throat,' Stella finally managed. 'And besides, my nerves still haven't recovered from my stand-in session.'

'Which is why I want you two to work together. I appreciate you've had a tough time at home, Stella, but I seriously want you BOTH to give it a go. That's why I'm offering you presenter training. And believe me, it doesn't come cheap.'

'But this age thing,' said Fran, coming to her senses. 'Won't we be laughed off the screen? What on earth would the unofficial Getting It website make of us?'

'And remember I got that hate stuff,' Stella chipped in. 'It was horrible.'

Paul grinned at them as he leaned back and put his Doc Martens on the desk.

'Look, everyone gets some flak when they first appear. Then it all dies down as the public gets used to you. You're not supermodels – you're real women. You're funny and vibrant women in your prime. That's exactly why I'd like you to give it a try. OK, I accept viewers expect glossy blonde bimbos. That's the aspirational end of the market. Women would like to look like them, men would like to, er, examine them a bit more closely. But I think most viewers, particularly women, would also like to deal with real women with real bodies, not stick insects.'

They both nodded dumbly, wishing they could down a swift gin and tonic to cope with the shock.

Paul was really revving up: 'Who is our average viewer? Let me tell you, she's probably slightly too fat, having never quite recovered from childbirth. She probably watches too many soaps, eats too many chocolates and saves up all year for Christmas, plus two weeks in an apartment in Tenerife. She lives in a world of elasticated waists, "buy one get one free" offers and has a chest freezer full of frozen white sliced loaves.'

'How do you know that?' Fran was suspicious, wondering if that was how he saw them. At least her loaves were wholemeal.

'Market research,' replied Paul simply. 'Now don't even

begin to think that I'm describing you two because I'm not. Absolutely not. But the slightly more down to earth, slightly more mature person, we think, would have a definite appeal. In fact we know it would because I commissioned the research.'

Fran and Stella looked at each other. Research? This was all sounding so planned, so set in concrete. Here he was, offering them fame. On a plate. And he'd also worked out that neither could let the other down over such an offer.

'If things go according to plan, I'd like you both to work on some of the fashion shows. I'm sure our middle-aged viewer would be far more comfortable buying a pack of T-shirts or a pair of trainers from you two than some anorexic, cocaine-snorting alien. Besides, you both have a great sense of style. You were easily the best-dressed women on the day of the launch.'

Easy with friends like Ginette lending you all the gear, thought Stella, deliberately avoiding eye contact with Fran in case they gave the game away.

'Right,' he said, 'I've already booked your training course. I'll get Fiona to email you all the details. Don't tell anyone yet. Do the course and then I'll look at the tapes.'

Fran and Stella walked out wondering whether to laugh or cry. They huddled in a corner of the canteen, unable to believe their luck, good or bad.

'This is going to take some getting used to,' said Fran, now trying to suppress an ear-to-ear grin. 'At least you've had a bit of a baptism of fire.'

'I'm glad the training's being kept quiet,' said Stella, 'especially if we totally mess up. We can then slink back from relative obscurity to total obscurity and no one need ever know. I don't know about you but I feel quite numb.'

'Me too,' said Fran. 'I certainly don't feel like a "not bad for her age" fashion guru.'

'Nor a "not bad for the age I lied about" fashion guru,' Stella reminded her. 'Clearly there's no going back on our little indiscretion about date of birth.'

'Nope. And the diet starts now as far as I'm concerned. Telly is supposed to put on seven pounds so that needs to come straight off.'

Neither of them slept a wink that night, both wondering if they'd somehow dreamed it.

'Someone called Des Ryder from the *Hartford Echo* called you,' Steve irritatingly managed not to stammer as he inadvertently let the entire production office know. Fran groaned inwardly at this announcement. She could already imagine the fingers pointing, the nudges and whispers. Despite Paul Dyer's assurances, she knew there must be some speculation that she was the grass. She'd better call Des back and make it public.

She dialled the *Echo* number. Within two rings Shirley had answered. Don't start chatting to me, Fran prayed, or they'll think I'm ringing up all the time. Mercifully, Shirley had her busy voice on.

'How are you, love?' she squealed, 'wish I could talk but this place has gone berserk.'

'Oh, why's that?' Fran could never resist her need-to-know tendency.

'Oh, this bloody Madame Chita thingie. I mean, half of Hartford keeps phoning in with sightings, theories. She's an alien, a ghost, even a dinosaur come back to life. Next thing we'll be selling Madame Chita T-shirts and duvet covers. Anyway, gotta go, another Chita call flooding in, I expect. Sorry, love, forgot to ask. Who do you want to speak to? Des? You sure about that? OK, love, good luck. Just putting you through.'

And listening in on every nicotined growl, Fran didn't doubt for a moment.

'Des, it's Fran Hallgarth.' Fran was aware that everyone in her office was blatantly listening. Subtlety was merely a word they couldn't spell.

'Hi sweetie. Bit of a first, you calling me back. How's things?'

'Get to the point, Des. I'm merely returning your call.' Fran wondered how she could somehow convey Des's comments so that the rest of the office could get a handle on his side of the conversation.

'Tiffany's looking particularly beautiful at the moment. Glad to see that older bag didn't get a look in. How's the stalker? Any more kinky magazines or letters? It all seems to have gone a bit quiet, or is that just the management putting the mockers on it?'

Aware of her audience, she decided to play to the gallery. 'Well, Des, that's an awful lot of questions. I have no idea why you're asking *me*. You seem to know more about what goes on at this television station than I do. I'll tell you what, I've been talking to my boss, Paul Dyer, about these horrible calls you keep making. How would you like to speak to him direct? You know, get the full story from the head honcho.'

She heard the click of a lighter and a first drag on a cigarette. Des was obviously flouting the *Echo* office rules by lighting up. No change there, then.

'Sounds good to me,' he drawled. 'But before you put me through, how about your thoughts on our mystery clairvoyant. After all, you were at the *Echo* for a very long time. You must have your theories.'

I certainly do, thought Fran, along with my virtual crystal ball and tarot cards. 'Sorry to disappoint but I haven't a clue.' She tried to sound casual. Could the office see her hands shaking at this turn in the conversation? Or, worse, could Des hear it in her voice?

'All this week I'm featuring interviews with various members of staff and their theories on the identity of our First Lady of Fortune. And I'm planning to include you.'

'But I don't work for the *Echo* any more,' Fran replied as firmly as she could.

But Des was not to be put off lightly. 'Just a few questions,' he snarled. 'When were you first aware that Madame Chita—'

'Like I said, I don't work there any more. I'm not interested in taking part in your feature, or any other for that matter.'

Des was straight back for the kill. 'Hmm,' he taunted. '"I'm not interested in taking part in your feature." That might not look so good in print, might it?'

'Don't care, Des, just leave me alone. Now I've got work to do and—'

Their conversation was suddenly drowned out by the unmistakable sound of the fire alarms going off at the *Echo* offices. Obviously Des's sly ciggie had been too near a sensor. Fran gratefully put down the phone. Everyone in the office, caught out by the abrupt end of the call, pretended to look deep in thought as they drifted back to their tasks.

At lunchtime, Fran made another pilgrimage into Hartford, bought a first edition of the *Echo* and retired to her regular car park to read the latest. It was worse than she'd expected.

The Chita story had gone into overdrive and now the

paper had turned it into a competition. There was a five grand reward awaiting the reader who successfully tracked down the mystery clairvoyant.

Fran gasped with shock as she pored over the small print of the competition. Employees of the *Echo* past and present were barred from entering. At least that ruled her out; it was the one competition she'd have won hands down. Des was also trailing a Madame Chita follow-up story that would be appearing the next day. Hartford's clergy were apparently going to hit back at the 'obscene and cruel way in which someone could hold such evil influence over people's lives'.

Fran suddenly realised her car windows had steamed up, probably due to all the tension. She wound them down and sat back against her seat, trying to assimilate what Des was up to. Today there appeared to be a five grand contract on her head and tomorrow she would be portrayed as a witch who ought to be burned at the stake. At least she had some twenty-first century consolation – poor old Joan of Arc probably didn't have access to wine and fags.

Her mobile cheerfully trilled in her handbag. It was Guy, ringing to apologise about the reward.

'Couldn't get out of that one,' Guy explained. 'I got overruled at a management meeting yesterday. I argued that it was immoral and infantile and made us as journalists look pretty flakey. You know, as though we can't even investigate something on our own doorstep.'

'Well, that's certainly true.' Fran managed a small laugh.

'I had to be a bit careful as I was the only dissenter. Didn't want to give the game away. My story is that the copy just arrives as regular as clockwork.'

'I must say I feel like a gangster on a Wanted: Dead Or Alive poster.'

'Bottom line, hon, is that the paper is selling its socks off. Advertising's way up. The whole of Hartford is buzzing about it. We're being inundated with calls, emails and letters. The competition is going to go large.'

'Des really has re-invented himself, hasn't he,' Fran muttered ruefully. 'I gather I'm about to be shunned by the dog collars tomorrow.'

'Yes, 'fraid so,' said Guy. 'And there's worse. It's finally dawned on some of our readers that the name Madame Chita is a clue. So the hunt's off for the little old lady in dangly earrings living in a kitsch little Romany caravan. It could now be anyone – even a bloke.'

'At what stage are we talking of DNA-ing the entire population of Hartford?' Fran forced another laugh.

'Dunno, but it's only a question of time,' Guy replied with a chuckle. 'Just calm down. Remember that you and I, plus I'm assuming Bob, are the only ones who know.'

'Yeah, that's all,' said Fran. Thank goodness he couldn't see her turning pink with embarrassment. She wasn't about to tell him that Stella also knew.

'Well, let's keep it that way,' said Guy firmly. 'And by the way, I'm phoning you on my mobile. Don't want to run the risk of Shirley, the newsroom or half of MI6 listening in.'

Fran put her phone back in her bag. So the clue in the name had finally dawned on them. She was amazed it had taken this long. Due to unforeseen circumstances, Madame Chita didn't want to be famous. Whereas, somewhat ironically, Fran Hallgarth was about to be. Possibly.

Chapter 24

Next morning Stella and Fran embarked upon a secret fitness regime to get into shape before their presenter training.

'Three decades wouldn't be long enough,' Fran wailed as they met up for their first early morning session at the local swimming pool.

She'd already tried calorie-counting years ago and had decided her maths wasn't up to it. Stella had tried different slimming powders which she pronounced to be 'so disgusting that you just have to go out for lunch'. They talked about having a stab at giving up alcohol but ruled that out completely on the basis that there'd be no point in living. Eventually they settled for trying to cut out carbohydrates. So bye-bye bacon sarnies, baguettes and pasta.

'Isn't it bloody ironic,' Fran mused as they tanked up and down the pool. 'I wait ten years for an oven so I can bake bread, cakes and jacket potatoes and now they're straight off the menu.'

Stella nodded agreement. She wasn't great at mornings at the best of times and this early swim was already nearly killing her. Unfortunately, their fellow swimmers were all grey-haired and much older and faster than they were.

'If we get famous,' Stella said as she finally regained consciousness, 'do you think we'll still be able to come to this pool?'

'Don't be daft,' replied Fran. 'Nobody'd recognise me and my symphony of cellulite as a fully clothed "not bad for her age" fashion guru. And let's face it,' she glanced briefly around her at the other swimmers, 'none of them are wearing glasses so it would never matter.'

The investigation into Tiffany's stalker was making very little progress. A casual audit of emails by the computer support team merely confirmed that both Tiffany and Kiefer had sent masses of emails to the unofficial Getting It website, voting for themselves as the station's most popular presenter. And they seemed to have emailed half the population, whom they counted as close friends, inciting them to vote as well.

Paul Dyer was keeping Fran up-to-date on progress. In return, she was giving feedback on the mood of the troops and how much they knew. No one had any idea, she reported, that their emails were being filtered. Nor did anyone have a theory on the identity of the stalker.

'Everyone seems to have auto-delete memories,' she told him during that morning's updating session. 'There was quite a flurry of gossip after the porn mag was planted. But that's all gone quiet now, probably because it was a one-off. Everyone knows Kiefer and Tiffany loathe each other and would prefer not to be in the same postcode. But that's old news. There's a low attention span here.'

'You can say that again,' Paul agreed. 'It's just possible that Kiefer planted the magazine to put her off and give himself more of the limelight. Or another theory the police are working on is that Tiffany planted it to grab even more attention for herself. This may sound cruel but I don't think her brain could quite cope with that one. I must say I've studied the tapes and I think her horror is genuine.'

Fran inspected her nails, wondering whether to say what was in her mind. Nothing to lose, she decided.

'This may sound bitchy, but Tiffany is an actress, after all. Is it possible that she was just pretending shock?'

Paul collapsed into hoots of laughter. What on earth was so funny? Had she gone too far by saying that? Fran worried.

'Tiffany, an actress?' he managed when he'd recovered. 'Depends on how you look at it. She came in on an "I've worked extensively in films and television" ticket, accompanied by a pushy agent who's got to be related to the Borgias. So did Kiefer, for that matter. But you won't find either of them in the audience at the British Academy Awards unless they buy their own tickets. They both talked themselves so far up their own backsides that they're now complete walking arses.'

Fran was taken aback, although his words merely confirmed what they'd all suspected anyway. 'Surely you could fire them for that?'

'Of course I could,' said Paul, grinning from ear to ear. 'But I didn't give a fiddling fart about their very creative CVs. The fact they could talk themselves up meant they could talk up the products. That's why I hired them, because they look like top totty and they can both bullshit for Britain. I doubt Tiffany could act her way out of a paper bag. And that's why I believe she was genuine in her hysteria.'

Fran suddenly felt rather small and naive. Why on earth was he sending her and Stella on the presenters' course? They weren't exactly top totty. Whether they could bullshit for Britain was as yet untested. She was dying to recount this conversation to Stella in confidence.

'So what happens now?' she asked him.

'Well, Tiffany's still getting the kinky mail. The police are examining it but, to be honest, they're not making any headway. They're not all that interested, between you and me, because there aren't any death threats. Clearly it's just a loony fan who's obsessed with her. The current theory is that he sees himself as a suitor and that Kiefer is his love rival.'

'But anyone watching them on screen will know that they hate each other,' said Fran, puzzled by this.

'Ah yes, but in his twisted mind the stalker thinks this is all an act and that Tiff 'n' Kief are actually an item. He's convinced that once she meets him, she'll fall madly in love and he'll whisk her off to Costa Shagalotta. So he's got to carry on rubbishing Kiefer in order to keep him off the case, so to speak.'

'Strewth, that's a bit Freudian, isn't it? What's your theory?'

'Just some dirty old raincoat somewhere with nothing better to do than to cut up newspaper headlines. Sadly this prat is probably our archetypal viewer.'

'Do you think they'll ever track him down?'

'About as much chance as Hartford Hotspur trouncing Brazil,' Paul laughed. 'To be honest, if I were the police I'd hire in this Madame Chita woman from the *Echo*. I think she'd have more success. Pity she's so bloody mysterious . . . Fran, you've gone quite pale. You all right? I hope you're not worried about your course . . . ?'

*

The full fury of Hartford's men of the cloth was unleashed on Madame Chita in that day's *Echo*. As Des had promised in his piece the previous day, this was to be a hard-hitting feature with various priests and vicars muttering on about hell, brimstone, Sodom and Gomorrah.

'Who is this cheater?' screamed one of the headlines. Des had written a long and rambling opinion piece hinting that the elusive Madame Chita was just an opportunist and a phoney. There was also an interview with Guy who, Fran had to admit, had played a bit of a blinder.

'Our old clairvoyant, Madam Irene, announced her retirement and we started to think about buying into a syndicated column,' Guy was quoted as saying. 'The following week, this plain white envelope arrived containing a week's worth of horoscopes from a mysterious woman signing herself as Madame Chita. We had no idea where it had come from but it was so outrageously different to the usual vague predictions that most newspapers run we decided very quickly to go with it. She was an instant hit with our readers. Then a week later another envelope arrived, and then another, and it's been like that ever since. No one has any idea who she is – and we're assuming she's a she – or where she lives. But Madame Chita's horoscopes are like no other.'

Guy went on to reminisce fondly about some of Madame Chita's achievements, including summer weather predictions, calling all the general election results to date and the odd tip at the Hartford Greyhound Track.

It's lucky he could remember the good ones, thought Fran as she nervously read the rest of the copy. On the downside was the day that Madame Chita had told all Capricorns to 'vent your feelings on the very next person you meet'. For several readers who'd taken her at her word, that next person had been their boss and they'd promptly been given the sack. One man had tried to sue Madame Chita and the *Echo* for loss of earnings but it had mercifully been thrown out of court at quite an early stage.

At least no one had come up with enough 'information' to claim the reward for rumbling Madame Chita. Fran figured she would probably have heard about that one soon enough from Guy.

She'd deliberately gone into town at lunchtime to read the latest onslaught in the *Echo* and have some time alone to think about it. She found herself a small corner table in Café Rouge, lit a cigarette and dialled Guy's mobile number. Drat, his voicemail was on. She was too scared to leave a message in case his mobile fell into the wrong hands. She was beginning to understand how Ronnie Biggs must have felt when he was on the run. Except that this was rainswept Hartford rather than Rio. She sipped a glass of mineral water, toyed with a salad and thought long and hard about the Chita problem. Then she tried Guy once more. This time he answered. Judging by the background racket, he was in the Slug and Lettuce enjoying a lunchtime pint.

'I can't go on with this,' she announced, trying to compete with the noise of the pub. Several people on adjacent tables began to eavesdrop unashamedly, thinking they were in ringside seats for the end of an affair. 'I want to pack it in,' she told him, trying to lower her voice but make herself heard to Guy at the same time.

'Sorry, hon, can't talk, if you get my drift,' said Guy, who was obviously afraid of being overheard. If he was discovered chatting to the legendary Madame Chita she'd be a legend no more.

'Look,' said Fran, taking control of the one-way

conversation and turning her head away from the nosy diners, 'I know there's a price on my head, I know your sales are going through the roof but I am stuck in the middle of all this whether I like it or not.'

Guy made grunts of protest as best he could over the din.

'It's no good you grumbling at me,' Fran continued resolutely. 'None of this is my fault. My only crime was to start sending you the stuff in the first place. Just because the paper's cashing in on it at the moment is nothing to do with me.'

'But, Fran, it's mega now. We've got a national TV crew coming in next week to do a bit for Channel 4, advertising hit record levels last week, beating Christmas hands down, and all the nationals are sniffing. Come on, Fran, give me a break, this is good for my CV. The Man Who Gave the World Madame Chita.'

'It might be good for your CV,' she remarked bitterly, 'but it's never going to appear on mine.'

'Hey, in another week or two it will all die down,' Guy tried to console her. 'You know what hype's like. One minute it's the ultimate in cool, the next it's yesterday's chip paper. Literally! Enjoy the moment.'

'Right now, I'd settle very happily for chip paper.' She ended the call and put the phone back into her handbag. She lit a cigarette and pondered at the crowd in the café through her exhaled smoke. Then she made her decision.

Chapter 25

The buying department was in a complete panic. In conjunction with the producers, they were preparing two separate programmes. Getting It On The Beach was devoted to products for beach holidays and was being produced by Fran. The other, Getting It On The Prom, featured strictly après-plage activities with Steve at the helm. A bigger than usual budget had been agreed – enough for a professional designer to come in and create a proper set. Naturally Kiefer and Tiffany were first choices to front the show, despite their personal differences.

With the course only a few days away, Fran and Stella found themselves secretly trying to analyse the presenting techniques both Kiefer and Tiffany employed. They'd still not breathed a word about the impending course to anyone at the station. And they were doing a lot of breathing in, hoping to shape up tired old muscles.

Right now, Fran needed to concentrate. Already tempers were fraying, mostly over Steve's incompetence.

'For God's sake,' Paul Dyer shouted at Steve, 'you must have been on a package holiday at least once in your life.'

'Er, no.' Steve looked distinctly uneasy. 'W . . . w . . . why on earth would I want to do that?'

'In that case, use your imagination,' came the reply. 'Or on second thoughts, perhaps you'd better not. God knows what goes on in that brain of yours.'

Paul immediately put Stella on to Steve's case and instructed her to knock some sense into him. She immediately dragged him into the canteen – Steve didn't do anything remotely as risky as smoking – and plied him with strong coffee in the hope that it might induce some sort of buzz.

'Look, love, it's very simple. Fran deals with all the "on the beach" stuff. Your show is about what happens after that. You need to get in the mood. On holiday, everyone gets burned to a frazzle during the day. Then they rush back to their hotels, shower and put on minuscule clothes they'd never be seen dead in at any other time of the year or in front of anyone they even vaguely know. Shoes more akin to stilts and jewellery that would make even the Beckhams blush. Everyone wears something white to really show off the skin that's been barbecued all day long. If you said the word melanoma they'd think it was a new dance craze. This is followed by an evening of drinking cheap cocktails with silly names, strutting up and down the sea front half-pissed and trying to look cool in a kind of night time peacock display. Geddit?'

Steve looked puzzled, the fading St Tropez-ed forehead now furrowed. Stella began to wonder if he'd ever had any kind of a life, as opposed to the secret world he seemed to inhabit. The glasses were a deliberate barrier, she decided. Unless his childhood hero was Buddy Holly.

Meanwhile Fran was up to her ears with the On The Beach end of the market. That night she drove home bored sick with everything to do with holidays. I need a break, she thought to herself as she finally swung into her road, but definitely not a wind break, and if I as much as glimpse another deckchair or parasol I'll book myself into The Priory. Do they do rehab for people who've overdosed on beach clobber?

She staggered into her kitchen and flung down her briefcase. She still found herself grinning at the new kitchen cupboards and gleaming paintwork. Bob had popped the casserole she'd made the previous night into the oven and it was bubbling away nicely. The smell of beef, tomatoes and garlic was heavenly. After dinner, she'd write the letter she'd been thinking about all day.

She boiled some water for the ribbon noodles (only for Bob, sadly, as pasta was now a banned substance) to go with the casserole and sat back at the table to enjoy a moment's peace. Ten seconds later it was shattered by the telephone – and Des's raspy voice down the phone.

'It's Kiefer, isn't it,' he announced triumphantly. 'He hates her and he's setting her up for a fall. Go on, admit it.'

'Well, Des, you seem to know far more about it than I do,' she replied tersely. 'Me? I only work there.'

'It's definitely Kiefer, and he wants the beautiful Tiffany off the screen so he can become the number one presenter.'

'Are you sure?' Fran hated herself for discussing it, even with old Des-perate Ryder. 'Many of our viewers think they make a lovely couple. Perhaps our stalker fancies the beautiful Tiffany and is jealous of Kiefer?'

'Don't be ridiculous,' Des mocked her. 'Why on earth would Kiefer fancy Tiffany? They're hardly an item, are they?'

'They might be, for all I know.' Fran bit her lip. She was

beginning to regret getting into this conversation. 'Look, Des, I only work with these people. I don't roster their sex lives.'

'But they're never going to be an item,' Des persisted. 'You must know that.'

'I haven't a clue what you're on about. If they're not now, they might be one day. We don't know that.'

There was a pause at Des's end. For one blissful moment, Fran thought he'd hung up.

'You don't know, do you,' Des said slowly.

'Know what?'

'Kiefer's gay. He's not interested in Tiffany, never will be.'

Fran mentally kicked herself. She'd never clocked that one. Of course he was; impossibly beautiful, immaculately dressed, groomed to perfection. And a better set of fingernails than all the women at the studio.

'How did you get to this one?' Again she couldn't resist.

'I have my sources. I've heard about Kiefer's very pushy boyfriend who clearly sees his bedmate as a rising star. Anything obstructing his route to the top is a threat. So Miss Tiff is simply in the way. Really, tut tut, Fran, I'd have thought you'd have worked that one out.'

Des laughed his horrible nicotined laugh and hung up.

Fran stared at the phone. She suddenly felt rather naive yet again.

So who was Tiffany's stalker? It certainly wasn't Des, she was now sure of that. But was it Kiefer, backed up by his pushy boyfriend? She still didn't buy that one. And anyway, the stalker had been quiet lately. Perhaps he'd gone away all together. She turned her thoughts back to the task she'd set herself tonight. She'd do it after dinner.

She called Bob in from the shed. They were dining in style these days – by candlelight at the new pine table.

'You look whacked,' Bob said, the picture of concern as she ladled out helpings of beef. 'Hope you're not overdoing it, love.'

'No, just Des on the phone again. His new theory is that Tiffany's stalker is Kiefer, because he's gay with an ambitious boyfriend.'

Bob sighed. 'This all makes my life at the bank seem boring. We never have that kind of excitement, except when people get stroppy when their credit cards are gobbled up. Anyway, are you going to write it tonight?'

'Yes, I've got to. I can't go on like this. It's making my nerves jangle.'

'Right then, I'll clear up this lot and you get started.'

Fran kissed him lightly on the cheek and then went upstairs. She put some paper in the state-of-the-ark typewriter, balanced herself on her rickety old stool and began typing.

To Whom It May Concern

I am very sad to inform you of the sudden and unexpected death of the clairvoyant Madame Chita. I am unable to give you any further details because one of Madame Chita's last instructions was that her identity must never be revealed, even after death. I am sure your readers and her many fans will be distressed at this sad news.

Madame Chita had completed her weekly horoscopes before her untimely demise so I am enclosing them, should you wish to publish what will be her last column. I am sure it would have been her wish for it to be printed.

Yours sincerely,

Madame Chita's sister

There, it was done. That should put a stop to all the stories. She opened one of her customary white envelopes and put the letter inside, along with the final horoscopes which she'd made particularly outrageous as a parting shot. It was weird writing your own obituary.

As she came downstairs, Bob was wrestling with the new filter coffee maker.

'All done and ready to post tomorrow,' she announced, collapsing into a chair. 'I hereby rest in peace!'

Fran left for work early the next morning in order to post her letter at the usual postbox. She thought back to that fateful night when she'd first sat down with her virtual crystal ball. She'd written it more as a joke than anything else. She'd grown to enjoy the secrecy of it all, of occasionally hearing women in supermarket check-out queues discussing Madame Chita and being a frequent subject on the Letters to the Editor page.

But it had outgrown its enjoyment and usefulness. The last few weeks had ground her down. To be revealed as the bogus clairvoyant who'd written such outrageous things would be too much to bear. This was the easiest way out. No more discussion, no more pleading from Guy. He might be revelling in the title of The Man Who Gave the World Madame Chita but by tomorrow he could play at being The Man Who Revealed Madame Chita's Untimely Death.

She was still wading through post and emails when a couple of headlines on an internet news page caught her eye. Unforeseen Whereabouts. Search for Mystery Clairvoyant. She clicked on the headlines and there it was. Guy had been right, the story had been picked up nationally. Remembering she'd left too early for the paperboy, she hastily found a copy of the *Daily Mail*. There it was, given full page treatment on page five.

Fran heaved a sigh of relief. Another good reason for posting her letter this morning. She sat back in her chair, taking deep breaths and trying to relax.

Her phone rang. It was Bob, quietly warning her that the story was in the *Express*, *Sun* and the *Mirror* as well. 'It's the talk of the bank,' he whispered. 'Did you post the letter?'

'Of course.'

'Good girl. RIP and all that. See you later.'

The morning progressed into a shouting match between the freelance set designer for the two beach shows – and just about everyone else on the studio floor. Stella and Fran nipped out for ciggies to mull it all over.

'Promise me you haven't told a soul about the Chita connection.' Fran knew she could trust her friend but still needed re-affirmation.

'Absolutely,' Stella answered truthfully. 'In fact, I've made myself forget about it so successfully that when I opened my paper this morning I was quite shocked and intrigued by the story.'

'I got a hint that it was happening, but it was still a bit of a jolt,' Fran confessed. 'And there's an even bigger jolt in store tomorrow.'

She then outlined Madame Chita's impending demise.

'That's absolutely brilliant,' said Stella in total admiration. 'Master stroke. And don't worry, my lips are sealed.'

Fran stubbed out her cigarette in the plastic bucket provided. 'That reminds me. The appalling Des told me something so obvious it was staring me right in the face.'

'What?'

'Kiefer's gay,' she announced. 'And he's got a very pushy boyfriend. Des thinks Kiefer and friend could actually be the stalker, trying to rattle Tiffany's cage so that Kiefer doesn't have to share the number one presenter slot.'

Stella gaped as she took it all in. 'Well,' she said finally, 'I suppose it's perfectly feasible. Do you believe Des, though? I mean, it's not exactly hearts and flowers between you two, is it?'

Fran threw her head back and laughed. 'No, but for all his faults, and believe me the list is endless, Des does tend to stick to the facts. He might do a bit of spin-doctoring, but when the lazy sod sobers up enough to find a good story it tends to hit the spot.'

'Do you think Kiefer and friend would stoop that low?' asked Stella, fishing out a packet of cigarettes from her bag and offering one to Fran.

'Oh yeah, definitely. I mean, Getting It is now the nation's number one shopping channel. It's dragging in twice as many viewers as its closest rival, for all the painful and farcical reasons we know about. So if you're Kiefer and you believe your own press releases that you are the undisputed queen of the shopping channels, then you've a queen-sized ego problem. Who wants to share the number one presenter spot with some stupid ditsy blonde?'

Back in the building, the stupid ditsy blonde and the undisputed queen of the shopping channels were having a very public row in the middle of the main studio. So they were conveniently lit for the benefit of the rest of the staff who were watching it on their screens.

'This is supposed to be a fun programme,' Kiefer was shouting. 'You look so bloody bored all the time. Every

216

time I say something and look to you for a reaction, I just get this vacant, out-to-lunch expression.'

'That's because you're boring,' Tiffany screamed back, tossing her blonde hair with a flick of a Cartier wristwatch. 'You just prat on all the time, hogging the screen.'

'You're so wooden.' Kiefer was going in for the kill by looking straight into camera one, knowing full well that they'd all be watching in the gallery. 'I'm surprised you didn't play a tree in your last acting job.'

'Huh. You're the one who's barking,' came the quick reply.

'Well, at least trees don't have lines to learn,' Kiefer hit back.

'I think our days working together are numbered,' countered Tiffany, straight to camera two. 'In fact, I'm wondering if it's you who's been sending all that horrible stuff and planted that disgusting magazine.'

'I'll have you for slander,' he thundered. 'Just think, everyone in this crummy building's been listening to what you've just said. You'll be hearing from my solicitor.'

'It'll make a nice change from all that other nasty stuff you send.' And without a backward glance, Tiffany strode out of the studio. Shortly afterwards, her agent phoned to say she was signed off with stress again, citing the stalker.

Chapter 26

'I think we're in for a long afternoon judging by the agenda,' remarked Fran as half a dozen of them filed into Paul Dyer's office for the monthly brainstorming session. 'Hush everyone, Diarrhoea.'

Paul swept into the room, eyes flashing. He flung another exquisitely cut Armani jacket over the back of his chair and banged several files down on his desk for emphasis. All idle chatter ceased immediately. His secretary, Fiona, looking particularly mutinous, sat down to take notes. Everyone ignored her as usual. She never made any attempt to be friendly. Today's brown dress looked like a potato sack, Fran thought, except that it was a shame for sacks.

'Right,' Paul announced, loosening his tie for effect. 'Tiffany's off the scene for the foreseeable future. Her agent phoned me after this morning's catfight to say that the stress of the stalker and now the row with Kiefer is proving too much. So I've had to write her off for at least a month.'

There was a quiet wave of reaction around the room.

'And I've put Kiefer on gardening leave for a couple of days,' Paul continued. 'He needs to cool off. He can't go around shouting his mouth off at people, especially people with whom he is supposed to have at least a vague semblance of on-screen chemistry. It's not much to ask really, considering what we pay these people. I will be reading Kiefer's horoscope for him when he comes back in and I'll keep you posted.'

At the mention of the word horoscope, Fran inwardly winced. At least she had a day's grace until Guy got her letter. Today she could enjoy a brief respite from the inevitable storm of protest that Guy would whip up.

'Pity we couldn't get the mad clairvoyant in from the *Echo*, what's her name? Chita? Ha ha. Yeah, get her in to tell him a few home truths.'

Fran felt herself going pink with embarrassment. She hastily fanned herself with a cardboard file. 'Sorry, Paul, bit hot in here.'

'Fiona,' he barked, 'open the window. Fran's having a power surge.'

Everyone allowed themselves a small laugh as Fiona grudgingly got up to oblige.

'Anyway,' Paul continued, 'I want to know what you lot think. Do you think we should keep on with the Tiff 'n' Kief combination or split them up permanently? Opinions please. Steve, you start.' He really was putting Steve on the spot these days.

'Split them up,' said Steve nervously. 'They're h . . . h . . . hardly Richard and Judy.'

'Pity,' said Tim. 'They do look good together.'

'Not today they didn't,' Paul announced firmly. 'I had hoped they would at least attempt to create a bit of chemistry between them, but today was more of a nuclear explosion. Clearly I was hoping for too much.'

'Don't see why,' persisted Tim. 'They should just learn

to bite the bullet and get on with it like the rest of us.' He shot a half glance in Steve's direction.

Paul leaned back in his seat, somewhat surprised at the range of opinion. 'Perhaps I should put it to the vote,' he concluded.

'Hang on a minute.' It was Adrienne, the production assistant. 'Look,' she said nervously, twisting strands of chestnut hair as she spoke. 'I'm not sure I should be telling you this, but you're all heading up the wrong path. It was never going to work between Kiefer and Tiffany. They'd never fancy one another in a million years.'

'R . . . r . . . really?' Steve stammered in amazement for all of them. Except Fran, who kept her eyes downcast just in case anyone clocked her reaction to what she now knew was coming next.

'Go on,' said Paul, eyes boring into Adrienne.

'Please don't say anything outside these four walls,' Adrienne pleaded, still twisting her hair, 'because I don't think he's come out, and I must say I never clocked it to start with, but Kiefer's gay. He wouldn't be interested in Tiff if she were the last tart on the plate.'

Fran tried to look as though it was dawning on her like the rest of them.

'You're kidding,' Tim blurted out in disbelief.

Fran caught Steve's face. He was wearing a very strange look. Perhaps he fancied Tiffany. Or maybe Kiefer was the object of his secret desire. Could he be Kiefer's pushy boyfriend, as described by Des? She hadn't thought of that before, but where Steve was concerned anything was possible.

At least that settled the argument. Everyone reluctantly agreed that Tiffany and Kiefer should never work together again. They then sank into the relief of discussing ordinary topics like the next two months' worth of projects.

'And just before you go,' Paul announced with a mischievous twinkle in his eye, 'we might be splitting up some of our presenters because of their tantrums and traumas, but we are also gaining a powerful new alliance. Fran and Stella are going to present a regular fashion show, beginning next month. I've already pencilled them in for a Friday night slot.'

All eyes immediately gravitated towards Fran and Stella, who sat open-mouthed, unable to react. He did have a habit of dropping bombshells.

But we haven't even done the course yet, thought Stella, panicking. He's railroading us into this. She looked across helplessly at Fran.

A ripple of quiet surprise went around the room. But the moment they were outside Paul's office, they were bombarded with questions all the way down the corridor.

Fran received another jolt when she finally got back to her desk. Guy had left a message to ring him. It couldn't be about her letter of resignation yet, unless the Royal Mail had broken all land speed records. She dialled his mobile number, praying it was unobtainable/unrecognisable/un-anything. But Guy answered after a couple of rings.

'Just keeping you posted, love,' he whispered. 'There's an ITN crew crawling around the town, doing an "And Finally" piece on Madame Chita for tonight's *News at Ten*. See how famous you've become!'

Fran shuddered. Famous? That was supposed to come later. They'd probably be back tomorrow looking for a body. She decided in a split-second not to mention the letter. He could find that out for himself. After all, she'd had quite a few shocks of her own lately. It was definitely Guy's turn for an astrological kick up the backside.

That evening, Fran settled down in her tatty sitting room to watch *News at Ten*. Would they run something on Madame Chita? Wasn't there a skateboarding duck somewhere in Britain who could provide a better story for their 'And Finally' slot?

But sure enough, Trevor McDonald mentioned a 'mystery clairvoyant' as they went into the commercial break. So Guy had been right. She sat through the second half, biting her nails to the quick. Suddenly Sir Trevor flashed a big smile and then threw to a pun-laden package about the mystery of Madame Chita and 'her phenomenal predictions'.

Fran watched the screen through her fingers, terrified to witness her alter ego finally making national television.

If they could see me now, she thought to herself, glancing around the room at the electrics hanging out of the walls, the empty doorway – the door propped up in the hallway for just the five years while Bob found the perfect brass plates with which to rehang it.

Fran dragged herself wearily up to bed. She was sick to death of Madame Chita. But she knew she'd feel better after she'd died.

Next day the billboards proclaimed 'Chita Dead'. So Guy had acted quickly. Probably delighted to have another story fall into his lap.

The letter from Madame Chita's 'sister' had been faithfully reproduced. As well as the story being front-page lead, there was a respectful tribute on the leader page, plus a full obituary. Well, as full an obit as they could come up with given no one had actually met the great legend.

Yet again Fran escaped from the mayhem of Getting It to take up her now habitual corner in Café Rouge to digest the paper over yet another salad and a comforting glass of mineral water. She had to admire Guy. He really did know a good story when he tripped over one and he'd exploited her bombshell for all it was worth. In fact, putting aside her personal involvement, she was rather proud of him. There was even a trail announcing that Madame Chita's last ever column would be published the next day.

Fran couldn't resist ringing him. Guy answered third ring, clearly larging it in the pub.

'Thought you'd ring,' he boomed over the din. 'I should be a clairvoyant.' He guffawed loudly at his own joke. Then he lowered his voice to be just about audible. 'Well done, Fran, you trounced me there. A master stroke, that. Never saw it coming.'

'Thanks for taking it in that spirit.' Fran was relieved. 'I thought you'd be furious.'

'Oh, I was,' Guy answered. 'Bloody seething. But you did tell me you wanted out. I suppose I should have listened.'

'But at least this way you get another story,' Fran continued. 'Very nice obit. Shame you didn't mention my birth on the end of a pier, previous convictions for stealing heather and my national collection of dangly earrings.'

'Oh shut up,' said Guy cheerfully. 'Gonna miss your stuff arriving in that envelope every week. Won't stop your payment for a while. Don't want to raise suspicion.'

'Hey, thanks Guy,' said Fran, pathetically grateful and thinking of new sitting room curtains.

Chapter 27

Fran and Stella arrived at the Soho address bang on 9.30 a.m. They'd got up at the crack of dawn to catch the earliest train from Hartford. The no-carb diet had certainly worked – both of them were down to a size twelve – just. It had been a struggle.

Ginette had come up trumps again with an outfit for each of them to wear on the course, just to give them confidence. She knew there was nothing in it for her – at the moment. But if they became overnight sensations, they'd all giggled, they'd be name-dropping her boutique everywhere from *Hello!* to *Harpers & Queen*.

As they were led upstairs by a minder to the 'mini studio' where their course was to take place, both of them were so overcome with nerves that they plodded around corners, up corridors, down stairs, up more stairs, without saying a single word. Finally they reached a huge studio door and were ushered in.

'Fran and Stella!' exclaimed a woman with a short ash-blonde bob. She glided towards them, brandishing a clipboard. She looked vaguely familiar. 'Welcome, come in, come in.' They all air-kissed.

They both blinked, taking in their surroundings. The

studio was massive compared to Getting It. Four huge cameras, standing idle, looked like creatures out of *Jurassic Park* waiting to pounce on them. It made Getting It's studios seem very basic.

Sheena Masters, as she introduced herself, was in her mid-fifties, Fran judged, but clearly fighting the ravages of age all the way. Whippet-thin with enviable legs, porcelain skin and delicate hands with no hint of liver spots, she was definitely a class act. Had she read the national news, presented programmes? Fran resolved to look her up on the internet later – and to start using handcream on a more regular basis.

'OK,' Sheena said with a smile, 'let's sit down and I'll run through the day.'

She motioned them towards a semi-circular sofa and coffee table, all rigged up with mics and hidden computer screens.

'The good news is that there are lots of boring things we don't have to cover today. Like autocue. Because you're going to present live shopping, there's no formal script to read and so no need for us to do any of that. Therefore we'll have two sessions this morning: firstly hair, make-up and colours. We'll find out what best suits you both. Then we'll have a little practice in the studio. Then we'll have lunch.'

Lunch, thought Fran, clocking Sheena's delicate ankles and wrists. I'll never be able to have lunch again.

'Then,' Sheena continued, 'we'll have a little more clothes advice, more studio and we'll round off with questions and queries.'

She paused and beamed at them reassuringly. Neither had yet uttered a word, overwhelmed by the whole experience so far.

'I must say,' she added, 'how pleased I am to hear that Getting It isn't following the well-worn path of only having bimbos on their programmes. With respect, we mature girls can offer just as good a performance. It's always been rather unfair, I think, that the chaps can go on until their teeth are practically dropping out, but most women are whisked off screen long before they're forty. As in my case.'

So she HAD been famous, they both thought, still racking their brains as to where and what she'd presented.

'I also think,' she continued, apparently unfazed by their continuing silence, 'that it's wonderfully innovative of your station to have more mature women presenting fashion for their own age group. I mean, I have never understood why magazines still insist on using stick-thin teenagers to model clothes aimed at their own mothers and grandmothers. By the way, I must say you two look terrific. I'm going to pinch the details off you for those fantastic suits.'

The both nodded, still unable to speak.

'Well, I'm sure you two get on like a house on fire so it won't be a problem keeping the dialogue going when you're on air,' she said, meaning they really did have to say something now or the whole premise of the course would be ridiculous.

'No, er . . .' Fran started. Stella opened her mouth and nothing came out. They both laughed nervously and then began talking at once.

'Don't worry,' said Sheena, 'everyone gets a bit fazed to start with.' She ushered them through to a dressing room where a make-up artist and stylist were waiting.

Next thing they were sat facing huge mirrors having intensive make-up lessons.

'Fran and Stella are going to be presenting women's fashion,' announced Sheena to the make-up artist, a pale, spotty girl who appeared to be called Jazza. Stella couldn't take her eyes off Jazza's terrible complexion as she worked away with her paints and brushes. Perhaps it was an occupational hazard, as it was for the women who worked in health shops. They always boasted the biggest zits in town. Jazza certainly knew her stuff though. Soon Stella looked quite transformed, her eyes larger and more sparkly and her face more contoured somehow. Then Jazza got to work on Fran. During all this, Sheena quietly chatted away on her thoughts about presentation as though she were swopping recipes. Except, of course, Fran and Stella had none to trade.

'Never lie on television. It always shows. If you don't know something about one of your products don't try and bluff. Viewers always know when you're not sincere. I once worked with a continuity announcer who never watched television. Never looked at the output. And they cut to her immediately after a horror movie where a man had been macheted to death in the closing moments and she just said, in honeyed tones: 'Hmm, that WAS fascinating, wasn't it?'

Fran and Stella couldn't help laughing. Sheena was a great raconteur. Suddenly they felt more at ease. Now that their make-up was done and their hair re-styled they returned to the studio. A couple of jackets had been laid out on the coffee table.

Sheena explained that they'd just have a little practice so they could then see for themselves how the make-up looked.

A small crew appeared from nowhere to man the cameras while they were both fitted with earpieces. They then found themselves on the sofa, listening intently to a man they hadn't yet met who was sitting in an as-yet-unseen production gallery. Sheena had suddenly disappeared – off to the gallery, they presumed.

'I want you to introduce yourselves and talk about those two jackets to each other. Ignore the cameras at this stage,' said the mystery voice in their ear. 'Fran, yours is the red one, and Stella, take the blue. Fran to start, in five, four, three . . .'

Fran took a deep breath and tried to smile at Stella. Her mouth had gone suddenly dry and her lips were stuck on her teeth. Yanking them back together, she managed to start talking. But she hardly recognised the squeaky voice that came out of her mouth. Stella did at least identify the territory from her one previous attempt and took over the conversation the second she saw Fran struggling. They managed to burble through three or four minutes on the jackets and were just beginning a spirited debate on the merits of dry cleaning when they heard a welcome 'Wind up now' in their ears.

They stopped, looked helplessly at each other and burst into nervous laughter. Sheena reappeared on the studio floor. 'Well done,' she exclaimed. 'You both look great. Paul told me you could do it. Come up and have a look.' They followed her up a short flight of steps and into a small gallery.

'Hi girls,' waved a bearded man with a now familiar voice. 'Sorry not to have introduced myself before. I'm John. Well done. Good make-up. See what a great slapper Jazza is.' He roared with laughter at his own joke.

They watched, stunned, as they both suddenly appeared on every one of the twenty screens in the gallery.

The morning then went by in a flash. They tried on

jackets of every colour and the hair and make-up were examined and recorded again and again until Sheena seemed satisfied.

'There aren't many rules in this game,' said Sheena in her gentle way. 'Black or white – not a good idea. No small patterns, they strobe. Big patterns add pounds, or rather stones. Even with digital television they don't look good. And also you're in a specialist field. You don't want to compete with the clothes you're selling. Same with jewellery, keep it simple and minimalist. Anything that rattles is out, so no charm bracelets, big belts or parking money in your pocket. That kind of thing.'

Soon it was lunchtime. Fran and Stella wolfed down tired-looking salads, both gagging for a gin and tonic, while Sheena tucked into a plate of pasta oozing with butter and pesto. It didn't seem fair. Soon they were back in the studio with Sheena now teaching them the art of talking to camera.

'Don't let your eyes dart around to see who's behind the camera. Talk right down that bottle. Pretend the lens is a friend, a lover. Look him straight in the eye. That's it, that's it,' she encouraged from the studio floor.

Up and down stairs they trailed, watching replays. As the afternoon wore on they learned how to move better, how to hold objects up for camera close-ups and how not to fiddle with stray bits of hair.

They were summoned to the gallery for yet another replay to be greeted by the whole of the team laughing. The director then hit a button and played back a couple of rather indiscreet remarks they'd made in between takes about Tiffany being cheesier than Parmesan.

'Everyone does that at some stage,' laughed Sheena. 'I once worked with a girl who thought she was having an

229

intimate chat with a floor manager about the size of orgasm she reached by sitting on top of her dishwasher. They piped the conversation around the entire building over the tannoy system.'

By the end of the day they had a shopping list of dos and don'ts that would have cleaned out half of Sainsbury's. Plenty of sleep, plenty of water, cut down on the red wine and sun-tanning, take more care of their hands for close-ups, and learn to breathe on air without goldfish-style gulps.

'Don't forget you're selling clothes. It's obvious you're both interested in fashion so make sure you pick out the pieces that suit you the most. Be brutally honest with each other – but not, of course, on screen. And remember, whenever you can recall what someone wore on television it's either because it was simply terrible or because it was so gorgeous you wish they'd given out the stockists at the end of the programme. Let's go for the latter.'

Sheena put down her clipboard with an air of finality. 'Girls, we've had a great day. I'm sure Paul Dyer will be delighted with the final results. Good luck. I'll be watching.'

With that, the gallery crew burst into a round of applause as Fran and Stella were presented with the tapes of their gruelling day.

'Still want to be famous?' Fran asked Stella as they lay slumped in an empty carriage on the last train back to Hartford.

'I decline to comment,' said Stella. 'But Sheena was a great teacher. So patient. It looks so bloody easy when you watch people like Tiffany sailing through it all. I'll never slag that girl off again, nor the others for that matter.'

'Ditto,' said Fran. 'But it's going to be a huge effort, keeping up this low-carb lark to look good. If Paul does give us the thumbs up, I'm going to have to put marigolds and dumb-bells on my Christmas list.'

Chapter 28

Fran couldn't wait to search the internet to find out about Sheena Masters's past career. Just as she thought, Sheena had presented just about everything from BBC national news to Radio 4. She felt rather embarrassed that she hadn't acknowledged such an impressive career during their training day. Sheena seemed entirely confident that the pair of them could present a fashion show. Fran, plagued with doubts, convinced herself that everyone got the same pep talk.

Still, the fruits of their labour were now on a VHS deposited safely in Paul Dyer's office. All that remained was the verdict. She and Stella had discussed that in depth and felt it was now in the lap of the gods. If Paul liked what they'd done, that was fine. But if he didn't, then perhaps they were sparing themselves a lot of heartache and future embarrassment. Then, after going through the motions of 'I don't really mind either way', they broke into a huge confessional about how it actually mattered hugely to them.

Paul, a mutinous Fiona informed them, was out of the office for most of the day so they'd have to wait anyway. As always, there was plenty going on in the studio to divert them. It was the first recording of Getting It On The Beach and the atmosphere was as far from sunny paradise as you could get. Stella was dashing around making sure all the beach equipment was in place. Piers, now fully recovered from his slipped disc, was doing all the heavy work. He'd taken to wearing a very strong aftershave, nicknamed Lucky Gym, which had the effect of warning people he was in the vicinity.

Stella and Fran were going through the final running order between themselves before they presented it as a *fait accompli* to Kiefer and his new sidekick, Alice. A perfect combination, Paul Dyer had decided. Alice was not in the same drop-dead gorgeous league as Tiffany but she was pretty. And, he had observed gratefully, pretty dumb. So no threat to Kiefer in any way, shape or form.

Half an hour to go and Fran and Stella were satisfied that the products were being presented in the right order, Kiefer and Alice seemed to have done their homework and Piers was just heaving the last plastic palm tree in place. Once they'd recorded the show, which was going out live, it would be transmitted several times a week over the coming month.

As always, the moment crept up on them. Fran and Stella took up their places in front of the screens in the gallery. They heard the production assistant start her count-down and shot each other an agonised look that said, 'This could be us in a couple of weeks' time.'

As Fran had discovered over the past few months, there was a kind of helplessness about sitting in the gallery watching the programme unfold. Live television went through a kind of fast-forward, rather like a runaway train. Within what felt like five frantic minutes Adrienne, the production assistant, was counting the presenters out of the hour-long programme.

A cheer of relief went up at the end as the screens went to black. Production-wise it had been one of the most complicated shows and it had gone perfectly. No mishap, injury or onscreen argument. Reps from the companies whose products had been featured went away with big corporate smiles on their faces. The call centre had reported huge business.

Fran decided that given today's success and her recent pay rise, she'd go and order those curtains for the sitting room.

'Good luck this afternoon, Stell,' she said as she picked up her bag. Stella was also involved in the afternoon recording of Getting It On The Prom.

Out in the fresh air and watery sunshine, Fran reflected once more on the untimely demise of Madame Chita, and on her job at Getting It. She felt problems lifting from her shoulders by the minute. Even the Des scenario wasn't bothering her so much, especially as Paul Dyer had shown so much faith in her. Knowing some of the innermost secrets of the company had somehow made her feel that bit more secure. The new kitchen had given her cooking renewed vigour. And even the spectre of presenting programmes with Stella – well, she'd cope with that if it happened. Yes, life was good.

Until the moment that she drove past an *Echo* billboard in Hartford High Street: JOB CUTS AT TV SHOPPING CHANNEL.

Fran almost did a handbrake turn into the nearby car park, didn't bother with getting a parking ticket and rushed round to the newsagent's. Two minutes later she was in her usual Café Rouge corner, ordering a coffee and reading Des's latest bombshell.

Billed as an exclusive story, it was difficult for it to be

anything else as the *Echo* was the only newspaper that covered Hartford. Staff were 'bracing themselves for a round of redundancies that would probably halve the number of jobs at the stricken channel'.

Fran lit a cigarette and pondered about the story some more through the smoke. Her mild elation at being a confidante of Paul Dyer was now right out of the window. How could she not know about this, nor even get a hint of it coming? Was Des's story correct? He'd been spot on in the past with what he'd written about Getting It. Surely her possible new career as a presenter wasn't doomed before it had even started? Had all that swimming, dieting and power-walking around Hartford been for nothing?

She re-read the piece. Was this mischief-making by Kiefer's pushy boyfriend again? It didn't quite add up. But, she had to admit, when Des got a whiff of scandal, he did check it out thoroughly. Pity he didn't apply the same rigorous scrutiny to his underarms.

'Shit,' she uttered, half aloud, remembering her reason for coming into town was to order the curtains. Can't do that now, not with redundancy rearing its ugly head.

She stubbed out her cigarette, put down some coins for the coffee and went back to the car park. The parking warden was just sticking down the last corner of a fixed penalty notice on her windscreen.

'Serves me right,' she said aloud, not even bothering to challenge him. 'It's my punishment for believing for a full ten seconds that my job was safe.'

Walking back into reception, the atmosphere was terrible. Kelly-Marie, in feather boa, tight black top, gold Kylie-inspired hot pants and thigh high shiny boots, was blubbing to her mum on her phone, convinced that her 'TV career' was over. She managed, between racking sobs, to warn Fran that Paul Dyer was coming in to address the staff at 4 p.m.

So it IS true, Fran thought to herself as she walked along the corridor to her office. She tried to ring Bob but he was in a meeting. So she left her desk and went down to the studio to see how Getting It On The Prom was coming along.

She was greeted by Stella, who just rolled her eyes to the heavens and nodded her head in the direction of Steve. 'All going tits up as we predicted,' she whispered. 'Not helped by the *Echo's* little time bomb. Not a good time to rally the troops.'

Despite the hopelessness of the situation, Fran had to stop herself from laughing at Steve who was flapping around like a big girl's blouse. He hadn't done anything remotely approaching the legwork required for the programme, relying as usual on people bailing him out on the day. Now he'd been caught out big time. The afternoon team were just in the mood, given the *Echo* story, not to salvage the mess as they usually did where Steve was concerned.

Kiefer, immaculate as ever in charcoal grey suit and pale yellow silk shirt, was in a foul temper, snarling over the running order, camera angles and so forth. Fortunately, meek Alice just stood there decoratively and did as she was told. With ten minutes to transmission, Steve was still faffing around over his running order.

'For God's sake, fuck off, McGuire,' the director's voice boomed out over the studio floor. 'I'll decide the running order. I seem to have decided just about everything else around here. McGuire, you couldn't run the hundred metres, let alone an hour-long programme.'

Everyone laughed a little too loudly to cover

mutterings about how Steve would be first out of the *Big Brother* house, if only he could find the address in the first place. The director, Dennis, absurdly chuffed that he'd made people laugh, albeit in a rather hysterical manner, warmed to his theme. 'Actually, Steve, there's one race you could run and win hands down.'

'What's that?' Steve wheeled around angrily towards him.

'The sack race!' Everyone started shrieking with exaggerated laughter.

'Cut!' shouted Dennis, bringing everyone to order. 'Eight minutes to transmission and here's the order of play.'

He gestured two fingers to Steve, now red-faced from anger and embarrassment at the back of the gallery, and calmly went through all the products in their correct order.

'Right,' he finally announced, 'that's settled. Now let's see about Getting It On The Prom as opposed to In The Neck. Let's make this another great one, folks. Quiet on the floor. Kiefer and Alice stand by . . . we're coming to you on camera two, right after the titles . . .'

The staff meeting looked rather incongruous being held in the studio among the palm trees, deck chairs and the general Mediterranean atmosphere of the set. The irony hadn't escaped anyone. Here they all were, crammed into a mock holiday set-up, awaiting the news that might send at least half of them on a prolonged 'holiday' – a no-expenses-paid trip direct to the job centre.

There was a ripple of subdued conversation. Several people had just taken out huge mortgages, convinced that their jobs were safe. The cars in the car park had also got a little trendier as people felt confident enough to trade up their motors. There were now so many soft tops that when it rained Kelly-Marie had to send out an email warning people to get their roofs up. The only good thing about the afternoon programme was that they had delivered another faultless show – in spite of Steve. Now it seemed almost too bitter an irony.

Paul Dyer strode purposefully into the studio. To everyone's amazement, he flashed an ear-to-ear smile as the laser eyes scanned the room.

'Everyone here? Almost? Good,' he announced cheerfully.

This doesn't make sense, thought Fran. If this is bad news, he's going to handle it very badly by being so jolly.

'I owe you a huge apology,' he began.

'Get it over with quickly,' shouted one of the engineers from the back. 'Shit and Shovel opens in ten minutes.'

'There are no job cuts, no redundancies.'

'Yeah, right,' mocked the engineer. His mates began supporting him by jeering.

Paul held up his hand for silence. He was still smiling.

'It's not what it seems and I'm afraid you have – albeit briefly – been the victim of a plot. I apologise for the stress that you were put under this afternoon, but I can categorically assure you that the story in the *Hartford Echo* tonight is a complete and utter tissue of lies.'

The whingeing undercurrent abruptly stopped. Everyone moved forward, craning their necks to see and hear every last detail.

'I will repeat myself,' Paul continued. 'The story in the *Echo* is a tissue of lies. And it was planted. Deliberately. By me.'

He paused for the whoosh of reaction around the room. Fran immediately reinstated her curtains and her onscreen career. Tim allowed himself a fantasy weekend in Paris with Stella. Dennis realised he wouldn't have to part with his beloved Mazda MX5 after all.

'Ladies and gentlemen, there has been a mole in this building, a mole who has been passing information to the *Echo*. Now I can't blame the *Echo* for publishing the stories. And up to now, they've been more or less accurate. We've had a bumpy ride, we all know this. But I haven't enjoyed reading about every last detail in the papers the following week, or in some instances the very next day.'

He paused to let that sink in.

'In some respects,' he continued, 'it has bizarrely worked to our advantage. The nationals have picked up on our various mishaps, reported them at length and bumped our viewing figures up to a level the board never ever envisaged. But this is, of course, a mixed blessing. It's all very well being known as the station that specialises in Getting It Wrong. Fortunately, up to now, our sales figures have been climbing—'

'Cut the crap, Paul. What's this about a mole?' Up came the engineer's voice again.

'OK, OK, I'll explain. For a time, with all the knocking publicity, the mole worked to our advantage in that she got us regular headlines.'

There was another gasp around the room at the mention of the word 'she'.

'But,' said Paul, 'we couldn't go on in this manner, knowing that one day this kind of leak wouldn't do us any favours. So yesterday I set a trap, fed some misinformation and; bingo, it appeared in the *Echo*. So, ladies and gentlemen, what you read in the *Echo* is – in two fairly brief words – complete bollocks!'

'Who's the mole?' shouted just about everyone.

Once again Paul put up his hand for silence.

'The mole is no longer digging up the dirt on us. Today's story about job cuts has come true – but only in the fact that she IS the redundancy. The one and only redundancy. She's been sacked and, just like Elvis, she has now left the building. Good riddance,' he paused theatrically, 'to my secretary, Fiona.'

Chapter 29

It looked as though the entire staff from Getting It had squeezed themselves into the local pub, with some of the young accountants already only a few pints short of a barrel. For someone who'd made so little impression, Fiona's demise was certainly enjoying a very alcoholic epitaph.

'The end of an error,' announced Dennis, raising his glass. The toast echoed around the pub, followed by a clanking of glasses and a brief silence as everyone took another huge slug of their drink. 'We should be toasting her with a glass of milk, considering she's such a cow.'

Fran and Stella stood in the quietest corner they could find, clutching gin and tonics and reassuring each other that Paul wouldn't have had time to watch their tape yet. Suddenly they were aware of him standing beside them, wielding a pint of beer.

'Didn't realise she would draw such a crowd,' he shouted to them above the din. 'For someone who said so little, yet blabbed so much, she's inspired quite a turn-out.'

'So why did she do it?' they both suddenly chorused.

'Revenge, because I didn't put her on the fast track to stardom,' he replied. 'She thought she should be the main presenter on Getting It – she even confessed to having planted the porn mag in the hope Tiffany would quit and she would get her chance. And the last straw was when I told her to book you two on to the presenters' course instead of her. By the way, you've passed! Your show tape's great. I'll give you some rehearsals and programme dates tomorrow. Now, if you'll excuse me, I've an announcement to make.'

Fran and Stella stood frozen to the spot. They wanted to hug each other but they were clutching drinks, ciggies and handbags. Instead they grinned ecstatically, speechless at the news.

Paul made his way to the centre of the bar and clapped his hands for attention.

'If you'd like to make your way upstairs, folks, there's a little supper laid on. This is my way of apologising again for the stress that you all went through this afternoon. It was unforgivable of me but, as I hope you now understand, I had to find out for certain.'

A drunken cheer went up as everyone lurched towards the stairs. With their lives, loves, cars and mortgages now reinstated, there was much to celebrate.

'So what happens now?' Stella asked Fran in between hiccups in the taxi on the way home. Having drunk a bottle of wine apiece, they were in no fit state to drive.

'I should imagine that the *Hartford Echo* will be well and truly Getting It in the neck tomorrow,' Fran replied. 'Publishing such a completely inaccurate story will require a major retraction at the very least. I'd like to hope that Des gets it in the neck too. He must be kicking himself for believing Fiona about the job cuts.'

'He's in for a rough ride then,' said Stella.

'Not half. And don't forget, it's not that long ago that Des was trying to pull his drink-drive stunt. But it's not like Des to take a story on face value. I'm surprised he didn't check his facts with the company.'

'Perhaps Des just went ahead. After all, he has written lots of stories about Getting It that were pretty accurate. And up to now, he hasn't been challenged.'

'He'd obviously found Fiona a good, trustworthy source,' Fran replied knowingly. 'He was probably feeling lazy, and you do tend to trust your contacts after a while.'

The taxi dropped Stella off and continued on its journey to Fran's house. She leaned back in her seat, enjoying the luxury of silence after a long and rather dramatic day. She admitted to a pounding headache but allowed herself a small smile. Des had really landed himself in it and it served him right. And what would he make of her news? Former *Echo* reporter turned television presenter!

The retraction in the *Echo* the following day was so small you'd have blinked and missed it. Des was clearly finding it hard to eat his fair share of humble pie. Paul Dyer was incandescent with anger and told Fran in confidence that he was instructing lawyers to press for a proper apology.

'At the very least I owe it to the staff after what I put them through,' he said. 'I've got to make sure they realise how safe their jobs are.' As an afterthought, he added: 'If you want to ring that disgusting Des character and give him a piece of your mind, you have my full permission.'

Hmm, thought Fran, it was tempting. Back in the production office, Steve was having a major flap.

'Got all these, er, kitchen thingies to deal with,' he stammered.

'So deal with them,' Fran replied dismissively.

'All these Useless Plastic Objects,' he pleaded with her. 'I mean, what on earth would I do with a p . . . p . . . potato peeler shaped like the Eiffel Tower?'

'Make chips and hum "La Marseillaise",' she snapped. 'Look, Steve, you're paid the same as me. I'm not sorting out your bloody mess. Sit down and read the instructions like everyone else.' Just the kind of conversation she needed to rev her up for a good row with Des.

She glanced around the office. Steve was now avidly reading the potato peeler leaflet as if his life depended on it, while the rest were engrossed in their computers or on the phone. She dialled the *Echo's* number.

'Fran! Hello, love,' Shirley exclaimed. 'How are you doing?' And before Fran could answer, Shirley continued: 'Des's in big trouble again, don't you know. A shouting match between him and Guy about your shopping station. They could almost be heard in the bakery department of Tesco's. Ever so exciting. Best fun I've had with my clothes on. I think Des's for the chop, don't you?'

'Dunno, Shirley, but he certainly deserves it.'

'Rumour is that he's getting his cards tomorrow morning. He's booked in for a meeting with the suits. Anyway, Fran love, who do you want to speak to?'

'Well, I was going to have a word with Des, but I think maybe I've just changed my mind.'

Fran replaced her phone. No, she didn't want to have anything more to do with vile, slimy Des. He made her flesh creep.

She turned her attention back to the Eiffel Tower spud-peeler. It looked more like an offensive weapon than a kitchen implement. Maybe a kitchen gadget show might be fun. Something she and Stella could do. She glanced across at Steve, who obviously had the attention span of a gnat. He'd already given up on the potato peeler and was looking intently at a website about flights to Guatemala.

'Planning to save the world?' Fran snapped. 'If I'd had the sense to shoot you when we first joined this station, I'd be out of prison by now.'

Then she had an attack of remorse. It wasn't fair to inflict her anger over Des on anyone else. Steve clearly didn't have a clue about shopping. She doubted his credit cards started vibrating every time he entered a shopping mall or felt the force when he walked past Lakeland. So what the hell was he doing on a shopping channel?

She glanced across at a magazine open on his desk.

'I was thinking of d . . . discussing this sort of stuff with Paul,' Steve said almost apologetically. 'I'd v . . . value your opinion.'

Fran picked it up suspiciously and flipped through it. Called *Spy World*, it was a real 'boys and their toys' magazine packed with pseudo spy and surveillance equipment and aimed at wannabe James Bonds. She could imagine Steve hacking into the Kremlin or the Pentagon to find out about Vladimir Putin's online grocery shopping or George W. Bush's favourite knitting patterns.

'It would make a great slot,' Steve announced, confidence bolstered up by the fact that she was showing interest. 'Could be a great r . . . ratings winner.'

'Why would our viewers buy this stuff?'

'Spy on their neighbours, check out a stray p . . . p . . . partner, that sort of thing.'

'Oh, I see. I just hope it's legal. Look, nothing ventured, nothing gained. Why not give it a twirl past Paul? In view of the recent demise of the company spy, he might just be interested in some of this kit himself.'

Chapter 30

The whiff of Lucky Gym was unmistakeable. It hung in the corridors like the stale smell of beer and fags in a pub the morning after the night before. No one needed to ask what was scheduled for the main studio that morning. Piers, in his element and a particularly unattractive yellow singlet, oiled muscles rippling, was setting up treadmills, ski and rowing machines and the ill fated Abdo Fabbo trimmer ready for yet another 'Home Alone' fitness show. This was still one of Getting It's biggest sellers and this time it had fallen to Steve to produce the show, much to his horror.

Rather than hire troublesome models, they'd bribed a small cast of 'extras' from the local gym. They arrived in lurid shades of lycra to form the background, happily pedalling away for no appearance fee whatsoever, just the possible ego trip of being recognised later on in Sainsbury's. Trina and Alex, the two new home fitness presenters, had already sussed Steve's shortcomings and were busily working out their own running order with the director. Meanwhile, Steve hung around like a chicken who'd stumbled into KFC by mistake.

General hubbub and whingeing suddenly fell away as

Kelly-Marie appeared through the studio door. In a neon pink sequinned thong leotard with purple tights and trainers, her blonde curls piled up high with a pink and purple sequinned ribbon, she looked so startling she'd have stopped the traffic in a grand prix.

Piers rushed over to greet her like an A-list celeb, insisting she took up her position on the exercise bike nearest the cameras. Unlike the rest of the planet, she didn't recoil from the heavy waft of Lucky Gym, everyone noted with interest.

'The couple met through their mutual love of lycra,' Trina whispered to Alex. 'Are they an item?'

'Her tits are going to be, judging by the lack of fabric in that leotard,' he replied. 'And another promotional coup for the Wonderbra. We're going to have our work cut out distracting our viewers from them!'

An hour later, out of the production gallery came a stream of smiling faces. Business at the call centre had been massive, largely thanks to Kelly-Marie's rhythmic cleavage. The vendors went off happily for drinks and nibbles, safe in the knowledge that they had a sure-fire winner which would be repeated half a dozen times in the next fortnight. Suddenly one of the PAs arrived, waving a copy of the *Hartford Echo*.

I KNOW WHO THE TV STALKER IS proclaimed the front page. Paul Dyer had got his retraction all right. He was quoted as saying that the previous *Echo* story had actually had ONE grain of truth in it – there had in fact been one sacking, although Fiona was not named. He then very neatly claimed that he'd discovered the identity of the evil stalker who had caused 'deep distress' to some of the station's presenters and that was the person who'd been fired.

Fran and Stella decamped immediately to the canteen to mull over this latest development.

'Paul is soooo clever,' said Stella, tapping the front page with her coffee spoon. 'Anyone reading that will assume that the stalker was rumbled and promptly sacked.'

'And at least Fiona's got her comeuppance,' Fran replied. 'She's hardly going to sue, is she? This is Paul's way of punishing her. And frankly, she deserves it, selling out on us all like that.'

Stella pondered the lipstick imprint she'd left on her coffee cup. 'She was certainly a cow and now she's been made a scapegoat.'

That evening, Fran practically crawled home. She was weary from the stress of the past few days, scared about the first rehearsals and very tired of dieting.

Bob was waiting excitedly for her in the kitchen. He was waving a copy of the *Echo*.

'Yeah, darling, seen it,' she said, giving him a quick peck on the cheek. 'It's been the talk of the studio all day. What with Fiona's departure and the redundancy false alarm the day before yesterday, I'm absolutely knackered.'

'No, not just that,' said Bob, still quivering with excitement. This state was unusual for Bob, who only got seriously agitated if his hammer drill conked out. 'You haven't seen the bit about Madame Chita, have you?'

'What?' Fran banged down the wine glass she'd just picked up.

'I didn't think you'd seen it,' Bob replied triumphantly. He plonked the paper down on the table. There, across the middle pages, was the headline: 'New Mystery Clairvoyant Joins the *Echo*'.

Fran feverishly read the copy. It seemed that another

mystery envelope had arrived at the *Echo* offices with a full week's horoscopes from a 'Madame Fay'. Guy was quoted as saying how shocked he was to receive the envelope, and that first of all, he'd wondered whether Madame Chita had contacted him from 'the other side'.

Fran immediately looked up Guy's home number and dialled.

'Aha,' he announced triumphantly when she'd explained the purpose of the call. 'Thought you'd be on the phone. It's you, isn't it? Madame Fay. Very clever, Fran, very clever indeed.'

'I don't know what you're talking about,' Fran replied.

'Absolutely,' said Guy. 'Very neat, very clever. And rather like arsonists who ring the fire brigade and then hang around to see them deal with the fire, you couldn't resist ringing to see how I'd reacted to your little ruse.'

'No, Guy, simply not true. I'm ringing because I've only just spotted it in the paper.'

'Yeah, well, you must have your little joke. I think it's fantastic, Fran, and just keep those white envelopes coming. It made a great story for us today – and took the spotlight off our slight, er, gaffe over your place. Well done, gotta go, people coming around for dinner. We'll just keep paying you as before.'

He put the phone down before she could utter another word.

'He doesn't believe me,' she said, shaking her head. She picked up her cigarettes and took one out of the box. 'It's so frustrating. He thinks I sent the envelope and that Madame Chita is back in business. Madame Fay, I ask you.'

'What will you do?' Bob asked.

'Oh, at least that's easy. Nothing. Nothing at all. I'm done with all that—'

They were drowned out by the smoke alarm going off. Once they'd recovered from the shock of the piercing sound, they looked around quickly to find the culprit. A pan of croutons that Fran had been frying for a caesar salad had now burned to a cinder.

Fran hastily snatched up the pan while Bob raced out into the hall to stop the alarm. Next thing there was an agonised scream. She raced out into the hallway to find Bob stuck in the most bizarre way. For a second, she couldn't quite fathom what he'd done. Then it dawned on her. He'd forgotten the missing floorboards in the hallway and had slipped down into the hole below. Clearly he'd hurt his ankle, but his leg left above the floorboards was bent awkwardly from where he'd fallen.

She summoned unimaginable strength and somehow hauled him out. Then, catching her breath once more, she dragged him, arms under his shoulders, back into the kitchen.

'I'm not going to say anything,' she puffed as she heaved him to the safety of a kitchen chair.

'No. You don't need to,' he gasped, propping a foot up on another chair. 'I must fix the floorboards. That's what I was starting in the shed tonight.'

Yeah right, thought Fran, pouring two glasses of wine and handing him one of them. 'Lots of famous people never got to finish things,' she said with a slight note of sarcasm. 'Schubert left a symphony unfinished, and that architect, whatsisname – Gaudí, that's it. He never got to grips with Barcelona.'

'Yeah, but they didn't get hurt in the process,' said Bob a touch bitterly. 'I'm sorry, love, I should have done those floorboards ages ago and got on with the sitting room, especially as you've got those curtains coming.'

Fran was just about to open another bottle of wine when she gasped in shock at Bob's propped-up foot. His ankle had swollen to almost double its normal size.

'I shouldn't have given you that wine,' she said. 'We'd better get you up to casualty and get that ankle X-rayed.'

Bob went quite white with shock when he looked at his foot. He could hardly moan or curse, considering it was all his own fault.

Hours later, after X-rays and a long wait, a doctor pronounced Bob's ankle broken and encased it in plaster. He signed Bob off work and gave him a telling off about drinking before hospital visits.

'I don't think I'll be able to get those floorboards done for a while,' said Bob sheepishly as Fran drove them both home from Hartford Hospital.

'Don't worry, love, Schubert and Gaudí had their stuff finished off by somebody else. I daresay we can find a chippy who'll sort out the floors.'

'If you'd still been Madame Chita, you'd have foreseen this,' said Bob, attempting a joke despite being in horrendous pain.

'It's a pity she couldn't have used her mystical powers to get the bloody floorboards fixed in the first place,' was Fran's reply. But in a rush of affection, especially after seeing him wince with pain, she added, 'I still love you though, Builder Bob. Despite the floorboards.'

Next day she found a message on her answering machine from Guy, apologising and grovelling profusely about his accusation the previous night. It seemed that Madame Fay was a hoax dreamed up by an over-imaginative young sports sub after too many pints in the Slug and Lettuce. Apparently a considerable amount of betting had taken place on the sports desk as to whether the *Echo* would print the horoscopes.

'Don't tell Shirley,' Guy begged in his message. By the tone of his voice he was obviously hugely embarrassed by the whole episode and frantically conducting a damage limitation exercise. Fran allowed herself a small grin. Served them all right for walking over Madame Chita's grave.

Chapter 31

D-day finally dawned. The rehearsals had gone reasonably well, despite the fact that both Fran and Stella were convinced they should have slimmed down to stick insect level to look vaguely acceptable on screen. They both studiously avoided talking about the unofficial Getting It website. The flak they were convinced they'd get was just too much to contemplate. Fran even had a nightmare about being pelted with bread rolls in the local Sainsbury's, just like Camilla Parker-Bowles.

They tried hard to concentrate on Sheena's tips. Lots of water, plenty of sleep. They ignored her advice about less red wine. Good for the heart, Stella intoned. Helps you relax, Fran contributed.

Ginette very kindly offered to come in and help them select their outfits. They were required to wear some of the clothes they were including in the show. Ginette winced at some of the seaming, the nylon hems and cheap buttons of the Getting It wardrobe for the more mature, post-disco woman. But with her usual flair, she helped put together some of the pieces and brought along a selection of really dramatic jewellery and scarves to make them look a million times better. That certainly helped their confidence levels.

One thing Fran noticed, to her great relief, was how kind, patient and genuinely helpful all the studio crew were. In contrast, their attitude to Tiffany and Kiefer was much more aggressive. It was always an 'us versus them' scenario.

Stella wondered how the other presenters would react to their forthcoming fashion show. Would they be jealous or bitchy about it? Not one of them had mentioned it, let alone offered congratulations or advice. They were all obviously so insecure that they viewed anyone else in vision as a threat. Piers and Kelly-Marie admitted to Stella one day in the canteen that most of the presenters hadn't spoken to them at all since they'd started making their cameo appearances.

'As if scrubbing a carpet or jiggling your tits up and down on an exercise bike is serious rivalry,' Fran scoffed when Stella told her. 'God help me if I end up as uncharitable as that lot.'

'You won't,' Stella assured her. 'If you do, I promise I'll kick your head in. It's a great leveller, I think you'll find.'

Paul Dyer had been extremely gentle with them. Having persuaded them this far, he wasn't going to let them duck out. The first two shows were to be recorded, so they could afford to make the odd mistake which would be edited out. Nevertheless, in a one-hour show there simply wasn't enough studio time to keep stopping and starting all over again.

'But not for long,' he grinned, wishing them luck in the make-up room. 'In the end, you'll prefer live. It narrows down the choices. You just have to go for it. Focuses the mind.'

Just like Stella's first dramatic appearance, the

recording whooshed by in a kind of nightmare haze. Apart from a couple of stumbles and a moment or two when the running order on their clipboards didn't seem to match what was appearing on the catwalk, they got through it relatively unscathed. A cheer broke out in the gallery and on the studio floor. Even the three models, who'd normally be straight on their mobiles to their agents to bitch about the fee for the next job, showered them with air kisses.

Fran couldn't believe an hour could whizz by so quickly. When Dennis got tape clearance and also double-checked that he could edit out a couple of stumbles, Fran burst into tears. She was immediately horribly embarrassed and then, of course, cried some more. Everyone knew the reason — sheer tension and fear finally being released. Stella, too, looked as if she'd done ten rounds in a prize fight. They couldn't really speak afterwards. In fact, they were so stunned they decided they weren't safe to drive. Stella didn't want to be on her own for the night so they went back to Fran's in a taxi, drank several large gin and tonics and deliberately went to bed early so they wouldn't have to watch the very first showing, scheduled for that night.

Next day being Saturday, they had the sheer relief of not having to face anyone at work. But from around 9.30, just after they'd both tottered downstairs for freshly squeezed orange juice and poached egg but no toast, their mobiles started ringing. One by one, various engineers, buyers and secretaries all rang to offer congratulations. Stella's colleagues at Bypass on Fashion screamed with delight down her mobile, and even Ginette couldn't resist phoning them to offer 'félicitations'.

Fran found herself pathetically grateful that no one from the *Echo* had called, especially Des. The programme was on far too late for Des who would have been ten pints down in some disgusting boozer by then. And she'd resisted the temptation of telling Shirley, knowing it would be all round town and then, of course, all over the *Echo*.

When Tim finally got through to Stella, he told her he'd been pressing the redial button for nearly an hour.

'You were fantastic,' he exclaimed. 'You're a star but then you are Stellar. Ha ha!'

Stella mumbled her thanks. She was already exhausted from this unexpected telephone onslaught.

'Don't forget our date,' said Tim cheekily. 'I know it's too soon but I—'

'Yes.'

'. . . said I'd ask you again and—'

'Yes.'

'. . . I just wondered if you . . . you said yes just then.' Tim had finally caught up with the conversation. 'You mean yes?' He was gobsmacked.

'Yes. Yes means yes, doesn't it?' said Stella, wondering how she'd suddenly agreed to this. A weak, tired, hormonal moment she admitted to herself.

It was difficult to decide who was more stunned, Stella or Tim. But they each consulted their diaries and agreed a dinner date for the following weekend.

'You're not going to mention this at work, are you?' said Stella finally. 'I don't know about you, but I just feel at the moment that it's best kept . . .'

'. . . quiet in case things don't work out,' Tim finished for her. 'Totally understand. It's also none of their bloody business.'

After she'd rung off, Stella found herself gazing at her mobile phone with a ridiculous grin on her face. Fran guessed the reason immediately. They fell into conversation as to what Stella would wear, where they'd go, what to order, how to say goodbye. Snog or peck? It was Born-Again Virgin territory after all these years.

Finally, as Fran loaded her new dishwasher, they got to the subject they'd been avoiding all morning.

'So do we want to do the presenting lark again?' Stella asked. 'And far more importantly, will Paul Dyer want us to carry on after he's seen the sales figures?'

'I'm sure he'll have been on the case all weekend,' Fran pronounced. 'As for whether WE want to do more, I'd rather see what Paul thinks first. And then decide. At the moment it feels like one of those fun retro things – a nightmare at the time but heaps of giggle potential when you look back on it. We'll dine out on this for years to come.'

'I hate to say this,' said Stella, lighting her first cigarette of the day and savouring that wonderful first puff, 'but I think we're going to have to watch ourselves on TV. So that WE can decide too.'

Fran disappeared into the sitting room to look at the Getting It schedule on screen. She came back a couple of minutes later. 'I can offer you a choice of screenings, caller,' she announced in a cinema booking clerk's voice. 'Ten minutes' time or midnight tonight. I suggest we get it over with now. Then if we're utterly riveting, we can be riveted again at midnight.'

They giggled like teenagers, took their coffee and cigarettes into the sitting room and collapsed on the tatty sofas to watch – mostly through their fingers. As soon as they saw themselves, they got hypercritical.

'I'm looking down at my clipboard far too much,' Fran observed, 'and I must get my roots done much nearer to the next recording.'

'I think I'm talking too much,' said Stella. 'In the section on the cropped trousers and tops I'm even boring myself. I've got to learn to shut up.'

'So, Stell, we'll get Paul's verdict on Monday,' said Fran, 'but do WE want to do this again?'

'At the moment it feels like having a never-ending series of operations lined up,' said Stella. 'Do you think we'll ever get used to the stress?'

Fran shook her head. 'Don't think so. Nor the constant dieting.'

'Nor the struggle to look good. The early nights.'

'The lack of a good fry-up.'

'Having to go swimming at the crack of dawn.'

'But we're going to, aren't we?'

'Yes, of course we are.'

There was no agonising wait for the verdict on Monday morning. As they came in through the reception doors, Kelly-Marie announced that Paul Dyer wanted to see them immediately. They marched in unison down to his office, not uttering a word, hearts beating with every step.

The moment they saw Paul they knew they'd passed the test. Fran couldn't believe how relieved she was. She didn't dare look at Stella in case the pair of them got overemotional. Sales had been slow, but overall it was a promising start. The companies' reps had been pleased with the results, particularly in a quiet slot with a great deal of opposition on the other channels.

'So, girls, the concept works!' His eyes danced and flashed. 'Women are happy to buy clothes endorsed by older women. With respect, it helped that we had younger models, but the message got across that you were two fashion-conscious thirty-something women . . .'

Fran and Stella both felt themselves blushing and deliberately didn't look at each other.

'. . . not in the first flush of youth.'

Nearer to the first hot flush of the menopause, Fran thought to herself. Suddenly she was aware of Paul asking about other presenters' reactions. Fortunately Stella was doing the talking. No, she was saying, they hadn't had any major problems with other presenters, other than no reaction at all. And no, they hadn't offered any advice either.

'Bloody typical,' Paul raged. 'Keeping it all to themselves because they think their craft is so special. They don't like newcomers, particularly those who might just be better than they are. Anyway, just to warn you, you'll go through a bit of a pain barrier now that you'll be doing regular presenting.'

Again, Fran and Stella couldn't make eye contact at the words 'regular presenting'.

'You'll get accolades, you'll get abuse. It's a funny old world out there, but basically you'll get a lot of flak to start with. Regular viewers like their regular presenters. New faces are disruptive. It takes a long time to build up that special kind of trust. You might get kinky calls, maybe a flasher or two, someone will follow you home occasionally and you'll get a fair amount of abuse down the phone, in the pub, on the street and in the supermarket.'

Fran thought immediately of her nightmare about Camilla Parker-Bowles and the bread rolls.

'Because you're in people's sitting rooms,' Paul continued, 'you'll find they can be very up front with their opinions. They'll actually be quite rude if it suits them. Take no notice. They're just sad.'

Fran and Stella went away wondering whether to cheer

or to get measured up for body armour. At least their next programme was three weeks away.

Tiffany was coming back. The word went around the studio quicker than email. The gossip was endless. Fran and Stella decamped to their little corner of the canteen to give the matter a thorough airing.

'To be quite frank, I'd rather hoped I'd seen the back of her,' said Fran, sipping a hot chocolate and inspecting her fingernails, wondering whether to try a French Manicure before her next presenting slot. 'She was always so unpredictable and downright difficult. She makes presenters like Alice and Trina seem like a breeze – and us, of course!'

'We're not a breeze, we're more of a hurricane,' said Stella. 'But at least the rest of us are used to coming up with ideas and making suggestions. Working with Tiffany is like being on a rollercoaster where the brakes have just failed. About as ridiculous as booking Keith Floyd into a temperance hotel.'

Chuckling, they slipped outside for a quick cigarette in the summer sunshine.

'Hate the thought of autumn,' said Fran, shivering as she lit up. 'All that rubbish about the season of mists and mellow fruitfulness. Wet leaves, sensible shoes, dark evenings – even the spiders come indoors. And then there's all that pre-Christmas ho ho ho crap.'

She caught the look on Stella's face and instantly regretted saying that.

'It'll be my first Christmas on my own,' Stella muttered to the dusty pavement.

'No it won't, because you'll come over to us, surely,' Fran insisted. 'Bob will be off the crutches and we'll have got the floorboards done by then. And Tim might be in the equation?'

Stella shot her a 'steady on' look. She took a drag on her cigarette and surveyed the studio's main entrance. 'Funny how we were so hell-bent on getting on screen when we walked in here that first time. And of course we didn't have a clue what it involved. The atmosphere was so raw with ambition it was quite scary.'

'How could I forget?' Fran replied, laughing. 'You stepped into the breach, and now we're both at it. But of course the fame thing hasn't hit yet. I wonder what it'll be like the first time we're recognised in the street.'

Stella stubbed out her fag with a kitten-heeled shoe. 'Exactly. Just imagine fans interrupting your meal in a restaurant for an autograph, or going through your dustbins. I hope you and I never end up needing a personal shredder.'

Suddenly a dark blue BMW swung in through the gates and purred slowly past them, finally pulling up outside the entrance. Out swept Tiffany, looking a million dollars in the most amazing – and clearly expensive – suit made out of a random patchwork of denim and tan suede. She was sporting dark glasses and wearing very high-heeled tan suede fringed boots with a huge shoulder bag to match, plus loads of gold jewellery gleaming against her tanned skin. This was NOT a high street purchase.

Tiffany looked across at Fran and Stella, acknowledging them briefly with a small wave of a suede-gloved hand, before disappearing inside.

'Milady,' Stella dropped a mock curtsey once she was out of sight. The pair of them had another good giggle about it all. 'She means business. Just hope Paul's got his flak jacket on. She looked like Annie Oakley in that outfit.'

'Or something off the Deadwood Stage,' said Fran, bursting into song. 'Talking of dead wood, I wonder how Clark Kent's getting on.'

'That damn home surveillance show,' groaned Stella. 'It was a great idea of his, to be fair, but where Steve's concerned he always needs propping up. He just can't read the instructions on the packet. It'll be under researched, appallingly organised and total crap. Except that we'll bail him out as usual because we always do.'

'I have to confess,' said Fran, 'that I've actually caught myself feeling sorry for him lately.'

'Well, I haven't,' said Stella. 'Don't forget, I've got to work with him on this.'

They went back to their separate projects – Fran to begin thinking about putting together a country garden show, and Stella to have a discussion with Steve about the spy show, which now had a title – Come Spy With Me.

The so-called military adviser that Steve had drafted in had had so much surgical work done to his face it was nothing short of a miracle he could see out of it. This, Steve nervously explained, was because the adviser had served with the SAS and had had to change his identity. Why he'd picked the 'Phantom of the Opera' look was anyone's guess.

'So why is Jabba the Hut appearing on a shopping channel then?' asked Dennis of anyone in earshot. He was not a fan of Steve's. 'If he's that low-key, being part of Getting It's hardly the route to a safe house, is it?'

Steve used his newly acquired convenient deafness to help cover up his inadequacies. He was attempting to look busy and creative at his desk. Stella wandered over to see what he was really up to. He was so preoccupied, he wasn't aware of her standing behind him. As well as his usual trick of staring intently at blank pieces of paper, he'd obviously been delving into Adobe Photoshop. There was a cartoon red heart up on his monitor. So maybe a woman in sight? Perhaps he actually had a sex life. That would kill the 'impossible virgin' rumours currently circulating around the studio.

'Sorry to hassle you when you're obviously under so much pressure,' said Stella quietly in his ear. Steve jumped as if struck by lightning, hastily collected up the blank pieces of paper, flushed deep red and quickly flicked his screen. Up came a game of solitaire he hadn't finished. He touched another key. Weekend weather forecast in Kathmandu. What planet was he on?

'Sorry, I can see you're rushed off your feet,' said Stella in a voice so laden with sarcasm it could have brought down the *Titanic*, 'but once the king of clubs has shown up and you've checked out the weekend weather in Nepal, perhaps we could get some sort of structure together for this programme . . . or on second thoughts, don't bother, I'll do it.'

For once, Steve knew when he'd been caught out. He didn't make an excuse or try to cover up. He did his other pathetic little trick, which was to change tack completely.

'Ah Stella, just the person. I've got this little phone t . . . t . . . tap hidden in a clock – really clever. You'd never guess looking at it. Would you mind, er, mugging up on it, playing with it, see how it works. You're b . . . b . . . better at this sort of thing than me.'

In other words, you can't understand the instruction manual, thought Stella. She stopped herself from saying it out loud.

'Why would anyone want to use this?' asked Stella, giving him a piercing look.

'Oh, state security, d . . . d . . . domestic problems, that sort of thing,' Steve replied nervously. It was obvious he hadn't a clue what he was talking about. 'Tell you what,' he continued, 'how about a cup of tea? I'll get it.' And he was off as fast as he could in the direction of the canteen.

Stella sat looking at the tiny clock which had an instruction book the size of *War and Peace*. She cursed Steve aloud. And then she had the most brilliant idea.

Fran took the inevitable call from Des. She'd just got over the doorstep when she heard the phone ring. It was as if he were watching her in the street.

'So the beautiful Tiffany's back,' he rasped in his sixty-a-day voice. Fran ordered herself not to put the phone down. She sank into a kitchen chair, reached for her cigarettes and lit one while she considered her reply.

'Yes, you're absolutely right, and what a triumph of deduction,' she declared. 'Along with all our other regular Getting It viewers, you saw her on screen today. Your powers of analysis are just amazing, Des. Anyway, you weren't ringing to show off. You want something. You always do.'

There was a silence. Des clearly didn't like being mocked. Eventually he spoke, hissing through the gaps in the nicotined fangs that she knew so well.

'This stalker business,' he growled. 'It's not Fiona.'

'Unlike you to come up with any facts,' Fran replied tersely. 'And more importantly, why should I bother to listen to any more of this drivel? You should check your sources, Des. You got it badly wrong before.'

"Look, sweetie, I was set up. By that bitch Fiona.'

'Serves you right for hanging around with pond life,' she retorted. 'You were entirely happy to run all the other

264

stories about the station before. And just because you get it wrong – and big time – don't start chucking your toys out of the pram. Our Baby's Tidy Toys Sack isn't on sale for another couple of weeks. Watch out for the promotions because there'll be lots of fantastic ideas to keep your toddler happy all day long—'

'Oh shut the fuck up,' Des interrupted.

'My sentiments entirely,' replied Fran, slamming down the phone. She went straight upstairs, ignoring the plaster falling off the bathroom walls, and had a long and very therapeutic shower.

Paul Dyer was in full flow. He'd summoned both the buying and the production departments to a think-tank, with a brief that they become more cohesive in sharing problems and in general policy. At least that was how it was billed. Paul had already told Fran that it was aimed at Steve, in order to give him a bit of a wake-up call.

Paul was waxing lyrical about the psychology of shopping. 'Remember, women browse. They want to make up their minds, compare price and quality, think about how their friends will view the purchase before they go for it. With men, it's look, decide, pay. Think of Julius Caesar clapping his eyes on Britain – I came, I saw, I conquered. Veni, vidi, vici, for those of you with some grasp of Latin. In today's world it would be veni, vidi, Visa card.'

A ripple of laughter went around the room. Paul was a charismatic speaker.

'So remember who your audience is for each product and think about it accordingly. Steve, why do you think women go window shopping?'

There was a pregnant pause, all eyes now on Steve. They were not disappointed.

'Er, when they want to b . . . b . . . buy windows?' came the nervous reply. Hands were hastily bitten to stifle the giggles.

'You've spent too long on Planet Krypton,' said Paul tartly. Clearly he'd heard all the jokes. 'It's about time you cut it in the high street. From the lack of consumer knowledge you display here, I wouldn't be surprised if you thought PC World was a policeman. Tell me, what does Monsoon sell? And don't say macs and wellies.'

'Er, I d . . . d . . . don't know.'

'Then perhaps you'd like to tell us why you wanted to work at Getting It.'

The question everyone wanted answered! Steve was beginning to squirm. Fran noticed that a muscle was going frantically in his neck.

'I, er, well, I er, needed a job,' he stammered, 'like the rest of you.'

'Fair enough,' said Paul. 'Bit more like it. Go on.'

'And I, er, well, I thought it would be easier than it is . . .'

'It's time you woke up and smelled the coffee,' said Paul sarcastically. His eyes clearly said, why did I get it so wrong when I hired you?

Fran wondered too. Perhaps she'd ask him one day if there was the right moment to do so. Steve just didn't fit in at all.

Chapter 32

'If you're like me, when you walk into a room you want everyone to notice you. And with this watch, with its gold-coloured bangle and thousands of tiny Austrian-cut diamonds, so many I lost count simply hours ago, you will create an entrance. Every woman in the room will shriek at you: WHERE DID YOU GET THAT WATCH?'

Tiffany was warming to her theme and smiling wantonly at the camera. Everyone in the gallery obliged with a stage-whispered, 'Where did you get that watch?'

'And you will be able to smile, flash your wrist and tell them that you got this totally gorgeous piece for just thirty-five pounds from Getting It. The station that sells jewellery to the stars.'

'Does it?' enquired Dennis, covering the talkback mic with his hand as he quizzed the rest of the production team in the gallery. 'All news to me.'

'And me,' said Fran, 'especially as it's a brand new range, first time on sale. But it sounds very convincing.' She was watching Tiffany's every move, trying to analyse why she did it so well. Being a size eight was certainly a factor, she decided, and also being drop-dead gorgeous.

Back on the studio floor, Tiffany simpered, 'On the

other hand, you might want to buy this beautiful watch for your friends for Christmas, so we'd better keep this incredibly low price a secret just between ourselves. I've got lots of friends who are going to be Getting It this Christmas.'

A huge snigger broke out around the gallery, loud enough to be picked up on talkback. Fran shivered momentarily. How long would it be before their honeymoon period was over and the gallery crew would be sniggering at her and Stella? She was suddenly taking much more interest in how Tiffany approached each product.

'I mean – getting this fabulous watch for Christmas,' Tiffany continued, completely unflustered. She then whipped through the product number and cost one more time and finally turned on her most seductive smile.

'At this price, you can't afford not to have it. So order yours from Getting It. I'm certainly getting it myself.'

'Cut,' said Dennis. 'Roll promo. Brilliant, Tiff. That crappy watch has sold its socks off. The vendor's just gone off to do a victory roll.'

The second the camera was off her, Tiffany's breathtaking smile came down like the final curtain on *The Mousetrap*.

'I am NOT Tiff and this is shite,' she announced to anyone who'd listen. 'This is going to damage my career, not to mention give me a life-threatening nickel allergy. People will start associating me with cheap and tacky jewellery for ever if I'm not careful. Can't we have a programme with some decent stuff from Aspreys or Boodle and Dunthorne?'

'People who shop there wouldn't dream of watching Getting It,' said Fran tartly. She'd come down to the studio floor to start taking all the jewellery away. 'That type of customer won't have heard of "Suddenly Essential, your favourite late-night warehouse clear out". They'll be too busy quaffing Krug and propping up the Met Bar.'

'Quite,' replied Tiffany, sneering.

Dennis jumped into the row. 'Our viewers have probably had a few pints down the local,' he told her. 'They've staggered home late and thought, "If I buy that for the missus, it'll shut her up and get me off the hook." And when she receives her watch, she'll proudly show it off to all her mates when they're out on the razz. And then they'll all want one too. Bingo! Oh, that's probably where they all were. Bingo.'

'Yes, well, I wouldn't put it past them,' snapped Tiffany, nose in the air.

'There's no need to be such a snob,' replied Fran before she could stop herself. 'Just because people lead different lifestyles to you, it doesn't make them inferior.'

Fran braced herself, waiting for another retort. Instead, Tiffany burst into tears. Fran instantly regretted going so far, but she couldn't help herself. A presenter throwing a tantrum because she was being paid mega-bucks to flog a cheap bit of jewellery was beyond Fran's understanding. Would she behave like that if she carried on being a presenter? Of course not, she reminded herself. Stella had promised to kick her head in.

'Let's go get a coffee in the canteen,' she offered, leading the sobbing Tiffany out of the studio.

As they made their way down the corridor, Fran noted that not one person they passed enquired after Tiffany and her obvious distress. Clearly she'd run out of road among the riders in the Tea and Sympathy Stakes.

Fran pointed to a corner table while she fetched two

cappuccinos. Tiffany had calmed sufficiently to dab her eyes with a tissue. Irritatingly, the immaculate mascara remained intact.

'Sorry, I didn't mean to upset you,' said Fran gently, still feeling guilty that she'd reduced the station's number one star presenter to floods of tears. Tiffany indicated through sobs that the problem wasn't her.

'Kiefer being horrible to you again?' Fran tried to guess.

Tiffany shook her head in silence, her blonde hair swaying to and fro.

'You won't have to work with him, certainly not on the current rota.'

Tiffany shook her head again. 'I've got to tell someone,' she finally spluttered.

'So it's not just flogging a few rubbishy watches that's upsetting you then,' said Fran, taking a sip from her polystyrene cup.

'No,' Tiffany sniffed and wiped her nose again. 'It's worse. It's much worse . . .'

Fran was baffled. How could anything in Tiffany's lightweight world be less than fairytale?

'Stalker,' she finally blurted out. 'The stalker's back and it's not Fiona.'

'I think we all know that now,' said Fran gently. 'So who do you think it is?'

'A man.' More sobs from Tiffany.

'Well, that narrows the field a bit,' said Fran, trying to be sympathetic. 'Do you think you know this man?'

'No idea,' said Tiffany, blowing her nose. 'But I've had these letters. You know, newspaper headlines all cut up. He wants to meet, thinks I'm ravishing. Desperate to take me out to dinner. Says he'll write again – and then phone.'

Fran suddenly became stern. 'He could be a nutcase.'

'Not that nutty. Bright enough to find out where I live, or follow me. The letters came through my front door. Hand-delivered.'

'Have you told Paul or anyone in the company?'

'No way. Not after the Fiona palaver in the paper. Not with everyone now thinking I was stalked by a woman. No, it's too, too embarrassing. I'm not going to tell them.'

Stella had just about mastered the art of the digital spy camera. She'd ploughed through the manual, cursing and swearing, and to celebrate her achievement she'd decided to take a break in the canteen. There she spotted Fran and Tiffany in the corner.

'Oh sorry,' she said when she got closer, realising Tiffany was in some distress.

'No, join us,' said Fran, beckoning her to a chair. 'Tiff's got a problem.'

Tiffany visibly winced again at the shortening of her name but decided not to protest. Fran outlined the story of the letters.

'She doesn't want to complain to Paul this time, especially after the fiasco with Fiona,' Fran explained.

'Yeah, can understand that,' Stella nodded. 'Any idea who it is? Someone who might have a grudge or want to upset you? Someone having a joke at your expense?' Just most of the studio, Stella thought to herself. They think you're a monster and that's just for starters.

'Kiefer? Obvious candidate, but perhaps too obvious,' Fran surmised aloud. 'But now you don't work together, surely he can't be jealous any more? I doubt it's him. Piers harbouring a crush? Kelly-Marie wanting your job and a more substantial brush with stardom?'

'I really don't think pedalling away on an exercise bike

271

in a thong leotard and flashing your jacked-up tits to camera constitutes a brush with stardom,' said Tiffany huffily.

Fran and Stella exchanged looks. Tiffany, having been off, evidently hadn't heard that they'd landed their own fashion show. This wasn't the time to tell her.

'Look, Stell,' said Fran, making a statement mainly for Tiffany's benefit, 'it could be anyone really, anyone with or without a motive. Someone we know or someone we don't. But all that matters is that Tiff learns to take no notice and that she feels safe at home.'

Stella suddenly banged her fists on the table, making the froth on the cappuccinos bounce.

'How very stupid of me!' she exclaimed. 'What a twit I am. It's all staring me in the face.'

'What is?' chorused Fran and Tiffany.

'I've got all this stuff at my fingertips. I'm working on the Come Spy With Me show. I'm sure I could persuade one of the companies I'm dealing with to let me borrow some kit, you know, to really get to grips with it in a more realistic situation.'

The other two were agog.

'Brilliant!' pronounced Fran.

'What could you do?' Tiffany asked, slightly miffed at decisions being made all around her without her involvement.

Stella took a sip of coffee and then proceeded to tell them about the various gadgets she was working on. There was everything a would-be Sean Connery would need – including sunglasses with mirrors so you could see if you were being followed and a safe that looked like a discarded Coca-Cola can. She described a home fingerprint kit that helped you check for raiders on your dustbin and a one-button personal alarm so loud that it would perforate the eardrums of just about everyone in your postcode.

'We could rig up a tiny surveillance camera outside your house,' said Stella, 'and watch to see who's delivering the letters.'

'Fantastic,' said Fran, clapping her hands in delight.

Tiffany was not so impressed. Probably, Fran decided, because it was not her idea and she hated anyone being remotely cleverer than her.

'Let's do it tonight,' said Stella. 'I've got the kit in my office. We'll have to get someone to install it. How's Bob's ankle? Is he up to doing this?'

'Well, he's hobbling but he'll do it,' said Fran. 'I'll promise to stop making him watch endless episodes of *House Doctor* if he does. I'll ring him now and we'll come round to your place tonight.'

Tiffany nodded miserably. 'Let's not tell anyone here,' she begged. 'I really don't want anyone else to know.'

'Good idea,' said Stella. 'Just in case it really is some little scroat from this place.'

At eight that evening they set off in Stella's battered old Renault Clio to Tiffany's house which was inevitably in the most expensive part of Hartford. Bob sat across the back seat, leg outstretched and moaning.

'Stop whingeing,' said Fran, laughing at him as they pulled up. 'I know shares sometimes go through the floor but husbands aren't supposed to.'

They phoned Tiffany from Fran's mobile as arranged. Tiffany then answered the front door of her Georgian townhouse, looking effortlessly glamorous in a pale pink and white tracksuit. They were ushered into a very elegant sitting room while Tiffany fetched glasses of dry white wine for the girls and a bottle of Becks for Bob. It was one of those terribly trendy minimalist houses where nothing was out of place – except themselves. A huge nude painting of a woman who looked suspiciously like Tiffany hung over the simple open fireplace. A set of shelves in the corner had only three or four artistically placed frosted glass vases on them. A coffee table – smoked glass balanced on a huge piece of driftwood – boasted a piece of pottery that looked rather like a couple bonking. No ashtrays, books or magazines, and definitely no slippers.

Everyone perched on the edge of their chairs, terrified of spilling their drinks on the cream carpets. Fran and Stella had instinctively asked for white wine rather than their preferred red – just in case. Once she'd served the drinks in the most fragile and enormous glasses Fran had ever seen, Tiffany brought in the letters she'd received over the past week. They were all in different styles, some consisting of newspaper headlines cut up into messages, others clearly written on a computer. All had the same message: Tiffany was a goddess and the writer was totally in love with her and desperate for them to meet.

Fran and Stella read them avidly. It was fascinating to have a ringside seat on how it felt to be famous. They both tried not to appear over-excited by them. Tiffany, meanwhile, was trying to contain her pleasure at the adulation. Bob concentrated on clutching his bottle of beer and trying not to moan.

Eventually they got around to rigging up the camera. It was surprisingly easy, even with Bob hobbling around on his crutches. Within half an hour the camera was installed, giving a fish-eye view of the porch on Tiffany's widescreen television. The camera could be set to take a still frame every few seconds, so that Tiffany could play back the tape to see if she had had any unwanted callers while she was out. Or she could record it on her video in the normal way.

Then, with a perfunctory peck on each cheek from Tiffany, they were all despatched into the night air. As they headed up the path, they heard the bolts shooting across Tiffany's front door.

'Not one of us,' said Fran to the others as they drove home. 'Very cool customer, wasn't she?'

'Yeah, and the house looked just like a photoshoot,' replied Stella. 'I mean, there wasn't even a dog, let alone a dog hair out of place.'

'Do you think she'll perform to the security camera every time she puts a key in the door?'

'Wouldn't surprise me. She'll be putting on lippy when she puts out the milk bottles. That's if she actually does that kind of thing.'

'Probably regards the fridge door as some kind of spotlight. You know, open it and bingo – lights, camera, action.'

'I felt very uncomfortable,' said Bob, butting in. 'But then I feel uncomfortable everywhere at the moment. I can't wait to get this bloody plaster off. Three more weeks to go.'

'I hated that house,' said Fran to Bob once they were home and she was tipping ground coffee into the cafetière. 'Too minimalist for me. You couldn't relax, not for a nanosecond. In all my years of property snooping for the *Echo* I never visited a house so bleak in terms of atmosphere. I think a stalker would probably liven the place up. You never know, he might turn out to be a

275

carpenter and then we could get him to come round here.'
She gave Bob a cheeky glance.

'If he is, we will,' Bob promised, propping up his plastered ankle on a chair. 'I wasn't mad about the place either. Mind you, I envied her floorboards. I'm so very sorry about that, love. I'm surprised you've stuck with me all these years in this mess.'

Bob hung his head in shame. Fran felt her usual rush of love for him.

'Didn't have any choice,' she said kindly. 'At least it was you who fell through the floor, not me. I'd have insisted on a complete recovery by a pool somewhere hot and expensive.'

'Tomorrow we get in a chippy.'

'Promise?'

'Promise. If Tiffany can have a bloody CCTV system installed, the least you can have is floorboards.'

Chapter 33

Stella's date with Tim turned out to be memorable for all the wrong reasons. Any first-date nerves were dispelled as disaster after disaster unfolded throughout the evening. Tim forgot his reading glasses so Stella had to read out the entire menu to him. He'd also unwittingly booked a completely non-smoking restaurant so Stella had to keep nipping out for a cigarette. During the 'between the main course and dessert' cigarette she was caught in a severe gust of wind and rain. She then had to return to the table and explain why one half of her dress was soaked and several dollops of water were now trickling through her hair and down her face. Tim just roared with laughter. So much so that he knocked over a bottle of burgundy which duly crashed to the floor, taking a glass with it. The last straw was when Stella pressed the button to open the window in Tim's car and it duly slid down, made a few ominous clunking noises and stuck fast. So she had to endure a second soaking as the rain poured in through the now permanently open window.

When they reached her flat, Stella found herself offering him some plastic sheeting and gaffer tape to patch up the car window. Standing out in the continuing downpour as they fixed it made them laugh even more. By the time they'd finished they were both soaked. Stella's normally immaculate dark hair, which she'd spent hours teasing into shape, was now plastered to her head, and her mascara was forming black trails down her cheeks. She was actually soaked through to her underwear but she wasn't about to tell Tim that. It was only after she'd invited him in to dry off a bit while she made some coffee that she finally had an attack of first-date nerves. They sat awkwardly at her kitchen table, waiting for the coffee to filter through.

'I'm so sorry about your car,' Stella started to apologise.

'Not your fault,' Tim insisted. 'It could have happened at any time. Just wish it hadn't been tonight. I can't remember a more disastrous evening that I enjoyed so much.'

'Me neither,' Stella replied, not quite meeting his gaze. Would he ask her out again? She hoped so, but she wasn't sure how one was supposed to behave in these circumstances.

'When's your next programme scheduled?' he asked.

'Two weeks' time,' she replied, grateful that they were moving for the first time towards a work-type conversation. 'In fact, tonight's meal was my last proper one for two weeks. It's the life of low-calorie lettuce leaves again until then.'

'That's a bit drastic, isn't it?' said Tim, remembering his beached whale of an ex-wife. 'I mean, you're not remotely fat. Why do you want to lose weight?'

'Oh, all the usual reasons,' Stella shrugged. 'Don't want to let the side down. Fran and I both agreed that although they've asked us to present this show as typical middle-aged women, we don't want to feel like fat and frumpy

278

middle-aged women. So we've got this regime going. We've rather let things slip since the last programme. Just the sheer relief of getting through it, I suppose. But we've got to get back on track.'

Suddenly she had a moment of depression. The evening HAD been fun, despite all the mishaps. And now it was about to end, along with the prospect of not a square meal in sight for the next fortnight.

'So I couldn't persuade you to come out for a meal with me again?' Tim teased her, a mock sad look on his face. Stella tried to contain her delight.

'I guess I could come out,' she replied, 'but I might not be able to eat much.'

'Good,' said Tim with a grin. 'And you never know, the evening might be less eventful.' He drained his coffee cup and got up to go. Stella found herself secretly embarrassed at how desperately she didn't want him to go. Tim gallantly kissed her hand and then disappeared into the night.

Tiffany was throwing a tantrum in Paul Dyer's office. If there'd been any fur handy, it would have been flying.

'I'm getting straight on to my agent,' she announced shrilly, flicking her blonde mane with a diamond-studded hand. 'I was promised star billing at this crummy little outfit, not to come in at God knows what time of the day to record some third-rate tacky little programme.'

'Suddenly Essential is NOT a tacky little programme,' said Paul firmly. 'And there's nothing in your contract that stipulates any such condition. You simply cannot make demands like this.'

'Oh yes I can,' she snapped back. 'I am the face of this station and let's not forget it.' She pointed to the blonde in the shopping trolley on the wall behind Paul's desk.

'Face but not the body,' said Paul, who was not rising to the bait. 'Let me remind you, Tiffany, that the body's Tracey's.'

Tiffany scowled in disgust. 'Not my fault your first presenter didn't cut the mustard. And the fact that it's not my body had better not get out.'

'Get real – the whole station knows. Remember they were nearly all here before you.'

'I'll get my agent to put a clause in my contract then,' she announced. 'Or better still, get him to get me out of this crap altogether.'

Paul sat back in his chair and gave her a long, stern look. 'And while you're on the phone, get him to update your CV. Or better still, delete some of it. Your film career, for a start. I'm not stupid. We didn't hire you for your acting abilities, but your next employer might not be so impressed.'

'Next employer?' Tiffany was now at full volume. 'What are you talking about? I come and go as I please.'

'Not here you don't,' Paul replied, going for the jugular. 'Tiffany, you're a bloody good presenter and a pain in the arse. You know as well as I do that there's no acting work out there for you. You're a pretty girl who can blab on about a pile of saucepans to camera and do it extremely well. But this is not Restoration comedy. It might seem like it at times but I can assure you it's not. So if you have any sense, you'll shut up, put up and turn in the performance of your life tonight.'

Tiffany immediately burst into a series of loud and dramatic sobs. Paul coolly watched her.

'Tears would make your distress a little more authentic,' he said eventually. 'Now bugger off and get on with it.' He indicated the door.

Tiffany got up to leave. 'By the way,' he said as her hand

reached the door handle, 'no more problems with the stalker I trust?'

'No,' she muttered huskily. 'None at all.'

She shut the door just a little too loudly. Silly girl, Paul mused after she'd gone. Why can't people who are good at their job make it easier for those of us who are struggling?

Tiffany, meanwhile, stomped up the corridor in a state of high dudgeon, heading for the production office. She had a job to remember where it was, as she usually swept into the building and straight to make-up. Not wishing to ask anyone and admit her ignorance after all this time, to her great relief she eventually found it.

Inside, she was greeted by a sprawl of desks, computers, paper and half-opened cardboard boxes, together with a distinct waft of stale garlic bread and a smattering of lunchtime pizza delivery boxes. Trying to hide her disgust, she was relieved to find Fran at her desk, hammering away on the computer and trying to last all day on raw carrots and a strawberry smoothie.

'Tiffany! Anything wrong?' Fran looked surprised to see her.

'No. Should there be?' Had Paul Dyer already been on the phone to Fran?

'Just that you don't normally venture up to our scruffy neck of the woods, that's all,' said Fran, taking in Tiffany's rather wan look. 'Tell you what, I'm exhausted with this script. Let's get a coffee.'

Tiffany looked vastly relieved. Once in the canteen, they bought cappuccinos and sat down in a quiet corner for a chat.

'So – is this about the stalker? Have you had another letter?' asked Fran.

'No, no,' Tiffany dismissed her. 'Much worse. I've had a big bust-up with Paul over this late-night warehouse rubbish. I really shouldn't be doing this at all.'

'Oh?'

'I mean, why should I wreck my reputation by flogging all that leftover stuff? I'm a star. I shouldn't have to dirty my hands on cheap trash.'

Fran was amazed that Tiffany could make statements like that in dead earnest. She wondered if that kind of ego came with the job, and whether she should watch out. Having seen Tiffany's immaculate, non-cluttered world, she could appreciate how some of the items would appal her. She'd have to choose her words carefully.

'Well, I guess that makes me a leftover producer,' she said with a half smile. 'Because that's the script I'm working on right now.'

'Oh, poor you,' said Tiffany unsympathetically. 'Or rather, poor me. I'm the mug who's going to have to say all that stuff.'

'I've been working on Suddenly Essential for a while,' Fran said slowly, 'and I always approach it with a touch of comedy. I try to work out ways of linking incongruous items together to give it a sense of fun. Paul's all for it. He thinks it could make cult viewing if we carry on like this. Probably why you're rostered on to present it. You can't blame the station for wanting to use their number one star on a very popular show.'

Strike me down, Fran thought, I almost believe this myself. Not bad for a spur-of-the-moment gush.

Clearly she'd sold it to Tiffany, who nodded wisely.

'Tell you what, give me an hour and I'll show you the draft script,' Fran continued, desperate to keep the upbeat mood going. 'It'll give you a sense of the tone we're looking for.'

Later that afternoon, Fran was still amazed that Tiffany had bought the whole story. She even showed up early on the studio floor to look at the products – almost unheard of – and had taken on board the idea of doing some of it tongue-in-cheek. That way, she wouldn't damage her reputation as a serious presenter, Fran had explained. Viewers wouldn't associate her with the products in quite the same way.

'Let's face it, if you think a plastic dog that barks and lights up outside your home when you have visitors is a must-have, you'll concentrate on saying he's clever and cute,' said Fran. 'The fact that you're not really endorsing it won't matter. If our viewer thinks it's incredibly naff, they'll realise deep down that you think so too. It's just a matter of how you deliver the lines.'

'Well, I am an actress, after all,' Tiffany smiled sweetly, 'films, television, West End.'

'Exactly,' said Fran, privately appalled at the on-going blatant lie. 'It'll be a doddle for you.'

Tiffany swept off to make-up, leaving Fran quivering with nerves about the monster she'd suddenly created. Should she tell Paul Dyer she was putting a new spin on his late-night show or risk their top presenter walking out?

She went back to her office to put the finishing touches to the script. Then she rang Paul's office.

'Gone home,' announced Kelly-Marie after the phone diverted to reception. 'It is half six after all. Don't ask me how to transfer you to his mobile. Haven't a clue.'

Fran sighed. It was going to be a long night.

Two hours later, everyone was ready. Lights, cameras, action.

'Hi there. I'm Tiffany Shire and I'd like to welcome you to Suddenly Essential. Loads of weird and wonderful items are up for grabs tonight. You might find them weird, you may think they're wonderful, but they're not just on offer. They're on SPECIAL offer – and that means dirt cheap.'

Tiffany flashed the smile that clinched her monthly pay cheque. In the gallery, Fran smiled back to the bank of screens – in sheer relief. Tiffany was entering into the spirit of it. She just hoped Paul Dyer wouldn't find it all too larky.

'First up tonight are some more of these wonderful German sausages. All vacuum packed so they're perfectly safe. I can't tell you what they taste like because I'm strictly vegetarian but I'm sure they're absolutely delicious. All the cooking instructions are clearly marked on the back – actually, they're in German and I'm afraid I only did Spanish at school. So can't help you there. In fact, I can't read them very well at all, the print is so small. Which brings me on to our next product – this wonderfully elegant magnifying glass in the shape of Admiral Nelson. Remember, Nelson was blind in one eye so this shows just how good the other one was. Camera three, can you come in close? There, good. If you hold up Horatio here, you can read that print on the sausages so much better. Prices and product codes in just a moment because I'm going to whip through a few more bargains first to give you a little flavour-ette – just like these fab sausages.'

Dennis in the gallery was already helpless with laughter. Even Fran, who'd written the script, was laughing at Tiffany's delivery. She'd really captured the absurdity of all the stuff they had to clear out.

'Now I don't have nasal hair,' Tiffany continued with her million-dollar smile, 'but I know heaps of people who

284

do. Half the staff here for a start but I daren't tell them. No, it's our little secret. So here's a useful gadget to snip away at those stray tendrils. Simple to use, with very sharp cutters – and if you're at all nervous then why not buy the Nelson magnifying glass to give yourself a better trim? We could do you a deal on the two; in fact, if you buy two or more products on tonight's show we'll throw in the postage and packing absolutely free. Oh, and guys, don't forget your ears. Furry lobes are sooooo last season.'

'Tiffany,' whispered Dennis in her earpiece, 'the phones are lighting up at the call centre. It's practically a power surge. Keep going. Brilliant stuff.'

Tiffany then sat down at a coffee table and picked up a brown plastic donkey.

'We have a name for these here at Getting It – UPOs or Useless Plastic Objects.' She covered her mouth with her hand in mock shame. 'Hey, naughty me, giving the game away. All our trade secrets. And talking of secrets, this donkey isn't just a UPO. Camera three, come in tight please. This donkey has a name – he's called a Fag Nag.'

Tiffany then squeezed the donkey's ears and a cigarette popped out from a small hole below its tail.

'Yes, it's the naffest cigarette dispenser I've ever seen. You just load up a packet of fags in the basket on his back, quick squeeze of his ears and ta da! Another cigarette – not from the horse's mouth but from the donkey's, er . . . well, let's not go there. Just think what a riot your dinner parties will be from now on. Prices in a moment. And still in this section of the show, how about this?'

Tiffany indicated two more items on the table in front of her. A do-it-yourself blood pressure monitor complete with cuff and stethoscope, all in a presentation case.

'OK, you smoke too much and you'll be smoking even

more once you've got your fantastic plastic donkey fag dispenser. So maybe it's time to check your blood pressure with this handy kit. No more traipsing to the doctor's to get the boring old lecture on quitting. Check it out yourself.'

She then moved on to a shiny black box on the table.

'So, blood pressure up from all that smoking? Relax, de-stress, put your feet up and let this mystery black box take the strain. It's an automatic card shuffler. It just needs two batteries, put your pack in here and in three seconds, hey presto, they're shuffled. Now we haven't got many of these so you'll have to be quick. I think this is a must-have for any card shark so get on that phone or go online to make your order. First come, first served.'

We've got four thousand of those bloody stupid boxes, thought Fran. Let's hope this shifts them.

Tiffany was now unstoppable. She'd really learned Fran's script and taken on board the humour required. The gallery crew was almost hysterical. The call centre was phoning out for reinforcements to cope with the calls. At this rate the warehouse would be completely empty.

And so it went on; the do-it-yourself back scratcher in the shape of forked lightning, a laundry basket shaped like Widow Twankey with a matching vacuum cover . . .

Fran went to bed that night absolutely stunned at the results. She'd taken a huge gamble but they'd virtually emptied the warehouse.

Chapter 34

There was a massive bouquet of flowers on Fran's desk when she arrived for work the next morning. It was from Paul Dyer, with an ecstatic note to say that last night's figures had broken all records known to man. Or at least TV Man. In other words, they had shifted a mountain of rubbish from the warehouse in two hours flat.

With sheer relief and weary delight, she arranged them hurriedly in a nasty yellow and white vase covered in horrid pink cherubs that had been left over from a previous warehouse clear out. Her next task was to ring Tiffany and tell her the good news. But before she could look up her number, the phone rang. It was Tiffany, sounding troubled.

Fran ignored the ominous tone in her voice and plunged straight into an excited account of the success they'd achieved the previous night. It completely failed to ignite Tiffany, who couldn't even draw on any of her limited acting ability to feign enthusiasm.

'What's wrong?' Fran finally gave in.

'Stalker visited while I was on air,' Tiffany announced. 'Knew exactly where I was – on the bloody telly, of course. So he knew the coast was clear.'

'Did you get him on camera?' Fran asked anxiously.

'Yes and no,' Tiffany finally replied. 'It was raining last night. He had a stripy brolly so I couldn't see his face.'

'Shit,' Fran exclaimed. 'We'll have to wait for a fine night. Trouble is, Tiff . . . any,' she remembered to finish her name, 'people always know when you're not at home when you work on live TV. Believe me, it's not difficult to find out addresses. Even the bloody electoral roll is on the net.'

Tiffany went on to relate that the stalker's latest note was the usual twaddle. 'But it's definitely a man,' she continued nervously. 'He left a message on my answering machine as well.'

Fran perked up at this. 'Fantastic. Sorry, I mean, oh good. What did he say?'

'Difficult to tell,' Tiffany replied. 'He had a thick foreign accent. Just grunted about the note he'd put through the door. I'll bring in the tape when I come in to do "warehouse" tonight.'

'OK. We'll have a listen later on. I once interviewed a voice expert when I worked at the *Echo*. I'll see if I can dig up his contact number again.'

'Thanks, Fran.'

'By the way, did you dial 1471 after you played back the message?'

'Yes. Caller withheld number.'

'Hm, pity.'

Later that evening, Fran, Stella and Tiffany huddled around a small tape recorder, listening to the message again and again. The accent, they decided, was somewhere between Newcastle and Budapest. Clearly someone disguising their voice. The script was hilarious, straight out of Mills and Boon.

'Your mother must have been a thief. She stole the stars and put them into your eyes. I worship you from afar, beautiful goddess . . .'

Fran and Stella didn't dare make eye contact in case they both laughed. Instead they did a lot of meaningful staring into the pattern of frothy milk on their cappuccinos.

'Well, Tiff – any, the system's in place now. It's just a question of holding tight, being sensible about personal safety and sooner or later this twit will let his guard slip,' said Fran as confidently as she could. She was building up to warehouse clear out mode again and desperate to get Tiffany up to the level of the previous night. Tonight's offerings included packs of joke tarot cards that only contained the death card, an amazing new superglue and a doormat you could have customised with a picture of your ex.

Once again Tiffany entered into the spirit of things, much to Fran's relief.

'Ever wanted to peer into the great beyond and sort out your life?' she announced with that winning smile. 'These tarot cards are just the job. Make those life decisions quickly and easily with one quick shuffle. Oh look, the death card.' She turned it over and held it up to camera.

'Maybe it's time to end your marriage. Get into the mood with this fantastic doormat. Just send us a picture of your soon-to-be-ex and we'll print it on the mat. Then you can wipe the floor with him, walk over him rough-shod or just get the mud off your boots. These mats are simply walking out of the warehouse so get dialling now.'

Fran transferred her attention to the screen giving figures from the call centre. Once again, business was going through the roof. Items not even delivered yet were selling out in their lorryloads. But then, nothing at Getting It was ever straightforward.

After the show Fran suggested she follow Tiffany home, an offer Tiffany gratefully accepted. As they drove in convoy through the dark wet streets, Fran began to wonder what would confront them. Pity it was raining again tonight. If the man paid another visit, he'd be concealed by the umbrella once more. They parked on the street right outside Tiffany's house and went inside without a word. No note on the mat. Straight to the sitting room, a quick rewind of the videotape produced nothing. But the small flashing light on her answering machine suddenly made them both draw breath.

'Let's have a drink before we listen,' said Tiffany. Fran noticed her hands were shaking. She disappeared into the kitchen and emerged a minute later with two gin and tonics.

'Don't worry, I've made it a small one as you're driving,' she said. 'Right, let's roll tape.'

A disembodied voice announced that there were three messages. They paused for a few agonising seconds for the playback. The first two sounded like wrong numbers. A woman with a rather unattractive Essex accent leaving two messages for 'Taffy'. One was a lot of fuss about collecting dry cleaning and the other announcing 'Your father's back on the pop'.

Fran shot Tiffany a look as if to assume they were wrong numbers. 'My mother,' Tiffany explained through clenched teeth. Fran realised she had just learned more about Tiffany in the last twenty seconds than she had over the past few months of working with her. Then came message number three. 'Hello gorgeous,' croaked the familiar Geordie

Hungarian accent through a lot of crackling. 'I'm new in town so could you give me directions to your bedroom.'

Both their faces fell. They involuntarily took a sip of gin for comfort.

'At least you didn't get a visit tonight,' Fran tried to console her.

Tiffany sank back into her vast sofa. 'Have you got hold of your voice expert chappie yet?' she whispered.

'No,' said Fran, 'he's on holiday for a month. We'll just have to get these snippets on tape ready for when he gets back. But I'd like to hope we can nail this weirdo well before then.'

She glanced around the immaculate house, such a contrast to her own shabby, moth-eaten sitting room. Yet at that moment she wouldn't have swapped places with Tiffany in a million years. She could imagine Tiffany lying awake upstairs in some sumptuous designer bedroom, waiting for a brick to come through the window, followed by a sinister Hungarian Geordie intruder picking his way through the broken glass. Whereas she'd be cuddled up in bed with Bob, happy in the knowledge that if an intruder chucked a brick through their window he'd probably wake them up to complain there was nothing worth nicking. She drained her glass and made to go.

'Thanks Fran,' said Tiffany, getting up and showing her to the front door. 'Really appreciate all you've done. Sorry if I've been a bit difficult now and again.'

They air-kissed goodbye and as Fran got into her car she could hear Tiffany putting a chain on the door and turning the huge mortise locks she'd had installed.

Neither of them noticed a car parked across the street, hidden by the shadows and the pounding rain.

Chapter 35

Fran dróve home chuckling to herself. Essex mum, drunken father and for Tiffany read Taffy. She wondered what the hell Taffy stood for. Clearly Tiffany had made the decision to reinvent herself down to the very last detail. Fran couldn't wait to tell Stella. They met up next day outside the studio at the first available opportunity.

'This sounds incredibly disloyal,' said Fran, 'but until I'd seen and heard the evidence for myself I'd never quite bought into this stalker story.'

'Ditto,' Stella replied, offering her a cigarette and fishing out her lighter. 'When it first started it was quite aggressive. All that stuff with the magazine was pretty awful for her.'

'I'm almost ashamed to say this,' Fran continued, 'but until now I wondered if this stalker thing was a figment of Tiff's overactive imagination. If Tiff and Kief were writing their own fan mail on the website, it's only a short step away from writing your own stalking letters. After all, these presenter types are such attention junkies.'

'Unlike us!' Stella laughed.

'Very unlike us. They seem to sail through all these programmes day after day. Here we are doing one a month and it feels like one long dental appointment.'

'Trouble is, they're younger. It's so much easier to look good. At our, ahem, age it's bloody hard work.'

'By the way,' said Fran with a grin, 'Tiffany's mother calls her Taffy. I heard it on her answering machine.'

'Taffy? What sort of a name is that?' Stella glanced up at the darkening sky. 'Do you think we should have changed ours – you know, before we started this presenter lark?'

Fran pondered for a moment. 'We could have gone for spoof names, I suppose. Called ourselves Voluptua Honeypot and Magenta Vermillion. But I don't think we'd have kept straight faces.'

'Also,' Stella sensibly pointed out, 'we have enough difficulty remembering our "ages" without adding names to the equation.'

As the heavens broke, they hurried back indoors. As they passed the reception desk they spotted Kelly-Marie looking somewhat reminiscent of a can-can dancer from the Moulin Rouge. She was obviously on the phone to a hopeful suitor. Her transatlantic drawl filled the reception area, along with an overdose of Issy Miyake.

'No, James, sorry, I can't go out tonight . . . no . . . I'm filming another fitness show. No, just sooooo busy. It's a late recording . . . no, I can't make dinner.'

'And no, she probably CAN'T make dinner,' Stella joked when they were out of earshot. 'Or boil an egg, come to that.'

'There's no fitness show tonight,' said Fran. 'Late recording? Perhaps that's code for what she and Piers get up to when they drag themselves away from the gym. Makes me feel very old.'

'And just how old? Thirty-seven? Thirty-nine? Forty-two?' They both laughed.

'Ssssshhhhh!! That's OUR little secret,' Fran continued. 'The "late recording" must be Kelly-Marie's excuse. By the way, have you told Tim your age yet?'

'Er, no.'

'Better do that. Otherwise you'll have to 'fess up when you get to the register office.'

'Oi, steady on,' Stella protested, pretending to clunk Fran with her handbag.

Back at her desk, there was an urgent message for Fran to ring Tiffany at home. Fran knew almost before she dialled what the subject would be. She checked that no one could listen in on the inevitable conversation.

'He came after you'd gone,' Tiffany said in a nervous whisper. 'I found another note on the mat this morning. Same old sloppy rubbish.'

'What about the camera?'

'Sorry, Fran, forgot to switch it back on after you'd gone.'

'Don't worry, that's my fault as well. I should have thought of it after we'd viewed the tape. Are you sure you wouldn't like me to tell Paul about this?'

'No, absolutely not,' said Tiffany. 'It was all too too embarrassing last time when everyone found out about Fiona. I don't want people to think I'm some sort of gay icon.'

'But we know it ISN'T Fiona this time,' Fran replied. 'Unless she can speak deep Geordie Hungarian.'

They hung up. Fran turned her attention to her next programme – the country garden show. A little more upmarket than the norm for Getting It, with a range of beautiful terracotta pots, trugs, brass watering cans, hurricane lamps and so on, to be shot on location.

She was also savouring the calm of the office without

Steve. His first Come Spy With Me show was being recorded that day so there was the delightful contemplation of a flap-free zone in the office all day. Bliss! She pitied Stella having to work with him and Kiefer. Today they were featuring the smaller, more straightforward gizmos. The surveillance camera they'd rigged up at Tiffany's house was due to make its appearance on a later programme.

Stella, meanwhile, was allowing herself a brief rêverie about her evening out with Tim that weekend. While Kiefer and Steve bickered about the running order of the programme, she was delightfully out of it, mentally planning a two-day beauty routine which would help towards the next presenting session. As the swearing started, she was in the blissful world of the face pack and the aromatherapy bath, and wondering whether she could fit in quick manicure, pedicure and cathiodermie facial appointments after work that evening.

So much so that she completely forgot her secret plan.

Fran got home that afternoon to find the house full of timber and a carpenter busily sawing away. As a gesture of solidarity, Fran had agreed NOT to tell the chippy why Bob's leg was in plaster, or the circumstances in which he'd been hired to replace the hall floorboards.

'There's always so much to do when you move into a new place,' said the builder cheerfully, surveying the ten-year nightmare that was Fran and Bob's sitting room. 'Blimey, mate, you've got your work cut out for you here,' he added with unintentional irony. 'Guess you're planning to gut this lot and start again. Kitchen's nice, but the rest is going to be a pull-out job.'

'Er, yes,' Bob replied, trying not to look too boot-faced.

'What rotten luck moving in here with all this work ahead of you and breaking your leg,' the carpenter continued. 'Still, at least it gets YOU off the hook. Brilliant timing, mate.'

Fran fled to the kitchen, trying not to laugh. All this was hitting home with Bob, who looked more downcast by the minute.

By nine o'clock that night Fran had a new hall floor, and she spent the rest of the evening walking up and down on it. She was just thinking of having a quick read of the latest *OK!* magazine before going to bed when the phone rang. She answered, half yawning.

'Fran? It's Tiffany.'

She should have known better. She tried to muster a more positive tone of voice.

'Hi Tiff – any,' she corrected herself. 'What's wrong?'

'He's been again,' announced a distraught Tiffany, 'while I was here.'

'What happened?'

'Tonight's warehouse clear out was cancelled at the last minute,' said Tiffany, breathlessly. 'Power problems in the studio, so they just ran last night's programme again. Nobody will notice, same shit, different day. So I came home early, locked the door and went upstairs to bed. I was reading when I saw the security light go on outside.'

'Then what happened?'

'I hid upstairs for about half an hour and then crept down in the dark,' Tiffany continued. 'There was another of those sloppy notes on the mat, handwritten this time. Not the cut-up newspaper stuff but ordinary writing. Quite stylish, actually, and no spelling mistakes. Good quality paper and ink too. Oh, and I caught him on camera . . .'

Trust Tiffany to leave the most important bit till last. No sense of priority.

'Whaaaaaattt?? What did you see?' Fran was now wide awake and almost dancing with nervous excitement.

'Just a hat,' she replied simply. 'No brolly this time, but he had a bloody hat on so I couldn't see his face. Picture was quite blurred actually. It could have been the milkman for all I know. Mind you, we don't have a milkman here so that probably rules him out.' She laughed, slightly hysterically. 'Oh, and then the phone rang. I didn't answer, of course. I was too terrified. It was him again, leaving the usual sloppy message on my answering machine in that strange voice.'

'Tiff – any,' Fran corrected herself hastily yet again, 'keep your door bolted, put the lights out and go to bed. I'll ring you first thing in the morning to see how you are, and then we'll discuss what to do at work next week. Keep your answering machine on just in case we can collect some more voice samples for my expert. The more the better.'

Unlike the time Stella had found herself in the midst of a personal drama, Fran couldn't bring herself to invite Tiffany over to stay the night – not given the state of the house, emphasised by the chippy's rather brutal comments. She knew there'd be a massive potential for flak if she did. Tiffany was definitely NOT Stella.

'Thanks Fran. I really appreciate what you've done.' Tiffany actually sounded sincere. Or had it been her specialist subject at drama school?

*

Monday morning dawned bright and clear – having rained all weekend, the sun came out to make the pavements glisten.

Stella returned to work in a contented haze. Her evening with Tim had been fun – and disaster-free. They'd gone to a new French restaurant that had opened in the next town on the basis that if they broke any glasses or wrecked the joint they wouldn't bump into anyone they knew. It also had a smoking area. Stella had surprised herself at how relaxed she'd felt. They'd laughed and chatted as though they'd known each other for years.

She'd worn a favourite outfit – a midnight blue pencil skirt with a matching beaded cardigan (one of Bypass's trendier ranges) that slipped on more easily thanks to the current diet regime. Tim had repeatedly told her she looked a million dollars. After coffee at her flat, plans for another evening out and a passionate snogging session on the doorstep, Stella had lain in bed for hours trying to remember if she and Ray had ever had that kind of magic. She couldn't even recall an occasion when he'd noticed what she'd been wearing let alone commented on it. If he had, it was so long ago it had been erased from her mind. Her only current image of the marriage was the solicitor's bill which had dropped on her mat a couple of weeks ago.

Fran, Stella and Tiffany met up in the canteen mid-morning with a tiny tape recorder to play back all the new evidence.

'I dunno,' Stella announced, scratching her head in confusion after hearing the latest message for the umpteenth time. 'It's a really weird accent. He's a nutter, of course.'

'Well, he does seem to fancy me,' Tiffany announced, without making any connection to the previous statement. Neither Fran nor Stella could believe that Tiffany might actually revel in this situation. Just shows that fame and flattery can ride every storm, Fran thought to herself. She couldn't imagine being anything other than terrified by a stalker.

'We've just got to pray for some fine weather,' said Stella, 'so we can get a glimpse of him on camera without that stupid hat.' Without thinking, she added: 'Come on, Fran, get your tarot cards out.'

Fran blushed scarlet, suddenly reminded of the horror that had been Madame Chita. The *Echo* campaign to expose her had long since fizzled out. It had died a swift death after the publication of Madame Chita's obituary.

'Hot in here,' Fran began fanning herself with a paper napkin. 'Maybe this summer's going to be a scorcher. That's my prediction anyway.'

It was another few days before Stella realised what she'd forgotten. She was in the middle of a row with Piers about a James Bond-style studio set-up for Come Spy With Me – black leather sofa, potted palm, art deco lamp and cocktail shaker – when it suddenly dawned on her. Dennis's voice boomed out over the studio floor. 'Ten minutes to air, folks. Let's stop arguing and get on. Running order goes like this: we start with the keyhole camera, go to the Watch Your Back surveillance sunglasses, we linger over the 007 cocktail shaker, then we smooth our way towards the Jaws shark repellent. Now according to my list, we still have the phone tap clock. But I haven't seen it. Piers, get your act together please. All the products should have been on the studio floor an hour ago.'

Phone tap clock, thought Stella to herself. Sounds familiar. What on earth did I do with the phone tap clock? With a rush of memory, she put her hand to her mouth in horror. She'd rigged it up near Steve's desk a couple of weeks ago for a laugh. Her brain began to race. She couldn't bring herself to confess to everyone on the studio floor and in the gallery about what she'd done. Especially not with Steve nearby, doing his best to look efficient while watching his brilliant idea slowly go down the tubes.

'Sorry Piers,' she lied, 'couldn't get our sample to work properly. Didn't want it to go wrong on air. So I'm waiting for another one. It hasn't arrived yet.'

'OK, don't worry, love. We'll skip it,' came Dennis's voice over the studio floor. 'We've got plenty of stuff to fill. Quickly please, everyone. I want to run through the camera positions before we go on air.'

Stella tried to conceal her relief. In the first flush of romance she'd completely forgotten about the clock. Must shape up, she told herself, and get a grip or this will all come tumbling down. She'd whip the clock out of the office after everyone had gone home, wipe the tape and then pretend a new one had arrived by parcel post the next day. She was actually shocked at how underhand she could be.

The next couple of hours were sheer unadulterated hell, with Dennis screaming in the gallery, Kiefer shouting back whenever they went to a promotion break and Steve sweating and stammering. Even Piers, who never complained, got exasperated with it all and his grasp of counting backwards collapsed. As usual, it all boiled down to Steve's incompetence. The top wouldn't budge on the cocktail shaker so Kiefer had to ask his audience to imagine what the 'martini shaken not stirred' tasted like. The keyhole camera refused to work properly and somehow Kiefer got himself tangled up in the fronds of a plastic palm tree when he attempted to demonstrate the surveillance sunglasses. The slight collision mussed up his hair and he completed the remaining half hour looking somewhat reminiscent of Ken Dodd. And not being the most popular chap on the planet, no one bothered to tell him. The tree was saved from collapse by an unusually quick-witted Piers who crawled out of shot along the studio floor and hung on to the base for dear life.

When the Come Spy With Me programme finally finished and they'd checked the recording, Stella left Kiefer, Steve, Dennis and Piers having the mother of all rows on the studio floor. She whipped back to the production office and grabbed the phone tap clock, which had gathered a good layer of dust since it had been sat there. She shoved it in her bag and made for the door. A long soak in the bath and a low-calorie boil-in-the-bag something or other would help her unwind from a pretty terrible day.

Stella's little garden flat had really taken shape since she'd moved in. She opened her front door, flung her coat and bag on to a chair and flopped down on the sofa with a glass of chilled white wine. Then, having relaxed a little, she put her dinner in the oven and started running a scented bath. Perfect. She was just going to put on some soothing Chopin piano music when she remembered the phone tap clock. It turned out to be a clever little gadget, voice activated so no long pauses between conversations. The range was quite small so it didn't pick up general office babble. Stella lay back in her bath, savouring the peace and relaxation as the tape started playing back what it had picked up.

Steve's voice blathered on, making very laboured calls, virtually all work-related. His private life seemed to consist of a bit of phone banking, chasing up his dry cleaning and constantly ringing his mother in Potters Bar to enquire about her angina. All incredibly dreary. Inspecting her toenail polish through the milky scented water, Stella couldn't be bothered to get out and switch off the clock. She might as well hear the rest of Steve's underwhelming life. She lay back for another few precious moments, and felt her eyes start to close. She was just fantasising about a holiday with Tim when a voice made her sit bolt upright in the bath. It couldn't be . . . or could it?

Chapter 36

Stella raced around trying to find her phone. She feverishly dialled Fran's number. The rings became more and more torturous. At last Fran answered.

'Thank God you're there,' Stella plunged in without any preliminary hello. 'The stalker, the Geordie from Hungary. It's Steve.'

'Whaaaaaat??' Fran dropped the phone and had to scrabble around to pick it up again. 'You're kidding? Aren't you? How on earth did you get to that?'

Stella recapped the story. 'I sneaked the phone tap clock home tonight to wipe any sound on it and then take it back as if nothing had happened,' Stella explained. 'To be honest, I wasn't sure I'd read the instructions properly. But it worked all right. It's only supposed to operate within a certain radius, so it just picked up Steve's phone calls. I was playing through all his dreary rubbish when up popped THAT voice.'

Fran couldn't suppress her hysteria any longer. 'What a total twit,' she said, wiping away tears of laughter. 'Hang on a minute though. It might be someone else in the office using Steve's phone. It's perfectly possible. Don't forget there are lots of times when that office is empty –

even in the daytime. Especially if we're all in the studio.'

'Yeah, suppose so,' Stella conceded reluctantly. 'But it does sound like him. We'll have to find another way of proving it. Let's compare notes in the morning. Oh shit . . . my dinner has been in the oven for ages . . .'

The rest of their conversation was drowned out by the kitchen timer going off.

Next day Fran met Stella outside the office before work. Stella thought they would be taking up their usual position outside for a smoke. But Fran kept on walking, beckoning to Stella to keep up with her. Next thing they were heading back to the car park.

'What's all this about?' Stella enquired.

'What car does Steve drive?'

'Just a bog-standard Peugeot, I think,' said Stella. 'There it is.' She pointed to a dark grey one that had seen better days. 'I'm sure that's his car. Why? What are we going to find out from that?'

'Wait and see.'

In fact neither of them had to wait. The evidence was there to behold.

Back in the studio, they rang Paul Dyer and asked to see him urgently. As luck would have it, they were able to see him there and then.

Between them they pieced together the events of the last few weeks, Tiffany's stalker, the messages and the love notes.

'Tiffany doesn't know we've come to you about this, but I'm sure she'll understand when she realises we now have irrefutable evidence.'

'And what is this evidence?' asked Paul with a twinkle in his eye. He was secretly over the moon at the possibility that Steve might have made a complete idiot of himself. He'd castigated himself many times over hiring Steve, putting it all down to a momentary lapse of judgement. He still couldn't reconcile the Steve who'd done a competent, if rather nervous, interview with the man who now drove everyone up the wall with his uselessness. Was this why he had become so distracted?

'We just checked his car in the car park. There's a stripy brolly on the back parcel shelf, together with a hat. That stupid Indiana Jones hat he occasionally wears to work. It could be the hat on the video. We just never made the connection. To be honest, the pictures on the security camera weren't that great.'

'Hmmm,' said Paul, leaning back in his red leather chair and putting his feet up on the desk. 'There's one way to flush him out. Rather like the way I outed Fiona. But this time I'm going to have to rely on the co-operation and trust of a very small number of people. But no one else must know. Here's the plan. Tell me what you think.'

Paul spent five minutes outlining what he had in mind.

'Perfect.' Fran clapped her hands in delight. 'We'll get it set up for tonight. Fancy coming along?'

'Wouldn't miss it for the world.'

Tiffany was surprisingly calm when they told her about the plan. She wasn't even cross that they'd discussed the stalker with Paul without her knowledge or consent. In fact, Fran suspected she was secretly flattered that so much attention was suddenly being lavished on her again. And at least this time the stalker was a definitely a man. That made it respectable.

The only people let in on the plan were Tiffany, Fran, Stella and Paul Dyer, plus Colin, the studio's most experienced cameraman, and his sound recordist, Rod. But only Fran, Stella and Paul knew that their expected quarry was Steve. Everyone else, including Tiffany, assumed they were hoping to catch a mystery visitor who owned a hat, a stripy umbrella and had a propensity to write sloppy love notes.

The rest of the day in the production office was a terrible strain for Fran. She felt she must be appearing incredibly shifty because she couldn't look Steve in the eye for fear of somehow giving the game away. And eventually, when everyone was packing up to go home, she gave him her prepared speech as casually as she could muster.

'Phew, I'm glad I'm not on warehouse clear out tonight,' she proclaimed, trying not to sound like first night at the Hartford Amateur Dramatics. 'They've got so much stuff to get through, there's talk of extending it by an extra hour. Poor old Tiff will be hoarse by the time she's finished.'

She picked up her bag and began putting on her raincoat. 'Anyway, what are you doing tonight? Anything exciting? Don't know why I need to ask you that, Steve, I'm sure you lead a far racier life than me.' She just couldn't resist it.

'Well, er, n . . . n . . . not really.' Steve pushed his glasses back up his nose. He was always taken aback when anyone asked him a personal question. 'Just going to visit my m . . . m . . . mother. She's not very well at the moment.'

'Oh dear,' said Fran, embarrassed that she knew all about the angina. Not to mention the waterworks problem and the lack of a good bus service in Potters Bar that Steve had also discussed on the phone.

They met at Tiffany's house at 9 p.m., a full hour before she would have appeared live on television. Except tonight the station was going to run a repeat. None of the engineers had batted an eyelid when Paul Dyer had quietly announced a last-minute change of plan. It meant the studio shift could rush over to the local pub for a few bevvies before finally heading home at the normal time, partners none the wiser.

'Nice place you've got here,' remarked Paul Dyer as they all sipped gin and tonics in Tiffany's immaculate sitting room. She was busily distributing tiny plates of sushi to everyone. So that's how to stay permanently slim, Fran noted.

'That'll keep the wolf from the door,' joked Colin. Everyone laughed nervously and took another gulp of gin.

Paul went on to outline the plan. He would keep watch in his car just a few yards down the street from Tiffany's front door. He'd be able to sit there in virtual darkness because a tree, overhanging from a front garden, very conveniently cut out the street light. From that position, he had an unobscured view of her pathway and front door. Stella would keep watch from a small bathroom window upstairs in Tiffany's house. From there she had a good vantage point to see the pathway and most of the street. Colin and Rod would hide in their people carrier parked outside. They'd all decided to put their mobiles on vibrate, just in case the mystery visitor heard a ringtone and was frightened off. They would all be ready to roll at the receipt of the text message 'Go go go' which Paul had already punched in.

At 9.30 p.m. they went out and rehearsed their positions. Throughout all of this, Tiffany and Fran would be in the sitting room, curtains and blinds drawn, watching the events on the front doorstep via the security camera.

Colin drew Fran aside. 'No one seems to be worried about possible violence,' he whispered. 'Is this just to allay fears, or do I get the impression that we might somehow know this gentleman?'

'Hmmm, I'll text you a few clues when we're in position,' Fran whispered.

Finally, convinced that the light from Tiffany's television screen couldn't be seen through the curtains, they all wished each other luck and took up their positions.

The waiting was interminable. For the first half hour they were all buoyed up with the excitement of the mission. But by ten to eleven Tiffany, who obviously suffered from a low boredom threshold, began flipping through a pile of glossy magazines by the light of the TV screen, in between moaning about her career. Fran, more used to hanging around outside courtrooms and council offices in her days on the *Echo*, couldn't take her eyes off the TV, even though it showed only an empty doorstep. Stella, positioned by the bathroom window, began to regret volunteering to be upstairs lookout. She was beginning to get a crick in her neck.

Only Colin and Rod were quietly chuckling in the people carrier. They'd read Fran's text message: 'For crazed stalker read Steve McGuire.'

'Didn't know he had it in him,' Colin whispered to Rod. 'I do hope he enjoys our little surprise.'

'Couldn't happen to a nicer bloke,' Rod replied sarcastically.

Eleven o'clock came and went. It started to rain, sending torrents of water down the gutters. Tiffany's leafy avenue was incredibly quiet. Apart from an occasional car whooshing past and sending up showers of water in its wake not even a late night dog-walker had ventured out. Eleven-fifteen, and not a single pub goer returning from a cheery night down the local. Eleven-thirty, and Fran began to regret telling Steve that the warehouse clear out was probably going to overrun. He still had at least another half hour if he was going to pay a visit. They'd all agreed that midnight was the cut-off. By ten past twelve Tiffany would have returned home from work anyway if the programme had been live.

Fran was suddenly racked with doubt. Maybe they'd actually got this horribly wrong. Maybe the Hungarian Geordie wasn't Steve but someone who'd just used his phone several times. Loads of people owned stripy umbrellas, just about every garage sold them. Maybe Steve actually WAS visiting his mum in Potters Bar. And what would Paul Dyer have to say if he'd wasted an evening as a result of their foolish theories? At least it was taking her mind off tomorrow's fashion show recording.

Another ten minutes dragged by. Stella was almost nodding off, leaning against the bathroom window. Even Rod and Colin, initially buoyed up at the thought of humiliating Steve, were getting cramp from sitting crouched down for so long. Tiffany was whingeing on about her beauty routine, the importance of sleep for a flawless complexion, and talking about going to bed and leaving them all to it. Fran remembered Sheena Masters's advice about lots of sleep and wondered how she'd look on screen tomorrow. A mess, she decided. But at least this was distracting. She'd have only gone to bed a complete bag of nerves and unable to sleep anyway.

Then it happened. A car drew up some thirty yards down the street. Car door quietly locked. Footsteps, faint at first, but coming their way. Although she couldn't see the car, somehow Stella instinctively knew that this was it.

'Footsteps approaching,' she whispered urgently down the stairs to Fran and Tiffany. As she sent Paul and Colin a text message to that effect, she could feel the hackles on her back rising. God, this was exciting. She went back to the window, straining her eyes to get that first glimpse of the person walking towards them.

The rain was now sheeting down, bouncing off pavements and windows and muffling the sound of the footsteps. Paul, hidden by darkness across the road, caught his first sight of the lone walker in one of the wing mirrors he'd already angled towards the pavement opposite. Concealed by the golfing umbrella, the man's pace was firm and purposeful. But weren't those trousers just a tiny bit naff? Confident of his prey, Paul fired his 'go go go' text message to the crew.

Upstairs, Stella could now see the umbrella. Colin and Rod, now confident that the stalker wasn't approaching from their corner, were able to slip silently out of the car, sheltering under the enormous boot lid to assemble their gear. Once loaded, they put up the hoods of their jackets to stave off the pounding rain. Then they gave each other a thumbs-up and pulled down the boot lid as quietly as they could. The rain was so loud that it drowned out the sound of the catch anyway.

They silently walked to the corner of the street to the vantage point they'd already agreed, camera now rolling. Fran took up her position on the other side of the front door, heart beating like a drum. Stella was now craning her neck to get a proper view of the pathway. Paul was ready to cross the road from his car at the given moment.

The walker got nearer and nearer. Only ten yards to go. His pace was still even and confident. Five yards, almost there. Still no glimpse of his face as the umbrella was pulled down to shield him from the torrential rain. Three yards now. Would he turn into Tiffany's path or would he carry on and probably bump slap bang into Colin and Rod waiting at the corner? Now he was level. Everyone held their breath, almost willing him to make that ninety degree turn into Tiffany's pathway. For a second Paul and Stella, who had the best views, thought he was going to carry on past, but no, he paused. That one second was agonising.

He made the turn, walked through the gate and up the path.

Paul slipped silently from his car, glad of the noise of the rain to cover his car door closing. Colin and Rod appeared around the corner. By the time the stranger was putting his foot on the doorstep, Colin and Rod were through the gate, camera and mic pointing in his direction, with Paul right behind them.

Tiffany's security light came on as usual. Then Colin flicked on his camera lamp. But the man, hidden from view behind the umbrella, didn't register the second light behind him. He was bent over, intent on pushing an envelope through the letterbox.

Upstairs, Stella was hanging out of the window, oblivious to the rain soaking her hair. Fran, just inside the front door and seeing the envelope coming through the letterbox, was shaking with fright as she picked it up off the mat.

Tiffany, with the best seat in the house, sat terrified on the edge of her sofa as she watched the whole scenario on her widescreen TV.

'Good evening.' Paul's voice came out loud and clear. The man wheeled round in shock and blinked at the camera like a rabbit caught in car headlights. He was too stunned to utter a word.

Paul's voice boomed out on the night air. 'And what do you think you're doing?'

Chapter 37

It took Steve a full five seconds to clock that he was being filmed. And other ten to realise that it was the voice of Paul Dyer firing the questions from the darkness behind the camera.

'I repeat,' came the unemotional voice, 'what do you think you're doing?'

'Well, I, er, don't think it's any of your business.' Steve laughed nervously. There was no smile on his face, only complete shock. 'And what are these people doing here?'

He indicated Colin and Rod as though they'd dropped in from Mars.

'You work with them. They're filming you.' It was almost an unnecessary remark. 'You're caught on camera, both outside and in.'

Steve looked completely stunned. 'OK, g . . . g . . . guys, I'm sure this is some kind of j . . . j . . . joke but,' he paused nervously to look at his watch, 'time's getting on.'

He tried to push past the cameras towards the gate without success. Paul blocked his way.

'As I said, you're on camera not just here but inside the house as well. Thanks to a surveillance system we've had installed. Thanks to Getting It!'

Steve turned back to the front door. Now it was open and Fran took a step forward. He was so startled at seeing her that she thought he was going to have a heart attack.

'That's right, Steve,' she said, beckoning him to take a look. 'There's a tiny camera up here watching the porch and we can view it on wonderful widescreen television in the sitting room. Come on in.'

Like a lamb to the slaughter, Steve followed her dumbly inside, his mouth still gaping in surprise. Standing in the middle of the sitting room was a very white-faced Tiffany.

'So it was you,' was all she could mutter to the soft cream carpet. She couldn't make any eye contact with him.

Fran brushed past the crew and handed her a letter.

'Found this on the mat, Tiffany,' she announced. 'Why don't you read it out?'

Tiffany glanced at the note, burst into tears and threw it on the floor. She flounced out of the room and upstairs.

'How . . . how . . . did you know it was me?' Steve managed to stammer, taking off his glasses to briefly rub his eyes.

'Well, you can thank Stella and Fran really,' said Paul firmly. As if Steve were really going to thank them, thought Fran.

'And it was also due in part to your very own show, Come Spy With Me,' Paul continued with a smile. 'That was such a great idea of yours. The tiny surveillance camera in the hall – that's one of your products. And thanks to the phone tap clock – another of your suggestions – we were able to pick up some of your phone messages to Tiffany. I must say that mid-European with a touch of Tyneside accent is very impressive.'

Fran, who had now calmed down from all the drama, had to look away to avert a sudden desire to giggle.

'Now take a seat, Steve, because we're going to give you a film show. Video in, Fran? Good. Let's roll tape.'

With the exception of Tiffany who was still snivelling upstairs, everyone crowded round to watch the huge silver television.

'Here you are a few days ago.' Paul was now giving commentary as he spooled through the tape to the relevant bits. 'Another rainy night, so that big umbrella's really useful. Pity we couldn't see your face. And here you are again, hat on this time. That looks like your Indiana Jones leather one, I think. Pity the picture quality's a bit poor. Oh, and here you are tonight . . .'

Steve had gone puce with embarrassment.

'Let's all have a drink and talk about it, shall we?' Paul said firmly. Fran went upstairs to fetch Tiffany. They all felt it was unfair to raid her drinks fridge without her say so. Fran was also terrified of breaking her expensive glasses.

A red-eyed Tiffany duly appeared and sat down without a word in the sitting room.

Fran handed round gin and tonics but pointedly didn't offer one to Steve.

'So why did you do it, Steve?' Paul questioned. 'We're all waiting to know and I think Tiffany's entitled to an explanation.'

All eyes bored into Steve.

'Well, I, er, don't know w . . . w . . . what to say,' was all he could offer.

'Not good enough,' replied Paul. There was a cutting edge to his voice. 'Answers please. You have abused the privacy of another member of my staff and caused her undue distress. This is NOT the time to decline to comment.'

Steve hung his head in shame. A nervous twitch was going in his neck.

'Steve, let's put it another way. Writing anonymous letters and leaving spooky messages constitutes harassment in my book. And probably the police's too. So talk, sunshine.'

'Sorry, I'm so sorry,' Steve muttered to his white sports socks and tasselled loafers. 'I'm just . . . I've always . . . I tried to . . . I'm just besotted with her. I've just w . . . w . . . worshipped her ever since I first saw her.'

He broke down in noisy sobs. Fran and Stella looked away, horribly embarrassed. Tiffany and Paul just stared coldly at him. Colin and Rod cheerfully kept rolling tape, having decided that it would either come in handy as police evidence or make a great contribution to Getting It's first Christmas outtakes tape.

Paul continued: 'So why this ridiculous campaign, these silly voices and notes? Why didn't you just ask her out like any normal bloke?'

'I didn't think she'd have me. She's a goddess, up on a p . . . p . . . pedestal. Why should she be interested in me?' Steve wiped his eyes.

'I must say I think you'd have had more luck going down the more conventional route of inviting her out for a drink. Call me old-fashioned but—'

'Are you going to c . . . c . . . call the police?'

There was silence around the room. Paul paused, considering his reply as Steve squirmed.

'No, I'm not. Unless Tiffany wants to press charges.'

Tiffany shook her head, transfixed by the carpet. She still couldn't look at Steve.

'So,' Paul continued, 'I suggest we all have a good strong coffee, if Tiffany doesn't mind. It has been a long night. And then I think we should all go home. You,' he indicated Steve with a nod of his head, 'are not in a fit state to drive so I will drop you off at your house myself. And then I suggest that we all keep this sad and sorry episode to ourselves until it's dealt with appropriately.'

Everyone nodded in agreement, except Steve who looked terrified.

'I'm sorry,' Steve repeated, 'so sorry. I never meant to hurt Tiffany. I just . . . can't help . . . how I feel about her.'

Paul insisted that Fran and Stella have a lie-in so they'd feel fresher for their fashion show recording in the afternoon. They both arrived at the studios at eleven, where they were immediately summoned to Paul's office.

'Aha, Miss Marple and Jessica Fletcher, my favourite super-sleuths,' he grinned as they came through the door. 'Grab a chair and I'll update you.'

They both sat down expectantly. They were not disappointed.

'Now here's the scenario,' Paul beamed, laser eyes flashing. 'I've had a full and frank chat with our friend Steve this morning. I've signed him off sick for two weeks, although with his particular brand of sickness I suspect it will need a lifetime's recovery. I've told him to come back in a fortnight, get his head down and concentrate for a change. If he puts as much energy into his work as he did into his Tiffany campaign, he'll start doing much better than he currently is. And I've come up with a punishment that he – and we – will remember for a long time to come.'

Stella had a fleeting image of a naked Steve in the stocks in reception with Kelly-Marie in bondage gear chucking wet sponges at him. She had to gaze hard at her newly manicured nails to stop herself laughing.

Paul patted a box in front of him. 'I've just viewed the

tape that Colin and Rod shot last night,' he said, 'and it's fantastic. Then of course we've got the footage from the surveillance camera itself which is perfectly good enough for transmission. It really does demonstrate how effective it is. It's not often I'd say CCTV footage could be classed as entertainment! So what does that add up to?'

Fran and Stella looked blankly at him.

'Sales, that's what!' he announced.

They both looked at each other in amazement.

'We'd never get a better sequence even if we hired top Hollywood actors. This is dynamite – much better quality than all those awful American 'snoop on your partner'-type videos. So I've told Steve that we're going to use it as part of the Come Spy With Me sales pitch.'

'Bet he didn't like that much,' said Fran.

'You bet right. He hated the idea but he doesn't get any say in anything just now. That's the price he's going to pay. He's lucky he hasn't been sacked.'

'What about Tiffany?' asked Stella. 'She won't want to be part of that.'

'No, she won't,' said Paul. 'We won't say where it was filmed and anyway, because it's dark and it's raining, you'd be hard-pushed to identify the street, let alone the house. She doesn't really feature in the confrontation anyway so it will be easy to edit her out.'

The women both laughed. 'That'll be a first for our Tiff,' Fran remarked. 'Not wanting to appear! Normally she'd go ballistic at the thought of being cut out of anything.'

Paul poured them a coffee each from the cafetière on his desk and continued: 'I have promised Tiffany that she will not have to work with Steve again. I've also told Steve to apologise to her. In the conventional way, by signed letter. Not via anonymous notes and silly voice messages.

Sad git that he is, I expect he'll derive some pleasure out of that.'

'"I'm just besotted with her,"' Stella mimicked Steve's outburst the previous night. '"I've just w . . . w . . . worshipped her ever since I first saw her."'

They all laughed.

'Well, I must say it's the best fun I've had in ages.' Paul concluded their meeting. 'I made a big mistake hiring Steve; I thought he'd bring a different personality to the mix. If he doesn't shape up after this, he'll be out. Anyway, well done again, girls, and remember, our lips are sealed. Now good luck with your show this afternoon. Let's have another ratings-buster.'

By lunchtime, word had got round that Steve was off sick. Instead of being concerned or even suspicious, most people seemed openly pleased.

Fran found herself feeling slightly sorry for him when she heard some of the crueller comments. She wondered what he was going through right now. Being off work for a nerd like Steve would probably be torturous, especially as he couldn't secretly drool over Tiffany on a regular basis. He didn't seem to lead any sort of life at all other than visiting his mum. Stalking Tiffany had probably been a high point.

Before they went into make-up, Fran and Stella received a brief email from Paul indicating that Tiffany had agreed to the use of the film in Come Spy With Me, providing it didn't give away the location or her involvement.

'I must say,' Stella remarked to Fran as Elle, the make-up artist, began her miracle work, 'the last couple of days have been so eventful they've taken away some of my nerves.'

Fran widened her eyes in warning to Stella. Elle, though good at her job, was generally regarded as a notorious gossip. There were no richer pickings than in make-up, where people offloaded all sorts of emotions as they psyched up to go out in front of the cameras.

'I hear Clark Kent's off sick,' said Elle, clearly wondering if this was something to do with the 'eventful days' Stella had mentioned. 'Superman isn't supposed to be ill.'

'Oh, just a bit of stress, I expect,' said Fran, trying to sound vague. 'I think his mum's ill or something. Or maybe it's over-exposure to kryptonite.'

To their slight surprise, Stella and Fran found their second programme much harder than the first. There were three false starts before they really got going. Two were technical but one of them was Stella's fault. To her huge embarrassment, she blanked on her own name.

Sheena Masters's words came floating back. You can so easily forget the things you take for granted, she'd warned them. Dennis and the gallery crew were very kind but Stella and Fran knew it wasn't going as well as the first time.

Afterwards, rather deflated, they went out to dinner to try to piece together what had gone wrong – before they had their post-mortem from Paul Dyer the next day.

'For a start, we didn't have Ginette on hand,' said Stella. 'Pity she's away on holiday. I'm sure she'll help us out next time.'

'If there is a next time,' Fran replied grimly. 'I must say I felt uncomfortable in the clothes. Ginette made me feel much more confident about how I looked. I really felt like a bag lady today and I'm sure it showed on screen.'

'Also, last night's scenario with Steve probably didn't help our concentration,' said Stella. 'But you're right, this pressure to look good is a bloody nightmare. I've always been a huge fan of Trinny and Susannah but they're right up there in my estimation now. I mean, they HAVE to look good all the time. They're at the top of the fashion guru premiership. We've just been signed up to Division Three.'

'Anyway,' said Fran, 'our next bash is another month away. Let's enjoy some decent nosh for once.'

Fran had only just got through her front door when the phone rang. Please don't let it be Des or Tiffany again, she prayed. But it was Stella, breathless with what sounded like a mixture of excitement and panic.

'Guess what?' she said.

'I dunno, give me a clue,' Fran replied.

'No, go on, guess.'

'Oh hell, Stell, I dunno. I've had enough excitement for one day.'

There was a pause. She could hear the click of Stella's lighter. '*Handbagged*. I've won.'

'*Handbagged*?'

'The competition. There was a message on my machine. I've won the first prize – five grand plus a star-studded celebrity night out. And you HAVE to come out on it with me. I promised you, remember?'

Fran's head was spinning. With all the drama at work she'd completely forgotten about *Handbagged* magazine. They rarely mentioned Ray, let alone the runaway redhead. The talk was all of Tim these days.

'Strewth, Stell, this is amazing,' Fran said, recovering some composure. 'Mind you, I don't suppose Ray and

Ginge will like it much. Does that bother you?'

'Nope,' said Stella, who sounded very hyped up. 'I put up with years of shit from Ray. It's pay-back time. You and I are going to have the most amazing evening.'

'Now hang on a minute,' Fran warned, trying to think on her feet. 'There's Tim to consider. If he means as much to you as I think he is beginning to then you ought to talk to him first. He's a producer, remember, not one of our publicity-junkie presenters. He might not approve of it.'

'OK, you're right,' said Stella, obviously a bit deflated. 'I'll talk to him.'

'And then there's our new-found fame to think about. We might be no spring chickens but we're appearing on the box. Paul Dyer might not like it either.'

'I hadn't thought of that,' said Stella, now sounding disappointed. 'I just played the message and then phoned you. I'll have to think this through.'

Next morning, Fran and Stella had a quick huddle in the canteen before the meeting with Paul Dyer. Both admitted they hadn't slept a wink the previous night. A combination of too much food and far too much on their minds.

In the post that morning Stella had received a letter from *Handbagged* outlining the details of her prize. Stretch limo at their disposal in London, a night at a five-star hotel, one thousand pounds to spend on an outfit (which Stella insisted they share), plus a night out at a film première at the Leicester Square Odeon, followed by cocktails with the stars. The downside, of course, was that *Handbagged* would be running a feature on Stella, the photographs and the story about how she came to take them.

They downed their coffee and headed for Paul's office, hearts thumping in anticipation of his verdict.

'You both looked like you've been run over,' he said cheerfully. 'The second programme is always the worst.'

They both looked at him, puzzled.

'It's a bit like second night at the theatre,' Paul explained. 'First night, everyone's geared up, nervous, focused, they've rehearsed the play into the ground. Critics are out there sharpening their knives. Second night, after great reviews, everyone thinks they've cracked it and that's when things go wrong. That's why I suggested at least two programmes should be recorded. Just to let you earn your spurs.'

They both heaved a sigh of relief. He didn't seem the least bit bothered.

'In fact,' he continued, amused by the glum faces, 'I'm getting good reports from the gallery about how willing and anxious you both are to listen and learn. But, more importantly, we did good business last night and the orders are still coming in. And that's ultimately what counts. This isn't Shakespeare, it's all about shifting stock.' He paused to tap his keyboard. Up came a complicated spreadsheet on his screen. 'Yup, selling well, and I'm going to compound your obvious misery by repeating this show a couple more times than scheduled. Oh, and talking of misery, don't look at that bloody Getting It website. You really don't want to know the rubbish they're putting on there.'

Fran and Stella both winced. 'We made a policy decision a while ago to give it the finger,' said Stella valiantly.

'Very sensible. Oh, and one other thing,' Paul continued. 'I've been talking to our PR company and they think they could place some features in women's magazines about you two on the basis of two late thirty-somethings

323

getting their TV break. You know the sort of thing, it's never too late, blah blah . . . What's wrong?'

Fran looked at Stella for confirmation. 'I think we'd better tell him,' she finally announced. Stella nodded her agreement.

Fran took a deep breath. 'Paul, we have a confession to make. We both told a bit of a porkie to get our original jobs. Trouble is, we never thought you'd give us this kind of break. And now it's coming back to haunt us.'

'Oh, and what's that?' It was Paul's turn to look worried.

'We're not thirty-somethings. We're actually forty-somethings. We were forty-two and forty-one when we joined. And now you can add another six months at least on to that. We just thought we'd never get interviews if we put down our true ages.'

To their relief, Paul roared with laughter. Up came the Doc Martens as he sat back in his chair.

'You're probably right,' he exclaimed, 'which just shows what a dickhead I am and how ridiculously ageist this business is where women are concerned. I reckon that makes the feature idea even better. Because you are even more fabulous forty-somethings, you'll have even wider appeal.'

'We don't actually want to be any wider,' Stella managed to joke out of sheer relief. 'But we hope to appeal. Actually, now you mention magazines, there's something else I have to tell you. And you may not like it.'

Paul looked at them both, intrigued. They were amazing value for money, these two. Stella quietly outlined the events leading up to her competition win. 'I entered the competition months ago when things were very different,' she finished, staring intently at her empty coffee cup, her cheeks flushed with embarrassment. 'Obviously the prize is tempting but the situation's changed and I'm not sure you'd approve of me and Fran doing it, especially if it involves a lot of publicity.'

'But it's brilliant,' Paul announced. 'I bet our PR company will think you two are heaven-sent. After all the other publicity this station has gone through, a bit of real life revenge won't matter at all. Anyway, you're both stars now. Go off and enjoy it and mention Getting It as often as you like.'

Stella and Fran left Paul's office completely stunned. No dressing down over the programme, no problem over their ages, and now the green light to accept the *Handbagged* night out. Only one more hurdle. Stella wanted to discuss it quietly with Tim over lunch.

To her relief, not only was he delighted that she'd won the prize, he quickly cashed in on her relief by persuading her to go to Paris with him for a weekend treat.

Steve's fortnight off whizzed by, much to the annoyance of everyone in the production office. They were just getting used to the nerd-free zone.

'I hope whatever he's got lingers on a bit,' said Adrienne as she idly flipped through the latest copy of *Heat* magazine. 'Don't want to sound unkind but it's so much easier around here without him.'

'I'm sure Getting It's share price must be soaring thanks to us not being hampered by him,' Tim remarked. He was surreptitiously thumbing through a holiday brochure. Adrienne, eyes like a hawk, spotted it immediately.

'Coo-err, Paris,' she announced just loudly enough for the entire office to hear. 'Whisking our Stell off to La Belle France, eh? You're pretty romantic for an oldie.'

Tim was just about to explain that even the over forties

were capable of having some fun when Adrienne was suddenly rendered speechless. She pointed dramatically at the magazine.

Tim took one look and went into Victor Meldrew routine. 'I don't believe it,' he said, shaking his head. 'I just don't believe it.'

Everyone in the office abandoned their desks and rushed over to take a look.

There were gasps and shrieks as they all clocked the cover of the magazine. In the bottom right hand corner was the headline: 'TV Shopping Babe to Wed', along with a small picture of a ravishing-looking Tiffany in one of her suede numbers. Arm in arm with a devastatingly good-looking man.

'Bloody hell, it's Steve!'

Inside, a double-page spread entitled 'Tiffany's Getting It At Last' greeted them. Everyone jostled for position to get a better view of the article. It was a simpering account of Tiffany's career, with all its embellishments, culminating in how she'd met Steve at work.

'Here, Stella, look at this.' Tim hastily kicked the Paris brochure out of sight as Stella walked into the office. He wanted to get their weekend organised and booked, just in case she changed her mind.

Stella had to practically elbow her way through the crowd that had now gathered to read the article.

'But that's ridiculous,' she announced. 'It can't be true.' Then she remembered to hold her tongue in case she revealed what the others didn't know.

Tiffany had managed to give Steve the makeover of the century. Gone were the geeky glasses, the lanky hair, the sallow skin. No more ill-fitting trousers and slip-on shoes. Instead, there were pictures of a tall, well-groomed, tanned and confident man happily embracing the beautiful Tiffany.

'She must have called up Trinny and Susannah,' said Adrienne. 'This is a completely new man. And to think, this was going on under our noses all this time.'

Stella shot a knowing glance at Tim.

All the phones started ringing as everyone around the building heard the news. Kelly-Marie, another *Heat* magazine devotee, had made it her business to ring as many people as possible.

'Just been summoned to a meeting,' Stella half-whispered to Tim.

When she got to Paul's office, Fran was already there, *Heat* magazine spread out on Paul's desk. He broke into a grin as he told them that *Hello!* magazine had just phoned, asking to be put in touch with the happy pair.

'All I can conclude is that when I ordered Steve to apologise to Tiff he must have done it rather successfully.'

'This is so unreal,' replied Fran. 'So what happens now?'

'Oh, it gets better, especially from Getting It's point of view,' said Paul. 'It seems that there's a bidding war for photo rights to the wedding. I can't believe I'm saying this but I think we're going to have to get Steve on screen.'

Chapter 38

'Only two days to go.' Stella rubbed her hands together in delight. 'Then you and I are doing the swank.'

Winning the *Handbagged* prize was keeping Stella's spirits up. She was finding the stress of being on screen tough. The pressure to look good was proving time-consuming and hard work. They'd also taken a further bashing on the unofficial Getting It website, just as Paul had warned them. 'Get those crumblies off the screen' was the gist of it, completely missing the point about breaking the taboo of older women on the box.

'Everyone has a right to be completely stupid,' was Paul Dyer's response. He'd secretly had their post screened so that the odd nutty letter didn't reach their desks. He'd also had a formal request from Des for an interview with Fran, along the lines of 'ex-*Echo* reporter turned TV star'. He'd quietly told Des to get lost, and threatened him with death by Super Suck vacuum cleaner if he ever dared to contact Fran again.

Stella was also secretly worried about a nasty Ray and Ginger reaction to the *Handbagged* piece when it came out but she kept that to herself, convinced that Fran would then try to talk her out of the trip to London. At least they could play at being real stars for one night only.

'Oh, by the way, had a word with Ginette,' Stella announced during a coffee break. 'She's going to lend us some nice gear to go to London, and she's coming along to give us a hand on the next programme.'

'Stell, that's fantastic. But I'm still worried about this magazine article. I hope it's not going to stir things up unnecessarily, especially as you've just got your life back on track.' Fran knew only too well how unscrupulous journalists could turn a straightforward story into something more sinister with a little interference here and there. And Stella's story was hardly run-of-the-mill. More naked-run-of-the-street.

'Honestly, Fran, I've had a good think about it, talked it over with Tim and he thinks it's probably quite therapeutic. They've already approached Ray for a comment, they told me this week. None forthcoming, of course. I mean, what could the bastard possibly say? And also they'll block out the bitch's face so she can't be identified. So they know it's happening. Anyway, people talk about their divorces and relationships all the time. Kilroy and Trisha don't seem to have any trouble filling all those studio seats day after day. So one more case won't make much difference. And I now view the whole episode as the best thing that ever happened to me.'

The big night out became in reality rather a blur. So much excitement crammed into one very expensive twenty-four hours. A bit like getting married or having a baby – except that neither divorce nor sleepless nights were likely outcomes.

When the white stretch limo turned up at Fran's house,

the neighbours' curtains didn't just twitch, they positively rocked. Fran and Stella made a point of giving a regal wave to the street as they stepped into the car. Inside, there were bottles of champagne already on ice. The driver of the limo, Charlie, a cheery cockney, insisted they toast him. In fact, by the time the limo had purred its way from Hartford to their five-star hotel, they'd toasted all their families, every friend they'd ever had, the Queen and even the kitchen cupboards.

'Thank gawd for Charlie,' Stella muttered, grabbing the driver's arm as he helped her up the steps and into the marbled and palmed reception area. Both of them were now regretting not having had a more substantial breakfast.

They soon sobered up when they saw their suite. It was breathtaking. Two bedrooms, each with a queen-size bed and ensuite bathroom, plus a huge sitting room with widescreen television, music system and a selection of the latest films on DVD. There were huge bowls of flowers and fruit everywhere and so many chairs, easy chairs and sofas they'd probably never get around to sitting on them all. The bathrooms each had Victorian roll-top baths in the centre of the room, as well as white drapes at the windows and piles of exquisite crisp white towels everywhere.

'Lunch,' proclaimed Stella, grabbing the room service menu and sinking into a sofa. 'Let's enjoy this gorgeous suite. Then we're off to get the frocks!'

While they waited for the food to arrive, they bounced on the beds and zapped through all the TV stations like a couple of giddy teenagers. Lunch was delivered by an army of waiters who transformed their beautiful dining table into a banquet setting, complete with candelabra, crisp napkins and the finest crystal glasses. They served up the meal with quiet aplomb and then retreated, leaving their excitable guests to feast.

'Wow, I could enjoy this for ever,' said Fran, who was suddenly feeling overwhelmed. 'Listen, Stell, this is such a wonderful adventure. Thank you so much for inviting me.'

They raised their glasses for the umpteenth time that day.

'You're a truly wonderful friend,' Stella responded. 'I have never forgotten how you helped me in my hour of need. And ever since.'

'We're in danger of getting over-emotional,' said Fran, coming down to earth a bit. 'Do you know, because of the state of the house, you're the only person I've ever allowed to stay. That's the measure of our friendship.'

They clinked glasses and began to eat. The food was quite divine. After coffee and petit fours, the thought of dragging themselves around the shops now seemed a bit of a nuisance.

'But,' said Stella, 'in the best female tradition, we don't have a thing to wear. And we have one thousand pounds to spend.'

'I just hope we find something in time,' said Fran. 'It would be ironic to have this prize money and not come back with anything.'

'Oh, we will.' Stella shot her a knowing look.

Charlie was waiting with the incongruous limo. The two of them swept out, pretending there was simply no other way to travel. The journey to the shops would have been quicker on one foot, let alone two, as the car slowly negotiated the twists and turns of the back streets and one-way systems of Mayfair, bringing them finally to Bond Street.

Again they bid Charlie farewell, and disappeared through the perfumed portals into shopping heaven. The search wasn't difficult. A cream silk tuxedo-style suit by Ben de Lisi for Stella. It looked wonderful with her dark hair. Fran also found her dream outfit, thanks to Amanda Wakeley – a long velvet two-piece in darkest purple, trimmed with silk on the collar, cuffs and revers. There was just enough left in the prize pot to splash out on cream silk heels for Stella and diamanté sandals for Fran. They blew the final few pounds on a tiny pot of face cream that promised eternal youth. Then it was back to the hotel, courtesy of Charlie, followed by a serious tart up. Finally, another couple of glasses of champagne later, 'to steady the nerves', they were climbing back into their limo to go to the film première.

Watching the flash bulbs popping at them was just about the most exciting thing either of them had ever encountered. Because they'd pulled up in a limo and were being ushered along a red carpet, the huge crowd and the photographers all assumed they must be really important. As the flash guns fired, the crowd surged forward at the crush barriers, attempting to get a glimpse of them.

'One wave and I'm inside,' Fran warned Stella, not liking the attention as much as she had expected. If only I hadn't eaten such a large lunch, she thought, desperately holding in her stomach muscles as if world peace depended on it.

'It's all so wonderfully absurd,' Stella replied. 'Everyone's waving and popping cameras just because we got out of a stretch limo. How ridiculous is that! Savour the moment. They've no idea we flog cheapie T-shirts on a shopping channel.'

They waved a little more, but when autograph books

started being thrust in their direction even Stella decided it was time to withdraw. Inside was a star spotters' paradise. Every It girl who'd ever been 'It' was there, together with pop singers, supermodels, supermodels' bits of totty, supermodels' agents and supermodels' agents' bits of totty. There were plenty of Liz Hurley dressalikes pouting, thrusting and posing, just in case the waiter holding the tray of canapés was in fact a Hollywood scout in disguise.

'Awful lot of women dressed in leather,' remarked Fran, scanning the room. 'Leather trousers, leather bustiers, leather skirts.'

'It's a turn-on for men,' said Stella knowledgeably. 'Reminds them of new cars. Omigod.'

Stella went white, almost spilling her glass of champagne. Unable to speak, she gesticulated with her glass. Hugh Grant was standing about ten yards away, surrounded by an adoring crowd.

They both adopted fixed smiles as they stood frozen to the spot, mesmerised by him. Fran recovered her composure sufficiently to mutter under her breath, 'He's coming this way. What do we say? Do we say we're from Getting It?'

'No, you silly tart,' Stella muttered back, her knees trembling. 'He'll never have heard of it. Anyway, if he does speak, you've worked in newspapers, interviewing stars. You know what to say.'

'Hugh Grant has never heard of Hartford,' said Fran wryly. 'I've only interviewed stars on their way down, or after court appearances for driving offences.'

They both resumed their fixed smiles, praying there was no lipstick or basil trapped between their teeth. Gradually, Hugh Grant was wending his way towards them, smiling left and right, acknowledging compliments, grinning to the ever-present cameras. Suddenly he was within five yards of them. Stella almost fainted with excitement. This was light years from Bypass on Fashion. This was *Four Weddings and A Funeral*, *Notting Hill* and *About a Boy* all rolled into one. Another couple of minutes and he'd be next to them. They'd practically be sharing the same oxygen.

For the second time that day they felt like giddy teenagers. Fran's heart was pounding in her chest. This was ridiculous. Here she was, a woman of forty-two, literally falling to bits at a man's feet. She half-glanced at Stella, and was relieved to see she was having the same problem.

'Darlings,' exclaimed Hugh, giving them a wave, his grin extending wider and wider. Stella and Fran grinned ridiculously back. Perhaps the magazine had primed him to meet them. Perhaps this was an extra part of the prize they hadn't been told about.

'Darlings!' It came again. This was it, they were just seconds away from touching him. Heavens, at this rate he might even peck them on the cheek.

'Caught you last week. You two are sooooo good,' came Hugh's next utterance.

'What?' There must be some mistake.

'Love your show.' They both looked around frantically to see if he was talking to someone behind them. He continued: 'So refreshing to see elegant women on the box. Not just fluffy bunnies. And you really know your stuff. I'm a great fan of Getting It. It's such a huge laugh. Well done.'

With that, he pecked each of them on the cheek amid another barrage of flash bulbs and moved on.

'Did I just dream that?' asked Fran. 'Or have we had too much champagne? I think I'm going to faint with excitement.'

'I won't be washing my face for at least a week,' said Stella, equally stunned. 'Hope Tim doesn't mind. What a night.'

Chapter 39

Handbagged magazine was everywhere. And not just on the news stands. Everyone at Getting It seemed to have their own personal copy lurking on their desk. Kelly-Marie was so glued to hers that several calls went unanswered.

Stella's story had made the front page of the magazine – 'Running for cover' – with an accompanying back-view photograph of 'the titian-haired temptress' doing her streak. Inside was a double-page spread with the caption 'It's not my fault she forgot her clothes'. The story had been given an alarming amount of spin. Stella was 'an attractive TV executive at Getting It' whose marriage had been 'an empty sham'. Ray was portrayed as a 'lazy, heartless slob', so idle he could have been related to the Royle family. It was cliché city. The only thing they omitted were the surnames.

'I think you're very brave,' said Adrienne in total admiration. She had spent hours on the phone to her mum and all her friends telling them that most of her workmates were now celebrities. 'Anyone who behaves like that deserves to get it in the neck. And as for Miss Ginger Minger, if you sleep with someone else's husband then you run that risk.'

'Well, she certainly made all the running,' said Stella, who was relieved at the enthusiastic reaction. She'd expected a much rougher ride.

'Anyway, that prize must have made up for it,' Adrienne continued, wide eyed. 'Top night out in London worth thousands?'

'Meeting Hugh Grant at the première was just amazing. Sadly, it's all a bit of a blur,' said Stella, recalling the pain of her hangover the next day. 'Too much champagne in the stretch limo.'

They got the thumbs-up from Paul Dyer. He'd been delighted at yet another publicity scoop for the station. With a further photo spread about their prize night out due in next week's *Handbagged*, Getting It was getting some much needed positive publicity.

'I must say,' said Paul at the conclusion of the monthly meeting, 'that it's a pleasant change to read some good news about Getting It's presenters, rather than having to read about them falling out of hammocks or dropping chairs on their feet.'

Everyone laughed.

'Now there's one last thing I want your opinions on before we adjourn to the pub,' said Paul. 'Now we know that Steve is a sex god, do we try him out on screen with Tiffany in a romantic double act? My head says yes, probably for commercial reasons. We'd probably generate heaps of publicity. But my heart says no. I'd be interested in your opinions.'

'No,' everyone screamed in chorus. 'No, no, no.'

Tim, as the voice of reason, spoke for all of them. 'I think, Paul, that we have finally reached a position here at Getting It where we are actually Getting It right. We've gradually got rid of the duff products. We know what works. We're at last managing to maintain sales figures without anyone having to injure themselves onscreen. We no longer have warring presenters. Instead we have loyal viewers. It's a treat not to pick up the *News of the World* to read about our latest disaster.'

'Good,' announced Paul, delighted at the verdict. 'Just to warn you, Tiffany IS stamping her pretty little foot to make sure I put the new and improved Steve on screen. That's one wedding wish that won't be granted.'

With that, they all adjourned to the pub for a warm-up session ahead of Saturday's big wedding, plus the placing of bets as to how long the marriage would last.

The marquee was incredibly beautiful. Set in the grounds of a huge Georgian manor house, it consisted of two huge rooms with midnight blue ceilings and thousands of tiny lights. A group of classical guitar players serenaded guests as they quaffed champagne and nibbled at the most exquisite canapés.

The guests seemed to have been divided into three factions: the entire staff of Getting It (apart from the unlucky few on duty), a clutch of celebrities, models and It girls, and journalists and photographers from every tabloid newspaper and celebrity magazine in the country. Tiffany had obviously decided to go for maximum exposure.

Fran and Stella, not yet on presenters' pay, had once again called upon the services of Ginette for the evening. Ginette had read enough about the impending wedding to know that the world and his photographer would be there so she happily invited them round to her boutique out of hours to choose what they fancied. The gilt-edged invitations had stipulated black tie so everyone seized a glorious excuse to dress up. Fran, in a long dark green velvet dress with satin bodice and matching bolero, and Stella, enviably slim in a midnight blue silk column dress and feather boa, both felt a million dollars. Bob and Tim looked particularly dashing as they'd matched their bow ties and cummerbunds to the colours the girls were wearing.

The Getting It crowd were still all of a twitter over the whirlwind romance. They'd found out more about it from reading various magazines than they had from the happy couple themselves, who'd hardly shown up for work since the bombshell of 'I'm Marrying My Stalker' had hit the headlines. Pictures of Steve and Tiffany wrapped around each other in various states of undress at a very trendy hotel had been accompanied by various breathless accounts of how Tiffany had been pursued by a mystery man who had turned out to be the besotted Steve. The account conveniently omitted the Night of the Long Lenses and concentrated on Tiffany's 'romantic discovery' that the man was her dreamboat Steve.

'He rang to apologise and invited me out to a wonderful lunch,' gushed the copy. 'Somehow it happened. That defining moment. That lightning strike when I knew Steve was the man for me. Lunch became dinner and by midnight he had proposed and I had accepted. Within twenty-four hours my life had completely changed. Forgive him? What could there possibly be to forgive?'

The article gave Steve an easy ride too. 'Tall, handsome Steve McGuire holds down a challenging job as a top producer at Britain's highest-rated shopping channel, Getting It. Yet this gentle giant with the Hollywood looks was too shy to pluck up the courage to confess his true feelings to Tiffany, the woman of his dreams.'

Another magazine helpfully explained: 'Some might think that this golden couple are rushing into marriage rather hastily, but they've actually been working closely together at Getting It for some months. Theirs has been the most romantic of courtships. Steve wrote more than fifty love letters and poems to the object of his desire. How could Tiffany resist such an ardent suitor?'

As more and more guests arrived, mingling, giggling and laughing, the more excited the Getting It crowd became. Piers and Kelly-Marie arriving as an item wasn't entirely a surprise, but at least they'd left the his 'n' hers lycra at home. Piers looked decidedly uncomfortable in his dinner jacket, which was straining at the seams. The snake tattoo around his neck didn't quite gel with the wing collar of his dress shirt. Kelly-Marie was in everyday office dress: a black lace mini flamenco dress with wonderbra-ed cleavage on display and the highest black patent heels known to woman. The whole ensemble was topped off by a black lace mantilla and black net veil over her face. The photographers loved it – and so did she.

Presenters Jason and Charleena appeared *à deux*, wrapped in each other's arms and smiling enticingly for the cameras. 'Auditioning,' Fran whispered to Stella. 'They actually hate each other but their contracts are up for renewal.'

Then Kiefer arrived, accompanied by a beautiful young boy. He'd obviously decided he might as well come out, seeing as Tiffany had been snapped up, so to speak. On a relative scale for Kiefer, he looked quite happy.

Then came the big surprise of the night so far: Adrienne, looking a little bashful on the arm of Paul Dyer. Paul looked devastating in his dinner suit, while Adrienne looked just as fantastic in a female version but with

340

nothing on under her jacket. The body language, everyone immediately decided, indicated that this had been going on for some time.

'Never guessed that one,' said Stella to Fran. 'But don't they look terrific together?'

Fran nodded, juggling a glass of champagne while she tried to wrest her cigarettes from a tiny evening bag. Another barrage of flash guns temporarily blinded everyone. Suddenly she felt a hand on her shoulder. She wheeled around to face Des Ryder, grinning at her through nicotined teeth and brandishing a notebook.

'We meet again,' he snarled at her. 'No, not gate-crashing. They invited the *Echo* along with all the others.' He indicated the photographers. 'So what's the real story behind the happy couple?'

'No idea,' she replied tersely. 'All I know is what I've read in the papers this week, same as you. So no comment.'

'Oh come on, Fran. I'm sure a good journalist like you would have found out a little more than that.' He was taunting her now. 'So come on, spill the beans.'

Fran looked around furtively for support, but Tim and Bob were several yards away avidly talking cars and Stella had gone off to hug Adrienne and get the complete lowdown on her relationship with Paul.

'Look, Des, I don't have any beans,' she snapped back. 'Why don't you try Jack, of Beanstalk fame. He gets his at the market. I'm sure they're going cheap.'

But Des wasn't to be fobbed off. 'Don't you mess with me, Fran. Or should I say . . . Madame Chita. The late Madame Chita.'

Fran felt her blood run cold. She was grateful for the racket going on around her. So many people were arriving and air-kissing that they were drowning out the poor

341

classical guitarists – and, more importantly, the noise of her heart as it crashed against her rib cage. She took a sip of champagne to buy herself some thinking time.

'Is that the best you can come up with, Des?' she tried finally. 'Me? Madame Chita? Don't be ridiculous.'

'But I KNOW it was you,' Des persisted. 'Guy let it slip last week over a pint too many in the Slug and Lettuce. And now you're on the telly. Makes it SO much more interesting.'

Fran knew when she was defeated. If Guy had blabbed while under the influence then she couldn't talk her way out of it. Her own resistance had also been lowered by several glasses of champagne on an empty stomach.

'What if I was?' she reasoned with him and mostly with herself. 'What's the *Echo* going to do? Run a story admitting they didn't know what was going on under their noses? Retract an obituary? Make you look a complete dolthead because your major investigation couldn't find the answer when it was staring you in the face? Doesn't make you look like any kind of crime correspondent, does it, if you can't solve a mystery in your own office.'

To her relief, Des looked extremely rattled. And to her even greater relief, she realised she'd just come to the joyous conclusion that she no longer cared. If Des wanted to out her as Madame Chita and make himself look an idiot, he could go right ahead.

She turned her back on him and walked away in the direction of Bob as fast as she could. She briefly explained to him above the din what had just happened. And suddenly – she felt free. The burden of the deceit had finally been lifted. Why on earth hadn't she done it earlier? Now that she'd kicked Des firmly into touch, she almost felt sorry for him!

But it was more than that. If she'd still been working at

the *Hartford Echo*, she'd have been among the press pack like Des tonight, goggle-eyed at the celebrities, envying the dresses, wishing like hell she'd been on the guest list. And here she was, invited, very much a part of it and mingling with the rich, the thin and the famous. And wearing one of the most drop-dead gorgeous frocks she'd ever set eyes on. Now that was progress!

As she, Stella, Tim and Bob all clinked glasses once again, they were all silenced by a toastmaster who, equipped with radio mic, was summoning everyone into the inner room of the marquee for the marriage ceremony. Everyone hastily drained their glasses, reminding themselves that they were here primarily for a wedding. The booze was only secondary. The noise dipped dramatically as they queued to bag the best seats in the rows of gold chairs set out ahead of them.

The air was thick with the wonderful scent of lilies. A string quartet was playing in spirited fashion to one side of the dais where the ceremony was to take place. Meanwhile, the photographers were all assembling on the other side of the dais, jostling for position with their tripods and stepladders.

Suddenly a whisper went around that the moment had come. Up the aisle came the completely transformed and smiling Steve, wearing a deep tan and a white tuxedo. His best man was the facially challenged SAS man who'd been 'adviser' on the Come Spy With Me show. Compared to the new-look Steve, he contrived to appear even more scary.

They now had a groom. Just needed the bride. A few minutes ticked by. The chatting resumed. Surely she wasn't going to duck out, not after they'd forked out for this lot? Another five minutes ticked agonisingly by.

Just at the moment when Fran and Stella began to wonder whether Steve would have the courage to ask for a volunteer from the audience, the string quartet struck up with Mendelssohn's Wedding March. All eyes turned to the back of the marquee for Tiffany's big moment.

Having absolutely no dignity, let alone a sense of occasion, everyone burst into a cacophony of applause and wolf whistles, drowning out the efforts of the quartet. The photographers snapped frenetically as Tiffany proceeded slowly towards the dais. As the flash bulbs popped and popped, her smile got wider and wider. She really did look a show-stopping million dollars – in the simplest of dresses. She wore an ivory silk strapless bodice embroidered with thousands of tiny pearls and a matching straight skirt with a puddle train. On her head was a delicate pearl tiara and in her hands a bouquet of cream lilies.

'Twenty grand's worth,' Stella mouthed to Fran, her expert eye roving over the dress as Tiffany wafted past.

Everyone turned to the front as the ceremony started. Fran suddenly remembered the night she'd heard the phone message from Tiffany's mother. She noted the ill-matched couple standing at the front on the bride's side. So this must be Essex Mum and Drunken Dad. She must try to find out later on what 'Taffy' stood for. She didn't have to wait long.

They began to take their vows. 'I call upon these people here present that I, Taffeta Diane . . .'

Tiffany had tried to dip her voice as much as possible but her secret was out. The front three or four rows caught the name, sniggered and told the rows behind who hadn't quite heard. As they passed it on, the sound of stifled giggling swept back like a Mexican wave over the rows and virtually drowned out the rest of the vows.

Fran and Stella didn't dare make eye contact in case they burst out laughing. Fran made a mental note to find out whether Shire was Tiffany's real surname. She doubted it somehow.

The registrar continued without batting an eyelid. Given the circumstances of Tiffany and Steve's 'love match', he could hardly expect it to be one of the more serious, moist-eyed ceremonies. He'd read the 'I'm Marrying My Stalker' accounts just like everyone else.

The ceremony over, guests were plied with more champagne and canapés while the photographers began their work proper, with no one keener than Tiffany to get maximum exposure and ensure her future livelihood. While the celebrity guests found themselves taking part in the longest photo call Hartford had ever seen, the main section of the marquee was now being opened for the wedding breakfast.

It looked so breathtaking that everyone burst into spontaneous applause. Themed in cream and gold, it was incredibly stylish. Everyone completely disregarded the place names and the seating plan and just plonked down with their friends. Soon they were tucking into a salad of warm quail, lardons and leaves and sipping chilled Chablis.

Fran, Stella, Bob and Tim managed to grab a table with Piers and Kelly-Marie, Jason and Charleena and Paul and Adrienne.

'Can't wait for the speeches,' said Paul, sitting back in his chair and beaming at everyone. 'Especially from Clark Kent in a tux.'

The flash bulbs were still popping through the main course. Kelly-Marie unwittingly provided some un-scheduled entertainment by getting one of her false eyelashes caught up in her net veil. Meanwhile two buttons on Piers's dress shirt finally conceded defeat thanks to the Abdo Fabbo trimmer nightly workout. They burst off into the air, leaving him with a gaping shirt and a hint of more tattoo. Aided and abetted by a bottle of excellent Bordeaux, Kelly-Marie and Piers confessed, slightly slurred, that they'd had 'his 'n' hers' tattoos done that day on their bums. Offers to show the assembled table were hastily declined.

Fran decided that a spot of fresh air and a visit to the loo would be a good idea. She wended her way across the marquee until she reached the exit. As she did so, she realised she was being joined by Tiffany's mum, whose bouffant hair, leopard-skin spray-on frock and tons of diamanté jewellery were hard to miss.

'You're Tiffany's mother, aren't you,' Fran said politely as they queued. 'Mrs Shire, how do you do? I work with your daughter.' She offered her hand.

'Pleased to meet ya, love,' came the Essex accent, 'but I ain't Shire. Me name's Scoggins. That's our Taff's as well but gawd knows why she went and changed it.'

Taffeta Scoggins, Essex Girl. No wonder Tiffany re-invented herself, thought Fran.

The pudding had arrived when Fran returned to the table. It had been billed as a palette of ice creams and sorbets. The palette was made of the finest wafer-thin biscuit and the ice creams and sorbets resembled dollops of paint.

'That reminds me,' said Bob, taking Fran's hand. 'I've got a confession AND a suggestion to make. I've taken out a loan.'

Fran went white. 'What for? Are you mad?'

'No, don't think so. Thought it was time we got

someone in to finish the house so I've arranged a cheap loan through the bank. It should cover everything.'

Fran flung her arms around his neck, unable to take in what he'd said.

'Bob, that's fantastic, that's brilliant.' She was almost crying. 'But what's the suggestion? You mentioned a suggestion.'

'Well,' said Bob, suddenly a bit tense and running his fingers through his wiry hair. 'Once it's done, how would you feel about selling it and buying something else?'

Fran looked thunderstruck. She could see her fantasy being snatched away. 'Oh no, not another DIY decade,' she begged. 'Please, Bob, don't put me through that. I couldn't bear it.' She began to get very agitated, emotions heightened by the amount of drink they'd now consumed.

'No, not that, I promise,' said Bob, trying to calm her down. 'I thought we might go for somewhere new.'

'Whaaat?' There was only so much a girl could take.

'Somewhere brand new,' said Bob firmly. 'In fact, while you girls were trying on half the dresses in Hartford the other night, I had a quick whizz round a showhouse on that new estate in town.'

'You're kidding?'

'No, I'm not. They're really lovely and they're being snapped up fast. I think it would make a good investment, so I took the plunge and paid a very small holding deposit on one of the plots. We need to look at it in the next couple of days, but if you decide you don't like it then it's not the end of the world.'

Fran was still in a state of shock. 'I'd love to live in a new house,' she spluttered. 'I'd never want to go out ever again. But this isn't like you to rush into something. Why didn't you tell me before?'

Bob grinned and kissed her hand. 'Because I thought you might be cross because we hadn't discussed it, or you might not believe that I was serious. Also, there's a big selling point to all this which I think you will find hard to resist.'

'What's that?' said Fran, immediately suspicious.

'There's no shed!'

'Done and dusted,' Fran cried in delight. She kissed him enthusiastically and turned to the rest of the table.

'We're moving house,' she announced. Everyone automatically raised their glasses to toast the news, but only Stella knew the enormous consequence of her statement. She beamed at her friend in absolute delight.

Fran leaned over and whispered in her ear. 'Brand new house and no shed! By the way, regarding the bride. How does Taffeta Scoggins grab you? Even Taffy McGuire will be a big improvement, and that's saying something.'

Suddenly a hush went around the room as the toastmaster appealed for silence. 'I give you, the father of the bride.'

At least they were spared the mention of Scoggins, thought Fran. Probably intentional. She really couldn't blame Tiffany for that.

Mr Scoggins, tie askew and very red-faced, rose to his feet, raised his glass to toast the happy couple and promptly fell backwards over his chair.

'Sorry, ladies and gentlemen, we'll come back to Mr Scoggins in a moment,' apologised the toastmaster. Now the secret was out. Howls of undisguised laughter went around the room as people put Taffeta and Scoggins together.

'In the meantime, I give you – the bridegroom.'

Steve rose to his feet, grinning nervously. He put his

hand up to quell the imagined applause. Paul Dyer sat forward intently to hear what Steve had to say. They were all expecting the usual stammering display of nerves.

But somehow Tiffany had achieved a miracle in that direction too. Steve efficiently thanked their parents, the bridesmaids, his best man, the registrar, the hotel staff and all the guests without as much as a hesitation. Then he managed a tribute to his new wife.

'Until I met Tiffany, I was the loneliest man in the world. She transformed me . . .'

'You can say that again,' Paul whispered to the rest of the table. 'Nothing short of a fucking miracle.'

'. . . into the luckiest man on the planet.'

'And not a phone box in sight,' joked Tim.

'Quite what a famous film and television star like Tiffany sees in me I can't imagine, but I know that at Getting It I got the biggest bargain of all.'

Raucous cheers from all the Getting It tables broke out around the marquee, followed by thunderous applause and wolf whistles. Steve, realising he might as well quit while he was ahead, sat down, looking relieved that it was all over.

Eventually the toastmaster regained control, announced that the 'bride's father was still a little indisposed' and informed the guests that a twelve-piece dance band was about to strike up. The band broke straight into a medley of Gershwin numbers, beginning with the bride and groom's first dance together. Their choice, somewhat ironically, was Billy Joel's 'Just the Way You Are'. Everyone applauded as they sashayed around the floor. They were so proficient that Stella and Fran suspected Tiffany had got Steve to take lessons. She certainly HAD been busy.

'Should have been "Strangers in the Night",' said Paul, who'd found the whole thing hysterical. 'You've got to hand it to Tiffany. She saw something in him that the rest of us didn't.'

During a breather from the dancing, Fran, Bob, Stella and Tim flopped down at their table. Stella suddenly sported a very foxy smile.

'Shall we, Tim? Shall we tell them?'

'Absolutely, darling,' Tim replied with a huge grin. 'Look, it's not quite the form to announce this at another wedding, but I don't think this one really counts. For all the reasons that we know.'

Stella nodded, wide-eyed with excitement. 'We're engaged,' she announced. 'We've just decided.'

'Fantastic,' announced Bob, summoning a waiter for some more champagne. 'What a top night.'

'I was going to wait to ask her in Paris but it just came out. We'll celebrate properly away from this circus,' said Tim, indicating the drunken dancing going on, 'but we just decided that we wanted to tell you two first.'

Fran and Stella hugged each other and the guys clapped each other on the back in congratulation. The four of them raised their glasses to Stella and Tim's future happiness.

They were interrupted by the toastmaster appealing for silence before the cutting of the cake. It was the perfect photo call. Gorgeous wedding couple standing beside a fantastic cake in a beautiful location. The music and conversation lulled for this important moment. Click, click, click went the cameras.

'That's her,' a familiar voice shouted out. 'The blonde in the dark green dress. That's Madame Chita.' Like everyone else, Fran whirled around to see what the fuss was about. Suddenly, to her horror, the press pack turned away from the cake-cutting and descended on her like wolves. In a blur of flash guns she was being bombarded with questions. How long had she been Madame Chita? Why did she fake her own death? Was she going to do more television? Did her TV bosses know about her secret life?

For what seemed like a lifetime, Fran just stood there, terrified out of her wits. Then she caught Des's face laughing at her from behind the lines of photographers. It was his voice she'd heard. In a split-second she realised he'd tipped them all off. The triumphant speech she'd made to him earlier had obviously fallen on deaf ears. Des was finally getting his revenge.

The marquee descended into chaos. Bob and Tim barged through the throng to try and haul her out of the mêlée. Meanwhile Tiffany, enraged that her big day had been upstaged, burst into hysterical tears and started screaming at the crowd to let her through. Moments ago she'd been sharing a special moment with her husband of just one hour. Now she wanted out.

As the action hotted up, more and more guests surged forward to see what was going on. Everyone had drunk a little too much champagne to be polite. One girl in a short slip dress and impossible heels lost her balance and tripped over a chair, dragging half a dozen other guests down with her as she fell. Tempers frayed as several people were pushed back against tables which promptly toppled over, scattering plates, glasses and flowers. Scuffles broke out between some of the photographers, all trying to grab what was now a much better picture story. Everyone now wanted two shots: one of the mysterious Madame Chita and another of the bride having a tantrum as she watched her wedding being wrecked.

Tiffany, realising how it was now going to look on the front pages, decided to cut her losses. She picked up her cream silk skirts and left the marquee, leaving a flustered Steve to try to calm the masses. In the spirit of a sinking *Titanic*, the band struck up with 'Just One of Those Things'. Eventually, when the press pack had disappeared, those guests who'd survived the scuffle decided to make a night of it. With plenty of booze left on the tables still standing, and the band game for more, the party really took off.

Fran, still in shock at her ordeal, was now dreading what Des would be telling all the papers about her Chita connection. She was sitting back at their original table with Bob by her side, his arm tightly around her. Stella, Tim, Kelly-Marie and Adrienne joined them, all white-faced at what they'd just witnessed. Even Fran in her *Hartford Echo* days had never seen such a vicious scrum.

Suddenly they all realised that Paul and Piers were nowhere to be seen. Minutes ticked by. Nobody had a clue where they'd gone. Fran began to get very worried. Could the media bundle have developed into a punch-up outside?

Tim announced he would do a circuit of the marquee inside and out to see if he could find them. Five minutes later all three of them returned, grinning like Cheshire cats. Paul and Piers, however, looked a little ruffled. Paul appeared to have lost his bow tie and Piers was missing a few more buttons off his dress shirt, so more tattoos were peeping through.

They all sat down amid clamouring questions and poured themselves some more champagne.

'We've been on a mission,' Paul announced. 'Young Piers here has been reading Des Ryder a few relevant sections of the Riot Act.'

One look at Piers convinced Fran he'd given Des quite a thumping. He was looking very pleased with himself as Kelly-Marie looked on proudly. All those hours in the gym had been put to good use.

'And I,' announced Paul, 'have been briefing the press on what a completely crap crime correspondent Des Ryder is. And how he caused a riot at a wedding by accusing a very valued member of my staff of being a dead clairvoyant. I've never heard anything quite so ridiculous in all my life. I have threatened him with further proceedings and I'll be lodging an official complaint with his editor tomorrow. And this time I want a proper apology. I'm sure the bride and groom will be doing the same. That man just wrecked a wedding.'

Fran looked hopelessly at Bob. He raised his eyebrows at her and grinned. Paul had just brilliantly and unwittingly solved the entire problem. Madame Chita could finally rest in peace.

'More champagne please,' Paul asked a passing waiter, who duly obliged. With the wedding party drastically reduced, there was plenty left. As the waiter reappeared with two more bottles and some fresh glasses, Paul continued: 'I hate to say this, but I have a feeling our viewing figures are about to shoot up again after this little shambles. We may have to rethink the new Mr and Mrs McGuire doing their own show.'

He raised a glass to all of them. 'The publicity from tonight's little fiasco is going to be mega. It could be worldwide.'

Everyone groaned at the thought.

Paul sat back in his chair, arm around Adrienne, now sporting a grin from ear to ear. 'Who'd be famous, eh?' he said, surveying the devastation around the marquee.

'Not us,' Fran and Stella chorused firmly. They linked arms. 'Let's go and get a whopping great piece of that wedding cake.'

IN CAHOOTS!

Jane Blanchard

Their New Year's resolution is to have some fun . . .

It seems a long time since Sarah, Vicky and Judith were bright young things. Middle age is looming and threatening to be middling. Romance is something that happens to other people. If life is meant to begin at forty, then where the hell has it got to?

Over a bottle of New Year champagne in their favourite local wine bar, Cahoots, the three friends decide to take control; to let their hair down and rediscover life – and love – all over again. Suddenly Vicky's on the run from half the television crews in Britain; Sarah discovers the truth about her marriage; and Judith learns that work isn't the only four-letter word on the street . . .

In Cahoots! is Jane Blanchard's sparkling debut novel – a corking romance comedy about three women determined to put the fizz back into their lives.

NAILING HARRY

Jane Blanchard

The strut of a peacock, the libido of a rabbit and the morals of a skunk. Meet Harry Hampton, office super rat and boss from hell.

Harry's media company HOT specialises in corporate TV, PR, marketing and advertising. Harry specialises in stealing other people's ideas, sacking staff he doesn't like and claiming credit where credit isn't due. Those above him think he's a bit of a hot shot. Those below would just like to see HOT shot of him.

After surviving yet another round of reckless redundancies, four female workers decide they've had enough of Harry's game. It's time to bully off, to show this womaniser just what women are capable of. And they're not the only ones to reach breaking point over Harry's antics. His much younger, beautiful wife Val also wants her revenge – and she's determined to make it as public as she possibly can . . .

HOPING FOR HOPE

Lucy Clare

When Liddy Claver visits her doctor a few days before her fiftieth birthday, she assumes she is menopausal. But instead, her doctor has some astonishing news for her: she is thirty weeks pregnant. Liddy is shocked, but not as shocked as her husband Martin is going to be. Liddy and Martin haven't had sex for five years.

Liddy learns that Martin has also been unfaithful, and she hopes that being honest with each other might bring them back together. But when Liddy gives birth to a baby daughter, Hope, it is a child that her husband wants nothing to do with, and equally problematically, that their three grown-up children – Laura, Miranda and Alex – each feel should be theirs to bring up . . .

Compassionate and compelling, Lucy Clare's debut novel is an emotive page-turner par excellence. It is a story about families – about hoping for understanding, hoping for support, but above all, about hoping for Hope.

WILD STRAWBERRIES

Emma Blair

In the lush countryside of West Cornwall lies the small fishing village of Coverack and the warm welcome of the Paris Hotel. It is an appropriate name because the owner, Maizie Blackacre, finds her life changed for ever by the arrival of a young Frenchman.

The Second World War has brought its own special turmoil to Coverack. When Maizie's husband Sam joins the Merchant Navy, she is left to cope with the hotel's dwindling trade and two young evacuees. Then the arrival of Christian Le Gall, a French lieutenant recuperating from a war wound, lightens all their lives.

When Christian reports back for duty, Maizie is surprised at how sad she is to see him go – and how much she dreads the return of hard-drinking Sam. Caught between loyalty to her unfeeling husband, and her growing affection for Christian, Maizie has to fight her own private war of emotions . . .

GETTING HOME

Celia Brayfield

There is only one rule in a suburb – never trust your neighbours.

Westwick, the ultimate suburb. Nothing ever happens in Westwick; that's why people live there. Nice people like Stephanie Sands. Loving husband, adorable son, dream job and a beautiful garden – life is just about perfect for Stephanie until the day her husband is kidnapped.

Big mistake, losing your husband in the suburbs. The neighbours turn nasty. The TV totty sees Stephanie as a media victim and the totty's husband sees Stephanie as 'lonely' – codeword for desperate. Stephanie discovers that she isn't the kind of woman to take this lying down. Suddenly it's a jungle out there – adultery, blackmail, sleaze in high places and lust on the lawns, until Westwick scrambles the helicopters and takes to the streets with an army of eco-warriors in the hilarious live-TV climax.

Getting Home has outraged upholders of Volvo culture everywhere.

'Deliciously comic – lightning flashes of wit and scalpel-sharp observation' *Daily Mail*

Other bestselling Time Warner Paperback titles available by mail

☐ In Cahoots!	Jane Blanchard	£5.99
☐ Nailing Harry	Jane Blanchard	£5.99
☐ Hoping for Hope	Lucy Clare	£5.99
☐ Wild Strawberries	Emma Blair	£5.99
☐ Getting Home	Celia Brayfield	£5.99

The prices shown above are correct at time of going to press. However, the publishers reserve the right to increase prices on covers from those previously advertised, without further notice.

timewarner
paperbacks

TIME WARNER PAPERBACKS
PO Box 121, Kettering, Northants NN14 4ZQ
Tel: 01832 737525, Fax: 01832 733076
Email: aspenhouse@FSBDial.co.uk

POST AND PACKING:
Payments can be made as follows: cheque, postal order (payable to Time Warner Books) or by credit cards. Do not send cash or currency.

All UK Orders	**FREE OF CHARGE**
EC & Overseas	25% of order value

Name (BLOCK LETTERS) ....

Address ....

....

Post/zip code: ....

☐ Please keep me in touch with future Time Warner publications

☐ I enclose my remittance £ ....

☐ I wish to pay by Visa/Access/Mastercard/Eurocard

Card Expiry Date
